For My Wife

THE PENITENT

Part One of The Scar Sea Wars

Jay Yasities

Being the memoir of Asheth Acellion, faithfully transcribed by your servant Meil Facilus

Asheth Acellion, Baron of Estwake

Born 643 FB, granted his Barony during reign of Emperor Domint III

Died 674 FB, killed during the siege of Estwake, succession war of Emperor Frachia the First

Resurrected by the foul necromancer Kroll in 344 AR at the ruins of Estwake to serve in his Raised army, during the war of the Scar Sea.

CHAPTER ONE

I woke up with a sword lodged in my ribcage.

The blade ended in a dull metal cross-guard and a leather wrapped handle, with a simple round pommel. The sword had me pinned to the heavy wooden door behind me, driven through me with such force that I was not touching the ground. The shadow of my leather-booted feet against the flagstones beneath me shifted back and forth. There was a torch on the opposite wall, and as it was fading its flame guttered and spat.

The room was a small stone cellar, with walls of old brick discoloured by damp and mould. The flagstones were uneven, and pools of water were sitting in the cracks and spaces between them and in shallow concavities in the stones where they had been worn by the tread of feet over many years. To my left I could see a dark doorway where stairs, also damp and badly worn, led up out of the cellar. Some running water trickled down them as if there were a deluge above. A little in front of me, laid on the floor, was the shape of a body. Although the shifting torch light gave some illusion of movement it was not alive. There was a pool of blood widening around it.

I felt no pain from the sword, even though it was struck through me. I was not bleeding. There was no flesh to bleed, nor to feel pain. My ribcage was exposed, unclothed by both skin and fabric. All of my bones were uncovered in this way. If I were capable of fainting I believe then I would have lost my senses, but I can no more faint than I can whistle, and for similar reasons. A lack of flesh, and no requirement for the breath that men take for granted.

I raised my hands to examine them. There were some pieces of armour bound to me. I had no breastplate, obviously, but I wore vambraces that had been tied tightly to the bones at my wrists and just below my elbows with leather laces. I brought my fingers closer to my face and examined them in the fading light. My finger bones were joined together by some dark, oily substance, which glimmered with a soft green sheen when I turned my hands to-and-fro. Thin black threads, like the roots of some forest fungus, grew between and into the joints, their dark tendrils sinking into the bone and disappearing from view. I brought my hands to my face. The sensation was a dull, distant echo of touch, as if my hands were numbed by cold. I could feel the hard edges of my cheekbones and the sharp point of my jawline with no covering of skin to cushion the structure. My fingers grated on my exposed architecture.

A horrifying thought occurred to me. My fingers crept up my face, tracing the ridges of my eye sockets. I reached for where my eyelids should be, protecting my fragile vision, and found there was no resistance. My fingertips encountered only space, and with sheer terror I pushed into the empty sockets with my skinless fingers and found nothing. The bones blocked all my vision, and the dim light around me was replaced by a dull green glow.

I heard my jaw *clack!* open with shock and pulled my hands away quickly. I tried to scream but no sound left my mouth. My mind spun and swirled, and my sanity left me, racing into the darkness like a frightened animal. I pounded my skinless fists and feet on the rotten door behind me, wrenching myself to-and-fro, only stopping when the blade in my chest scraped against my ribs and threatened to shatter them.

Rack came to collect me. Of course, I did not know his name then.

I heard him coming down the stairs, muttering and grumbling under his breath, and the noise startled me out of my whirling madness. I stilled myself before he entered the room. He was a tattered ruin of a man, with rat-like, sharp, and strikingly ugly features. He was small of stature, stooped and bedraggled. His skin was pale and dirty, with open lesions and sores visible around his eyes and mouth, and his hands seemed almost black with filth. He wore a long, black, hooded cloak, and looked like he smelled awful. One of the few benefits of my nature is that I do not have a sense of smell. He was carrying a torch in his left hand and swept it in front of him as he entered the room. He took a look at me, shook his head, and wandered around the small cellar, talking to himself.

"What have you done 'ere? Silly old bones, this is a mess, what have you been gettin' up to?"

He spoke a coastal Sechian dialect, one I understood, as I had picked some up in the old campaigns.

He trotted over to the corpse lying on the floor and using the tip of one sandalled foot he rolled it on to its back. He brought the flame of his torch down closer to the dead man to inspect him. The corpse was some kind of soldier, though not wearing any colours to show his allegiance. He wore light leather armour, strapped over dark clothing, with patches of metal at the joints and a breastplate. He had on a grey, hooded cloak and wore a heavy pack on his back. There was a small hatchet in his right hand that his fingers had tightly gripped in his last moments.

"Well you don't look so well, do yer? We'll have to take you back to Master Kroll, see if he can find a use for yer." He spoke to the corpse as if it were the most natural behaviour.

Rack rifled through the dead man's pockets with his free hand, retrieving some coins and trinkets and stuffing them into pouches and pockets in his ragged clothing. Realising he also needed to search the pack he jammed the spiked end of his torch into one of the corpses' eyes, and once he had determined that the dead man's head wouldn't move to the side too much and douse his light, he cut the pack away with a dirty blade and then rifled through it, pulling out and either pocketing or discarding the contents. He squirrelled away some rations and some small items and threw the camp gear into a dark corner of the room.

Finished with his looting he pulled his torn and dirty cloak back around his body and turned to examine me.

"Silly old bones... got yourself stuck there haven't you? And what's this mess all over you?"

He reached out to my body, just under where the blade protruded from my chest. Dabbing the tip of his fingers against the underside of my ribs, he quickly drew his hand away, as if it were hot metal. There was some oily black slime on his fingertips. He pulled a face and quickly wiped his fingers against his cloak, trying to remove the substance that was clearly causing him pain. The new stain blended into his already prodigious collection.

"Hmm." He said. "Never seen one of you leak before."

The man shook his head, and was still shaking his fingers, which had blistered where the foul-looking slime had touched them.

"Right," he said, "best get you down. Can't have you hanging around here all day, hehe, Master wants his skellies back, no waiting around!"

He grabbed the sword hilt with his right hand, seemingly expecting to be able to just pull it out, but it didn't budge at all. He frowned, leaning in to look at where it was embedded in the door behind me. Then he grasped it with both hands and braced himself against the wood with his right foot. He heaved and let out a loud groan, and his pale skin darkened with blood and breath as he strained to pull out the sword. His efforts came to nothing, and he stopped, bending double and coughing with the exertion. When he finally got his wind back he stood up to show an expression of exasperation that was battling valiantly and vainly with his natural features.

"Ooooh, this is a pickle make no mistake, a pickle. I'm going to have to get some of your brethren to help aren't I?"

He trotted off back up the stairs after reclaiming his torch with a wet, wrenching sound. I heard him voice his complaints and woes under his wheezing breath as the noise of his displeasure receded into the darkness above.

During his activity I had remained as still as I could. My mind was anything but. My thoughts wheeled in great twisting gales of distress, a storm of horror and panic howling through my mind. I tried to recollect how I had come here, what had thrown me into this pit of terror. My memories were fractured and piecemeal at best.

The first memory that returned was my last living one.

I was fighting. Alive and clothed in flesh, and in my armour. I stood and fought in the courtyard at Estwake. The gates had been breached, shattered, and Frachia's forces had swept in, cutting down all that opposed them. I recalled the clash of armour and weapons, the stench of spilled blood, steaming guts, the foul leavings of dead and dying men. Why smell remains in my memory when the sense is absent to me now has never been clear to me.

My brothers-in-arms were Lucien and Balus, and

they fought by my side, the three of us back-to-back and defending each other. The courtyard was overrun with ruffian men-at-arms, mercenaries under Frachia's employ who had rushed through the breached gates. There were still remnants of his main forces, treacherous knights in armour, glimmers of steel in a sea of unkempt and shoddy uniforms. My armour was slick with blood on the outside, blood and sweat within. My chainmail was rent in a dozen places. I held a sword in one hand and a dagger in the other, and I was cut and pierced all over. A wound in one armpit where a low-born soldier had tried to reach my heart. A deep slice in my thigh, above my greaves, where an attempt had been made to cut my legs out from under me.

We were losing.

Lucien fell. One sword punctured his armour, and as he tumbled to his knees a rabble of cut-throats had pounced, striking with hammers, swords, the edges of shields. He was being beaten to death on the paved courtyard floor while his life ran out of the breaches in his cuirass.

I heard Balus cry out behind me, and whirled to see him impaled on a pike, blood frothing from his mouth. He tried to cry out but just made a wet, choking, gurgling sound. I lunged for his assailant and clubbed down over the attacker's head with my sword, cleaving his brain from his skull. There was no artistry here, just brutality, all coaching in swordsmanship forgotten. I turned, bringing my sword across in a low, sweeping arc and slicing across the belly of a man behind me. His innards fell to the floor, and he dropped his weapon and tried to grab at the hot wet ropes of his guts, stuffing them back inside him as he fell to his knees, screaming.

I could not stand. My injured leg gave way beneath me, and my vision became red and black around the edges, as if I were looking through some gore-drenched tunnel. Our forces were gone, and I was surrounded by the enemy. My home, my fortress, had fallen. I felt an impact, and the shock made me drop the dagger in my left hand. I reached over my shoulder and found the handle of a weapon protruding from my back. There was an axe buried between my shoulder blades.

My last thought before the darkness took me, before my death, was of my family. I hoped Helena and my children had escaped. We had planned so much, and I grieved for them, for the loss of the happiness we had and for the pain that had come to us. I had tried to live with honour, to serve my Emperor, to be a good father and a good Lord. It had come to this. Kneeling in my own home and waiting to die.

I lifted my head and cried out in sorrow and fear, and darkness fell with the last blow.

In the cellar, I hung my head, but I could not cry or make a sound. My ability to express my grief was another thing that had been taken from me.

Wise men say that the flesh is weak. This is a weakness I lack.

Living men are at the mercy of their own flesh.

They can revel in it, indulging in violence and lust, or they can be betrayed by it. Emotions are partly physical. The heart beats faster in fear. The lungs seem to reduce in size as you gasp for breath in panic. The muscles tire, ache with fatigue, or twitch and contract of their own accord as the terror sets in and horror grows. The bowels loosen when the war-horn blows, whether it be your first battle or your fifteenth. Any man that tells you he is not afraid of the battlefield is a liar or a fool.

So, though I was teetering on the edge of a fit of madness, my body did not react in the way you would expect. I did not panic physically. My mind wanted to flee but my body did not respond.

I began to assess myself, as calmly as I could. It was as though a part of me could detach from the screaming in my head, suppress it, push it deep down until it was just a small sound underneath my thoughts. Like music heard from another room.

My death was self-evident. I died in the siege, fighting the usurper's traitorous forces. Frachia had killed his brother Domint, claimed the throne of the Western Gate that led from the Scar Sea to the greater ocean beyond, and had then moved to consolidate his fiefdoms along the Northern Shore. Mine had been the last to fall, being the furthest from his seat of power. Frachia must have achieved his precious ascension. A poisonous snake of a man, a foul beast of envy and spite.

I examined myself again and tried to think as clearly as I was able. The man who had come to free me from the door already knew me. He had greeted me with almost endearment, speaking to me as if you would to a family dog. I must have been animated for some time before I had regained my senses.

I looked at my hand again. My bones, and how I loathed the sight of them, were clean. I had seen rotten corpses, the remains of men in various states. Such sights were difficult to avoid in war and stay vividly in memory no matter how much you wished to forget them. These bones had not been recently uncovered, and lacked any obvious stain, or mark of grave-dirt.

My wrists and forearms were armoured with rusted, dented plates, as were my shins. There was a worn leather belt around my waist, with a tattered dark cloth underneath that wrapped around my thighs, though I needed no garment to protect my dignity. I was wearing boots that had seen better days, and they had been stuffed with rags to ensure a tight fit against my fleshless feet. At the top of the boots leather strips were bound around my ankles to stop the footwear from shifting position.

There was a sword on the floor to my right-hand side. This also looked rusted and badly made, and it had broken, its blade in several pieces scattered around me. It was evident I was a soldier of sorts.

I had the bare minimum of armour. Enough to avoid broken arms and legs, but no breastplate and no helmet. A breastplate would have been superfluous I supposed. I had no heart to reach with a striking blade. The lack of helmet concerned me as my head still seemed to be the seat of my thoughts. Did this mean my consciousness was also not worth protecting?

I was a cheap soldier. Minimum armament and armour, little concern for my protection. A conscript then. Forced to fight, thrown onto the frontlines to flood the enemy with bodies.

I had heard stories as a boy, told around fires by older children, of terrifying things that come in the night. Walking corpses, animated bones, wailing and tortured spirits hunting for souls or driven by the will of evil men. As a grown man I had always considered such things tall tales to scare children, a bit of merriment for the old at the expense of the young. I had done the same with my own children. Now I seemed to be part of such a story. Unless this was but a feverish dream and I was soon to awake.

I determined there was no sense in waiting to wake up. I would have to travel through this nightmare until it reached its conclusion.

I couldn't speak, I couldn't smell, but I could hear. I heard footsteps.

Rack appeared at the bottom of the stairs, torch in hand, and he was flanked by a pair of soldiers, skeletal like me. If we had been placed alongside each other you would not be able to tell us apart. Both were armed and armoured as I was, their decaying and battered swords in scabbards at their waists. Their black eye-sockets betrayed a slight green glow, deep inside their skulls.

"Come on then," Rack said, addressing me, "let's

get you down."

He turned to face his entourage and pointed at one of them to gain his attention.

"You, grab the sword in the door and pull it as hard as you can."

The dead man hesitated, thinking through these apparently complicated instructions, while Rack pointed at the other.

"You, grab his legs and hold him, don't want him cracking his skull on the floor do we, eh?"

The first skeleton had begun walking towards me, and he started to heave on the sword as the second skeleton finally seemed to understand what was required of him and moved forwards to grab at my dangling legs.

Unlike Rack's poor attempt, the first skeleton removed the sword from the rotted wood behind with little effort. Rack had to instruct the second skeleton to let go of me once the sword was removed, else I would have remained held in the air in his bony embrace.

Rack pointed at all of us and then gestured to the corner of the room.

"All right you lot, stand over there out of the bloody way."

I hesitated for a moment and then obeyed his command, as did my brethren. My delay was a little greater than theirs, but it did not matter, as Rack paid no attention to us after issuing his instruction.

He shuffled over to the door I had been pinned to and opened it, lifting its old, rust-encrusted handle. The door's hinges screeched and moaned, and the wood had become misshapen through damp. The base of the door caught on the flagstones and Rack had to put his shoulder against it to open it fully. Behind the door was a small storeroom, festooned with cobwebs and dust. There were a few barrels inside, some sacks, and some shelves covered in empty bottles and various broken pieces of pottery. Nothing in the room seemed of any value.

Rack shook his head. "Silly shore-people, all that effort for a room full of crap."

He closed the door, again having to lean against it to get it moving against the rust and the filth, and then he turned back to face us.

He pointed at me.

"You follow me. Need to get you fixed up and kitted out again, don't we? And I'll have to replace the bloody guards. Kantus won't be 'appy, not that he ever is mind..."

His instruction tapered off into grumbling complaint, and then he caught himself and continued to issue commands. He pointed at my brethren.

"You two, pick that carcass up and follow us upstairs. At least we can do some recruiting, heheh."

He laughed at his own little wit, but it swiftly became a series of choking and sickly sounding coughs, and I followed the sound of his hacking lungs as he moved back up the stairs.

The other dead men picked up their soon-to-be brother, each taking one end. There was an awful, wet, tearing sound as they peeled the corpse from the flagstones, the blood it leaked having stuck it fast to the floor. At the top of the stone spiral staircase the door was open, and we stepped into a small, enclosed courtyard, surrounded by a high stone wall. The wall was not in good repair, and chunks of old masonry were strewn about the space. The courtyard was open to the sky but the light was dim and there were dark rain-clouds stretching overhead. The sensation of rain falling on my bare skull was not pleasant, and I could feel water running into my eye-sockets and the cleft gap of my nasal passages. It was impossible to tell if was dawn or dusk.

The courtyard lay at the base of a small tower, a keep of sorts, which we had exited the basement of, flanked by a few scattered outbuildings in poor repair. The tower itself was tumbling and ragged, and from where I stood, I could see spiral stairs that wound to the top of it exposed by gaps in the masonry. The stairs ended in the middle of the air. There were the partial remains of a crenelated platform at the top of the tower, but this looked like a most unsafe standing place. This was a watchtower, and it was in ruins.

In the courtyard was a ranked assembly of the dead. They numbered thirty or so, a full regiment, and they stood still and at attention. Beside them was a covered wooden wagon lashed behind a starved and diseased looking horse. There were a handful of corpses on the ground here as well, in the same skirmisher's garb as the man in the basement. A handful of the dead worked to peel them from where they had fallen and load them into the back of the wagon.

Rack walked towards the regiment and pointed at three of the dead to issue them with instruction.

"You three – guard duty. You two at the top of the stairs, you at the bottom. Go now."

They considered these instructions carefully, and then broke rank and moved to their assigned positions. Rack turned his back to the regiment and addressed the two who had accompanied him.

"You two, load the body in the wagon then rank up. You, join the ranks with them. We're marchin' back to Estwake."

This last instruction was for me, and I dutifully joined the ranks of the grim soldiers.

We left the courtyard in file, two by two, and I thanked my luck that I had been a soldier in my old life, before I was granted my title. I knew enough to keep my march paced well and to pay attention to my orders.

The watchtower was on the Coast Road, the main artery of travel that linked all of the Baronies of the Northern Shore, along the Scar Sea. Coming out of the courtyard there were the remains of a gatehouse to my right, and I could see where iron gates had once stood, the rainwater of years having left red-orange stains on the stonework where the hinges had decayed in their settings. The ruined stone gate post on the opposite side of the road met up with a cliff edge that tumbled down to the rocks and crashing waves of the Scar Sea. The cliffs were the height of many men. There was a road leading to the water's edge, behind the watchtower, and this trailed down steeply until it reached Estwake Harbour, and beyond it the Scar River. The river fed into the sea through the Scar, the great fissure that ran along the foot of the Sagaran Mountains. It emptied into the bay before the sea widened into the Great Crossing.

I risked a look back and could see the light chasing the waves all the way to the west as the sun struggled to rise through grey and heavy clouds. The Western Gate lay many leagues that way, as the ocean tapered again from its wide expanse back to the narrow passage that held the seat of Empire and the fortress island.

I knew this place. More memories arose from the depths of my mind, still dim but slowly coming into focus. This gate and keep were the most westward edge of the Estwake Barony, of my estates. The cliffs here rose to a height and then met the plateau of my holdings along the ravine of the Scar. A natural rampart that had hampered Frachia's forces for some time when I defended my lands.

The rain continued to fall, heavier than before, and we marched in silence through the morning. Rack led the procession on his wagon, and he never looked back to check his entourage. I stole glances at my fellow skeletal brethren but could not gain any attention from them. I even dared reach out to touch the shoulder of the one to my left and could not raise a response of any kind.

We made our way along the cliffs, and then into the highlands where the trail we followed ran alongside the great crevasse of the Scar. During my lifetime Estwake had been a place of lush and verdant pine tree forests, wild scrubland and crags, beautiful and fierce where men had not tamed it. Now a malaise hung over all, the darkness of the rain and cloud mixed with foul mists that rose from the ground and curled around our feet as we trudged on through the landscape. The trees looked threadbare and sickly. The wild grasses and flowers were grey and bleached. We passed places where I knew sheep and goats should be on the rolling hillsides, yet there were no flocks and no shepherds tending them. I had never seen my holdings so bare of life. The oppressive atmosphere extended to wildlife as well, as there were no birds, and the only sound that marked our passing was the syncopated slap of boots on the ill-kept road surface. It was as though we marched through a graveyard.

In my time there had been many bridges across the Scar to join the two halves of my territory, and these had been proudly kept and well-maintained, vital as they were to the business of the estate. The ruins of these remained in some places, ramshackle piles of stone marking where the footings had been, some with rotting timbers clinging in ghastly likeness to my own uncovered bones. Many had collapsed completely, falling into the ravine below and then swept to sea by the river. Others had been maintained or repaired but with little care.

New wood had been hammered haphazardly into ancient timber, and pillars of stone had been shored up with no thought to design or aesthetics.

We passed villages that were devoid of all life and activity, their buildings empty, their doors and windows gaping open and gazing sightlessly into the cold grey morning.

The first sign of life I saw was at Estwake Town, the settlement opposite my old residence of Estwake Castle. The town itself lay on our side of the ravine, joined to the castle by a wide stone bridge. A wall enclosed the town, joining up with the edge of the Scar in a wide semi-circle, although even in my time Estwake had spilled the boundaries of this wall. There were stables, blacksmiths, stoneworkers and even some dwellings outside of its protection. We passed these on our way through the main gate and they were filled with industry, although I did not recognise the men and women working there. They were clothed in a similar manner to Rack, with dark and filthy cloaks and dirty hands and faces. They were of all shades of skin and varieties of feature, and yet shared the same diseased and sunken look that Rack wore.

We entered the town gate, flanked and guarded by more of my undead kind, and then marched along the main cobbled thoroughfare towards the keep bridge. The buildings either side of us were in disrepair but still occupied, and wary eyes looked out at us from muck-encrusted windows and dark doorways. There was no-one in the streets; no children playing, no family dogs scampering. The only sign of life beyond the suspicious house-dwellers were rats racing along the gutters and out-matching our pace. I recognised some buildings from my time living here, but many things had changed. Streets had shifted position, become more enclosed, and the houses hung over them, blocking out any weak light the sun could drive through the clouds. The whole town was more warren-like, as if it were a nest of rodents rather than a place for men and women to live.

We came to the keep bridge and marched across the yawning chasm on its uneven and broken road surface. We passed through the bastion gate, the one that had fallen to Frachia, and I was back in the courtyard where I had been slain.

The bleached and battered stone of the keep loomed above us, the height of twenty men. It had been built directly into the mountain behind it, many hundreds of years before, and had always been an imposing and intimidating structure. Now it was a monument to darkness and death. Black ivy and white threads of fungus clung to walls and buttresses, reaching up to encompass its crenelated towers, and pikes were thrust into the stonework in places where cracks had formed. These pikes were surmounted with many severed heads, in various stages of decomposition. Some were bare skulls such as the one on my shoulders, and some had rotten flesh of many shades and hues still clinging to the bone.

Rack pulled back on the reins of his drawing

horses, shouting a command to stop, and then stood and turned to face the assembly of dead still marching behind him.

"Cease march! Stand to!" he yelled as loudly as he could, and then was stricken by a series of choking coughs that led him to bend over yet again, holding his chest. The ranks of skeletons obeyed his command and stood still and silent, waiting patiently for his instruction to resume.

Elsewhere in the courtyard other skeletons stood in rows, silent and unmoving. In one far corner there was a row of cages, constructed of wicker tied with iron wire. The greatest noise in the courtyard came from these cages, a susurration of moans, shuffling, scratching and wailing. There were more of Rack's compatriots here too, ambling to-and-fro on quiet errands and carrying armour, weapons and leatherwork, but so close to the darkness of the keep they did not speak and they tried to move as quietly as they could. They paid us no attention at all.

A single sound rang out, the *clip-clop* of horseshoes on stone, and a dark figure on horseback slowly made his way towards our assembly.

The horse was skeletal, and armoured, with dull metal plates on its shins, its chest, and a spiked and armoured helmet. Barding ran along its sides, with black cloth underneath to stop it from grinding against exposed bone.

Its rider was a grim and terrifying apparition. It was armoured from head-to-toe, and its black-stained armour was ornate, etched with scrolling curlicues across every plate. It had a black cloak around its shoulders, not a ragged one like Rack's and his brethren, but an ebony velvet cape that shimmered as it moved in the weak sunlight. On the rider's head was a helmet with a pointed visor carved to look like a hunting bird, with black feathered wings sweeping back to rise to two points above his head. The rider reached up with one armoured gauntlet to lift its visor, and beneath the mask was a face like mine, all flesh removed, all skin shorn. The eye-sockets of the rider gave off the soft green glow common to my kind.

It spoke, and its voice was like the peal of a broken bell. Its mouth did not open, but I knew the source of the sound with no visual cue.

"Rack", It said.

Rack got down from his wagon, moving stiffly after his long ride. He walked towards the armoured rider and knelt before him on one knee.

"Sire Kantus," Rack said, "the tower at the western border has been raided. I've switched the guard and recovered the bodies of some Shore scum."

"Did they achieve anything of value, Rack? What was their purpose?"

Kantus' voice came from nowhere, from everywhere. I could feel it in my skull like a cloud of flies buzzing in a stone cell.

"Not sure, Sire," replied Rack, "they broke a couple of the guards and made a mess, but there's nothing there to take, and they didn't come into Estwake at all. Bloody pointless really…"

Kantus ignored Rack's muttering. Another undead approached the mounted warrior from across the courtyard, this one in similarly ornate black armour, and he knelt before the horse-rider, his head bowed. His helmet bore the image of some lizard-like creature, scaled and fanged. Kantus addressed the newcomer.

"Hallek. They are testing our defences. Scouting for weaknesses. We have hidden our activities as best we can, but we are moving forward now, and the alarm has been raised. We mustn't underestimate them."

"All they have done is provide us with new recruits." Hallek's voice was like his commanding officer's, a dull hollow echo issuing from under his helmet.

Rack chuckled at Hallek's statement, but then broke into another coughing fit, thumping his chest with one filthy fist to try to clear his airways. Sire Kantus ignored Rack's ailments, and trotted his steed over to the wagon, reaching down to turn over one of the bodies that lay in its bed.

In the daylight I got a better look at the dead soldiers. They wore light armour, leather with some steel plating, patches of mail in places. Skirmisher's wear like the body in the watchtower basement, not the clothing of a front-line soldier. Some had dark cloaks around their shoulders, and I saw one had his pinned at the neck with a small silver clasp, shaped like the fin of some predatory fish. Most had fair skin, although some had the darker skin of the lands to the far south or the Outer Islands in the

Western Ocean.

Kantus turned back to Rack and spoke. His voice began to pain me, like a headache caused by a bright light stared at too long. He began to issue commands and each one was like a spike thrust into my mind.

"Take these to Lord Kroll. He'll determine which are suitable for raising. Our enemies reduce while we grow in number. Hallek, rotate the regiments. Send a new garrison to the Western Watchtower to hold the pass there."

Kantus gestured to the front rank of the skeletons that had accompanied Rack, which included me. "You four, take this wagon down to the crypts."

Three of my brethren stepped forwards, and I matched their tread. There was no hesitation this time. Kantus' command was like a compulsion in my head, as if a hand had pushed me in the small of my back and forced me to move. He could reach into me and make me obey every word. I did not attempt to resist.

The four of us unhitched the wagon from the starving horse that drew it and then lifted the wagon's wooden spars over our shoulders. We marched towards the yawning dark gate at the base of the main keep and headed inside, leaving Sire Kantus and his underlings behind.

More memories came to me then. This had been my home. I remembered how well I had lit the keep when I had been Baron of Estwake. It was easy for the mountains to seem oppressive and the light up here could be dull and grey, so I had made great efforts to illuminate the inside of the castle, to make it a place of cheer and warmth. There were torch emplacements in the central corridor of the keep that used to burn day and night. Now there was only thin light from the door behind us. I was shocked that I could still see clearly, but it was not natural. I only perceived shades of grey, with a slight green caste. It seemed that another small advantage of my new state was excellent vision in darkness.

We passed the stairs that reached to the upper floors of the castle, my old suites, my guest rooms, my children's bedrooms. My despair increased as I noted the bedraggled and forlorn state of the keep, the cobwebs and dust, the rotted and splintered furnishings, the tattered remains of tapestries hanging threadbare from damp and mouldy stone. We reached the main hall at the middle of the keep. All the furniture here had been removed. There had once been a great table, where we held feasts for the local gentry and farmers at festival times. Now the flagstones were bare, and rotted rags hung across the walls where once had been luxurious displays of hunting trophies and rich cloth. There were open doors dotted around the hall, side rooms that had been kitchens, pantries, guard quarters, servants' quarters, armouries. We passed all of these and headed further into the rear of the keep. We were headed for the very back of the castle, where its walls bled into the mountain stone. We were going down into the catacombs.

The castle had been built over them, long before I had been Baron there. The caves nearer the surface had been used as storerooms, billets for visiting nobles' soldiery, but as the cave system wound down into the mountain the rooms became crypts and mortuaries, resting places for the Barons and families that had preceded mine and who had held the castle for centuries. As we neared the old entrance to the catacombs, I could see that the portal had been expanded. It had once been a stout oaken door embedded in the rear wall of the keep. Now it was a great gaping mouth in the side of the mountain, roughly chiselled and dug away into a wide and shadowed opening. Torchlight flickered in its depths as we led the wagon down a roughhewn passageway. We could have fit two more wagons alongside ours, such was the expanse of the tunnel. The passage led down many strides into the mountain side, and I saw that all the old catacombs had been opened up and run together, with only remnants of side passages holding scattered piles of bones. Rats scuttered here and there, sniffing at our passing and vanishing into crevices at our approach, and a miasma of flies and other carrion insects moved in waves and clouds around us. As we lurched further into the mountain some side rooms became visible. They were little more than extended alcoves in the walls, and in each stood a regiment of dead at attention, closely packed together, unmoving and silent. There were many of these alcoves. There were the beginnings of an army down there.

At the far end of the long sloping tunnel there was a wide, torch-lit, bowl-shaped cavern, its edges interrupted only by a pair of dark caves adjoining it on the far wall. At the base of the cavern, down a ramp of dirt and stone, there was a dark lake, not of water, but of some black, oily liquid. Its surface was occasionally lit by a sparking flash of green, shimmering light. Looking into the lake was like staring into some unnatural storm cloud. In the far corner of the cavern, on the opposite side of the dark tarn, there was a large metal cauldron, wider than it was tall, like a serving bowl. It was lit from beneath by a stone-ringed fire pit and held upright on black metal posts. Inside it a viscous white liquid bubbled and turned, and macabre shapes broke the surface of the boiling stew, hands with flesh running from them like wax, scalps of melted hair and ruined skin. Around the bowl and across the cavern many of Rack's colleagues hurried at their business. There was a stack of bodies stripped bare of almost all flesh alongside the cauldron, and these were transferred in piles to the waiting black-green lake. Other workers passed us and moved back up to ground level bearing bundles of clothes, armour, and removed weaponry. It was an industrious room. Standing and watching the activity, and occasionally issuing directions or moving to stir the caustic pot, was a dark, slim figure. He leant on a long black iron pole, that he occasionally used to fish a part out of the cauldron and inspect it before letting it sink once more into the stripping fluid. He wore simple black leather boots and linen trousers, and a long green tabard hanging halfway down his thighs. He had a dark grey cloak around his shoulders, with the hood drawn back to reveal skin that was a deep yellow ochre in the torchlight. His features were rough and lined, and he had a short grey beard and long, grey, straggled hair, greasy and untamed. When he was not directing the industry around the cavern, he muttered to himself, chanting some language I did not recognise under his breath.

He looked up from his activities, and if I could have drawn a breath I would have.

His eyes bled, red life fluid running where tears usually fall, and the irises of his eyes were black, the whites, pink. His stare sang with madness and horror, and the impact of his glance struck me like a blow to the chest.

He propped his iron stave up on a hook at one side of the cauldron and walked around the edge of the dark lake to meet us. He was a small man, almost two heads shorter than me. He had a pronounced limp, as if one of his legs was misshapen or truncated somehow. This made his head bob a little from side to side, and the shadow he cast on the cavern wall behind him shifted back and forth as if it were trying to escape its ties to him. He did not rush towards us. He paced slowly and calmly, shifting his weight to accommodate his ungainly gait, and held himself up as if he were a noble moving around a banquet or a dance. His awful stare seemed to burn into me, and for a moment I feared he knew I was conscious and watching him with intelligence. Thankfully he passed me with little regard, and turned to face us as a group, with no regard to my individuality.

"Attend me", he said, in a deep, sonorous voice, an unexpectedly pleasant sound in those unpleasant surroundings. I knew exactly what he required of us with no further instruction. This was not like Rack's clumsy control, or even like the commands that Kantus had issued with seemingly physical force. Kroll's words were spoken, and his needs appeared in my head as if they were a thought of my own.

He strode to the back of the wagon, and we followed him, two of us on each side of him. he leaned into the carry-bed of the trailer and inspected its contents, and then reached out to the corpse on the top of the pile, having to stand with one foot on a wheel to reach due to his short stature. He grasped the edges of the breastplate it wore, one hand on each side of the corpse's chest, and then lifted the body from the pile and placed it down on the ground in front him with no effort at all. He was unnaturally strong. He knelt next to the body and placed his hand on the dead man's forehead. He began to chant again, a low sibilant drone, and after a short while he removed his hand from the cold skin of the corpse and stood up.

"The stripping bowl for this one. You two, remove his clothes and boil him."

Two of my companions stooped and started to remove armour and clothing from the corpse, taking no care at all, ripping and shredding garments. There was no respect for the dead here. They were materiel to be used, grain for the mill of Kroll's dark industry.

While the skeletons carried out their instructions, Kroll lifted another body from the pile, knelt beside it, and repeated his chanting inspection.

After a short time, he shook his head and gave a little sigh of disappointment.

"This one is no good. Just useless meat. You two, take this one through to the Lesser Chamber. Nisht can have him."

Understanding immediately, and without hesitation, I moved forwards and then reached down to grasp the corpse under its arms as my companion lifted it by the legs. The weight did not discomfort me. I seemed perhaps a little stronger, or less prone to physical tiredness certainly, than I had been in life. That being said the body was awkward to manoeuvre, as I had to walk backwards, and the corpse swung to-and-fro as my helper and I shuffled around the circumference of the lake.

We headed towards the left-most cave at the rear of the lake cavern, and as we left Kroll's presence I suddenly felt as if a cloud had lifted and my full thoughts and faculties were my own again, to the extent they could be in my current predicament. We entered a low, unlit tunnel, and carried the body down it until we came to a small antechamber. This was the brightest and most well-lit room I had been in since I had entered the castle. There were torches spaced evenly around the walls, and shelves festooned with candelabra that were filled with large, lit candles, each with a small, polished plate behind them to increase the effect of their light. A greater version of these silver plates hung from the ceiling on chains, reflecting the candlelight around the room and focusing it onto a long wooden workbench that lay beneath the shining surface. On the workbench was another corpse, strapped down with long leather belts. It wore an iron collar around its neck, with a hoop to fashion a chain to, and its skin was mottled and rotten. The flesh was blackened in some places, a pale yellow-grey in others. A long ugly wound ran from the side of the dead man's belly up to his ribcage, crossing his midriff diagonally. The poor man had been disembowelled. A woman leant over the corpse and was roughly stitching together the wound with black twine and a curved iron needle.

She was tall, taller than me, and shaven-headed, with pale skin and cadaverous features. At first I mistook her for some undead creature herself, but then she looked up from her work and sighed, rolled her dark and blood-shot eyes, and lay down the hooked needle on a small tray next to her. She moved around the workbench and walked towards us, both my companion and I still holding either end of the body, having not been instructed to put it down.

She ignored us and leaned in to inspect our cargo.

"More of his cast-offs then. What use is being an apprentice if all I do is stitch together his rejects? When is he going to let me do some proper work?"

She spoke in Sechian, like the others, but I recognised her accent as being of the noble classes. She certainly had a more noble bearing than Rack and others of his ilk. I felt her questions were rhetorical and she did not expect a response.

She brushed absentmindedly at the dark leather

tabard she wore over her clothes. She, like Kroll, wore garments that seemed a little more well-made than that of Rack and the other workers. The long robe she wore under her protective apron was trimmed with silver thread.

She addressed us directly and gave instruction. She was not as compelling as Kroll, but she didn't have to try hard to make us understand.

"Put that in the basket over there. I'll get to it in a bit, I must finish this piece first."

She gestured at a large wooden crate in the corner of the room. There were slats in its sides where its contents were visible, and even if this were not the case its lid was propped open. It was filled with dead men and women in various stages of decomposition. One stray arm hung over the lip of the box. Grey fingers with blackened fingernails splayed in a spider shape from the dead limb. A single, staring, white and rotted eye could be seen near the bottom of the crate, gazing out blindly through the gaps in the wood.

My companion and I stalked over to the crate, and with some awkward and clumsy manoeuvring managed to discard our load and add it to the pile of dead. We turned back to face Nisht but she had already forgotten our presence and resumed her work at the bench. She was finishing her stitching, and singing, rather tunelessly, an old Sechian lament. She tied off a stitch and leaned forward to bite off the spare thread hanging from her repair. Then she stood up and reached for a bowl that sat on a shelf behind her. I could see from where I stood that the copper bowl contained a portion of black liquid, the same as that in the lake of the main chamber. She held the bowl with her left arm underneath it and moved her right hand in small, graceful patterns over the surface of its contents. A dim green light reached up from the bowl and illuminated her palm and the underside of her fingers. She lowered her hand into the bowl and with the tips of her fingers scooped a small amount of the black slime out. She winced as her skin touched it but ignored the pain and began to chant under her breath. I heard no words I recognised, but one phrase stood out from the others.

"R'Chun", she said, over and over again, with an entreating tone.

She put the bowl back on the shelf. Holding her fingers, still dripping with the foul ooze, over the body of the dead man, she parted his lips with her left hand and rubbed a portion of the black liquid into his exposed gums. She did this with almost motherly care. She closed the mouth of the corpse and then wiped her fingers on the front of her apron. They were blistered and raw from where the substance had touched them. Then she pressed her palm to the body's forehead and began to chant again.

The corpse twitched. Its fingers clenched slowly, opened, clenched again. Its eyes opened, and they were white, grey, pink, blind. It let out a low, rasping sigh. Then it sat up with a jerky and ungainly motion.

She turned her back to the undead creature and addressed my companion and me.

"Take this one up to the Lesser's Cage. Then rejoin your regiments and refresh yourselves."

The corpse stood of its own accord and lurched towards us. We each gripped an arm. I was filled with revulsion and horror but showed as little reaction as I could. Certainly, Nisht did not seem to notice my hesitancy, although she could hardly have read my expression. The dead man struggled against us a little, like a wriggling and unruly child being dressed for court. We marched it back out of the antechamber, down the unlit corridor and back to the cavern of the lake. I was lucky my companion had some idea of what our instructions meant, as by this time I was near insensible with terror and confusion. My mind had almost broken, and If I could have made a sound I would have been gibbering with horror. I was moving in a dream, a nightmare, every moment since my waking in the watchtower adding another crack in my sanity. All I could do was keep going forwards and hope that some answer would find me.

We marched back through the central cavern, around the black lake where Kroll and his followers, engaged in their grisly industry, ignored our passing. I saw Kroll dragging dripping bones from the boiling cauldron with his long iron stave, and his assistants arranging them on the ground beside the wide dark pool. One man took a bundle of bones, and carefully slid them into the liquid, which flashed green as the surface was broken by the new dead offering. We left through the main cave entrance, back up the long slope through the catacombs. We marched past the alcoves filled with waiting skeletal soldiers, and through the battered and tumble-down remains of the keep. We reached daylight again, and dragged our charge through the courtyard, stalking towards the cages I had seen on my first arrival. They were huge, lining one entire wall of the yard, and they were roughly constructed of tree limbs, twine and wire. At the fore of each was a gate entrance, fastened with a chain. One of Rack's compatriots, a small dark-skinned woman with a tattered and balding scalp of grey hair, scarred on one side of her face by horrible burns, scurried to the gate of the nearest cage and fished a brass key from inside her cloak.

She unfastened the gate but held it shut, and a commotion began inside as shapes lurched towards the opening. Inside the cages were hundreds of walking corpses, wearing only spare cloth and clothing, each bearing the evidence of some repair. A stitched-on limb. A filled and patched eye-socket. A splint, nails hammered into rotten flesh and dead bone to fortify a leg.

The horrifying mass of animated and dead matter moaned and rattled and screeched as they perceived our approach. They moved too slowly to escape their prison. We were able to add to their number through the gate opening before they reached us. The woman who kept the cage door shoved the new addition inside and closed the gate behind him before any of the dead could leave their captivity. The raised man stumbled around his new confines and joined in with the wailing and growling of his brethren.

My skeletal companion, who in all this time

had not acknowledged my presence, strode away, back to the keep. I followed him inside and we marched through it once more, back to the catacomb entrance and the slope down into darkness. He reached one of the alcoves set into the tunnel wall, already filled with many others like us. He turned so he was parallel to the dead behind him, and then stepped backwards. He aligned himself in a gap shoulder to shoulder with another of the silent skeletons. I followed his example, although without his precise movements, and stood next to him.

That was the first day of my new existence.

CHAPTER TWO

The undead do not sleep, as such.

That is to say, it is not like a living man sleeps, to regain energy and reform his thoughts. We do not have muscles and hearts and lungs so these need no rest. We do have minds, of a kind, though some of us have more mind than others. One of the first things I learned of my new being was that sometimes we needed to rest. Kroll and his people call it being 'refreshed'. For my brethren it was a matter of clearing old instructions, as their small and primitive thoughts clutter up their heads. After some time spent functioning, no matter the task, they begin to behave erratically. They fail to follow commands, or follow old commands long rescinded. They become stuck in repetitive routines, or fail to perform any action at all when instructed. A Raised, for that is how we were referred to by Kroll and his cult, could start to march away with no direction, not even stopping when reaching a barrier but instead pushing forward as if they could walk through walls and becoming frustrated when they could not. I heard talk of Raised becoming berserk and attacking their living handlers, or even each other, but there was never any inference from this that they had made a conscious decision, or that they had rebelled against their control deliberately. It was simply the idiot nature of them.

For me, this refreshing served another purpose. I used the time I was given to retreat into memory and attempt to re-construct my sense of self. The memories of my last moments in life were clearest, though I tried to shy away from those as it was a ghastly recollection. Memories of my family and my life before the siege of Estwake were harder to grasp, and they came in flashes and drips, as though my history were a bowl being filled by intermittent rain.

After refreshing alongside the other Raised I always felt clearer for a few moments, until the reality of my circumstances crashed through. Sometimes I could accept that what was happening to me was real. Sometimes I determined to convince myself that this was simply an extended night-terror, and I would soon wake in my bed with Helena. It was these moments, after refreshing and being given awareness of my surroundings again, that filled me with the greatest sense of despair.

Another method that Kroll used to maintain his grip of control on the Raised was to continually change the disposition and roles of his forces.

The Raised, the numbers of which were growing daily, were rotated through duties and postings with great regularity. A regiment may be guarding the keep and castle at Estwake one day, and then be sent out on patrol, down by the

Scar or up into the mountain passes on another. The wider estates of Estwake, the holdings by the Scar River, the farmsteads, the pastures up on the mountain sides that had once ran with sheep and goats tended by caring shepherds, all of these had been laid to waste. We marched in formation past bleak and bleached meadows where the grass lay grey rather than green as though all life had been drawn from it. It should have been harvest time yet there were no legions of farmhands with scythes to attend to the wheat and barley, and the crops lay dead in the fields. I saw the ruins of farmhouses, their timbers burned, their roofs caved in and only the stone chimneys standing.

Sometimes we would be accompanied on patrol by an officer. Kantus was the first one I served under, and I grew to loathe him. He would trot at the head of our march on his skeletal steed, pontificating about the glory of the Sechian Empire, and the faith he had in his god R'Chun and his Emperor, who had furnished the Sechians with a fearsome army that would conquer the Northern Shore. He was addressing a captive audience who would not voice any criticism of him, and he took full advantage, being by turns boastful and grandiose. I realised fairly quickly that he had little in the way of military experience. No soldier who has been in the field speaks of war in that way. His armour, though ornate, was impractical and over-burdening, for display rather than battle.

There were still small areas of Estwake, nearer the harbour and up along the border with the neighbouring barony of Tresh, that were viable farmland. Members of Kroll's cult who were not engaged in raising the dead were working this land, and if we had to interact with any of them it was Kantus that did so. The cult all treated him with deference and respect, kneeling before him before addressing him in any way. There were still mouths to feed in Estwake, as even though the dead outnumbered the living, Kroll's followers required sustenance. In my life Estwake had traded grain and other goods with the other Baronies along the Northern Shore. Now nothing went west along the Coast Road. Only Estwake Harbour itself remained in anything like good condition, and still seemed to welcome ships from all along the Northern Shore, or at least it did the few times I was given sight of it. It appeared the Harbour was the mask that Estwake wore to hide from the rest of the Baronies.

Our people's custom had been to give the honoured dead to the water, if they gave worship to Omma T'Lassa, the Mother of the Sea. The common folk further inland often gave their worship to the Lady of the Forest, G'Rath, the Serpent under the Mountain, S'Gara, or the hungry god of the cold north wind, Th'qa. These inland folk buried their dead. We were often tasked with exhuming the graves of these poor souls and adding their leavings to the growing legions of Kroll's army. This was foul work, and I did what I could to ignore the repercussions of what I was doing and focus on the labour, convincing myself that I was simply performing farm tasks of a kind. I was not always successful in distancing myself from these activities, and would often pause, stood in the pit of a shallow grave, despair and horror circling inside my skull like chasing animals as the rotted parts of some unfortunate peasant were unearthed from the soil. Fortunately, my hesitancy at these times was ascribed to stupidity rather than intelligence.

Our most important duty was to guard the border with Tresh. The eastern border of Estwake was mountainous and near impassable, but the western border was open in many places, not just the pass at the Coast Road. These entrances were overlooked by the remains of more watchtowers and guarding keeps. In my life they had been well-maintained and well-manned. Now just the ruins of these buildings stood like broken teeth in rotted gums, ivy- and moss-covered stones scattered around them. We sometimes stood guard while exposed completely to the elements, the wind and rain howling and slicing through the gaps in my ribcage and the holes in my skull. I stood and stared out from broken crenelations atop unsteady and crumbling towers. As autumn drew on the nights grew darker, and I and my fellows would be left watching the shadows creep across the forests and crags of Tresh under stormy clouds that lashed us with all their fury.

I retreated into memory often, trying to seek solace in the past, and I had ample time to do so. I had been a young man when I was granted my title. I had been a Captain in Emperor Domint's army, and then a Commander, and he had rewarded me for my actions against the Sechian Empire during his campaigns. He had given me

Estwake. The Barony was a natural fortress, mountainous to the East and South with a few easily defended passes, and it was also a fertile and productive land with much resource of food and timber from the mountain pines. To the North were leagues of dense forest, the territory of G'rath, the Lady of the Forest. Only wild beasts resided there, and men were not welcome.

The Sechian Empire had been reduced, pushed back and crippled. I took my men, our belongings, our titles and our families to Estwake and turned the castle and its holdings into a thriving, bustling and busy centre of life and light.

My wife Helena and I had a son and a daughter, Ascus and Aisha. We played. We hunted. We feasted. We loved each other. I miss them still, and if I had a heart in my empty chest it would break again at the thought of them. My brothers-in-arms, Lucien, Balus, had families of their own, and helped to run the holdings. It was a wonderful, peaceful time, of joy and bright summers and cold sparkling winters. We thought we had left war behind. The memories of bloodshed and filth and horror in Sechia faded. We had ten years of peace and prosperity, of love and growth.

Then the Emperor Domint, third of his name, died.

He was discovered on the floor of his chambers, blood and froth running down his chin, convulsing as though he were being struck with hot irons. It was foul and ignominious death for such a great man, a man I thought of as my friend and benefactor.

The messengers raced to my estate on fast ships or fast horses, telling tales of poison, treachery, betrayal. Domint's wife had been put to the sword. His most loyal retainers were hanging from the bridges at the Western Gate or were impaled on spears to stand against the skyline. The guards of the fortress had betrayed their leader and lined up behind his brother Frachia in a military coup, and mercenary companies that had fought with us in Sechia joined his forces, no loyalty in them except to the promise of coin. Frachia had bought or threatened or black-mailed all the Baronies along the Northern Shore, and many turned without fighting, having little thirst for another war after such a peace. Only a few of us, myself and my comrades included, refused to kneel to the Usurper. We fought well but could not prevail against the tide turned against us and we were pushed back, encircled, and finally destroyed.

There were things I learned about my circumstances later, and things I learned from Kroll's followers during my captivity. Kroll's cult were a strange, twisted lot, prone to prattling on, speaking to themselves like madmen. All of them were demented in a variety of ways, and they often spoke to the dead with a strange affection, as though they were addressing small children or family dogs. They were more likely to engage the dead in one-sided conversation than they were to speak to each other, and this habit, though strange, was useful to me at least.

"You've got t'know yer place, y'see?" said Clasp, as he leaned in to rub my skull with a dollop of brown wax.

I was being cleaned and repaired. When on patrol, or in combat, a Raised can find himself covered from skull to toe-bone in mud and filth, and the nature of our form meant we had many crevices that could harbour dried earth. I had had the misfortune of having mud in my eye-sockets on more than one occasion and it was extremely uncomfortable as well as partially blinding. Kroll's people took more care of our cleanliness and well-being than they did their own, so on my return from one of the mountain patrols I had been given to Clasp so he could perform maintenance. Obviously, I could not reply to his question, whether rhetorical or not, so I simply stared over his shoulder as he wiped me down and inspected my anatomy.

Clasp was a little taller than most of his colleagues, less stooped. He was still filthy, and his clothes were hanging from him in torn loops, but he took pride in his work. The sword that had been embedded in my ribcage a moon or so earlier had left notches in the bone, and he had filled them with some sort of compound that he smeared into the gaps and then let dry to a hard finish. Once it had set, he sanded down the rough surface and then bound the repair with strips of cloth soaked in tree-sap, which then hardened and served to strengthen the bone. He had cleaned the dirt from me, having to use a stiff brush to dig the muck out of the joints of my feet and ankles. He had then decided I needed a polish so had worked his way across my skull with a rough cloth.

"Kroll's got a plan, y'see, he's goin' ta sort these Northern Shore bastards out, just you wait. Think they can sit here on all this food and gold and what-'ave-you and not let us 'ave anything but scraps. Y'don't know what it's like in Sechia. Y'can't grow a bloody thing except weeds, and y'ave ta scrabble around in the swamps and scrublands to find food that dogs wouldn't eat. Is' no right…"

I'd heard similar muttering complaints from other members of Kroll's entourage. They had travelled here by ship some years ago, passing through Estwake Harbour in dribs and drabs until their numbers were enough to enact their plans. They had occupied the ruin of the castle early on. This I did not understand at the time. Why was the castle in ruins when it had once been a great fortress? Why was my old home empty?

The cult had expanded their territory and their army piece by piece, growing over all the Barony of Estwake like the shadow of a rising storm cloud, taking the farms and the smaller fortifications and recruiting to their cause where they could. I could not fathom how they could have achieved all this undetected and with no repercussions.

There was a hierarchy here, and Clasp knew his place in it. At the bottom were the Lessers. They were dead who, by the judgment of Kroll and his apprentices, could not be controlled sufficiently to serve. They had souls that could not be drawn back into their bodies to be refashioned for his purposes. They were instead inhabited by something else, some force I did not comprehend at the time. Nisht led the faction of Kroll's followers who worked on these, overseeing their new purpose and containment. It was not worth the time or effort to remove their flesh, so they were stitched up, awakened, and then herded for use as terror troops. I saw them unleased several times during our raids over the border and the results were horrific. Their flesh worked against them. They were stiff of gait and slow to react, but when they fell upon the enemy they gouged and bit and tore with all their strength, fighting like diseased and maddened animals with no thought to tactics or finesse. Their victims would either be paralyzed by terror or take flight rather than face such an enemy.

Next in this hierarchy of death were the Raised, of which I was one. We had been treated with more care because we could be governed, and had minds of a sort, though most of us had small and simple thoughts. All flesh was stripped from us using the caustic cauldrons that Kroll's cult employed, as the liquid they called the Blood of R'Chun did not react well with living tissue. We were placed in the lake in the catacomb chamber, and some force there re-assembled us, and gave us movement and purpose.

Higher in these rankings were the living, who could command all of those below, or at least drive them forward as they did with the Lessers.

Above all, aside from Kroll himself, were the Greater Raised. Kantus was one of these, as was Hallek. These creatures I did not understand until much later. They held dominion over all of the dead and seemed to think for themselves as I did. They, however, could speak, whereas I still could not. The Greater Raised came and went as they pleased and could to an extent decide their own courses of action, although they deferred to Kroll's command and intent. They were devoted to Kroll, and to the distant Emperor of their own land. Above all they were devoted to the great god R'Chun, to whom they ascribed their strange condition. I knew nothing of this so-called god, having not being particularly knowledgeable of religious matters during my life.

Clasp had finished. He put down his cloth and held my chin with the tips of his fingers, turning my skull this way and that to inspect his workmanship.

"Ahh, y're looking well now. Fresh as a new-born. Got to keep you all in good nick, 'eh? Need to be ready, Kroll's got plans for you!"

I kept still and continued to stare over Clasp's shoulder. It is a lot easier to maintain one's composure when you have no flesh to betray you.

I was placed back in my alcove to refresh with the rest of my brethren, awaiting my next task. The horror I suffered daily had become almost tedious, as though I had absorbed it into my being, and it was now a part of me. Early in my new existence I had contemplated ending myself during one of these periods where I was stored away with my fellow undead. I could not conceive of a way to do it quickly and surely. I had already been in minor skirmishes at the border, and it seemed destruction of the skull was the only sure way to end my kind. I had witnessed skeletal soldiers with only a torso, a head and a single remaining arm still crawling towards their enemy with thoughtless determination. If I attempted to end myself and failed, what would become of me? I did not want my affliction of intelligence to be discovered, as I feared the consequences greatly. My existence was torture, that was sure. What greater torture could lie in being found out? Kroll and his subordinates were cruel, fanatical people. I recalled the heads on pikes, which stared out over the courtyard from the keep above me.

CHAPTER THREE

It was late autumn. The rain lashed the ground with bile and hate, churning the earth to mud.

Kroll was becoming more aggressive. We had claimed the whole border with Tresh, the Barony directly to the west of Estwake. Although the Coast Road was the widest and most accessible thoroughfare between the Baronies, there were still trails and passes between the hills and valleys to the north that needed to be defended, and Kroll had garrisoned these areas, using the ruins of what towers remained to store his forces. Now his army had grown sufficiently in number he was beginning to push westward.

We had raided, pillaged and defiled every graveyard, village, farmstead and hovel in Estwake, and the dead were now a fully-fledged army of conquest.

There was a small township a few miles into Tresh called Gallin. It was little more than a square of stone buildings, a few shared halls and inns, a market, and some wooden dwellings scattered around within a defensive wall made of tumbled stone and badly maintained wooden fencing, hardly a robust fortification.

Its surrounding farmland petered out into the surrounding valleys and pastures. This was to be the first battle I took part in that was not simply a defensive action at our borders. We were to raid Gallin and make it a stepping-stone into Tresh.

Kantus and his lieutenant Hallek led our rag and bone army. We had been assembled in the courtyard at Estwake Castle, ranks upon ranks of skeletal Raised. We had gained cavalry recently, having captured horses from farmer's holdings and from the higher pastures where the herds of animals had escaped into the countryside. Stripping them of their flesh and raising them had been a significant undertaking and had taken a great deal of work, so increasing their numbers further would take time. There were thirty or so Raised sat astride the dead animals, and both they and their mounts had to be monitored carefully; if they failed to follow commands, retrieving them would be a task of immense difficulty.

Kroll's followers milled around, assigning weaponry, fixing padded plates of armour to skinny fleshless forearms with leather strapping, and setting the roles for the forces. We had a regiment of pikemen to lead, their pikes poorly made but useable, little more than sharpened stakes with crude metal hooks hammered into their shafts. I was assigned a sword as before, and I stood there at attention with the rest of the dead, my scabbard belted around my waist over the cloth kilt that covered my pelvis and thighs.

The Lesser Raised were being loaded into caged

wagons drawn by living horses, who whinnied and protested at the stench and sound of their cargo but did not bolt. Some of the shambling rotted creatures had to be dragged from their confinement using long leather loops on poles, tools that Kroll's cult members wielded with the skill of long practice.

Kantus assumed the role of Commander for this expedition, and Hallek was assigned to lead the potentially unruly cavalry. Kantus trotted his steed to the front of the assembled ranks to address his forces. His voice still pained me, its booming and buzzing timbre reverberating inside my skull and making my exposed teeth fizz and crack.

"We are to move upon our neighbour!" he bellowed. "Thus begins our campaign proper against the oppressors of the Northern Shore! They have forced our people to starve in squalor for too long. They feast and fatten and grow idle while we scrabble for scraps in the *dirt!* They drink wine while our people thirst for *clean water!* This will stand *no longer!*"

His horse reared and he raised his unsheathed sword, a weapon as overly ornamented as his armour, above his head in salute. His voice carried easily across the courtyard, though the autumn gale was forcing the rain ahead of it as if herding a stampede of cattle. It was not the voice of a man anymore, but of a ghost.

The living in his audience cheered and clapped and stamped their feet. I spied Rack in the crowd, his pallid face and diseased skin flushed with excitement, his cheering reaction only broken by a round of the hacking coughs to which he was often victim.

The dead did not react. They stood silent and still, unmoved by Kantus' speech and the passion of the crowd. I stood with them, detached, distant, retreating from this circumstance as far as I could into the maddened wanderings of my mind.

The assemble ranks marched for Tresh

A dead army on the move would be faster than a living one, were it not for the baggage train of living it must carry with it. Raised do not tire like common soldiers, or grouse and moan at the weather or the ground conditions, or complain of sores of the feet, aches in the legs, the weight of their kit, the meagreness or quality of their rations, or the thousand other things a soldier on campaign can find to whinge about.

I had been on campaigns in the south and east, when we had fought the old war with the Sechian Empire, defending the borders of the baronies and claiming new ones. The complaints of the rank-and file were a constant source of background noise. It is a statement of some truth to say that you should only worry about a soldier when they stopped whining. Chatter around the fire at camp was always of the comforts of home versus the dire discomfort of the Soldier's Lot. I had on occasion joined in with this pastime myself, even though I was of noble and ranked stature. It was always easier to maintain morale if the men thought you were one of them, even if just for a moment, before re-establishing discipline. When I was young and on campaign, I thought that this was wise of me, that I was playing a role to engender loyalty and obedience. Now I know that these were moments of truth, and my time with the common soldiery on campaign was a time of growth for me. I had been quite full of myself when I was a proud young man.

This dead campaign was not like the living ones I had partaken in. The cavalry led, the only noise they generated being the splash and crack of hooves on mud and stone. The pikemen and swordsmen were next, striding in orderly fashion through the hills and valleys of the Baronies, ignoring the damp seeping into their strapped and padded boots. At times our feet sank into the earth and each stride was accompanied by a *slurp* of mud and water rushing into the space left by our tread.

Behind us in the caravan were the wagon cages of the Lesser Raised, and they moaned and whined and growled as they always did, no meaning of complaint or sign of intelligence in their voices. Further back in the rear-guard were covered wagons carrying living men and women, a portion of Kroll's fanatics here to mend weapons, mend bones, herd the Lesser undead and control smaller forces if needed. Some acted as Sergeants-at Arms if required but were hardly attired for the part and still wore their ragged and dirty clothing. They were not dressed to fight but simply to be present. I saw Rack riding the fore of one of the wagons, Clasp riding another. Clasp gripped the reins tightly of the wagon he drew, and behind him was a great cauldron, the match of the one in Kroll's cavern. Clasp had a pipe lit against the chill, sticking out from under his filthy hood. Behind his wagon was another loaded with many barrels stacked high, which leaned to-and-fro as the muddy and uneven road surface pitched the wagon from side-to-side.

At nightfall we pitched camp, as the living needed to rest, and the dead needed to be kept under control via refreshment. The Raised were arranged in ranks and ordered to re-set themselves, and I gladly took the opportunity to retreat into my memories.

We broke camp just before dawn, and it was early morning, the sun just rising over the mountains behind us, when we reached Gallin. We had passed small, wooden lookout towers on the hills moving down into Gallin's valley, and our approach was marked by the peal of bells and the sound of horns shouting warning to the town. Kantus had not approached with any care or subtlety and did not seem overly troubled by these defensive alarms.

I could see from our higher vantage point, moving down the hillside, that the men and women of the town had assembled along its walls to face us. Most seemed like farmers and workers, shepherds and craftsmen, and they were armed with a variety of tools, farming implements, scythes, shovels, rakes. They were accompanied by a small force of men and women wearing the same skirmisher's garb as those who had raided the watchtower on the Coast Road. These leather and plate-armed soldiers were attempting to organise the defence, though it did not seem as if it was going well.

The cultists with us began some kind of chanting ritual. Dark clouds gathered, and the wind rose. The autumn sun was hidden by the rising storm. Cold and icy sleet began to fall, great freezing drops of water, obscuring vision and churning the ground even further until it was a sticky, sodden morass. The gales howled down from the mountain passes behind us and drove the chill rain at the defending village.

Kantus unleashed the Lessers first. The caged wagons were drawn to the front of our ranks, turned, and opened, and their contents spilled out in a pile of rotting and stitched flesh. Flies and maggots spilled from the ragged dead as they staggered and stumbled and lurched down the hillside like a foul wave. Some were confused and just stood with their blackened mouths opened, howling into the sky above them and gazing into the falling rain with blind white eyes. These were encouraged in their progress towards the village by prods from Kroll's cultists, who carried long barbed poles to drive the Lessers ahead of the rest of the army. Some of the unfortunate dead fell to pieces before they even made it halfway to the village.

The wagons were withdrawn, and the rest of the army began its stride forwards, the cavalry circling wide to our left as a flanking force. I watched as the Lesser Raised approached the villager's defensive line.

I had already partaken in some smaller battles at Estwake's borders, minor actions defending the keeps and watchtowers, but this was the first time I has seen Kroll's forces in a pitched battle. It was not like the old wars. Living men had to be trained, cajoled, ordered to fight, given motivation of coin or glory. They needed good reason to risk their lives, to fight with purpose and objective, and a commander of any competence would not throw away his men in needless battle. Some casualties in battle are inevitable but often it is the line that broke in fear first that lost. The tally of the dead can sometimes mean little to the outcome. You could win the battle but come out of it bloodied and far reduced in number, unable to continue prosecuting a campaign. Or you could lose but withdraw in good time and with good numbers so your forces could be re-applied to the enemy elsewhere.

Kroll's army did not take any of these things into consideration.

The Lesser Raised reached the defensive wall first. When the gathered townsfolk and farmers got a clear view of what they were facing, through the torrential rain, they broke immediately. The few that had the courage to remain were quickly overwhelmed as a wave of death and rot and horror lurched towards them and scrabbled over the poorly made fortifications. The Lessers fought like beasts, tumbling over the wall circling the village and then rising to gnash at throats with black and rotten teeth, to claw at eyes with shattered and ragged fingernails. If a man or woman fell before the horde then two or three Lessers would cease their advance and stoop to feed on them, the howling of their victims as flesh was torn and gouged only adding to the pressure of fear on the defenders. A Lesser would be impaled on a pike or a sword or a long-tined farmer's fork, but then the holder's weapon would be wrenched from their hands, and two more of the dead would drag them down to the ground to feast. Blood spouted from wounds and filled the air like mist. It ran into the mud at the feet of the melee and was churned into the earth until the ground was a sticky and slippy swamp of blood and offal and the shit of men dying in fear and pain.

The skirmishers fared better. Their leather, mail and plate served to protect them well from the snapping teeth of the dead, the claws of the Lessers finding little purchase. Some had crossbows and they removed their targets with great accuracy. These soldiers fought with discipline, keeping their nerve even in the face of this ghastly enemy. They stood back-to-back in twos and threes, covering each other and ensuring that no one of their number could be overwhelmed and brought down. Losing your feet in this battle would be a death sentence. They struck back and managed to make progress forwards, hacking their way through the wall of rotten flesh before them.

The Lesser's advance stalled. Kantus trotted alongside our regiments and gave the order to engage.

We advanced as a line and began to clamber over the wall of the village, using the mass of Lessers as a makeshift ramp. Once within the defences we began to strike out at the soldiers, our pikemen first pushing them further into the village until their backs were against some of the outlying buildings. Once pinned our swordsmen, me included, filtered through and began to attack. The battle then lost all sense of order and became a desperate struggle in the mud.

I will not lie. I killed in that battle, as I did in others. I tried to avoid a killing blow where I could, and fought defensively, raising my sword to block blows, but where I had to strike to preserve myself I did so. The urge to survive is strong. I had not had the courage to end my own existence, and neither did I have the courage to allow another to end it.

A moment came during the brief battle where I lost my footing. My boots slid from underneath me. One of the leather-clad soldiers, covered in mud and with his face a mask of fear and rage, loomed over me. He raised his sword over his head, ready to bring it down and crush my skull. I lunged upwards, and my blade struck underneath his exposed chin. I remember the look of surprise in his eyes. I could see the shining metal of my sword behind his teeth. He jerked, his eyes rolled, and he fell forwards onto me, blood pouring from the wound and covering my exposed ribs. It mixed with the rainwater and the mud. My sword was still fixed in his head, and his fall had torn it from my grasp.

I lay there underneath him, ashamed, afraid, my wits gone. I looked up at the sky, the dark grey clouds barely lit by the morning sun, the rain filling my eye sockets, the last remnants of the defenders dying around me at the hands of my dead brethren. I stayed there until the slaughter was finished, unnoticed in the midden of the battleground.

Kantus had no cause to engage with his cavalry. Instead Hallek led them on a grand and giddy hunt through the countryside surrounding the village, riding down any surviving peasants and then dragging their bodies back to Gallin as if they were the trophies of a noble's sport. The Lessers who were still feeding were allowed to finish their meals and then rounded up and herded back into their cages. I was lifted from the mud by some of Kroll's cultists and placed back with my regiment, and we left the broken defences behind us and entered the village.

Old men, women, and children were rounded up out of their hiding places, shallow cellars beneath floorboards, crawlspaces under roofs, shadowed corners of rooms or gaps beneath furniture. We stalked from house to house, dwelling to dwelling, and dragged these poor people to the village square to form one squalling, screaming, crying mass of bodies. There were hundreds of them, shivering in the rain.

I found a girl, hiding in an empty barrel. She had dark skin and hair, and when I pushed the barrel lid to the ground she looked up at me out of the opening and screamed and cried and howled for her mother. I stepped back and lifted my palms, trying to communicate. If I could have quieted her screams then I may have been able to stop her from being taken. I was not quick enough. Another Raised appeared beside me, and he reached into the barrel and grasped her by her hair to lift her from her hiding place, carrying the girl away to join the villagers in the square. I was filled with shame at my impotence, yet still half-believed this was simply a night terror from which I could not awake.

Kantus had the villagers separated into groups, the men and women in one, the children in another. Grandmothers reached out and cried and screamed for their grandchildren. Old men tried to fight and were struck down, beaten, whipped with leather straps until they submitted. The cultists then assessed their new cattle. Rack was one of them, and he and his comrades moved among the captives, using sticks of charcoal to mark some with a black cross, some with a black circle, and leaving others untouched.

Once this task had been completed the villagers were separated into groups, organised by the marking they had been given. The marked ones were marched out of the square to be put through whichever process had been decided for them. The children were tied by long ropes and assembled behind the wagons drawn up outside the village gate. Some of them were quiet with shock and fear, whereas others still screamed. Tears and snot ran down their faces, cutting clean paths through their grime-coated skin.

The last group of prisoners left were the unmarked. These were the ones who were too old or too infirm to serve any purpose to Kroll, even in death. They were gathered together, surrounded by the ranks of the Raised. Kantus gave the order and we closed upon the captives, striking them down with pike and sword. To my ever-lasting shame I took part in this brutal butchery, still half-convinced I was in an awful dream. We hacked away at limbs and necks. Outstretched fingers were separated from desperate hands raised in a last defence. Blood sprayed and I was coated, drips running down my skull, into the spaces where my absent eyes formed no barrier, into the cavity of my nose, drying to scabs between my exposed teeth. We continued our monstrous work until the howls of terror and pain died out and there was nothing left but a mound of dead meat and a widening pool of blood seeping into the ground.

I stepped back from the mound with my fellow butchers and watched as Kroll's followers poured pitch over the cooling mass. They lit the pyre of flesh and capered and sang and yelled praise to their god, as the flames surged into the stormy morning sky and black smoke bled into the clouds above.

I stood to attention with my brethren, and inside my skull my reason fled.

CHAPTER FOUR

The marked people from the village had been stored in a barn, pressed together closely with little room to sit and made to await their fate. The Raised stood guard through the village as Kroll's followers went about their business, emptying houses of useful supplies, rifling through store cupboards and family chests for anything useful or valuable. There was a village hall, just at the side of the central square, and this they emptied of furniture and dressing, adding what would burn to the still-blazing pyre.

Some of the Raised, myself included, were tasked with digging beneath the village hall. We stripped out its floorboards with little care and began hacking away at the foundations and the bare earth beneath, until we had created a wide crater, deep enough for a man to stand in and not be seen from above. This hole was sealed with waxed linen, weighted down around the edges of the pit with stones, and then barrels were fetched from the supply caravan. The barrels were filled with the same black-green, viscous substance as the lake in Kroll's sanctuary. Their contents were poured into the waiting pit until it formed a smaller sibling to the great lake in the cavern.

Once complete, the dark metal cauldron we had brought with us was installed alongside the pool, and this was carefully filled with a milky white liquid from another set of barrels. The living members of the entourage took great care not to be touched by either the black-green ooze or the caustic, flesh-stripping fluid, and they stood well back while the dead did the work. When the white liquid splashed and encountered wood or cloth it sizzled and popped and smoked.

Now the cultists were prepared to begin their recruitment process.

Townsfolk marked with a cross were brought into the hall in twos, marched between four Raised with drawn weapons. The victims had been stripped of their clothes. When they entered the hall, they were marched to the cauldron. Some of them kicked and screamed and fought, struggling against the bone clasped around their arms, yelling insults, crying and howling with horror. Others walked in a stilted manner, their faces blank, all sanity driven from them by the grisly scenes they had witnessed. It didn't matter. Once they reached the cauldron, Rack and one of his comrades muttered a prayer. Then they grasped each captive by the hair, lifting their necks to expose their throats, and ran a sharp sickle blade across the skin. These actions were quick, practiced and efficient, and did not allow for any resistance. With throats cut and blood pouring the villagers, not even dead yet, were loaded into the cauldron. It was only wide enough to accept a couple of captives at a time. More than once a victim tried to climb out, still having the strength to move regardless of their open neck, and I could see the liquid was eating their skin, flesh running in red and pink rivulets into the frothing and churning solution, mouths working but no sound coming out. The cauldron shook on its supporting framework, and I assisted another Raised in steadying it. It took little time for the movement to cease and all but tatters of flesh to be removed. Once the process was near complete, and mostly bone remained, the contents of the cauldron were transferred to the waiting pool using long metal hooks. I noticed that Rack and his fellows did not have the same fastidiousness as had been displayed in Kroll's lair. They weren't as careful to remove all the meat before passing the bones to the pit. The black liquid sometimes reacted with the remaining flesh, making it jerk and writhe as the parts sank into the ooze.

It did not seem to matter if the parts poured into the pool were jumbled together, or if the workers had to fish around in the bottom of the cauldron for errant limbs. The black liquid flashed with green light as the bodies slid into it. Its surface became still very quickly, until, after a little while, a fresh pair of raised would stride up out of one sloping side, the ichor dripping from their bones where it had not seeped into their joints.

This horrific ritual continued for hours. I was often part of the guard or was made to assist with retrieving struggling victims. I can offer no excuses for my participation other than my own cowardice and broken mind. Kantus occasionally came to watch and review our progress, and I recall feeling hate for him, even through the cloud of madness in my skull. He shouted prayers to the glory of R'Chun while the poor captives were brutally slain and resurrected at his direction.

At other times I was assigned to a local Inn, where the tables had been cleared to serve as workbenches. Here the circle-marked villagers were being made into Lessers, and if the process in the hall had been brutal, here it was barbaric. The victims were dragged into the Inn, laid on a table, and then struck through the heart with a dagger. There was little ceremony. The fresh corpse was fed a portion of the Blood of R'Chun, a swift and illegible prayer was said over them, and when they jerked and twitched and rose, they were led to the caged wagons, to allow Kantus to recoup his losses.

After days of this foul work there was not a living soul in Gallin other than Kroll's cult.

Kantus consolidated his gains. The village was garrisoned, its defences rebuilt and strengthened. A handful of the living cult members were left in control, with a small force of Raised to act as a forward post for Kroll's conquest. The rest of us were marched back to Estwake, leading a caravan of stolen livestock, supplies, and enslaved children behind us. Any children too young to make the journey were left for dead, some simply discarded at the side of the road. When we made it back to Estwake the children were shackled and put to task, feeding the animals, clearing stables, and tilling the last few workable fields. They performed their miserable duties under the ever-watching empty eyes of corpses.

Our actions at Gallin were repeated many times in the next few moons, all along our border with Tresh. We slowly expanded our territory, raiding and pillaging, and establishing new spawning places in every town and village we took. After weeks of this I was barely capable of thought. I trudged along with all the other dead men, and I partook in many atrocities. I performed acts of violence that far eclipsed anything I had done in the name of my Emperor. Any attempt to keep my fleshless hands clean was futile. I wanted to die but could not end my own life without risking more horror. If I fell in battle, I ran the risk of being trapped in my lifeless state in the muddy ground, my conscious skull trampled into the earth by the boot of some soldier. How long could I remain in that state? Would I still be there five years hence? Ten? A hundred? I admit I was a coward, although what man would not dread being buried in such a way, or trapped in an immobile state for all eternity?

My thoughts attacked me. In the old campaigns, when I crusaded into Sechia at the behest of Emperor Domint, I had planned and executed battles. We had raided and pillaged. We had burned villages and crops, had destroyed homes, had salted the fields after our passing to take any chance of succour away from our enemy. But that was a just war.

So I told myself.

We did what we had to before they did it to us. I believed that, then. I questioned myself and compared this war to that. Was the old war as vicious, as brutal, as awful as this one? We had not slaughtered prisoners wholesale and without reason... but were the reasons just? We had not captured slaves... but we left the people with nothing to eat, nowhere to live, no hope for the future. We broke their spirits and burned their beds. No. I had not been a monster then. I was a monster now. My fate could not be changed. I had once had honour, and now honour was out of reach. I remember the day I changed my mind.

There was a village called Farrow, further into Tresh than Gallin had been. We took it in the middle of the night, as our advance had not been marked, and there was no great need for tactics or subterfuge. We burst through the village gates with little effort, and then stalked from home to home, breaking down doors and capturing the villagers, slaughtering any that resisted. Most of the people there were too stricken with fear of our leering skulls to fight back.

I remember the wife of a farmer, her husband's corpse still gutted and bleeding on the floor of their hovel. She was trying to fend us off, with a short sword in her hand, while her children screamed and cried in terror behind her skirts. She was backed up against a chimney, the fire still lit and silhouetting her, her spine against the stonework. I had tried not to kill women and children, only doing so if forced by circumstance or if my actions were to be witnessed. A misguided attempt to salve my conscience. Here I hesitated as she swung her weapon before her. My brethren were a few paces behind me, and I did not want to strike the killing blow. She was afraid, that was obvious, and her blonde hair was stuck to her field-tanned face by sweat and tears and blood. But she was defiant, and there was pride and rage on her face as well as terror. She reminded me of my wife, Helena, who had been a fierce, spirited and intelligent woman. A man could not have asked for a finer partner. I remembered her skin, and her eyes, and her voice, and I was struck suddenly by a tidal wave of sorrow and regret. How little she would think of me.

More Raised pushed past me, into the modest space of the farmer's home, and they struck the woman, though not without her slashing at them in return. She shattered the skull of one of my companions before she was killed, and he dropped to the ground in a heap. A black cloud of dust rose from the hole in his head, lit by small green flashes and sparks.

I watched the fear and anger leave the woman's face. I return to this memory often. The look in her eyes, of horror, of loss, of hope leaving forever. I will never let myself forget.

I was part of the garrison at Farrow, the rest of Kantus' forces making their way either back to Estwake with their gains or moving onto the next village to victimise. There were not many of us left to guard this captured settlement. It was barely a village, just a handful of farmer's houses, a blacksmith, an inn, but it had good farmlands and many sheep and cattle. It was also close to the border that Tresh shared with Salis, the next

Barony along the coast. The birthing pool had been dug and filled. The victims needed to feed it had been collected. Farrow was to be one of the launching points for the invasion of Salis.

To one side of the village was a large and densely wooded forest. It was winter, and the trees were covered in frost and snow, dripping with shards of ice. It is often said that men feel chill in their bones, but I felt no chill in mine as I trudged through snow drifts and crunched frozen leaves and pinecones underfoot. Our patrol was small, just me and a handful of other Raised, tasked with guarding the borders of the village and ensuring that Kroll's people were not disturbed. Our patrol route wound through forest trails that had been trod for generations and were now only walked by the dead. The living that had helped create these paths had been taken away and given a new, dark purpose.

We came across a clearing in the forest sometime after midday, where there had been a fire-pit, and small stone benches set around it for gatherings in the evenings. A place for the villagers to come for celebrations and feasts. The pit sizzled and smouldered in the falling snow. It had been used recently, although my nature prevented me from sensing any warmth. There was a noise, just the quiet crack of a branch in the trees opposite the meeting place, and my companions and I drew our swords.

Several fast, dark shapes rushed out from under the snow-laden branches of the forest and charged us, knowing they had been discovered.

They were kin to the skirmishers we had fought at Gallin, wearing dark grey cloaks around their leather and plate armour, and a silver fin brooch at their necks. Their drawn weapons glinted in the winter sunlight filtering through the trees. They struck one of my brethren down with crossbow bolts before reaching our patrol, but then they were close upon us, and the melee was joined. There were four of them, three men and one woman, the men fair of hair and complexion, the woman dark-skinned, with black hair woven in tight rows over her scalp. Her teeth were bared in a fierce smile of hate and anger.

They had the element of surprise, and one of the men swung his sword in a wide arc and immediately beheaded the Raised soldier to my right. He did not wait for the skull of his first opponent to hit the ground, but kept moving, and tried to take my head on the backswing. I was a better swordsman than my fallen companion and parried the blow, and then ducked under the slashing blade to strike back at my attacker. I could not bring the edge of my weapon to bear from my position, and instead struck the man neatly at his temple with the pommel of my sword. The metal cracked against his skull, and he fell to the ground, his senses knocked out of him. I turned to finish him, his momentum having carried him past me, and I stood over his prone body with my sword raised and pointed down, the hilt gripped tightly in my hands. I held it over him and considered killing him where he lay.

Instead, I turned back to the melee behind me,

and saw that the rest of my patrol had gained the upper hand. One of our attackers was already dead, and the remaining man and the dark-skinned woman were on the back foot, unable to pull away. Now the surprise of the engagement had passed they were being encircled and driven back. They were hampered by the cold conditions and the poor ground in a way that we were not. They were separated, and the woman was being driven back towards the tree line, her back against the trunk of an ancient pine, and although she was defending well, she couldn't turn to escape for fear of being struck down. The strength and regularity of the blows coming towards her were wearing her down. Her companion was faring worse, his offense slowing through fatigue and chill as the dead pressed the attack. Finally, he lost his footing on the slippery ground, and fell back, one hand trapped beneath him to break his fall, his sword raised in front. One of the dead warriors slapped his sword away with a bony hand and struck the man through the heart.

I stood there, watching as my skeletal comrade pulled his blade from the dead man's body. He stalked towards the other duel, intent on overwhelming the woman with numbers and forcing her death. It was now three of us against her.

The memory of the farmer's wife, in Farrow, flashed before me. The same look was in the dark-skinned woman's eyes. Defiance. Fear. Anger. She was going to die, and she wasn't ready.

I could not watch this happen again. I had had my fill of compliance and atrocity. I ran up behind my comrade, and I cut the head from his shoulders with one sweep of my blade.

He fell to the snow as if he were a child's doll, empty and lifeless. I stepped over his unmoving bones to engage with the last remaining Raised. My sword in my right-hand, I grasped the base of his spine with my left and pulled him backwards as hard as I could, turning him in a circle and tossing him to the ground behind me. He tumbled, a clacking and clicking pile of bones, but quickly regained his feet. He still held his sword in his hands, but did not raise it, and he stood there unmoving, regarding me.

The dead do not have facial expressions. If they did, I would have said he looked confused.

His hesitation gave me an opportunity, and I lunged forwards. He did not even attempt to defend himself, having no capacity to understand my actions. I swung my sword with both hands and ended him there and then.

Then I stood still in the suddenly quiet forest clearing. I looked down at the snowy ground at my feet and saw small green shoots and ripped grass uncovered by the desperate battle. I looked up and watched as snowflakes fell from the low grey clouds. Some of the delicate falling flakes entered my eye-sockets and flashed with small green sparks before they disappeared. An old, old memory came to me then. Children. My children, playing in the snow, tossing it as snowballs at each other and me, screaming in joy as they struck home. They built great round men from the cold white snow, and made shapes in the smooth white surface, and tracked their boots through the freshest patches, and dove into drifts on the hillside to come bursting up from the frozen powder shivering and grinning. An overwhelming sense of loss and sadness came over me then, as though I were lost in a snowstorm alone with no hope of reaching home.

I heard a rustle of noise behind me. I turned, but I did not raise my weapon.

The woman stood, her back to the trees, her sword still drawn. She was panting and sweating with the exertion of the battle, her breath making clouds of steam in the cold air. She stared at me, and her face was filled with puzzlement and fear.

She spoke to me.

"Why... why did you do that?" Her voice was shaky.

I took a step towards her, and she started and raised her sword to keep the distance between us. The tip of the blade was pointed right at my skull face.

"Don't move. Why did you do that?"

I wanted her to finish me. I was tired. I had resolved to let her remove my head and attempt to release me from my tortured existence. She could strike me, quick and clean, leave my body in the forest, let the snow bury me. If I remained conscious at least I would be in the forest and be able to watch the passing of the seasons as I waited for darkness. I wanted the rest after death that I had been promised in life.

To that end I slowly got to my knees before her, placing my sword on the ground beside me. I tilted my head to gaze at the ground, put my hands together in the Sign of the Wave, like a penitent worshipper, and presented myself to her as a compliant and willing victim.

I don't know how long we remained like that. It could have been moments, or it could have been a lifetime. To this day I am still not sure why she did not finish me there and then. She had no reason to trust the dead.

We remained as still as a tableau in a temple. I could hear her breath, and the unconscious snores of her remaining companion. The forest made small sounds, tumbling snow from weighed down branches, the scrabbling and rustling of tiny animals and birds.

"Can you speak?"

I looked up. She still had her sword drawn but had lowered it a little. Still cautious, but curious too.

I turned my head slowly from side to side, and to be clear, covered my teeth and my jaw with both hands, one over the other to mime a gag.

She shook her head, as if to clear her vision.

"By Omma, what is this? I… wait. Wait. You understand me? You understand what I'm saying?"

I nodded, slowly.

Her lips pursed together, and she frowned.

"Pick your sword up. Throw it over there". She gestured quickly, with the tip of her weapon, towards the far side of the clearing. I stood up slowly and did as she asked, throwing it as far as I could, and it clattered over one of the stone benches and disappeared into the snow.

Not taking her eyes off me she walked over to her still-dazed colleague and knelt by his head, slapping his cheek to try to bring him round. He stirred, coughed, and rolled over towards her, dried blood visible at his temple where I had struck him.

"Wasss goin' on… fuck, ow" he slurred, rubbing the side of his head and sitting up with a groan. "Fenna, I think I got hit in the head."

"Well it's not gonna do *you* any harm is it, there's nothing to damage in there. And that's Captain Fenna when we've got company, I don't care if you've had your skull cracked. Can you stand Bor? We've got a bit of a problem here."

Bor got to his feet, wobbling a little, and Fenna supported him under his arm. He was a big man, at least my height, and had long, lank, dirty red hair that came down over his face, some of it wound into braids, some of it plastered to his scalp by the blood that had leaked from his split temple. His face and hands were criss-crossed with white scars that stood out against his ruddy skin. He looked like he was used to brawling. He looked at me, and immediately grabbed the sword he had dropped from the ground at his feet, adopting a defensive pose. He was very fast for such a big man, even after being knocked out of his senses. He was, however, a little uncouth.

"What the *fuck?*" he said, and Fenna had to put a hand on his chest to stop him from charging. He still looked shaky on his feet, and I doubt he would have made it, but I was strangely impressed with his resolve.

"Wait. BOR, WAIT! I'm still trying to figure it out. It… it saved my life. Cut down a couple of these other dead to do it. It hasn't attacked me. I think it understands what I'm saying."

Bor looked at her as if she had lost her mind.

"So? So what? What do you want to do, go drink an ale with it? It's fucking *dead*, Fenna, it's not your new best mate!" He looked back at me, and I knew that if he moved to kill me, she would not be able to stop him. So be it, I thought.

Fenna still had her hand on his chest, pressed against his breastplate, and she leaned into him, trying to make her voice soft.

"Just calm down. I have an idea what might be going on, but I need to talk to it."

"Yeah, you go talk to it, and then I'll cut the bastard's head off. They killed Sal and Verrik. That thing is not walking out of here." Bor gestured to the bodies lying cooling in the snow, and his face was stone. Fenna looked around at them, closed her eyes and took a breath.

"I don't think he killed them. He was the one fighting you."

"I don't fucking care Fenna. I'm going to smash his head in."

I was glad at this point that Fenna would be the one trying to talk to me, as Bor seemed unable to form a sentence without a curse word. He did not appear a noble gentleman to me, although I was the last person who should speak of appearances.

Fenna walked towards me then, Bor circling around me so that he was to my right, his sword raised and ready to strike if necessary. His boots crunched in the snow.

"You can understand me?" Fenna asked.

I nodded.

"I've got some questions, I'll try to keep it yes or no, alright?"

I nodded again.

"You're one of Kroll's soldiers, yes?"

A nod, yes.

"From Estwake?"

Yes.

"Did you kill either of these men?" She gestured to the corpses of her companions, which were slowly being hidden by the falling snow.

"Oh yeah, like he's going to tell-"

"SHUT UP BOR! Did you kill either of these men?" she repeated herself, with a hint of frustration.

I shook my head. No. I pointed at Bor instead.

"You hit Bor?"

Yes.

"I'm gonna kick his fucking teeth in." Bor took a step forwards and Fenna held up her hand and shouted *"Stop!"*.

Bor shook his head, angry, but obeyed the

command. Fenna looked at him.

"He could have killed you Bor. He had you. You were out cold."

"Good luck to him trying to kill me. Bigger men than you have tried, you bony fuck." He pointed to me with a snarl on his face, although it was just bravado. I could have killed him, but had spared him instead, and he knew it.

I nodded at her, and at Bor, answering the implied question. Yes, I had chosen not to kill him.

Fenna frowned, her eyes looking down at the ground, silent in thought. Bor's breath came out in great clouds of steam, his anger being shown by the wreath of mist around his head.

The Captain was leading to something, although interrogating me was a slow and impractical process.

"Have you been… like this, for a long time?"

I shrugged. A difficult thing to do when your shoulders have no flesh.

"More than a few moons?"

Yes.

"There's a watchtower. On the Coast Road, just at the border of Estwake and Tresh. Were you there?"

This question surprised me. I took a short step back and put my hands to my face. That was not a memory I cared to revisit often. My awakening had been distressing, to say the least.

"Were you at that tower?" She repeated.

Yes.

"Pinned to a door?"

Slowly I nodded *yes*, and she took a step back, looked away from me, into the forest, and back to her dead friends still lying in the clearing. The snow had almost covered them now, and it was also sticking to me, as I did not generate the warmth my captors did, and so could not stop it from settling on my bones. Fenna wiped her hand down across her face and pulled at her top lip between thumb and forefinger, deep in thought. Bor had not taken his eyes off me.

"By Omma." Fenna said

"What?"

"It was Dela. That stuff he gave us. The bottle." Fenna stared at me.

"It didn't fucking work. We lost a load of friends, and it didn't work."

"Maybe. Maybe not straight away. We got interrupted, remember? We put it on the skeleton and it kept trying to get off the door after you stuck it there. Then Sal said there was a patrol coming down the road from Estwake and we had to go. It must be him."

"It. That's not a him, that's a fuckin' IT. Listen, Fenna… it doesn't matter. We have to get *out of here.* We've stayed too long already, and all we've got to show for it is more dead friends and one weird undead. This was a waste of time."

"No." Fenna shook her head. "It wasn't. We've got something here. we need to get back to Dela."

"And tell him what?"

"That it worked. We need to take him with us."

"Haha, yeah, no. That's a fuckin' stupid idea." Bor was red in the face now, and pacing from side to side, his sword still in his hand and pointing towards me as he argued.

"It could be what Dela's looking for-"

"*I DON'T CARE!*"

Bor was definitely going to kill me if Fenna couldn't convince him. I had already resolved not to defend myself. She turned to me, sighed, and asked the right question.

"Do you have a name?"

I nodded. Yes. Then I crouched down, slowly, with my hands held open and raised so they could see I meant no harm. I picked up a piece of broken branch from the ground at my feet and walked over to a patch of snow drift left unblemished by our melee.

I used the stick as a quill, and wrote in the snow in large shaky letters:

ASHETH.

CHAPTER FIVE

Fenna had me strip off my vambraces, and my shin-guards, but allowed me the dignity of retaining the cloth skirt and belt I wore, even though the flesh it would have covered had long since rotted to nothing. She clothed me in a large grey cloak they reclaimed from one of their dead compatriots. Bor was clearly disgusted to assist in this. They stowed my armour and my weapon behind the treeline, and after removing a few trinkets and keepsakes from their bodies, they hid Sal and Verrik in the forest, laying them down amongst the pines and covering them with tight-packed snow. The ground was too hard to bury them, and Fenna and Bor did not have the time. It was unlikely their bodies would be discovered before the spring thaws. Fenna muttered a prayer under her breath to Omma T'Lassa, apologising for not being able to offer them to the sea.

Once their tasks were completed Bor tied a rope from his camp-pack around my wrists, doing his level best not to touch me in the process. He was still furious but had acquiesced to Fenna's intentions. He grumbled and swore under his breath as he tightened the rope. He passed it around my waist and then brought it back to my front to act as a leash. I was a prisoner of war now.

The light was beginning to fade, as it was late afternoon by this point. My patrol would surely have been missed by now, although in fairness, Kroll's people were not particularly fastidious about such things. Fenna and Bor packed up the rest of their gear, and then Fenna lit a torch using a small metal box she had in her pocket, some form of mechanical flint that I had never seen before. Bor grasped my leash and yanked me forwards roughly, and we made our way out of the forest, away from Farrow and towards the border Tresh shared with Salis.

We trudged on for several hours, and the sun set, replaced by a yellow, crescent moon. Once we had cleared the forest there were miles of scrubland and crag, the roots of the mountains and hills here petering out until they reached the Scar Sea. We were travelling parallel to the Coast Road but taking a more difficult trail, one that would help to avoid scrutiny from any more of Kroll's forces. Fenna and Bor did not speak until they had determined we had crossed the border into Salis. They found a small depression in the terrain, surrounded by bushes and some withered looking trees, and made a camp for the night. Fenna arranged rocks into a small circle and again used her mechanical device to quickly light a fire of dead winter branches. Bor held my lead and bade me sit on the ground in the fire light where he could keep an eye on me. He laid a blanket out on the cold and stony ground and sat down a few paces from me. Fenna sat opposite us on the other side of the fire, and started pulling out items from her pack, searching for field rations.

"We'll have to take turns watching him", Fenna said, around a mouthful of biscuit and dried meat.

"I still don't fucking get it, Fenna. We should have left him with the others."

"He's important."

"Why? I don't care if he's decided he's got a name, he's still a murdering undead bastard. He could be a spy. This could all be a trick."

Fenna nodded. "You're right. Dela will know if that's true. But that's up to him. We'll keep a close eye on him and let our esteemed Councillor work out the rest."

A look of frustration passed over Fenna's face, and she finished chewing and swallowing her food. She wiped her mouth with the back of her sleeve, and ran her right hand over her braided hair, as if gathering mental strength for the argument ahead.

"Listen, Bor. Kroll is gaining momentum. He should have been nipped in the bud years ago, and the Council wouldn't listen. They didn't listen to Dela. He tried to do what he could to convince them and this... Asheth... is the result."

"So? We don't need the Council. We can fight them."

"Tresh couldn't. Kroll's taken most of the Region already, and they should have been able to defend themselves. By Omma, they're moving on the port at Gariss in a few days at most, you saw that. If they take Gariss, if they take the capital… and they raid the graves, Bor, all of the inlanders bury their dead. Kroll's legion is getting bigger, and we've barely got an army at all. He can have ten soldiers ready while one recruit of ours wouldn't even know which end of a pike to use."

Bor shuffled in his seat and poked at the fire with the end of a branch, letting it blacken and turn to charcoal. Debate was not one Bor's strengths.

"So… what do you think Dela is going to do with… it?"

Fenna sat back a little, seeing that she had finally gotten her point across, for now at least.

"I don't know, Bor. I just know it's important. We get back to Salisson, we hand him over to Dela. He'll know what to do."

As they talked, I just sat there, staring at the fire. I could not sense any warmth from the flames, just as I had sensed no chill from the snow. Back in the catacombs, back at Estwake, it had never occurred to me to question these things. I had been walking through a dream.

I remembered other fires. Burning bodies. Thatched roofs set to the torch. Images of horror and gore, death and misery. The thoughts of my family and of the good times in my life were faded and grey, but memories of war and brutality were always in bright colours, flame, blood, the flash of metal.

I wanted to weep. I wanted to scream and howl. I was ashamed of what I was and what I had done. But no tears can fall from empty sockets. I did not hear Fenna's question, so lost was I in my reverie. I looked at her, turning my head so it was clear I was responding to her address.

"I said," She repeated, "do you know where you are from?"

I nodded, and slowly, so as not to make my captors any more nervous, I picked up a stick from the floor in front of me. I pulled against Bor's grip on my leash a little as I did so, and he held the rope taut. I cleared a patch of earth in front of me with one skeletal hand, to serve as a page, and wrote in the dirt in letters large enough for Bor to read. I was surprised the brute could.

Estwake, I wrote.

Fenna shook her head. "We know that, that's where Kroll took over. I mean before... before you were this."

I nodded and underlined the word several times to confirm my answer.

"You were from Estwake? When you... when you were still alive?"

I nodded.

Her forehead wrinkled in a frown.

"Asheth... Estwake. That sounds familiar. Something... hmm. Something Dela had in one of his books."

"You spend too much time in his bloody library- "

"*Shush!* I'm trying to remember something. Back before the Baronies collapsed. There was a famous battle there, at Estwake, one of the last of Frachia's coup. Dela thinks it's why Kroll went there in the first place, there was a mass grave outside the castle walls. Lots of recruits I guess."

I paid little attention to the last part, so shocked was I. I took my stick, cleared the ground again to have a fresh page, and wrote frantically.

Baronies? Gone?

Fenna looked at me, frowning again, this time in puzzlement rather than recollection.

"Of course? Years ago."

I cleared my page again. *How?*

Fenna sat back, and closed her eyes, seemingly reciting from some text she remembered.

"Frachia the Usurper could not hold the Baronies, after he assassinated Emperor Domint III and caused the Civil War of the Northern Shore. The Baronies fell, one by one, to either war or treachery. Estwake held out the longest. After the war, Frachia had lost too many men to retain control, and a wave of plagues swept the land due to the number of dead left unattended, decimating the population and further reducing his power."

She opened her eyes.

"There was a people's rebellion against Frachia, after the plagues. Lots of the old families died, either during the revolt or from disease and famine. The Barons were toppled. That's why we have the Council now."

I wrote. *No Emperor? No Barons? Who rules?*

Now Fenna seemed most confused. "Rules? No one 'rules'. We have a Council, at the Western Gate, and each Region has an elected Councillor who serves on it. Dela is ours."

I dropped my makeshift quill and sat back. No Barons? Hundreds of years of nobility, of legacy and honour and tradition, and Frachia had destroyed it all with his envy and his greed.

She leaned forwards.

"How old *are* you?"

I wiped the page clean again.

What year?

She narrowed her eyes, regarding me most intently.

"Hmm. It's 344, measured from the rebellion. That's the new reckoning. The baronies fell in 680 by the old reckoning but the Council re-started the calendar. If you fell at Estwake…"

"You definitely spend too much time in the fucking libr- "

"Shut up, Bor."

Fenna was still staring at me. I know I have no facial expression, but there must have been something in the way my shoulders fell. I still held the stick in my hand. For a moment, just the smallest flash of something like compassion showed on her features. Just for a moment.

I took up my false quill again and wrote in the dirt.

Nearly 400 years.

Even Bor stumbled over that. He looked at me, and back at Fenna, obviously struggling with what I had written. Fenna raised her hands and lifted her shoulders questioningly, impatient to find out the answer. His relaying of my response to her was less than delicate.

"*He's 400 fucking years old!*"

Fenna snapped her gaze away from Bor and dropped her hands to her lap. Her expression was filled with horror.

"By Omma. That's… no. Oh no. No. I know who you are."

I hung my head again and discarded my quill. For the first time in my undead state, I was recognised for the man I had been.

"You're Baron Acellion."

I nodded. Then I gathered my cloak around me, to keep out a chill I could not feel and yet seemed to sense anyway. I lay down, turned away from them, and stared into the darkness, away from the firelight.

Bor took the first watch. He held my rope-leash in one of his hands, and alternatively scratched himself, fed himself, and tended the fire with his other. It was a few hours later, in the small hours of the morning, when I realised he had fallen asleep and failed to wake Fenna for her watch. The rope had slipped from his fingers. He was undoubtedly still suffering the after-effects of my blow to his head.

I sat up, and pulled the rope gently towards myself, taking care not to wake my snoring captors. I worked at the knots around my wrists for a while and finally slipped my bindings. A lack of flesh was again an unsought advantage.

I could have left them then, if I had wanted to. Taken to wandering across the crags and wastelands. Maybe I could have assumed a new role as a haunt of the wastes, or perhaps found a way to finally end my existence. I could have smashed my skull open on a rock or found a blade somewhere and tried to cut my own head off. No doubt any such attempt would risk being unsuccessful, and leave me stranded in the wilderness, inanimate but still conscious. The thought filled me with terror, my earlier courage about this possibility now dissipated.

I stood up and climbed up the slope out of our hiding place to stand on a craggy outcropping near the top that overhung the gully below. The snow clouds had cleared, and the moon and stars were bright and sharp in the cold winter night.

If I had walked away, then I would have had to carry the weight of my guilt with me. I had partaken in awful things, far from the honourable life I had lived - or so I believed at the time. I did not know if I could ever clean the stain of my actions from my bones, but here at least was a possible path to redemption. I stood there for some time, in the wan light of the moon, as if waiting for some sign. The night sky was silent and gave me no answers.

After a little while I made my way, carefully and quietly, back down the slope. I took my place opposite the fire and waited for dawn.

Fenna woke first, just as the faint rays of the sun touched the top of the gnarled trees above us. I saw her open her eyes a little, enough to take in her surroundings. She saw me, unbound, and sat up with a start, scrabbling for her weapon. I did not move.

"Oh F- BOR! BOR, WAKE UP!"

Bor shot straight to his feet from his prone sleeping position and drew a dagger from his belt in one smooth movement. He did not even open his eyes. It was rather impressive.

"I'LL FUCKING KILL YA whass wha'happening?" he yelled and slurred, finally opening his eyes while holding his knife before him.

"You fell asleep! I'll have you whipped when we get back to Salisson you useless *prick!*"

He shrugged, but still held the knife out.

"We're still alive, aren't we? No harm done… where's the rope?"

I gestured to the neatly wound bundle of rope I had left at the foot of his blanket.

"Oh." Bor's face reddened.

"Yeah, *oh.* He could have cut our throats in the night and that would have been the end of us and it would have been *your fault!*"

"Yeah. Um. Sorry Fenna."

"That's *Captain Fenna!* Just because… never mind. You'll address me as Captain for the rest of this march… And don't think I won't tell Dela."

She turned to me, still furious.

"We've got another day's march at least to get where we're going." She sighed. "I guess you could have gone if you'd wanted to. So we'll forget the rope. But you're going to have to keep the cloak, if someone sees you it'll cause a whole mess and I don't have the time to explain it to anyone. Can I… by Omma… can I trust you?"

I nodded, and gathered up the cloak around myself, hiding my form as much as I could. I pulled the hood up over my head and then forward, so it hung over my face.

She continued. "If we meet anyone stay back, and if they ask, we'll say you're... that you're deformed by disease or injured or something."

I nodded my assent to her orders and waited patiently as they doused the fire with dirt and gathered up their packs and belongings.

As they did so I picked up another makeshift quill and wrote on the ground in front of me.

Would you like me to carry anything?

Fenna and Bor both shared a look, Fenna still angry, Bor red-faced and shuffling his feet. They both seemed exhausted, and I wanted to help. After a moment Fenna shook her head and gave a wry little smile, almost a grimace, and then used the discarded rope to tie a pack of supplies together for me to carry. Not weapons, I noticed. I lifted the load onto my shoulders, and we set off, back up the slope out of our camp-ground. We made our way across the craggy and bleak landscape, heading for Salisson.

We avoided people where we could. When we got to more populated trails we passed farmers and traders, driving cattle or pulling wagons of goods behind them, drawn by tired old horses. No one looked at me twice. The cloak and the pack I carried helped mask my shape and features, and I still wore boots, so my feet didn't appear strange to anyone. The only real problem was my hands, as I had no gloves and had to hold the ropes over my shoulders to stop the pack shifting too much. Whenever we came close to anyone I did my best to hide my hands away under my clothing.

The nearer we got to our destination the busier the rough roads became, and now we were passing columns of refugees, families who had escaped the horrors being perpetrated in Tresh. They were forlorn and bedraggled people, some carrying all their belongings, if they had any, on their backs, and some dragging makeshift barrows and wooden carts behind them. Children cried and babies squalled and raged at the indignities heaped on them by travel. Many of the rabble were near starved, their faces drawn and pale, and they shivered under their ragged cloaks and did not look up as we passed, simply trudging through the ice and mud.

It was nearly sundown when we reached the outskirts of Salisson. Unlike Gallin and Farrow, which been more villages than towns and had little in the way of defences, this was a city. Not as grand as the Western Gate by any stretch, but busy and bustling, full of life and light and noise, if of a grim demeanour. The river Salis encircled it on both sides in a moat, making the city an island, a fortification I recalled from my visits here hundreds of years ago. The river on the eastern side, where we approached, was natural, but I recalled the moat on the western side of the city had been constructed by damming and splitting the river in two, making it a formidable defence.

Across the river leading into a barbican gatehouse was a wide bridge, lit by tall oil lanterns and cobbled with stone. Looking along the walls to my left I could see where the harbour wall extended out into Salisson Bay, and there was a beacon at the far end, whose light swept in a great circle at regular intervals. I could not recall the light being so bright or turning in such a fashion on my previous visits. The oil lamps as well were of a design I did not recognise and seemed far more efficient than those in my recollection, shining very brightly. Strange pipes led from their tops and seemed to lead down into the stonework at their feet, and they let out a strong blue-white glow, instead of the yellow-tinged flames I was used to. Much time had passed, and many things had changed.

Traffic over the entrance bridge was controlled by a gate and guard house on our side of the river, and the well-armed and well-armoured guards checked travellers, inspected wagons, and generally controlled the flow of traffic.

Fenna turned to me as we waited in the mass of bodies awaiting entrance into the city. She whispered into my hood.

"Keep yourself covered. We don't want to cause a panic. They'll let us in – they know we work for

Dela – but you're going to be a problem."

Bor surreptitiously grabbed the back of my pack, to make sure I made no aggressive move while we passed through the crowd. We edged forwards slowly as the queue for the bridge made its way towards the city. No-one looked at me. The vast majority were refugees, like the ones we had seen on our way here, and they seemed downcast and dejected.

I tightened my cloak around me as much I could. I felt a spike of guilt and fear in my spine. If I were discovered I would be torn apart by the crowd, and I would not blame them for it. We made it to the front of the queue. Many before us had been turned away. The city was bursting at the seams with desperate people. I could see lights along the riverside, opposite the walls, indicating that many refugees had opted to set up camp there rather than seek shelter elsewhere. Most of the petitioners at the gate were sent to these camps rather than given entrance.

The guards raised their hands for us to stop, and a senior officed addressed Fenna. he was a tall, dark-haired man, red in the face, and showing the greying hair and puffy features of a drinker nearing middle-age. His armour seemed too tight on him, and he shifted his overly ornate breastplate with a grunt of discomfort as he approached us. He wore a crested helm with a row of black feathers running from his forehead to the back of his skull.

"You're back then. Where are the rest of them?"

"Sal and Verrik didn't make it. We got caught by a patrol outside Farrow, had to make a run for it."

"Then who's this then?" the guard said, gesturing at me. I was stood behind Fenna, trying to keep myself in shadow.

"A prisoner. We're taking him to Councillor Hevigne, he'll want to question him."

"He'll need searching then."

"We've searched him. He's not carrying anything. And this is Councillor Hevigne's business, not yours."

The guard smirked, breathed in to puff out his chest, and put his face right down into hers.

"Listen, you and your *Wardens* might be Dela's little pets, but *I'm* in charge of who gets in and out of here, understand? I've got a *responsibility,* y'see? I know that's not somethin' your rabble are used to. I can't just go *gallivantin'* around the countryside like you and your rats."

Fenna stood her ground. I had no doubt she could have cut his throat without a moment's hesitation. I had seen her fight. This man seemed far outclassed by her.

She gritted her teeth. "This man is not to be touched, searched, spoken to or even looked at,

Garet. He's Dela's. if you so much as breath in his direction I will take your manhood and have you wear it on your head instead of your silly feather hat."

"We'll see about that." said Garet, and he reached over Fenna's shoulder to grab at me. Fenna immediately assumed a fighting stance and began to draw her sword. Bor had his dagger in his right hand already, his left still holding onto my pack. The guards behind Garet stepped forwards with their weapons drawn, and the crowd of refugees behind me immediately panicked and tried to back away. The mass of people behind them crowded forwards, attempting to see what the commotion was, and suddenly we were in a crush. No blows had been struck yet, but it was about to become bloody.

In the confusion and press of bodies someone grabbed at my cloak to stop them from falling, and my hood was pulled from my head. There was a brief, awful moment of silence, and then a high terrified scream came from a woman behind me. Garet saw my face and retreated, far faster than I would have thought him capable of. In his haste to get away he stumbled and fell on his backside, his sword wavering in the air in front of him in one outstretched hand. The other guards stopped dead in their tracks, and their swords dropped to their sides in shock.

Suddenly everyone was screaming and crying

and howling. People behind us panicked and gibbered and started to retreat, and the great mass of the crowd fell back, trampling and stamping anyone unfortunate enough to fall. For some there was no room to move, and I heard splashes as people were forced over the low walls of the bridge and into the river, the freezing water drenching them to the skin and slapping the breath from them.

Fenna turned, grabbed my hood and pulled it back up in one quick movement. She strode towards Garet, who was lying prone before the gate with a terrified expression. She used her sword to strike his weapon away, and it fell from his hand and clattered on the cobbles. Then she leaned towards him, bringing the point of her blade to his face and pressing it against the tip of his nose.

"Get. Us. Inside. NOW." She had to raise her voice to be heard over the tumult behind us.

Garet scrambled to his feet, grabbed two of the still reeling guards, and we passed through the gate with an armed escort.

CHAPTER SIX

Inside the city was chaos. The streets and alleys were overflowing with people, filled by the bodies fleeing Tresh. Some had lit small fires to keep warm in the winter chill, and families were huddled around them, covered in blankets, all their worldly belongings around them on the cold ground. The smoke from these fires hung in the air throughout the city, a thick fog lit by sparking embers, and the guards accompanying us had to press through the mass of refugees and the choking fumes, pushing and shoving to make space for us to progress.

We passed through the gatehouse, and I risked a glance back from under the darkness of my hood. I recalled the layout of Salisson, a little, and saw that the general shape of the walls inside had remained the same, but that the inner wall had long since fallen. Frachia had been forced to besiege the city when he had made his thrust for power, and it had been taken through treachery rather than application of force. Now the dwelling places and working buildings of

Salisson butted right up against the outer walls, and the defensive positions inside the city had been over-run by the needs of its populace. I even saw that there were stalls and a promenade of sorts that ran along the walkway at the top of the walls, and the archer's loops positioned along the crenelated tops were being used as seating places for the merchants there. There was little indication that Salisson had faced a siege in a very long time.

As we got nearer the centre of the city the buildings became larger and more imposing, some of them faced with marble and various layers of ostentatious ornamentation. Most of these places were not well kept and were weather-beaten and shabby, faded from their days of grandeur. It took a little while to reach what had been the central keep of Salisson, back when it had been part of the Baronies. It had been encircled by walls when I knew it, but these were gone, and now it only boasted a small, enclosed forecourt laid before its main entrance. There were more guards stationed here, and Garet strode ahead of us to speak to them. I could not hear what he said over the noise of the city, and as the sun had gone down, he was lit only by the oil lamps stood outside the keep, and the fires that were burning on the street corners. The nearby flames made his facial features shift in the light and meant his expression was difficult for me to read. He seemed afraid and furious, yelling to be heard over the hubbub and racket of the crowds.

The guards at the forecourt gate moved aside, relenting in the face of his abuse. Fenna, Bor and I were bundled through the gate and led up to the front of the keep, and we were taken through a pair of heavy and ornate double doors. Two of the guards followed behind us. We stepped into an entrance hall. This room had many adjoining corridors, lit by more of the strangely bright oil lamps, and they led off in many different directions. There were framed paintings on the walls, scenes of old battles, coronations, and noble figures posed in regalia. My captors and I were led down a corridor to the right of the entrance, that turned a corner and ended in a barred and armoured door. One of the accompanying guards fished in a satchel at his side for a set of brass keys and unlocked it, lifting the bar away and stowing it to the side of the entrance. The bar was attached to some sort of mechanical arm that held it upright against the wall. Beyond the door was a set of spiral steps leading down into a basement dungeon, this lit only by open-flamed torchlight rather than the efficient oil-lamps above. Passing down the stairs we came to a row of cells, each with a wooden door resembling the one above, heavy and stout and with the same barring mechanism. Each of the cell doors had a grate at eye-level that allowed for sight of the prisoner contained within, and for conversation if necessary. There were small gaps at the base of the doors where trays of food could be passed to-and-fro. I knew a gaol when I saw one. One of the forecourt guards unlocked the nearest door and I was relieved of my pack and my cloak and gestured into the cell. The guards had obviously been forewarned of my nature but could not hide the expressions of disgust and horror that passed over their features. I did not resist them but walked quietly and calmly into my cell. Inside there was little furniture, just a low wooden bed with a threadbare blanket, and a small wooden bucket, filled with dirty water. I was glad I would not need that. The door closed behind me. It was at least better quarters than I had enjoyed in the catacombs.

I heard Fenna speaking to Garet.

"I need him kept safe here. Can I trust your men not to communicate with him, or interfere with him in any way?"

"I don't know who you think you are- "

"LISTEN, Garet. Dela is going to want to talk to him. He's an important asset, and we *cannot* risk him. I lost two good friends to get him here, and I won't have you wasting their lives because your men couldn't follow orders."

"My men will *follow orders*. But don't think Dela won't hear about how you spoke to me."

"Tell him what you like Garet, I don't care. As long as that prisoner is in that cell, unharmed, when Dela comes to get him. If he isn't I will personally have you hanged."

There was silence for a moment. Then Garet grunted assent, turned to one of his subordinates, and had them lower the bar and lock the door. Then he gave his orders.

"You, and you. Watch that thing. If he tries to get out, smash him to pieces. If he tries to talk to you, smash him to pieces. You hear me in there, you fuckin' skeleton bastard? You try anything and I'll have you ground into fuckin' *dust!*"

At this I heard him leave the room, closely followed by Fenna and Bor. The guards left behind took up station either side of my cell door. I lay down on the bed. The only illumination in the cell came from the torches outside, but I could see clearly even in the low light, my nature allowing me greater vision than other prisoners would have in my circumstances.

I waited. If there is anything the dead have in abundance it is patience.

I lay there for several hours, lost in memory and reflection. I hoped I was doing the honourable thing. I carried such a weight of guilt. I thought about the awful actions I had carried out, the torment I had inflicted on others through my cowardice. I had been pushed to do evil and had not stood my ground.

I heard footsteps coming down the stairs. It was now around midnight, and I stood up to peer at my visitor through the metal slats of the door-grille. The guards stood to attention. They were lucky to have stood in time, as both had been sat reclining against the stone walls for a while, and I had heard snoring.

The visitor was carrying a small, portable oil-lamp of ornate design. I could not help recalling my first meeting with Rack moons ago. There could not have been a starker difference in presentation. This man was of a dark, midnight-black complexion, and clean shaven, both his face and his scalp. The light gleamed from his oiled and carefully tended skin. He was so well-kept his age was hard to tell. He could have been in his fifties, or younger, or older. Only his eyes betrayed experience through age. He wore simple black trousers and a long, plain white shirt, closed at the neck with a silver pin, the mirror of the fin-shaped ones worn by Fenna and her people. Other than this he was unadorned and conservative in dress, with none of the noble trappings I would have expected of someone in his position.

He paid the guards no attention and walked towards the door. His eyes were bright and piercing, shining with intelligence and reflecting the light of the lamp he carried. When he spoke, his voice was rich and deep and laden with authority.

"Captain Fenna tells me you claim to be Baron Asheth Acellion."

I nodded, as he regarded my features through the cell-door slats. He showed no emotion.

"Well, we will see. Nothing is as it appears these days. You may be who you say you are, or you may be a hook dangled in the water for me. Kroll can be cruel and subtle, as well as a brute."

He stepped back a little from the door.

"I am Dela Hevigne, Councillor for Salis. I am trying to protect my people, and I'm going to find out if you can help me. We will speak at length tomorrow. Can I expect your continued co-operation?"

At this I stepped back a little myself, making sure I could still be seen in the glow from his lamp and the torches on the far wall. Then I bowed to him.

Dela gave a wry smile at this.

"Very good. We shall re-convene in the morning."

He turned to the guards, still stood to attention.

"I'll send down a relief for you two

momentarily... and if I catch either of you sleeping on watch again, I'll have you both flogged, do you understand?"

Both guards shuffled their feet and mumbled "Yes, Sir", like naughty boys caught stealing orchard fruit.

Dela left then, and I lay back down and waited for morning.

The guards came into my cell not long after dawn. There was some difficulty in binding me for transport. At first, they tried to apply iron shackles to me, but found that none they had were small enough to imprison my wrists. I would obviously be able to slip my bonds. After some discussion between them one of the guards was sent to fetch a handful of leather cords, which they used to tie my hands together and link my feet closely, reducing my gait to a shuffle. My new captors wrinkled their noses with distaste as these fastenings were put into place. It was clear they had no desire to touch me or even look at me. My presence filled them with loathing.

Four guards escorted me back upstairs, their weapons drawn, two ahead of me, two behind. We exited the basement dungeon back onto the ground floor corridor, and then moved deeper and higher into the keep, up more floors and along more corridors, passing rooms filled with people deep in industry, writing in ledgers, scrawling on chalk boards, and counting on bead-racks. I was cloaked again for my interrogation, but knowledge of my presence must have been passed as whispers through the keep. Where my passage was noted, by the various scribes and ledger-men, their rooms fell silent, and I could hear the movement behind us of people rising from their seats and rushing to view my parade through the building.

We reached a room at the end of one corridor with a stout wooden door, painted black. The doorknocker was a silver fin on a lever, its point towards a round plate of metal. The lead guard rapped on the door with the fin and a voice inside the room bade us enter.

The room inside was large, appearing to take up almost half of this floor of the keep. It was well-lit, with a wide bay window overlooking the town below. The glass of the window had been inlaid with coloured plates held in with leadwork, and the morning sun sent lines of blue and green and gold across the room, lighting dust-motes floating in the air. There was a desk in front of the window, and a chair behind it, so that the occupier could turn to gaze out over Salis if they wished and take in the sight of the city spread below them. Across the desk were books, parchments, a bead-rack for counting, a sextant and other instruments of a kind I did not recognise, maps, and a couple of empty wine glasses. Dela sat in his chair. In one corner, to the right of the brightly coloured window, Fenna sat in another. There was an empty stool in front of the desk, and this is where I was ordered to sit. The guard's voice betrayed his nerves, and after he had seated me, he and his companions tied my ankles to the legs of the stool so I could not move easily. My hands were left bound together.

I looked around the rest of the room. The walls were covered in shelves that were filled to overflowing with books, more than I had ever seen in one place. I thought that Dela must have been a very rich man to be able to acquire so many precious volumes. On one wall was a large map of the continent. I had seen rough maps before and could compare this assumedly modern one with the old campaign maps from Domint's time. The general shape of the old baronies was still there, running along the Northern Shore of the Scar Sea. Estwake lay to the East of the map, with the Sagaran Mountains beyond it that separated us from the northern parts of Sechia. The mountain range curved down and below to run into the Southern Shore, forming the wall that prevented Sechia's expansion in our direction. The other Baronies, or 'Regions' as they now seemed to be, were still named as they had been in my time - Tresh,

Salis, Avania, Burus, Prain, on and on in a row all the way to the island of the Western Gate, the capital, that served as the only means of egress from the Scar Sea to the Western Ocean. I could see the gains we had made on our campaigns in the south as well. We had taken Teris and Nedra from Sechia, and these lay on the opposite side of the Western Gate Island. The Sechian Empire had been pushed back to the East and South, its access to the sea had been reduced, its power curtailed. It seemed we had kept what we had taken from them.

"Does it look familiar to you, Baron?"

Dela addressed me, and I turned and nodded. I leaned to my left and ran my pointed fingers along a row of books just out of my reach, and then looked at him, trying to convey my confusion at his collection with a shrug. After a few moments he took my meaning.

"My books? Of course! In your time these would have been relatively uncommon, and expensive too. We have achieved much in the years since your… life. There have been many mechanical and technological advances, amongst which the greatest has been the printing press. It is a machine that allows us to reproduce writings, quickly and much more cheaply than in the past."

I shook my head in wonder. As I thought on this

Dela dismissed the guards, who voiced protest at leaving me in his office. He ignored their pleas.

"I'm perfectly safe. I need to question our guest in private, and Captain Fenna will protect me if need be. I think it unlikely the Baron could do me any harm. You've done a good job, so run along now please gentlemen."

They left, the rear one looking back suspiciously as he closed the door behind him.

Dela sighed.

"Well. There we are. We can have a civilized conversation now. I suppose offering you any refreshment would be pointless. Would you mind at all if I had some wine? I realise it's a little early, but I find it does wonders for my work in the mornings."

I nodded, to show my assent, and watched as he moved to a nearby shelf, retrieved a stubby glass bottle, and re-filled one of the empty glasses on his desk. The amount of glass in the room also seemed extravagant to me, another sign that I was no longer in my own time.

Dela offered a glass of wine to Fenna, who raised a hand to decline. She rolled her eyes a little when Dela turned away from her. He sat back down and faced me.

"I know I drink a little too much, but I'm afraid you and I both suffer from a similar affliction, in that neither of us sleeps a great deal. I find the wine gets me through the pain of the morning until I can drink through the pain of the afternoon. Luckily my tolerance is remarkably high for wine. Can't stand spirits. Leave the harder stuff to the younger generation. I like to be able to taste what I'm drinking."

He seemed completely unafraid of me. Almost comfortable in my company. He took a sip from his glass, set it down carefully after making a little space on his cluttered desk, and sat back with a sigh.

"So. Fenna tells me you can write."

I nodded. He collected a sheaf of parchments from the floor next to his feet and placed them on the desk in front of me. Then he leaned forwards and passed me a small, silver tube, with a point at one end. I took it from him, but then held it up to my face so I could examine it. The point was split, a fine dark line down the flattened silver. Dela again noticed my confusion, and began to speak, but I had already realised its purpose. I put what I assumed was some sort of mechanical quill to the parchment in front of me and wrote quickly, and the ink, seemingly held in the body of the device, flowed onto the page. Its metal shaft grated against my skeletal fingers as my hand moved.

Yes. I can write.

I turned the parchment around to show him. He seemed pleased that I had worked it out.

"Excellent. Can you confirm your full name for me please?"

Baron Asheth Acellion, 14th Lord of Estwake, Commander of the Sechian Crusade.

"Hm. Difficult thing to verify, I'm afraid. I have some documentation from that time, various histories and accounts have been written. I would have to spend some time preparing a test of some sort, a way to establish that what you say is true. I must say, it seems extremely unlikely. I know that Kroll used the burial sites at Estwake for his initial… ah… recruitment. But the odds against you being that *particular* individual are… Hm. Let me show you something. Fenna, pass me that box, would you?"

Fenna stood up and walked over to the shelf Dela was pointing at. She fetched back a black lacquered wooden box, that had a small lock in its front. She placed it on the desk in front of the Councillor, and he reached down the front of his shirt and retrieved a small key that hung on a loop around his neck. He unlocked the box, reached inside, and pulled out a small glass vial. Inside was a viscous black liquid, that occasionally flashed with a green iridescence in the light from the morning sun.

"Do you recognise this?"

Yes. Kroll uses it.

"Yes. Yes, he does. This was taken from Estwake, a few years ago, before Kroll began to generate his forces in earnest. He and his followers arrived in Estwake by ship some time ago, posing as religious refugees from the Sechian Empire. They managed to ingratiate themselves with the Councillor for the Region, a forked-tongue serpent of a man called Sern Cellin. Kroll has some kind of hold on him, or at least a means to gain his loyalty. They brought this… substance with them and have made more since their arrival. Kroll is a cultist, a worshipper of a Sechian God of Darkness and Decay, who they call R'Chun. They call this filth the Blood of R'Chun."

Dela put the bottle down on his desk. Its surface reflected the colours from the stained-glass window, but seemed to generate its own green ambience, just visible in the sunlight.

"The Cult of R'Chun now controls the remnants of the Sechian Empire. Kroll and the other cult leaders have the ear of the Emperor and they are intent on expanding their territory, to give them greater access to the Western Ocean. They want the Western Gate, and to leave the Northern Shore in ruins. They might succeed."

Dela took a sip of wine and turned to look out of the window behind him as he continued to speak.

"My spies brought me this bottle. I tried to use it to convince the Council of the threat. I can't take any captured undead to the Western Gate. By the time we got there any example would become inactive, the dead seem to become inanimate again if removed from the cult's influence. Last time I tried Kroll's forces were still small and well hidden, and Cellin argued they were just settlers, suffering religious persecution. Usually, it would be a noble endeavour to protect such people, we aspire to be a tolerant society. But in this case…"

Dela turned away from the window, leaned back in his chair, and closed his eyes. He rubbed his eyelids with his fingers and pinched the bride of his nose.

"The council has accused me of paranoia. Since the Sechian conquest, since the plagues, since the revolt… we have grown insular and weak as a people. We believed the Sechians were no longer a threat. Our population was severely reduced, and though we are trying to build a new, modern society… it's all very well and good trying to be noble and forward-thinking. But we should still be prepared to protect ourselves."

Fenna coughed into her hand and looked at Dela with bemusement. He glanced at her and gave a little smile, shaking his head.

"My apologies. Fenna has heard all my rantings

before. Her organisation, her Wardens, exist because of my paranoia and caution. They are my eyes and ears. And my blade when necessary."

He picked up the bottle again, examining its contents.

"This is not the same as the cursed mixture that Kroll uses for the bulk of his forces. He has several types, as far as I can tell. Some of his... creations are more advanced than others. This is the formula he uses to create his elite soldiers, his leaders. It gives them consciousness, and speech, and free will. Somehow. I don't pretend to understand the sorcery involved. But I know a little of Kroll's beliefs. Certainly, he only gives it to his most devoted followers. They must be volunteers, you see. Fanatics. Else he could empower someone who would oppose him."

He looked at me.

"Moons ago, I asked Captain Fenna and her people from the Salisson Wardens to lead a mission to the edge of Kroll's territory. It was rather dangerous, and possibly blasphemous. I asked her to test a portion of this liquid on one of the undead, so that I could have an example to put before Council. I believe, and Fenna believes, that you are the result of that mission."

I sat for a moment. My mind reeled, and my memory rushed back to that first day. I had been pinned against the door so I could not move.

Some of the Blood of R'Chun had been on my chest. Rack had touched it.

I picked up the strange quill again.

I cannot speak.

"No. The liquid does not act on its own. It needs to be accompanied by... a ritual, prayers, words in an old Sechian tongue. I gave Captain Fenna a scroll to read from. She was interrupted before the process was completed."

Can it be finished?

Dela regarded me with his sharp, intelligent eyes.

"Hm. Perhaps. We need to prove your identity first. And your allegiance."

My allegiance?

"To Kroll! To darkness!" He raised his voice, and now there was a touch of emotion in it, his anger rising beneath his calm mask. "Do you still serve that *madman*? Are you a spy, or a distraction? Are you an assassin, a misguided fanatic, waiting to strike me when my guard is lowered? Did you volunteer to become this... this *thing*?"

My own anger had risen during his rant, and this last accusation pushed it to boil over. I turned and threw the metal quill against the shelves to my left, and it shattered, spraying its contained ink in an arc across Dela's books. Fenna reacted immediately, leaping to her feet and drawing her sword, and Dela had to reach out with his arm to stop her from rushing towards me and striking me down. I tried to stand, but my feet were still bound to the stool and it was difficult to move. I stared eyelessly at her

"WAIT!" yelled Dela. He calmed a little, and I paused mid-rise. "Stop. Both of you. Baron, if that is who you are... what do you expect? You are a walking dead man. You have been raised from the grave by foul, ancient, *blasphemous* sorcery to wage war on the living at the behest of a lunatic. You serve an empire of death that should have long since crumbled, that has only been kept together by the darkest means. I cannot just take your word."

I sat back. I had no expression, so he could not see my rage and confusion. Could he not understand that I hated Kroll, I hated what he had done to me? I hated my own bones.

"Moreover, *Baron*. I... *we* represent the people who overthrew your dynasty. We tore down the Baronies. If you are Baron Acellion then... *we* are also your enemy. The brutal actions you performed in Sechia, for your Emperor, are testament to what a dangerous man you could be."

At these last words I turned my head towards him sharply, my body betraying my shock. Dela smiled a cold, bitter smile.

"What, Baron? I know the time you come from.

I am a historian and reader by inclination. Why do you think the Sechian Empire turned towards the dead to fight its battles? Why it became so desperate it would sink into such darkness? The weight of history bears down on them. The war Domint began broke the empire, crippled it, starved it. But their rulers wouldn't relinquish their grip, as ours had to. They had no revolution. There was no appetite for continued struggle. They were ravaged by famine, by plague, by loss on an unimaginable scale, and they did not recover as we did. You murdered a generation, burned their crops, salted the earth and stole what good land was left, and took all access to the seas beyond the Gate. Then you sailed back to your keeps and your holdings believing you were honourable men."

He took a sip of his wine, and placed the glass back on the table carefully, turning it so the crystal cut edges of the container caught the coloured light from the window.

"Put simply, Baron... you were butchers."

CHAPTER SEVEN

Little more was gained from me in that first conversation. Dela offered me another of his metal quills, but I refused to take it. I was untied from my stool and taken back down to the gaol by the guards.

After being placed back in my cell I was left for some time in contemplation. I could not accept Dela's assessment of my history. We had gone to war with Sechia because their lands encroached upon the western end of the Scar Sea, on the Southern Shore. The Baronies held only the Northern Shore then. There had been attacks on coastal villages, raiding parties arriving by ship to steal food, gold, supplies, and to take captives for trade as slaves. As far as I knew, our war against them had been justified by these raids. They were the aggressors, not us. Domint, my Emperor, my *friend*, had raised his armies and his fleets to fight back, and I had followed him. We pushed along the Southern Shore from the Western Gate, pushed the Sechians back from the coast, and established new Baronies there.

Most of their ports were taken, leaving only minor holdings at the far eastern end of the Great Crossing. They were left with little access to the Scar Sea, and none to the Western Ocean that lay beyond.

We pushed deep into their lands. We crusaded through the south and the east, and at every turn removed their ability to wage war. If we had not, they could have raised their armies again, could have tried again to take what was ours. Yes, Domint had been ruthless. I had been ruthless. We left them nothing. But that did not mean that my friend was the same kind of man as Kroll.

And yet.

I remembered the old crusades. My memories had returned to me almost completely by this time, still muddy and unclear in places, but with far fewer gaps. I had fought in brutal battles, yes, and I believed I had fought with honour. But afterwards... afterwards my fellow nobles and I would retire to our camps or our ships, and plan for the next battle. While we studied and conversed and schemed and strategized, the men would ravage the towns, burn the fields, and act as they wished. I did not care about that. Neither did my comrades.

When we were done – when the crusades had been completed, and we had retired to our lands, satisfied that we had broken the enemy – we had claimed new lands, new harbours for our ships, and a new border. Now, beyond the Baronies we established on the Southern Shore, there were only wastelands.

Surely this was right? Surely Domint was acting to protect what was his, what was ours? Was that not what a leader should do?

I felt then as if I were standing on shifting sand and staring into a black ocean.

After a while I was retrieved from my cell. It was late afternoon then. Dela's study was no longer lit by the light from the window, but several bright blue-white oil lamps were affixed to the walls, and they provided ample illumination. The setting sun was behind us now, and the only lights visible through the coloured glass were from the lamps and torches strewn across the city below. Fenna had once again taken up her position alongside her patron, watching me and ready to draw her weapon if required.

Dela said nothing as I was once again bound to the stool, and a quill and piece of parchment were placed in front of me.

He dismissed the guards and regarded me intently. Once they had left the room he leaned forwards on his desk, his elbows on the dark wood, his fingers steepled in front of him. The smooth, dark skin of his head gleamed with golden reflections of the lamps surrounding him.

He spoke.

"I have some more questions for you, Baron. I require some proof of your identity. I have been reading today, trying to find as much detail of your life as I can, in the histories I have collected here. I do realize that if... if you are who you say you are, then this is a most painful experience for you. Please try to see things from my perspective. I am trying to wage a war with *nothing*. The Regions have no standing army. Each Councillor is responsible for their own guards, militia, whatever they require. Some have organisations like the Wardens, although theirs are perhaps a little more... conventional than mine. They are used to fighting bandits, and sea raiders, and breaking up criminal gangs. None of the Regions have ever tried to fight another openly, and there would be little purpose in it. Now I am trying to martial the Regions, to build a force of men and women who have never known a real war. There is great resistance, and not even an acknowledgment of any threat."

He sat back. "I need to know the truth, and then perhaps you and I can help each other. But I must have your co-operation, else you are of no use to me."

He let the implied threat hang in the air, and I took his meaning. He stood up and faced out of the window, picking up his ever-present glass of wine as he did so.

"My city is on the verge of violence. We are packed with refugees. If I cannot get control of events, then control of this city will soon slip from my grasp. Panic is in the air." He turned back to me. "Will you help me?"

I waited a moment, and then reached for the quill.

What do you want to ask me?

"You had children. What were their names?"

My son was Ascas. My Daughter was Aisha.

It pained me greatly to write about them as being in the past.

"Your wife?"

Helena.

"How did you die?"

I doubt anyone had ever been asked this question in all of history.

I fell at Estwake. Frachia's men had driven us back. The walls were breached through treachery. We were killed in the courtyard.

"We?"

The last of my men and I. Lucien. Balus. My friends.

"Hm. All of this is knowledge from written records, Baron. Kroll is cunning. He has lived in Estwake for some time, and Cellin also is well-read in the history of that Region. There is nothing you have told me that Kroll could not have learned and taught to you. We need some detail, some truth about you that can be leveraged as proof."

His brow was creased, and his lips were pressed tight together. This was not working. Was this all my life amounted to? A family tree in a book, a painful, shameful death? Was this my legacy?

I picked up the quill once more. There was something I could tell him that would not be in the books he had read. A secret I had kept for a long time, but felt I had to reveal to prove myself.

Ascas was not my son.

At this Dela leaned forwards, frowned, and whispered "*What?*"

I underlined the sentence. He took another sip of wine, and sat back again, a quizzical expression on his face.

"How?"

Ascas was Domint's son. A Bastard. Helena was on campaign with us in Sechia, she was a field nurse. Domint had made her with child.

"Then why did you raise him?"

I pressed the quill to parchment again. Dela and

Fenna waited patiently as I wrote. This was no simple thing to explain.

I loved her. Domint did not. He had to disavow Ascas, as he had a wife, but no children with her. When the campaign was over I took her back to Estwake, as far from the capital as we could go. Domint arranged it. Estwake was my reward, but also Helena's refuge, and a hiding place for Ascas. No one could know. But Frachia found out. It enraged him. That's why the war started. Frachia was no longer the successor. Ascas was.

I waited while Dela read aloud, so that Fenna could follow our conversation.

"There's no evidence of any of this. How can you prove it?"

Is Ascas' birth date in your histories?

"Yes. Perhaps. Why?"

I was on campaign, in the far south, when Domint took Helena. They were still at the Western Gate then. She was sent South after she was with child. She gave birth in Sechia. I could not have been his father.

Dela sat back in his chair, his fingers steepled in front of him again.

I placed the quill back on the page. This was a shameful thing to have to share, but I could not think of another way.

Dela took a deep breath and spoke.

"This might be enough. I will have to research it. There are good records of the campaigns in my library and it's unlikely that such records will have been present in Estwake. If what you say is true it does lend you some credibility, that is certain. We will reconvene in the morning."

I spent a restless night on my cell cot. I could still refresh myself from time-to-time, and retreat into memory, but it was not sleep. I felt little benefit from it other than the passage of time. I also felt that my memories were no longer a safe space.

I remembered bringing little Ascas to Estwake. He was so small, so fragile I had not resented him. My love for Helena simply grew to encompass her child as well. When we had Aisha a little while later Ascas doted on her, and the two of them filled the castle with their bubbling, joyous laughter, running through the rooms and halls and gardens, jumping and hiding and playing. I was proud to be their father. I was proud of my family.

Now my pride turned to grief, and sorrow, and regret.

When I was retrieved again it was already midday, and the remnants of a meal were still on Dela's desk, amongst the assorted pile of parchments and bric-a-brac he appeared to store there. Fenna had moved from her guard station in the corner of the room and was now seated to the right of Dela. Not all caution had been abandoned. I was still tied to the stool before the guards left the room.

"Helena gave birth seven moons after reaching Sechia." Dela took a sip of his wine and continued. "It's possible that you were the father, but very unlikely, especially considering the conditions in camp at the time. I doubt such a premature child could have survived. You were already married to her when you came back from campaign."

I nodded.

Fenna turned to address her patron.

"This would be a lot easier if you gave him his voice."

Dela looked troubled. "Yes. Perhaps. It's a risk, Fenna. It was a risk when we tried to use Kroll's sorcery in the first place... not just a physical risk, but a spiritual one. I don't know what effect this... magic... this foul curse-work, has on the soul. I regretted you trying the first time. I should not have requested it of you."

"I'll take the risk." Fenna's face hardened. "We need him, Dela. He knows so much about Kroll, about what is happening. We need to know what he does, and as soon as possible. The Council need to see the truth. Kroll is already at our border... he'll push into Salis soon, and as things stand, we *cannot* stop him. The Wardens aren't enough."

Dela sighed and stood up, picking up his wine glass as he did so. He sipped at his wine and gazed down at the industry of Salis through his ornate window.

"Fetch a priestess." He said.

The priestess was a young woman, timid and small of stature, dressed in the long blue robe and skull cap of the Order of Omma T'Lassa, the Mother of the Sea. She folded her hands one over the other when she saw me tied to my cell cot, in the sign of the Blessed Wave, her right hand pointed up over the curled knuckles of her left. She started to babble prayers until Dela put a hand on her shoulder and whispered urgently into her ear, and she stilled a little, though her hands still shook.

Dela stood with his back to the cell door, holding an oil lamp, and the priestess stood against the wall, chanting under her breath and occasionally bringing her hands together when she ended one stanza of a prayer and began another. Fenna knelt at my head, a piece of parchment in one hand, the open bottle of black liquid in the other. She read from the stolen incantation, anointing my skull occasionally with a small drop of the Blood of R'Chun. The words of the spell were in Sechian, but an old dialect, and I did not recognise much of it. Dela had copied the words of the original out as sounds for Fenna to make.

It did not take long for the ritual to take effect.

I suddenly felt light and airy, as if I could float from my bed if I were not tied to it. Then a low noise began, a ringing sound like a distant, high bell, somewhere over the Sea. I did not know if the others could hear it or if it was just inside my skull. It grew in volume and intensity until I could no longer hear Fenna's voice. The room grew dark. Until then I had been able to see in darkness, but at that moment it was as if I had been thrown into the deepest bowels of the earth, accompanied only by the cacophony of ancient bells.

Then I was flying. Part of me could again see the dim room around me, but another part soared, as if I were in two places at once.

A dark ocean churned and rolled below me, and above me was a sky of high and angry storm clouds, sparking and flashing with great sheets and streaks of green lightning. The bolts of light were striking the ocean, and each time they did a great boom rolled over me, and the water where the forks touched boiled and spat tall towers of swirling brine into the air. I was rushing over the surface of the sea, the storm chasing close behind me. Under the waves a shadow stirred, a huge, leviathan shape, curling and twisting and keeping pace with my flight, and I was sure it regarded me, and was drawing me forwards. I felt a prickle in the base of my skull. Turning to look over one bare and bony shoulder I gazed into the high anvil of cloud behind me and saw the shape of a hooded figure, impossibly tall, the trailing edges of its cloak bleeding into the vapour below it. Bright green sparking eyes glowed from a face in shadow, and it filled me with such terror I was glad I could not see its features.

Land was visible ahead of me now, a city, and I knew it was Salisson. I could see the harbour, and the river-moat, and the bridges packed with desperate bodies. It was all still. The people on the bridges and in the camps at the river's edge stood silent as statues, bleached of all colours apart from the reflected green light of the chasing storm. Below me, in the tumbling waves that rolled into the harbour, I heard a voice cry out my name, almost yearningly. It was a woman's voice, but there were tones beneath it that made me think of other sounds, the cry of a sea bird, the deep wailing song of an ocean serpent, the soft sigh of a wave drawing back from a sandy beach, the bubbling last breath of a drowning man.

Dela's keep was in the distance, and as I drew closer my speed did not decrease, and I feared I would crash into its walls. Instead, I passed through, a brief flash of grey stone and dark-green lichen visible to me, and then I saw the people inside, frozen at their desks and their counting beads. I passed through them also, their flesh a smear of red across my vision, and then down through the floors, carpet, woodgrain, stone, moving through all of it as if it were mist.

In the gaol cell I saw myself, tied to my cot, the statues of Dela and Fenna and the young priestess caught in a pose by the still golden light of their lamps. I had a moment to examine my own bones and though my mind recoiled from the sight I was not given time to react before I was plunged back into my own decayed form.

Then the pain began. First a seed in the centre of my skull. Then a blossoming flower of agony, unfurling to touch my face and grind against my teeth, running tendrils down my spine, into my arms and legs, until burning, winding roots of torture infested my whole frame. It grew, and grew, and so did my fear. It built up to an intolerable pitch, making me fear for my wits, until I was suddenly released. A gale blew through the cell with such fury even the covered flames in the oil lamps were snuffed out, and I thought I could hear a distant roar of frustration and rage. The priestess fell to her knees, babbling and crying, and Fenna was thrown back, cracking her head on the cold stone floor.

I screamed.

CHAPTER EIGHT

The priestess bolted from the room with remarkable speed, her shadow from the torchlight racing up the stairs beside her. I heard her screaming and crying prayers and accusations of blasphemy as her voice receded into the distance.

I was still bound to the cot, and the room was only illuminated by the last of the torches outside. Dela reached inside his jacket and produced a mechanical flint, using it to light his lamp again. Fenna stirred a little from her position on the floor, letting a low groan escape her lips.

"Fenna, are you well?" I asked, out of some gentlemanly reflex, and immediately regretted speaking.

I sounded like Kantus. There was still some trace of my old voice, but now it was a hollow, soulless boom, like a distant horn on a foggy coast. The sound did not come from my mouth, but emanated from inside my skull, and I could feel a buzzing vibration in the bones of my scalp and jaw. I had opened my mouth to speak, unlike Kantus.

Fenna winced at the sound and sat up. In the glow from Dela's lamp I could see her face. One of her eyes was swollen nearly shut, the other a little less, and a thin trickle of blood ran down the sides of her nose, running where tears usually did. She touched her face and brought away some blood on her fingers.

"It worked then?" She said, trying to get to her feet. She stumbled a little and Dela had to catch her arm to steady her.

"Apparently so," He said, "Although I fear we may have upset Daughter Corriss. How do you feel?" The concern in his face was all too visible, even in the dim light.

"Like I've been kicked in the soul. Hungover. My face hurts." She rubbed the blood away from her eyes with her sleeve and winced when she touched her swollen eyelids.

"I'm sorry Fenna. I should not have asked this of you." He said, shaking his head.

"It needed doing."

Dela nodded, and swallowing his guilt for the moment, turned towards me.

"Baron? Are you yourself? Or have we allowed an evil spirit into our midst?"

I was still tied down, but I could turn my head to

look at him.

"I feel... I am still myself. I believe so anyway. I do not like the sound of my voice." I was trying to whisper, but it was difficult, and my words seemed to bounce from the walls of the small stone cell.

"Can't say as I do either, Baron. You are a little painful to listen to. I am not sure that you are speaking as such, my ears don't seem to be the only organs involved in the process." He rubbed his temples a little, as if nursing a headache.

"I can only apologise, Councillor Hevigne. I will try to keep my speech to a minimum." I turned my head back to stare at the low ceiling and watched the lamplight chase shadows across the stone.

We reconvened in Dela's study. The guards escorting me through the corridors regarded me with even more fear than before. Word had spread of my new-found voice, it seemed, and they watched me with trepidation as I stalked alongside them. I both disgusted and terrified them.

In the study I was placed back in my customary position, hands still bound together, ankles tied to the stool, and I was ready for interview or interrogation once again. It was nearly evening, and the lights were being lit across Salisson, visible from Dela's window.

"So, Baron," he said, "Let us have a conversation. First, some history. Let me try to put all of this into some context for you." He paused and took a sip of his wine.

"Domint. I know he was your friend, or at least you respected him as a leader. He was greedy. Perhaps. From my perspective it is difficult to tell."

"Greedy?" He was in danger of raising my ire once again. I had had quite enough of my Emperor's name being besmirched.

"I said, perhaps. Please do not take offence, Baron. To me... this is a man that lived a long time ago, and made decisions that permanently shaped our society, and that led to our current conflict. History cannot be changed. Were I in his position, perhaps I would have made the same decisions. It is hard to say. I believe... I hope that my driving impulses differ from his."

"And what are your driving impulses, Councillor?" I tried to keep the anger out of my voice, but I did not have a great deal of control over tone or volume at this point.

"Mine? I wish to serve my people. Protect them. Lead them into prosperity, and peace, educate them and raise them up."

"My Emperor had similar goals. Made similar

speeches."

"Did he? His actions contradicted his words."

"How *dare* you!" I raised my voice. Dela winced.

"I'm not trying to judge Domint, Baron," he said, "I am trying to explain how we got to where we are."

He stood up then, refilled his glass from a bottle on the shelf, and sat back down. I seethed and stared at him with eyeless sockets.

"Domint was trying to expand his Empire. He saw Sechia as a threat to that but did not have the political or military backing to lead a campaign against them, until the piratic raids on the coastline increased. There's no evidence Sechia was behind those attacks. In no way am I saying they were innocent. The Sechian Emperor of the time had expansionary goals too. But Domint used the raids as motivation to strike first."

He took another sip of his wine. Fenna still sat in her chair, listening, watching me.

"Domint pushed into the lands on the Southern Shore, having secured the support of his court and his military assets, like you. He invaded Sechia, sent crusading forces to take what they could and destroy what they couldn't. He drove the Sechians to their knees and then left them to their fate. He over-reached, however. Frachia saw weakness and struck."

Dela turned to look out of the window. It was dark outside now, and the coloured glass would have been black in the shadows if not for the lights of the city.

"Frachia was cruel. There was little support for him from the people. The Baronies were fragmented. Then the plagues came, and with them famine, violence... change. A group of scholars, religious leaders, merchants, led a revolt against Frachia. Afterwards they set up the Council and our new political template. We – that is, the rest of the councillors and I – are answerable to the people. They can vote for or against our leadership. We can be removed, peacefully, if we fail in our remits. This system has given us many benefits. Advances in medicine, engineering, mechanical wonders..."

"It's not perfect." Fenna spoke up from the chair in the corner, leaning forwards with her elbows on her knees.

Dela turned to her with one eyebrow raised, and one corner of her mouth curled in an apologetic smile.

"Oh, come on," she said, "you're giving him the clean version... there's been all sorts of dirt as well. It works, most of the time, but it can be corrupt. And it's *slow.* We weren't prepared for war. My Wardens... we deal with pirates, brigands, gangs. This is more than we were built for." She looked at Dela, and he shook his head and rolled his eyes.

"Quite." Dela agreed, turning back to me. "It's true, it has been difficult to... *motivate* the council. The current Sechian Emperor is Velst. He has been cunning, and he has turned to dark powers. His Empire did not revolt like Frachia's did... they have suffered for years, and they still struggle with resources. So, they use the dead, as some nations use slaves." He shook his head.

"Convincing the Council of this has been difficult. I was accused of spreading ghost stories and falsehoods. Councillor Cellin has been Kroll's advocate, and he is a talented liar."

At this Dela sat back, a troubled expression on his face.

"I believe you are the answer. I can use you, Baron, to prove to the council that the threat is real... or perhaps create more like you."

At this I jerked, and the clack of my jawbone falling open echoed around the room.

"NO! No. You cannot." His suggestion horrified me, and I did not try to temper my voice. Both Dela and Fenna winced at my volume.

"Why, Baron? Should I not adopt the weapons of my enemy?"

I had to make him understand. My existence was torment.

"You... you cannot use this sorcery again. I am a prisoner in my own bones, I have lost everything... I have awakened 400 years after my birth and everyone I loved is dead. To make more like me would be an act of great evil. You would be no better than the ones you fight."

"Then you must help me, Baron. You must go before the Council and show them what faces us."

I sat in silence, my mind reeling. I had always believed I was an honourable man. I had believed in my Emperor. I wanted to still. But this was too much, too much. I could not continue like this.

"I will do as you ask. But I want something in return." My voice still boomed.

"What would that be, Baron? What can I offer a dead man as a reward?"

"An end to it. I miss my family, my friends, my *brothers-in-arms*. I should be at rest, not locked in a cage of bones. Help me to die, Councillor. I am so very, very tired."

Dela regarded me, thoughtfully, considering my price.

"So be it. You have my word, Baron. When your task is complete, I will help you."

We spoke at length after that. I described the cavern in the catacombs at Estwake, the structure and disposition of Kroll's forces. I told Dela and Fenna of the new pools of sorcery created in every town and village Kroll had attacked, how he had grown his numbers and expanded his influence, how he threw waves of lesser undead against defences to break the wills of men. I spoke of the leaders Kroll had created, and the thought that they had volunteered to be like me filled me with disgust.

We were finally interrupted by a commotion outside the door. Bor burst into Dela's study, wild-eyed and panting after racing through the keep to give warning.

"Councillor, Captain, there's... you need to come downstairs, quickly. The High Daughter is here and she's not fuckin' happy."

Dela and Fenna looked at each other, and Dela covered his eyes with the palms of his hands. Then he rose and Fenna followed him, after ordering Bor to watch me.

They hurried from the room and Bor turned to me, angry.

"This is your fuckin' fault. Knew it was a mistake to bring you here."

"What is going on?" I asked, and Bor recoiled at the sound of my voice.

"By Omma, don't you say another fuckin' word. When did you learn... never mind, just keep your trap shut."

I turned away from him and sat still on my stool. I hung my head and regarded my bound hands. I could hear yelling and singing coming from outside the window, old ocean hymns. There was a large crowd of people gathering below, and the glow of their lanterns and torches was visible through the glass.

I heard many footsteps, running down the hall that led to Dela's study.

The door burst open, and there stood Daughter Corriss, accompanied by several men and women with tools, hammers, and wooden clubs. Assisting them were a handful of Garet's guards. Bor turned to face them, his dagger drawn already, and the priestess addressed him in a high shrill voice.

"Stand aside! By the order of the High Daughter, we are to remove this... *abomination!* This *filth* will not be tolerated! I order you to let us pass!"

"You don't get to order me around, y'fuckin' wethead." Bor was perfectly willing to engage all of them, numbers be damned.

"STAND ASIDE! This is the work of Omma T'Lassa and *it will not be denied!*"

Bor would die defending me, out of loyalty to Fenna. The mob were crazed with fear and the priestess seemed on the verge of madness, spit flying from her mouth as she spoke, her eyes rolling in her head.

"Bor!" I yelled.

Everyone in the room snapped their heads to look at me and fell silent in an instant. Some of them made the Sign of the Wave. One man dropped his hammer to do so, and stooped to pick it up, cursing and scrambling for his makeshift weapon.

"Bor, let them take me. If you fight them, you will be killed. Do not do that for me."

He looked at me with confusion, and the distraction allowed more of the mob to enter the room, until he was outnumbered more than ten to one. They had closed the distance on him, and one man reached out and grabbed Bor's dagger arm while his attention was on me. Bor turned, ready to strike with his clenched fist instead, but he was already overwhelmed. Several of the intruders held him and began to punch and kick him while he struggled and howled at them, cursing their mothers and their children. The priestess directed the others to pick me up and they did so, stool and all, and carried me out of the room as if they held aloft an ancient chieftain on his throne.

The frenzied procession carried me down through the keep, back through the small courtyard and down the steps outside, where

Dela and Fenna faced an angry crowd. There were hundreds of men and women, many of them the rag-dressed refugees that we had passed on our way through the city. They held their torches and lanterns in the air, and yelled and screamed and prayed, punctuating each stanza of their worship with gestured weapons. Their noise redoubled as they saw me exit the courtyard gate, high on my tawdry makeshift palanquin. Some of the crowd fell to their knees when they saw me. The hood of my cloak had fallen, and my skull was visible to the multitudes. The mob surged forwards, knocking many at the front of the throng to the hard cobblestones and sending them sprawling.

A line of Garet's men held back the tide as best they could. A few paces behind the struggling guardsmen there was a smaller group of people, and I recognised Guard Commander Garet, who wore a look of leering victory on his face, smug in his snug armour. The young priestess stood behind him, and they both watched as Dela argued with an older woman, tall and severe in a long blue gown and an ornate headdress, decorated with ocean waves made from silver and sapphires. She wore her chains of office around her neck, silver links threaded with seashells.

Dela was clearly furious.

"High Daughter, you must *understand!* You must

stop this! We are at WAR! I need this man... he is invaluable to our defence!"

She was taller than Dela, and looked down her nose at him with cold, hard eyes.

"This is no man, 'Councillor'. It is an abomination. You have blasphemed against Omma T'Lassa and imperilled all of our souls in the process. You must give yourself to The Mother of the Sea in penance for your sins against her. Remove this thing from my *sight!*" She turned her back on Dela and addressed the baying crowd behind her.

"It must be DESTROYED!" she screamed, and the crowd roared in response. Dela took a step back and looked up at me, and then to Fenna, who was standing by the gate behind me.

A small coterie of Garet's men assembled at the High Daughter's direction and took control of my portable prison. One held each leg of the stool, and I was ferried towards the crowd, the guardsmen forcing a passage through the mass of people with unrestrained violence. I turned back to see Bor had joined Fenna by the courtyard gate. The wound at his temple had re-opened and his face was covered in blood, black in the lantern light. Dela strode towards them, and with yelled and pointed commands that I could not hear over the baying mob they were both urged away from the scene. They set off at a run, circumventing the gathered people and heading down towards the docks.

I was carried aloft by the guards, moving deeper into the city and reaching a square where throngs of chanting and singing people circled a wide stone plinth. An execution site had been prepared. An anvil had been placed on the plinth, and a large man stood behind it, wearing a hood over his head and a long, leather blacksmith's apron. He held a sledgehammer in his hands, its heavy metal head placed on the floor between his feet.

Garet walked alongside his guards as they carried me towards my fate, and he looked up at me, a dirty grin plastered across his ruddy face.

"Told you I'd have you smashed to pieces, you fuckin' undead son of a whore."

I returned his gaze and replied to him. "Do as you wish, Commander. I care *NOT!*"

This last word came from a place of spite and with it I unleashed the full force of my voice at him. I had been curious as to what I sounded like if I decided to shout.

The effect was immediate. Garet recoiled as if he had been struck by a bolt from a siege crossbow. He lost his balance, and the crowd behind him parted, so that he stumbled and fell on his backside, just as he had at the bridge into Salisson.

"You spend a lot of time on your arse, Commander!" I yelled over the crowd, and if I could have smiled then I would have. He looked up at me with fear and embarrassment, and I took some amusement from that.

I was set down, and the leather binds that tied me to the stool were cut. Garet's men grabbed me at each extremity, the whipped-up frenzy of the crowd helping them to overcome their disgust, and I was lifted aloft again, this time spread-eagled and splayed. They carried me up the few stone stairs to the plinth and set me down next to the anvil. I was forced to kneel before it, although I did not offer much resistance. I had accepted my fate, glad I was to be finally freed. I craved the peace I hoped it would bring.

I was forced down over the anvil's horn, and it dug in underneath my ribcage as my head was pressed against the bare metal at the other end. My hands and legs were bound underneath it, and I was tied like a hog for the roast.

The High Daughter arrived with her entourage and stood alongside me to address the crowd.

"We commend to you, Omma T'Lassa, Mother of the Sea, this unholy form. We will render it to dust and pass it over the waves of the ocean. Let its blasphemy dissipate in your holy waters. Let its sin be diluted by your changing form. Let the dead lie! Let them no longer trouble the living!"

There was a commotion, somewhere behind me. I could not turn my head to see. I heard a dull *thump* and the masked executioner fell beside me, face up, his covered features just below and in front of mine. There was a crossbow bolt embedded in his head.

I heard the High Daughter scream "You *DARE?!*" and the guardsmen on the plinth drew their weapons. There were several more thuds and clangs as crossbow bolts hit home, and the crowd panicked and began to scatter, scrambling to get away from the carnage. I heard heavy footsteps cross the square behind me and run up to my executioner's block. The figure arrived beside me and bent down, and Bor's head appeared in my field of vision. His face was still a mask of blood. He produced a knife and began to cut away my bindings, grunting with the effort. He looked at me and spoke.

"Don't fuckin' make me regret this, bonehead."

He finished his work and hoisted me to my feet, again covering me with one of the Warden's cloaks. The square around us was filled with screaming chaos. Most of Garet's men had fallen back, and the crowd were running for the surrounding alleyways and streets. I saw Fenna, drawing her crossbow with a lever and re-loading it. Alongside her were others, a grim looking rabble dressed in leather and metal armour. Her Wardens. They charged the remainder of Garet's men and pushed them back with great swings of their weapons and a flurry of bolts. The town guard did not have their discipline or skill and broke under the ferocious assault, turning to join the escaping populace.

The High Daughter and her subservient priestess were still on the plinth with us. The younger girl hid behind the robes of the old woman, crying, while the raging harridan shrieked angry prayers, pointing at my cloaked form.

"FOUL CREATURE! ABOMINATION! *UNDEAD FILTH!*" She howled epithets and curses at us as we retreated. Bor and I reached the Warden's line, and he ran to Fenna.

"What the fuck now, Captain?" said Bor, one of his meaty hands still clamped around my upper arm.

"Head for the Sea Snake. You need to get him to the harbour - we'll cover the retreat. Dela is boarded already, we need to leave. We're headed for the Western Gate."

"I don't think we'll be welcome here again."

"Can't say as I liked it much here anyway." Fenna bit her lip, and then gave Bor a quick embrace before patting his back to send him on his way.

We raced through the town, Bor dragging me

by the arm and not once letting go. The locals and refugees cowered in windows and crouched in doorways, watching our passage. We reached an inn, dark inside and apparently unoccupied. The sign hanging above the door showed a crude picture, just visible in the ambient light of the city. It was a coiled and twisted sea serpent, holding a struggling figure in its fanged jaws.

Bor dragged me into an alley by the side of the building, and still holding my arm he fumbled at his belt for a set of brass keys. He chose one and unlocked the back door of the inn, quickly pushed me into the darkness beyond, and then closed and locked the door behind us. I could see in the gloom inside the door. My night sight had not deserted me with the addition of my voice. Bor knew the layout well enough not to need light.

He pulled me through the entry room and then headed for a door that led to basement stairs. At the bottom of the stairs was a lantern, which he lit, using one of the strange flint mechanisms the Wardens carried. Once he had light he unlocked a further door at the rear of the basement, and this led down more stairs to a low, stone clad tunnel, which stretched off into the darkness, in the direction of the harbour.

After a long while in the cramped, twisting tunnel we climbed another smaller set of stairs and emerged underneath a wooden storage crate that lifted on disguised hinges, hidden at the rear of a dock warehouse. The harbour was in front of us and I saw a ship, far grander and more advanced than any I had seen in my life. It had many tall black sails, and on the main sail was a stitched representation of a sea-predator, lined in silver, with a great broad fin on its back. We ran to where it was docked and passed a handful of Wardens who busied themselves with preparations for launch. Bor dragged me up the boarding ramp and onto deck.

Dela waited for me there, enraged, ranting and pacing the deck, all pretence at calm dropped.

"Ten years! TEN YEARS I've built what I could for this Region, and *this* is my reward! Undone by that, that short-sighted, intolerant, pious *bitch!*"

He rubbed his face with his hands and growled into his palms. I could hear noises on the dock, men and women bustling to-and-fro, shouting orders and grabbing supplies to load onto the ship. Fenna appeared at the top of the boarding ramp, joining Bor, and she clasped his shoulder and then turned to the enraged Councillor. Dela was still cursing and sputtering insults, but then caught himself and tried to get hold of his temper.

"Ahhh, apologies for the language, Fenna,"

"It's fine, I hear worse from Bor. Anyway, the High Priestess *is* a bitch. What now, Councillor?"

"We cast off. Are your Wardens on board?"

"There are a few stragglers, but we'll be ready soon. We need to leave before Garet's men regroup." She moved back to the rail of the ship and leaned over it, shouting down to hurry the activity below.

Dela turned to me.

"You have cost me a great deal, Baron. All the progress I have made here, all the gold I spent to try to drag this Region out of the mire. Gone in one night. I am a rich man, Baron, but no amount of money will repair this."

"I will repay what I can, Councillor." I said. "As you can see, I have little to offer, other than my service and my honour."

He smiled a little at this, his anger subsiding. "Then that will have to do."

I gave a short, nodding bow. Shortly afterwards we headed out of port, and into the Scar Sea.

CHAPTER NINE

The crew were not happy I was on board.

I had been bundled away into a dark corner of the hold, placed under guard and bound again, this time to one of the wooden braces that reinforced the ship. We had left in the middle of the night. This was not an ideal time for a ship to slip its moorings, and a winter storm appeared to unleash its wrath upon us as soon as we were in open water. The ship tossed to-and-fro on the violent and angry sea. The Wardens standing guard over me had to steady themselves against the contents of the hold and the hull of the ship. One of them seemed badly affected by the rocking motion and had to run into a far corner to empty his stomach of its contents.

The sailors blamed me for the poor conditions, or so Fenna told me. They believed the sea resented my presence, as I was an unclean spirit. The wind howled and the waves rushed over the deck, and the water seeped down through the planks to fall on my head and the heads of my guards.

This continued for the rest of the night and most

of the morning, until the sea finally let go its fury and relented in its attacks.

Near midday, as far as I could tell, Fenna came down to sit with me. She dismissed the guards and pulled up a barrel opposite me.

"How do you feel?" She said, and again there was some glimmer of compassion in her expression.

"Not seasick, if that's your concern." I bobbed my chin towards my midriff. "Although I do not have the stomach for sea travel."

"Was that a joke?" She winced and smiled a little, with gritted teeth.

"Yes. Sorry. I expect you find that a little tasteless."

"Not necessarily tasteless. I just didn't know you had a sense of humour."

I shifted my position, with some difficulty. I had been sat cross-legged on the floor, still cloaked, with my hands tied in front of me, one length of ship's rope around my wrists and ankles and threaded up through the beams. I managed to turn myself to face her.

"I was famed for it, once. When you are on campaign... war is a brutal pastime. Men die, friends die. You see things that stay with you. Many soldiers tell jokes and stories that they would not share in polite company. It is how we reconcile ourselves with the darkness."

She rubbed her head, wiping some water from her braided hair. There were still drips falling from the wooden ceiling.

"Yeah, I understand that. The Wardens... a lot of us have a dark sense of humour. We've seen some things."

"How did you come to be a Warden? How did you end up working for Dela?"

"Heh, that... that is complicated."

"I have very little else to entertain me down here. Tell me."

She shifted on her seat now, getting as comfortable on the barrel as she could. Her legs dangled.

"Dela... he arrived in Salisson a decade or so ago, as far as I know. He used to be a pirate, although don't say that to his face. He insists he was a privateer, heh. He used to board Sechian ships on behalf of the Council... they still have some ports on the Southern Shore, and they attack our vessels when they can."

She brushed another drop of water from her head.

"He lost his taste for it. He made a lot of money from his time as a seadog but the Council were squeamish about it, about what he did and why he did it. He told them a war was coming but they're too busy with their own interests. So, he used his money to run for office in Salis. He used to berth there most of the time."

"And you? How did you come to be here?"

"I... we, Bor and I, Sal, Verrik... we were street runners. Thieves and bandits. Orphans in gangs, most of us. We'd fallen into the cracks. He approached us, in person. Said he needed help, would pay well for us to go straight like him. Some turned him down. Most of us didn't. We were all old before our time. My parents died when I was eight years old. Bor won't talk about his." She ran her hand over her head again, her expression thoughtful.

"I owe Dela a lot. He's not perfect, not by a long way. But I think he's right. About you, and Kroll, and Sechia. So I'll follow him where this leads."

"You think he's right about me?"

She turned her head away from me to hide her face.

"I think, I believe, that you *are* Baron Acellion. I think you want to do the right thing. I think you can help us. I made a choice to save you and now I can never go back to Salisson."

She looked at me then, her face hard, teeth clenched.

"Tell me I'm right. Tell me I haven't made a mistake."

I leaned forwards a little and tried to speak as

softly as I could.

"I do not know, Fenna. I want to help. I will do whatever Dela asks. But you must understand... I am nothing but sadness and anger now. This will need to end."

She stared at me, the care on her face evident even in the dim light of the hold. I do not know, even now, if I deserved her care. Under the martial aspect of her dress and the hard lines of her face was an old soul. Fenna had the heart of ten women.

"I will help you, Asheth." She said. "When the time comes. I promise."

I was brought to the Captain's quarters, later that afternoon, although in the grey light of the squalling sea the passage of time was difficult to track. I was hooded again so my form did not upset the crew any further, although I heard muttered curses and prayers as I passed them on the deck. One grizzled old dog stepped out of my way and then spat at my feet as I was led to the stern of the ship. I was becoming used to such treatment, a far cry from the respect I had commanded when I lived. Most of the crew studiously ignored me, working on cleaning the deck. One man was hammering away at a rail, repairing some damage they had not had the opportunity to fix while at dock, as we had left with some haste. He kept his back to me as he swung his tool over his shoulder, pounding a post into the edge of the deck.

I was walked into the Captain's cabin by Fenna and Bor, and sat at a chair facing the rear window of the ship. The glass was made up of joined coloured panes and bore a resemblance to the one in Dela's study. Dela was there, lurking at the rear of the small room, gazing through the ornate window at the churning waves that marked the ship's passage. Behind a large wooden desk sat another man. He had a long dark beard, twisted into braids and tied with ribbons, and he wore a long black jacket, like Dela's, but worn open, with a white shirt underneath. His black hair was tied back in a tail with another ribbon, and he had a deep scar on his face that ran from his left temple down to the side of his mouth, a white crevasse standing out against his tanned skin.

Fenna and Bor stepped back from my chair and stood behind me. I was not bound.

Dela turned away from the window to address me.

"Baron, I would like you to meet Captain Berisio Shand. He is a friend of mine, and he also works for me. I own the ship we are travelling on, the *Silverfin*... however at sea his orders are to be followed absolutely, and I defer to his decisions in all matters during voyages, as is proper. No ship can have more than one Captain. Your coming aboard was a hurried choice, made under some duress, and in the interests of peace onboard he has determined to meet with you. Please speak to him with all due deference and respect, as you have done with me." Dela placed a hand on the Captain's shoulder, squeezing it, and then stepped back to re-assume his position at the window.

The Captain said nothing, and just watched me. His gaze was unblinking and calm. In front of him, laid on the desk, was a wide-bladed and curved sword, drawn from its scabbard and within easy reach.

I bowed my head, raised it, and pulled the hood back so that he could see my face.

"A pleasure to meet you, Captain. Thank you for your hospitality."

I had become accustomed to a severe reaction from anyone meeting me. No such instinct seemed to trouble the Captain. He grunted, laid one be-ringed and sun-damaged hand on the hilt of his sword, and leaned forwards.

His voice was low, a whisper, almost a growl. His accent was thick, from somewhere to the west.

"Met your kind before. Y'don't scare me none. All sorts of things floatin' around out here."

His fingers drifted back-and-to on the handle of his blade, tapping out a rhythm to a song only he could hear.

"My crew don't want you here. They've fought your kind as well, on Sechian ships, on raids on the Southern Shore. They're not usually as talkative as you, mind. My crew think you've cursed us. Are you a curse, dead man?"

I shook my head. "*I* am cursed. I do not believe, so far, that my ill-luck extends to anyone else."

He smiled at this. Some of his teeth were gold.

"Time'll tell."

He continued to question me for a little while. Most of his inquiries mirrored Dela's. Some time into my interrogation a mate knocked on the door behind me and then barged straight in, shoving Fenna and Bor out of the way. Bor regarded him with violence in his eyes, but Fenna put a hand on his chest and the brute held his temper. The mate pulled up to a halt when he saw me but then shook off his shock and spoke.

"Captain, we have a ship trailing us. Maybe a couple of leagues behind. Lassin thinks it's flying Treshan flags but it's too far away to be sure."

Fenna turned to Dela. "Kroll was lining up an attack on Gariss when we left Tresh. He could have taken the port by now."

Dela frowned. "It could be a friendly vessel, but

we must be careful. Our mission may have been compromised... I suspected there were spies in Salisson. Berisio, what do you think?"

"I think we shouldn't stop for nothin'. Until we reach safe harbour everyone's an enemy." Shand turned to face his mate. "Can we outpace 'em?"

"I dunno Captain. *Silverfin* is the fastest ship in these waters, but we don't have the wind for it. Whoever she is she's gaining on us. It's not natural."

Shand got up from behind his desk, grabbing the hilt of his blade as he did so, and left his quarters with the mate. I heard him outside barking orders in his broad accent, his voice suddenly loud compared to the quiet growl of our conversation.

The weather was an enemy. The wind came in fits and starts, but no matter which direction it rushed from, the sails of the *Silverfin* could not find purchase on it, and our pursuers gained on us with supernatural speed. The gales whirled around the ship like a legion of tormented spirits, changing direction with little sense, rattling the rigging and ripping the sails to-and-fro, and removing all hope of being able to tame the tempest. Shand ordered that the oar deck be used to try to gain some speed, but it offered little benefit.

I remained in the Captain's cabin during this time, continuing to provide what insight I could to Dela while he, Fenna and Bor sipped wine from small wooden cups. We did our best to distract ourselves from the stern chase, as for now we would only be in the way and could not influence its outcome.

We could see the trailing ship growing larger in the Captain's window.

The *Silverfin* was prepared for battle. Ports were opened in the hull of the ship. The mechanical skill of the Regions had extended somewhat towards armament, and over-sized crossbows ran down the port and starboard sides of the ship, held on a deck made only for the purpose of mounting them. They used a lever and winch mechanism to load bolts nearly the height of a man, and the points of these missiles extended out into the brine and foam-flecked air. On deck were small catapults, again with winch-driven loading mechanisms, and these were loaded with tar-soaked balls of iron and rag, to be lit upon the commencement of hostilities.

As the chasing ship drew nearer figures were visible stalking across the deck, even through the gloom of the storm and the growing darkness of the sky. They did not move like the living, and their silhouettes were thin and spindly. Although the wind was still howling, voices carried on it unnaturally, and the chanting of

Kroll's cultists could be heard calling the tempest down upon us and twisting it to their purposes.

The crew of the pursuing ship raised a large red banner at their prow, the signal that they wished to communicate. They pulled alongside, barely ten paces from us over the waves, and as they did so the ocean immediately around us calmed, as if we were trapped in the eye of the cursed storm. A low phosphorescent mist rose from the still water, curling around the sharpened bolts of the great crossbows that extended from our hull and sending ghostly fingers crawling up our suddenly dead sails.

A single voice called from over the water. I heard it through the open doorway of Shand's cabin, and it filled me with dread. All hope for release drained from me at that moment. I cannot feel the cold, and yet a chill passed down my spine, and I held my fleshless face in my hands.

It was Hallek. His voice was like a temple bell, tolling doom.

"I address Councillor Dela Hevigne of Salisson. You have found one of my fallen brothers. I wish his return. If you give him to me, you and your crew will not be harmed. We do not wish conflict with you."

Dela was still in the cabin with me, and he rose to leave the room and respond to the request. Fenna grabbed his arm and shook her head.

I heard Captain Shand reply, his now bellowing gruff voice carrying easily even through the muffling effect of the mist.

"This is a private vessel out of Salisson, and I don't know who yer speaking of! We have no passengers! We're a trading ship, headin' fer the Western Gate, and I'd be obliged if y'd let us pass!"

"You lie, and so dishonour yourself. I did not wish to engage you in battle, but you would force my hand."

Shand's response was not a shy one.

"DO WHAT YOU LIKE! My honour is not for the likes of you to question, foul spirit. And ye'll not find *THIS* ship an easy conquest, so be gone with yer!"

At this a great shout of "SHAND! SHAND!" went up from the crew, and battle commenced.

The Captain screamed "STRIIIIIIIKE!" and the tensed crossbows let their bolts loose. They crashed into the enemy ship and pierced its hull with great cracks of splintering wood. The catapults on deck were lit and the flaming arc of their missiles glowed through the mist as they landed on the opposite deck and burst into starry fragments, lighting sails and the dead alike.

A few of the huge crossbow bolts had great, barbed arrowheads that hooked into the enemy's hull, and these were attached to the *Silverfin* by long chains. These were wound by the straining and sweating crew turning huge reels, and as they were pulled in, they drew the enemy ship nearer to us until the decks were adjacent. Shand had not waited for his ship to be boarded like some common merchant. He was a privateer and was not about to be anyone's victim. He was the pillager, not the pillaged. Boarding planks were extended from the deck of the *Silverfin* from recesses beneath the deck, wound forwards on turning cogs until they touched the dead ship, and Shand's crew attacked the enemy vessel as a prize to be taken. The dead dropped planks of their own, simple wooden lengths as opposed to the mechanical extensions that the *Silverfin* boasted.

The enemy ship was not equipped like ours. It had some weaponry like Shand's ship, but its dead crew were unused to sea warfare and were slow to react. Hallek may have assumed that fear of the dead alone would be enough for him to prevail. Shand's crew weren't afraid of the dead, but they did hate them, and that hate drove them onto the enemy deck in a wave of violence and destruction.

Dela and Fenna were still in the cabin with me, Bor having joined the crew on deck. The Captain of the Wardens drew her weapon and moved towards the door, but the Councillor stopped her.

"*NO!* We must protect him. Otherwise this has

been a waste of time."

Fenna turned and she stepped back, sword still in hand. Her face was filled with fury, but she obeyed Dela's command, and closed the door to try to protect the cabin's occupiers. Outside we could hear the clash of weapons and howls of rage from Shand's crew. It seemed at least some of the dead had managed to board us in the confusion of battle.

Suddenly the door burst open again, and two Raised soldiers entered the cabin, with more behind them defending the entrance from the privateer crew. Fenna immediately lunged forwards, sword raised, and jammed her blade into the eye socket of the lead undead, splitting his skull in two and driving him back into his comrade behind him. She pushed as hard as she could and her charge forced the dead back out through the door. Dela moved around Shand's desk, drawing a short sword from beneath his cloak, and stood guard in front of me. I saw Fenna tumble to the deck, surrounded by dark skeletal forms, lit only by the lanterns of the ship and the burning enemy vessel. The light of the flames cut through the mist and smoke.

I could not sit there and be watched like a frightened child.

I stood up from my chair, my dark borrowed cloak still around my shoulders. I pushed past

Dela to come to Fenna's aid, forcing my way through the door and ignoring his cry of alarm.

One of the Raised loomed over Fenna, preparing to strike, and I hit him with all my speed and weight, knocking him to the deck and causing him to drop his sword. Another Raised turned to face me and again, just as in the snowy forest days ago, the dead man hesitated, as if not sure I was friend or foe. I took his moment of confusion as a gift, and reaching out I grasped his face, pushing my fingers into his eye sockets. I turned, shifting on my feet, and with as much force as I could produce I slammed his head into the frame of the cabin doorway. His skull shattered in my hand like an eggshell.

One more dead man stepped forwards, standing astride Fenna's prone form, and as I turned to face him he overcame his confusion and slashed at me with his sword. I leaned back to dodge the blow, the sword passing a finger's width from my neck, and I struck out as he was off-balance, grabbing the blade with my right hand and reaching under his ribcage to grasp his spine with my left. I lifted him, more easily than I thought I would, and held his struggling form above my head. I stalked to the edge of the deck and tossed him into the waters below.

The dead cannot drown, but neither can they swim. Perhaps he made it back to land, eventually.

I turned back from the deck-rail to see that more of the dead had made it on board. Shand's crew fought like wild beasts, snarls of hatred and rage loosed from their mouths with every blow, but Hallek had no interest in keeping the ship he had used to chase us down. He wanted this one, and me with it. He was throwing every Raised he had at the *Silverfin* with no concern for defence.

My anger grew. I felt that I would have no respite from this evil, that I would never be free, and it enraged me. I have said before that emotions can be curiously limited in me. I can feel anger, or sadness, or fear, but usually these impulses retreat quickly. I have no heart to race nor flesh to quicken. Yet at that moment, stood on the deck of the assailed ship, I felt the heat of battle and wrath rising in me as it had in the old days. All fear left me, and the rage grew until it took me over.

I quickly looked around for a weapon. There are many tools on board a sailing ship that can be turned to violent purposes. I had seen that swords were not ideal against the hard bones of the dead. Near my feet, against the newly repaired deck railings, was a long wooden box. Opening it I found a set of shipwright's tools. Quickly discarding the smaller items, I fished out a broad-headed hammer with a long handle, the cousin of the one that had nearly demolished my skull in Salisson. I dragged it from the box, turned, and launched myself into the fray.

My first victim had his rear to me and was clashing with a single member of Shand's crew. The sailor had been driven back to one of the ship's masts and impaled with a rusted sword, and blood was visible on his teeth and lips. I swung and slammed the hammer into the base of his attacker's spine, cracking it in two almost immediately. The skeleton's legs buckled, his scrabbling torso fell to the deck, and raising the hammer over my head I smashed it down into his skull to cease his movement. I turned to look behind me and then swung my weapon in a wide arc, crashing it through another group of the flailing dead, throwing them back against the deck railing. I kicked out and one toppled backwards over the rail and fell into the ocean, his bones immediately sinking from view into the dark brine.

The battle lust was in me now. I swung back, cracking the heavy metal head of my hammer against the skulls and ribs of all who stood before me. I drove them into the deck as shards of bone and dust, cracking the planks beneath my enemies with the force of my blows. I smashed their faces with bellows of hollow-sounding rage, watched their teeth fly, their jawbones split, their skulls shatter. I felt something like joy, as many moons of horror and pain and fear were released in a single frenzied dance of wrath. Bor appeared alongside me, a sword in each of his hands. He had seen I was the only cloaked Raised and had realised my identity as I struck at my former captors. We exchanged looks, nodded at each other, and then threw ourselves into the melee. He had wits in battle he could not reach in conversation. He spun and struck and laughed with glee at the release of combat, efficient and wild at the same time. Between us we carved a path through the dead.

The enemy ship was burning from stern to bow. Some living followers of Kroll had ceased their chanting manipulation of the storm and were trying to put out the flames with panicked and futile efforts. Shand's men had withdrawn to the *Silverfin*, and the mechanical bridges they had employed were withdrawn with them. What dead were left had abandoned their vessel and were clawing along their boarding planks trying to reach us. I lifted the hammer again, both hands grasping the long handle, and brought it down on the end of one these beams. It snapped in two and the dead scrambling along it fell into the sea. Along the side of our ship others in Shand's crew were lifting the enemy timbers and tossing them into the ocean below. A handful of Raised were trying to clamber along the chains linking the two hulls, but some mechanism inside our ship was released and the metal links slipped into the water, carrying their dead load with them.

I turned away from the edge of the deck and saw that the last of the Raised onboard were fighting on our bridge. Shand and some of his officers were pinned there, their backs to the railing as they fended off attacks. A dark armoured figure paced towards them, sweeping the deck with his sword. Hallek was going to kill Shand. The dead man's armour, laid on top of bone instead of flesh, was nearly impenetrable. None of the defenders could land a telling blow.

I raced for the steps leading up to the bridge deck. I clambered up the incline, and as I neared the top I swung my hammer at ankle height to the dead, sweeping several from their feet. I continued my ascent and brought my boots and hammer down on their skulls as I reached the top. I swept the dead overboard with low swings of my weapon and crashed into the others that turned to face me until finally Hallek was alone. A handful of men stood their ground before him, and I stood at his rear.

"*HALLEK!*" I screamed. I wanted him to know I knew him.

He turned then, and I did not hesitate. I brought the head of my hammer down on his armoured skull as if it were a star falling from the firmament.

He tried to avoid the blow but was not fast

enough. My hammer glanced the side of his helmet and struck it from his head. The lizard-carved helmet clanged and clattered across the deck and was swallowed by the ocean, and he snarled in his hollow, cracked bell voice and moved to strike me back.

The dead do not, in general, fight well. Lesser Raised fight like beasts. Raised fight like men of simple training, just thrust, parry, slash, thrust; no art or skill evident in their strikes. One on one any decent soldier can beat a Raised in combat. They rely on fear and weight of numbers to carry their battles.

Hallek and I were not like them. Our memories, and thus our skills, were intact. Hallek was no great warrior, but he had obviously trained with his weapon, and this fact coupled with his armoured form meant I was suddenly on the back foot. I desperately tried to parry his fast and unpredictable blows, and I was struggling to find a way through the defence of his plate and mail. He drove me back step by step, until I was leaning with my back against the railings and the hungry sea below me. I was to be consigned to the depths, just as I had disposed of others.

I was lucky.

The wooden shaft of the hammer I held split under a great swing of Hallek's sword, and suddenly the weapon I held reduced in size, the head of it still in my right hand. As he tried to swing back, I side-stepped and slammed the metal of the hammerhead into the left of his skull with all my strength, and this cracked one side of his face. A stream of black smoke and green sparks flew from the fissure, and Hallek staggered and cried out in distress. I lunged forwards and we tumbled to the planks together, rolling across the varnished and brine-soaked wood, and by sheer chance we ended the tussle with me sat astride him. I raised my weapon and with a scream of fury I smashed it into his eyeless, howling face. I did not stop. All my rage and desperation was unleashed in this final violent assault. I raised the hammer again and again, pounding it into his head until all that was left was dry, pottery-like fragments of bone, and the dented and cracked deck below them.

At Hallek's death the stillness that held the *Silverfin* ceased, and the fog swirled up into a whirling funnel. A great screaming gale erupted from the ocean, a sudden squall accompanying the wailing of his spirit as it left the broken shell of his skull. The two ships were tossed violently in the quickening and churning sea, and the attacking vessel was tipped in the water, the rents in its side from Shand's bolts now a wound through which the ocean found ingress. The Treshan ship lurched, and the screams of fear of the remaining living crew were still audible over the howling wind as they found themselves caught between fire and water.

As their ship sank the last remnants of the dead boarding party were thrown into the waves by Shand's men, who roared and raised their weapons in victory. I stood on the bridge, the wind and rain whipping and snapping my cloak around me and whistling through my skull. The half-length hammer was still in my hand. Shand leant against the railing and he and his men stared at me. They were bleeding from many places and panting with exertion. I turned to them, still standing astride the broken and decapitated body of Hallek, and I lifted my weapon as the crew had, roaring defiance through lipless teeth into the raging storm.

Lanterns that had been snuffed out during the battle were re-lit. The crew still avoided me while the bridge and deck were cleared and the wounded and dead were accounted for, but they did not spit at me or curse at me. Some had seen me fight and word had spread. Fenna appeared at the bridge steps, wobbly on her feet and bleeding from some cuts and grazes, but whole and mostly unharmed. Bor joined her, a look of concern on his face as he checked she was well. He leaned down to whisper in her ear and grasped her shoulder with a squeeze of affection.

Finally, Dela made his way up the steps, his sword still in his hand. A swelling on the left side of his face was beginning to close his eye. He walked towards Shand, and they clasped wrists and then embraced, holding each other for a moment.

I stood there, watching them. I still held the hammer, and I looked down at it in my hand, its broken handle held in my skeletal grip. I had nearly forgotten I had it. I walked slowly to the edge of the bridge, right to the rear of the ship, and placed it gently on the wooden planks. Then I turned back to face my captors.

Shand pulled away from Dela, nodded his head at the Councillor, and then turned to speak to me.

"Seen a lot of things on the Scar Sea. Things yer'd scarce believe. Never seen one eh'yer fight y'own."

"They are not my own. I have been Raised against my will. Enslaved. Conscripted. Made to participate in horrors beyond my limits. No more, Captain. I am Baron Asheth Acellion, Lord of Estwake, and I am no-one's slave."

The Captain grinned then, his glimmering golden teeth catching the lantern light.

"So it seems. Y'r welcome on my ship, Baron. The crew'll come around after what y'did. Y'saved my life, and I'm indebted to yer." He reached out his hand, and I grasped it firmly in mine, the first time someone had touched me with respect since I had awakened in the watchtower.

"No debt is due, Captain Shand. I have much to pay for yet, and this is but a fraction of what I owe Kroll."

The crew worked hard to repair the ship. The dead had caused much damage. Holes and cracks in the deck were hammered over with planking and sealed with tar, sails with rents in them where rusted swords had slashed were brought down, stitched with strong twine and raised again. The fresh and cold winter wind decided on a direction and allowed us to make headway. We sailed out towards the centre of the Great Crossing and onwards to the Western Gate, the Scar Sea momentarily our ally.

I thought of the voyages I had partaken in when I lived, when we campaigned against Sechia. We relied more on the oar than the sail then. We took the Sechian ports early in our conquest, and most of my experience of war had been on land. I stood on the prow of the ship, gazing out through empty eyes over the rolling waves. I had never been a seafarer, but that day I took in the beauty of the sea, and watched it change its aspect from one moment to the next. By turns it was green, wild and angry, then blue, calm and majestic. I watched the waves broken by sea life I could not identify, jumping fish that split the water in leaps and dives, their scales a rainbow of colours and flashing light. I saw long, bearded serpents chase the shoals for their meals, striking from below and grabbing at the darting panicked fish with wide-open jaws. They clamped their gaping maws shut over their catches and crashed back into the surf, diving for the depths again.

There was beauty, and there was death, and I stood somewhere between the two, on the waves of the Scar Sea.

I spent my nights still in the hold, away from the crew, but I was no longer bound. I had visitors, on occasion. Fenna came to talk to me and told me tales of how she and her Wardens fought bandits, chased down brigands and murderers, and provided information and insight for Dela's use. Dela came, and told me of his days as a privateer, a term he used with some insistence and a barely hidden smile. He had tired of that life, and had left behind close friends, like Captain Shand, who had served as his First Mate many years before. Dela had feared for the future of the Northern Shore and felt he would serve it far better as a Councillor than as a raider. He felt he had yet to prove this.

The Captain himself joined me for conversation, out of curiosity, and told me of what Sechia had become over the years since my campaigns. It was an empire of the dead now. He had seen Raised on pirate raids, but the Council didn't believe the tales of sailors. Shand and his crew, and the other privateers like them, were fighting the dead with little support. They had developed their own tactics to combat them, as he had amply demonstrated.

I, in turn, spoke about myself. About my campaigns, of how we had fought the Sechians in the old days, and the battles I had been in, and the comrades I had lost. Eventually I spoke of my wife, and my children, and how much I loved them and missed them. I told them that I was glad my family could not see me in my current sorry state.

My most surprising visitor was Bor. He came to the hold one night, holding a bottle of some lethal liquor in one hand, and a deck of worn gambling cards in the other. He drank for both of us, and we played games of chance, with a handful of small glass beads taking the place of coin. He soon became frustrated with the lack of expression in my face. I could bluff better than anyone he had played with.

He admitted, in his cups, that he and Fenna were lovers, as I had suspected. He dreamed of one day taking her for a wife. I told him she would make a fine wife, but not a tame one, at which he laughed and said he didn't want that anyway.

"What use do I have for a quiet mouse when I could have a wild fox?" He said.

He was a funny and jovial drunk, and his expressions of dismay when I bluffed him again and again were bellowed in jest and made me laugh. He was the first person to make me laugh since I had been unearthed.

CHAPTER TEN

It was just after dawn when we got our first sight of the Western Gate, nearly half a moon since we had left Salisson. The tops of its towers, lit by the rising sun, glinted red and gold.

The Gate Island sat between the two westernmost tips of the Northern and Southern Shores. A citadel had existed there for many centuries and had built up over hundreds of years to be the greatest city in the old Baronies. It was known as the Gate because for any ship to leave the Scar Sea, and thus make its way down the Jagged Coast of the Western Ocean or to the Outer Islands, it had to first pass beneath two fortified bridges that linked the island to the Shores. These bridges were huge, arched constructs, high and wide enough to allow several ships access beneath at any one time. They were defended, with dangling chains that could be raised and lowered on reels, ranks of catapults, and ramps filled with stones, ready to be dropped on any ship attempting entrance or exit without permission. By this mechanism the

Baronies and now the Regions of the Northern Shore could police all traffic in and out of the inland Scar Sea. No trade- or war-craft could enter or leave without running this gauntlet. This control had been maintained for seasons uncounted.

As the city grew on the horizon I was fetched from the hold and stood on the bridge with Captain Shand, Fenna, Bor, and Dela. Dela spoke first.

"Getting you into the city could be difficult. We need to cover you in a way that will hide your nature… your cloak only works as a disguise in darkness. I asked the Captain to help me create a solution. There are crew on board who have some skill with craft other than fighting. I have something for you."

A package was brought to me by one of the mates, a heavy parcel tied with twine. On top of it was the hammer I had used when we were boarded. The handle had been replaced, and the new shaft was a piece of hardwood, varnished until it was nearly black, and wound with metal wire to help prevent the breakage it had suffered during the fighting. Etched into the wood at the top of the shaft was a circle of skulls. The hammerhead itself had had the rust and patina of age ground off and it gleamed silvery in the dawn light. Both faces of the hammer had been stamped with Dela's fin heraldry. Finally, a pair of leather grips had been added, one at the base of the shaft, and one nearer the top, so that I could wield it two-handed, and my bony hands could keep better purchase on the smooth wood.

I nodded my thanks to the Captain and placed the hammer head down on the deck. Then I opened the rest of my gift. Inside was a set of leather armour and thick clothes, plated in places and mailed in others, in the same style as that worn by the Wardens. The leather had been stained black. I felt at one of the sleeves and saw that it had been padded, to help compensate for my lack of flesh. There was a metal helmet, with a leather face covering that could be lowered and tied under my chin, and a hood that would cover the whole of my head. Anyone seeking to discern my features would have to examine me very carefully.

"I'm allowed an entourage when I enter the Council chambers," said Dela, "and you are to be my bodyguard, Asheth, if that is a part you are happy to play."

I nodded my assent, somewhat humbled by the growth of his trust in me. "I might need help putting it on," I said, "My joints can be awkward, and it is a long time since I have had to dress myself."

Bor grinned and volunteered, for his own amusement, and he and I retired to the hold so he could assist me. He was hardly a gentle chambermaid but between us we managed to strap me into the padded outfit, amidst much cursing and spluttering.

When I strode back to the bridge, I looked more like a living man than I had in centuries. The padding restricted my movement a little, but not as much as I had feared, and I could sling the hammer across my back on a loop fitted for that purpose. The hood and face covering were deep and dark enough to hide my empty eye sockets, so I was unlikely to cause anyone a shock at first glance, although I realised I cut quite an intimidating figure. I had been tall in life, and now I loomed over my companions like some avenging wraith. I re-wrapped my dark cloak around my shoulders and stood to face them.

"Splendid." Said Dela.

"He's going to scare the living shit out of the city guard." Said Bor.

I had been to the Western Gate before, when I lived and Domint ruled. We had assembled all the forces of the Baronies here before we sailed to conquer. The city had grown in the time I had spent in my grave, and was now a busy, vibrant, walled metropolis. The pale sand walls were broken by huge bronze gates, inlaid with gold and marble panels, and crenelated guard towers loomed high over the harbour as we made our way into port. The Western Gate's defences seemed in a far less ruinous state than the ones in Estwake, Tresh and Salis. A small boat came out to greet us, steered by well-groomed guards in gold-plated armour and off-white tabards. We were guided into port, passing over a long, heavy chain that served as a barrier and was lowered into the water so that we could enter. We came to rest in the hectic harbour, bumping our hull against a floating pontoon that extended out into the sea. It was one of many. The harbour seemed bigger than I recalled.

I said my farewells to Captain Shand, and he clasped my wrist as I clasped his, and nodded with good will. I was touched by his gesture. As I disembarked one or two of the crew nodded their heads to me also, a response far removed from the insults they had hurled my way at first. I had gained some respect from them, and some trust, although none of them were likely to take me dancing.

We made our way along the floating pontoon and onto the stone paved slabs of the dock proper. A handful of the Wardens joined us, and the rest melted into the crowds of the port and disappeared from view. I fell in behind Dela, playing my part of bodyguard, as we made our way through the crowded harbour and towards the main promenade that cut through the centre of the city. The chill of winter was pronounced now, and the breath of people around me was visible in the air. I of course gave off no such vapour, but I was still lucky it was cold, as my padded and cloaked form was unremarkable in such conditions. It was a bright, clear day, and I felt my spirit lifted a little by the life and sunshine surrounding me, as the chilly people of the city went about their business.

I moved with greater purpose and vigour than I had in many moons, and I had some sense that I was becoming more like myself again. I had only to look down at my padded hands for the truth to break back into my thoughts.

We passed the main gate into the city with little incident, despite Dela's fears. He produced some papers from inside his jacket and presented them to the guards, who inspected them professionally and courteously, with none of the supercilious tone the Salisson guard had exhibited. As Bor had predicted, they did regard me with some caution, but there was none of the shock and horror we had feared, and my disguise held up well.

After we passed the gate, I leant down and attempted to whisper in Dela's ear.

"Why were your guards not like that?"

He turned and looked over his shoulder at me.

"They weren't my guards!" he said sharply, "They

came with the city! I'm not the only one who's at the mercy of the voter's whims. Garet had his hooks in too many places. That's why I had to create the Wardens. I didn't trust that brute as far as I could throw him, but unfortunately, you're not allowed to keel-haul public officials. Now keep quiet! You can't speak here... your voice is too distinctive. You'll frighten the children."

"Then what do I do if I'm asked anything?"

"Let me answer! Or mime a response. You're mute, as far as this city is concerned."

"Wonderful."

I turned and saw Bor was grinning, evidently finding my predicament quite funny.

We made our way through the city, and I marvelled at the advances that had been made while I 'slept'. Much of the wooden construction I recalled had been replaced with sandstone, marble, granite and brick. The roads were even stone slabs, mortared together tightly and well-maintained. The streets were lined with merchants selling fabrics, jewellery, fruits and vegetables from up and down the Jagged Coast and the Outer Islands, pastries and liquor, sweets and spices. I no longer felt hunger but looking at this wondrous variety of food and drink made me feel hollow. The city was colourful and densely packed, and we had to push our way past travellers, haggling customers and salesmen, ponies drawing carts filled with goods, street entertainers juggling silver balls or performing acrobatic routines, and a hundred more variations of colourful life at the Western Gate.

Fenna especially seemed entranced by the markets and the goods on offer, and on occasion we stopped for Bor to haggle over an item for her. He was a very good negotiator, being quite an imposing fellow, and between his fiery temperament and my looming presence in the background we acquired some fine bargains. Although Dela tapped his foot in irritation and impatience, he was clearly loathe to deny this small measure of entertainment after our forced voyage, and allowed the young couple their fun. Thus our procession through the city to the Council Chambers was not a quick one.

The Council was housed in a sprawling, walled enclosure of stone buildings, the largest surmounted with a glass domed hall. It was near the centre of the city, on high ground, and was surrounded by a public park where the locals strolled, taking in the fresh air and sunshine available there. There was frost on the ground and the small lakes and ponds dotted around the park had a skin of ice, but the sky was blue, the chill breeze from the ocean was gentle, and seabirds flew silhouetted against white clouds, their plaintive cries carrying easily on the cold wind.

Past the dome of the hall, beyond the park, I saw a crumbling, ill-kept tower, occupying the highest point on the island. It was the most dilapidated building I had seen there, but I still recognised it. It was the remains of Domint's castle, the old imperial fortress where he had held his throne. The seat of the Empire's power was now a broken toothless thing, a tumbled ruin of shattered grey stone and smashed battlements.

We reached the entrance to the Council enclosure and were again stopped by guards who reviewed Dela's documentation and then escorted us inside. We were led inside the walls and then along airy, arched and covered passageways, lit well by the winter sunshine, until we reached a suite of rooms and lodgings set aside for the Councillor and his entourage.

Dela had his own rooms, with a study and desk, and a window overlooking a small garden that was reserved for him. Fenna and Bor and the rest of the Wardens were directed to a barracks opposite, where they made themselves comfortable on wooden cots, removing their armour and packs and relaxing immediately like the veterans they were. They sent servants off to retrieve food and beer from the kitchens.

I was given a small antechamber just off Dela's suite, accessible only from within his room. These were bodyguard's quarters. There was a neat and well-made bed, with fresh sheets, a chair and desk, a trunk to store armour and weaponry, and a window that overlooked the same private garden that Dela had access to. In the small walled garden there was a bench, and a pond with a thin coating of ice over it. The few plants hardy enough to be still thriving in winter were dusted with frost.

While I hid in my room Dela sent for a messenger, and after determining he was not the only Councillor present, wrote a request for a Council meeting as urgently as possible. After the messenger left he bade me to come back out of my chamber and sit with him.

I did so after removing my padded gloves, my hooded cloak, and my helmet. There was little point in trying to extricate myself from the rest of the disguise. I was not uncomfortable, I did not sweat, and there would have been no end of bother trying to put it all back on. Bor would have been in his cups by then anyway.

Dela sat looking out of the window into the frost-rimed garden as he spoke to me.

"I've made arrangements for a council meeting tomorrow. We are somewhat early for a full conclave... it wasn't meant to be for another few weeks, as we only meet in full four times a year. It's too far for so many to travel so often. There would usually be more of us, but only seven of the Regional Councillors are currently present... only some of whom I trust."

"Why would you not trust them? Are they not servants of the people, like you?"

Dela smiled and rolled his eyes in amusement.

"You're no politician are you, Baron? I suppose it was simpler when you were... well, in your day."

"I do not know. I was a soldier, Dela, not a court lackey. Politics bores me. I prefer a fighter in front of me to a man scheming behind my back. At least then I can see the knife in his hand."

"Quite right!" Dela said, grinning.

He stood up, went to the cabinet in the corner of his study, and retrieved a bottle of wine and a crystal glass. He sat back down, poured himself a drink, and continued.

"However, unfortunate as it may be, we need political allies right now. The Regions may be one united entity according to our treaties, but in reality, we all compete... for resources, for funds, for status even. Decisions that affect the Northern Shore as a whole are taken by majority vote, but every man or woman on the Council will always try to tilt things towards their benefit. I try to do what I can for Salis. My intentions are... well, mostly, for the good of the Shore entire. Not everyone on the Council is there with the same motivation."

"It seems a lot easier to have an Emperor and be done with it." I said, already wearied by the idea of such manoeuvring for position.

"Hmm. You believe that?" Said Dela, his face suddenly growing hardened. "After all you've seen since your rebirth? In times of war, yes, I concede that perhaps there is a benefit to a single, strong leader. It allows for swifter action and decisive strikes in a way our system does not. But at what cost?"

He took a longer swig of his wine.

"Your... your Emperor, and all of the Emperors before him... carved the land up, ruled with violence and fear under a mask of love and holy mandate, and presided over centuries of feudal, miserable life for the common man. Farmers tilled the earth only to give the greater of their earnings in tithe to the Lords above them, having none left to better themselves or improve their lot. Just scratching away at the land with no hope of education, no influence over their own lives. Shepherds tended to other men's flocks rather than owning their own. We are moving towards a brighter future for *everyone*, Baron, not just those that hold title. Every man and woman should have control over their own destiny, and not be beholden to the assumed destinies of others."

I was taken aback by his sudden passion. I had never seen my position, my title, through another man's eyes in this way, and I felt suddenly as if I was in enemy territory. I had to respond.

"Please Dela, be calm. I am far removed from the Lordship I once held. I see some of the truth in what you are saying. It is true, I never gave much thought to the common man or common soldier when I held land or led armies, although I always tried to behave honourably towards them. I know some of the other Lords did not treat their subjects well, but I hope I did not follow their example. I wanted honour and glory and the words by my name that went with them. I am now paying for those ambitions. But I do not see much evidence yet of the progress you aspire to. Farmers are still enslaved by the fields of Estwake and Salis."

He held my empty gaze for a moment, and then relaxed a little, taking another sip of his wine.

"My apologies Baron. I lived my life as a free man, on the sea. My remit from the Council allowed me great latitude. I have never been a slave, or a conscript… the very idea repels me."

He gazed out of the window into the frosted garden. A small winter bird, its breast bright yellow and its beak black, landed on a branch on one of the small icy bushes and started to sing and chirp. He watched it for a few moments and then continued.

"You're right, of course. We still have some way to go... and perhaps I am not so different from the nobles of your day. The trappings and benefits of my office afford me many of the same luxuries. Progress is a slow turning wheel, Baron. We plan for the future... we change what we can. But conflict like this could undo many of our advances." He shook his head.

"I never wanted a war in my lifetime. Now one is here I find our system has flaws even I could not see. We need to turn the Council to this new purpose without undermining everything we have built, and plan to build. I do not know if I am strong enough to bear this burden. I must encourage them to fight, without allowing us to slip into tyranny. I do not want to be a new Emperor, nor do I want to serve one."

"You would have made a fine Emperor."

"That is not a compliment to me, Baron. I am on occasion at war with my own nature. I was a violent man in my youth. Now I just want to be a good man."

"I believe you are."

"Hmm. We shall see. I will be tested. The greatest test will be tomorrow, when I face the Council.

There is one among them we must guard against, who will twist what I say upon itself and make any truths I tell sound like madness, or weakness. You will be my hidden blade in this matter."

"Who is this person?" I could not envisage, at that point, someone who could match wits with Dela. Up until then I had only seen him as a strong and astute leader. He seemed fiercely intelligent to me.

"Cellin is here, the Councillor for Estwake. Kroll's creature." He lowered his eyes, looking at the polished wood of the desk. He rubbed the smooth black skin on his close-shaven head.

"He's here to muddy the waters. To cast doubt, to sow mistrust, to keep apart what needs to come together. His every effort will be bent towards undermining me."

"Then you must make a strong case."

"I am hoping your presence alone will do that." He said.

CHAPTER ELEVEN

The following morning a runner was sent to invite us to the Council Chambers. Each Councillor was allowed one bodyguard or escort, and I was to be Dela's.

We moved along the sunlit, arched and open corridors, the morning sun just starting to reach into the internal courtyards of the Council building. We were escorted into the main hall. This was where the dome of the building rose, a glass and lattice framework that served as the ceiling and filled the room with streams of green, blue and yellow light. It reminded me of Dela's study back in Salisson, but with brighter, cleaner stonework, and it was far grander.

Beneath the dome was a large table. It was a circle, open at one end, with an empty round space in the middle, a raised area where petitioners could stand before the Council and plead their cases, make appeals, or lecture the assembled Councillors on any information pertinent to their business. Off to one side of the great circle was another raised dais with three chairs on it, and another smaller but no less well-made table. These chairs were occupied by three key members of the Western Gate's organisations. The First Daughter, the highest representative of her religion. The head of the Merchant Union. The Captain of the Guard of the Western Gate.

Each was patiently waiting for the meeting to begin, leaning in to whisper in each other's ears on occasion. The First Daughter wore the azure robes and gold-and-silver seashell trinkets of her office, and on her head was a tall, ceremonial headdress, curled to look like an ocean wave and stained a dark blue. She seemed very old, and wizened, and had to be nudged to join in the conversation with her neighbour, the Merchant Boris Quist. He was a well-fed man, with golden rings festooning his fingers and greased dark hair plastered across his balding scalp.

The Captain of the Guard, a powerfully built man named Francyn, with gold-brown skin and close-cropped brown hair, sat at the far end of the table. Considering my last interaction with a guard commander, this man seemed much more professional. He watched the room with dark, predatory eyes while his companions nattered with each other. He wore the ornamental helmet of his office, an assembly of gold trim and sharp, bright silver edges, but the sword laid in from of him on the table didn't look ceremonial at all. It was clearly a weapon, not a badge of rank. I surmised it was his job to intervene if any political disagreement became heated.

Around the edges of the round hall were stations for the Councillor's bodyguards, and a myriad of other representatives, administrators, secretaries and officials. I took my place as directed by Dela, standing with my back to the wall in a small nook a few paces behind his chair. Dela greeted his fellow councillors, some warmly, some more formally, and shook hands with a few of the other functionaries milling around the room before the Council meeting started. He finished his greetings and took his seat.

There were six Councillors present so far, spaced unequally around the circle table. Dela had gone through their names and responsibilities with me the previous evening, in preparation for our business, and had named them for me as we entered the chamber.

Their nominal Head of Council, Adrianna Wain, was the Councillor for the Western Gate itself. She served the function of organiser and chair, in addition to representing her own interests and those of the capital region. She was a tall woman, wearing a long and flowing gold-and-tan robe, with severely cropped dark hair. She had an air of sophistication and intelligence, but she smiled at Dela when he took his seat and seemed to regard him with some affection.

This was in stark contrast with the scowling look Councillor Yast gave Dela. Yast was the representative for Avania, the Region adjacent to Dela's own. He was older than Dela, with long grey braided hair and a trimmed-sharp grey beard, and he regarded Dela with a contemptuous stare and a grunt of welcome.

The other Councillors, for Burus, Nedra and Prain, took their seats, emanating varying levels of warmth or chill towards Dela and their other colleagues.

Last to arrive, and the seventh Councillor to join that day, was Councillor Cellin, the representative for Estwake.

I had expected a dark-cloaked, sinister figure, a mirror of Kroll's dirty and dishevelled followers. Instead, he was handsome, bright-eyed and well-dressed, dashing and charming. He had blond hair that came down in fine ribbons over his eyes, which he could brush away from his forehead to reveal piercing blue eyes, an affected gesture calculated to make him seem harmless and coy to those he addressed. He wore a fitted green silken tunic, buttoned with gold, and pale riding trousers ending in polished knee-high black boots. His presentation made him appear the perfect country noble, as if he had stepped out of some romantic fable. His age was hard to tell, although I guessed he was older than he looked.

He seemed familiar to me. I had not met him in the caverns or catacombs at Estwake, nor in any of my travels around that blighted Region. I suspected he was one of the few that lived in the harbour and presented a living face to the rest of the Northern Shore. Yet some resemblance tugged at my memory, and it took some effort to remain in the present. Cellin was accompanied by his own bodyguard, who wore the bright green tabard and plate armour of Estwake before its fall, the same as I had worn when I had lived.

After Cellin finished his greetings and took his seat, the room's conversation and hubbub settled to a lower, whispered level, and the Council of the Northern Shore began its day's business. The scribes and secretaries dotted around the room took notes as the meeting progressed. Dela was not the first to speak. Councillor Wain began the meeting, running through an order of business, and then for a long while various representatives and petitioners were allowed into the chamber to speak to the Council, plead their cases, raise concerns, address complaints and injustices, and match wits with other officials over matters of policy, economics, security, business, and agriculture. I found, remarkably, that I still had the capacity for boredom, and found myself drifting off into reverie. If I were still capable of sleep, I believe I would have nodded off in no time.

Dela seemed to share my lack of patience. He shifted and fidgeted in his seat, occasionally let a sigh of boredom leave his lips, and at least once I thought I saw his head nod forwards and jerk back, as if he was on the verge of slumber and had caught himself just in time. His focus on Kroll had perhaps reduced his attention span for the general matters of Council.

By contrast Cellin was animated and engaged, charming and incisive. He was the very vision of the ideal politician. He spoke to every representative, from farmer to official, as if he knew them personally, as if he had known them all their lives. He made friendly jokes, raising laughs from around the room, and spoke with authority and passion on every subject presented to him. He was incredibly likeable, and I could see how he could have manipulated the Council. He shone with charisma. I knew then how difficult this was going to be. We needed this man to make a mistake, and I could not see what could sway the Council to our cause if we could not outmanoeuvre him.

After several hours of interminably, infuriatingly boring business, it was Dela's turn on the docket, and he rose to present his case.

He left his chair for this, walking around the table, and entering the centre of the circle as the petitioners had done before him. He stood on the raised platform, brushed his tunic down, as if removing the dust of boredom, and cleared his throat to speak. Councillor Wain was attentive. Yast slouched, already disinterested in what Dela had to say. Cellin sat up straight and steepled his fingers in front of him, the very image of care and concern. A wonderful mask if you have the gall to wear it.

"Councillors," Dela began, and cleared his throat again, as if he had gravel in his gullet. I realised at this point that I hadn't seen him drink wine for the entire meeting. Indeed no one had been having wine. There were only glasses of water, and jugs for its distribution. Dela's hands were shaking, and if I had a stomach, I believe it would have sunk.

"Councillors," he began again, "I come to you today with an update regarding the situation in Estwake and Tresh, and now in my own Region. Dark forces are moving against us. A shadow has been cast over Estwake, and it is now creeping down the Shore, infecting all it touches with darkness and death."

"More ghost stories, Dela?" said Cellin, with a feline smile.

"Not stories, Councillor. I know you do not spend

a great deal of time in your Region, preferring life in the capital, but if you did you would know what I speak of is real. The dead walk in Estwake, at the behest of the man you sponsor, the Priest of R'Chun, Faris Kroll. The dead walk, and they march on Tresh, and they are soon to march on Salis. If Kroll's ambitions are not curtailed soon the dead will far outnumber the living, and we will not be able to defend against them. Kroll is a tool of Sechia, and is a weapon being used to weaken us."

"Kroll is a religious leader, and a friend. He and his people ran from Sechia due to intolerance, persecution. Accusing him of such things is cruel, prejudicial, and beneath you, Councillor." Cellin seemed disappointed, but sympathetic, as if he were worried for Dela's mind. A pretence, but a masterful one.

"I welcome all creeds and races to the Northern Shore, Councillor. We should be a refuge, a light to guide all peoples towards progress. You know I am descended from such refugee stock." Dela had already begun to lose his temper. His lips tightened and grew pale against his dark skin. "Kroll has taken advantage of our good nature. He is a monster. He is raising an army, from the ancient graves of battle-sites, from the graveyards of common men and women, and from the living he strikes down. This infection needs to be cut out."

Cellin smiled, seemingly amused by Dela's oration.

"Tell me, Councillor Hevigne. From where I sit this looks like a common dispute between Regions. What evidence do you have for these fantasies? The whispers of superstitious pirates? The tales of those brigands you surround yourself with? Or do you simply investigate a wine glass and see the dead looking back up at you?"

There were titters and giggles from a few places in the room. Councillor Yast made a point of laughing loudly and openly, clearly mocking Dela.

The standing Councillor shuffled his feet and tried to hide his embarrassment, not entirely successfully. He composed himself and continued. "May I ask, Councillor Cellin, where is the Councillor for Tresh? Should Cres Alann not be here?"

Cellin shook his head and curled his lip. "You know as well as I do, this Council meeting was called by you, early. Not all the Region's representatives were available. You are the one that wanted to raise a Shore-wide question."

"And yet he usually arrives here early, does he not? I know he won't be here, either today or in the days to come. Tresh has fallen. Its capital Gariss has been taken by the dead. I know this as we were attacked by a Treshan ship on our journey here."

"That is quite an accusation, Councillor. To state that an aggressive act was taken by Tresh against your ship."

"I did not say it was Tresh, Cellin, I said the ship was Treshan. It was not crewed by living men. it was crewed by Raised warriors, created by Kroll and his followers."

"I find that quite hard to believe, Dela. Does the rest of the Council share my suspicions? That these are the ramblings of an old seadog, with a weakness for wine?" Cellin stood up and spread his arms wide in a dramatic and sarcastic gesture, looking around the room and grinning. It brought more laughter from the assembly. Yast was positively overjoyed. He dabbed at the edges of his eyes with a small silk cloth in a mannered and mocking fashion, forcing more laughter out of himself than was really required.

Cellin took his seat again, smug and pleased with himself, and Councillor Yast leaned forwards to speak.

"Councillor Dela, we have heard such paranoid tales from you before. You aren't fighting errant Sechian pirates anymore. I questioned your suitability for office when you were first elected in Salis, and I question it again now. I believe the strain of being responsible for a whole Region, rather than just a ship, is telling on you." Yast gave a humourless smile and raised his palms in contrition. "Perhaps it is time you accepted you cannot bear the burden of leadership."

"I believe it is up to the people of Salis to make that decision for me." Dela replied.

"Yes. Of course," Cellin said, re-joining the argument, "although I am told that you have been rejected by them. Did you not leave Salisson in some haste? It seems you were run out of the city after some… falling out with the Temple?"

I wondered at the time how Cellin knew that. We had left Salis at speed. I did not see how this news could have preceded us.

Dela was clearly puzzled as well and furrowed his brow as Cellin continued to twist the truth.

"I have spoken with the First Daughter and advised her that you have lost the support of many of your constituents due to… religious practices that could not be tolerated, even in an open and accepting society like ours. Is this not correct? Perhaps we should ask the First Daughter her opinion?"

At this Cellin turned to address the old woman, sat at her table.

Merchant Quist gave the First Daughter a nudge with his elbow to wake her, and the old woman sat up with a start and said "Yes! Yes, yes, quite intolerable…" before appearing to nod off again.

"You see," Cellin continued, "your position in Salis is tenuous at best if the Temple does not support you."

Dela hung his head a little, and a flash of frustration passed over his face. He took a deep breath. Losing his temper then would have been an error, and he knew it.

"You are correct in what you say, Cellin. I may have lost the support of the Temple. I may have lost the support of the people. I have taken risks, and I have had others take risks on my behalf. I have done whatever I deemed necessary to stand here before you, I have sacrificed my position, my standing with this Council, and the lives of the people who serve me and fight for me. If after today I am no longer welcome, then so be it. Ten years I have tried to make this council accept that our defence must be a unified effort, and I have only one thing left to try."

"And what would that be?" Cellin said, clearly believing at that moment that he had the upper hand. I guessed he already knew of my presence, if he knew of our exit from Salisson, and he was waiting for the opportunity to undermine me as well. Or stop me from speaking at all.

"I have a witness. He wishes to speak to you all."

"I hardly think that is appropriate. No further petitioners have been added to today's business.

We cannot allow anyone to just come in here and address us with no preparation."

"You do not speak for all of us, Cellin." Councillor Wain had stood up, having observed the debate quietly until now, and she leaned forwards, both of her hands on the table in front of her. She looked at Cellin as if she were examining a kill after a hunt. She turned her gaze this way and that, looking into the eyes of everyone sat around the table.

"I do not suppose to, Councillor Wain," said Cellin, now a little more subdued, "but we have procedures in place so that these meetings are orderly and well-documented. Dela cannot be allowed to circumvent them, with lurid gossip and ridiculous fantasies."

"Ordinarily I would agree, Councillor. But I have a higher authority over this chamber, however slight, and I am allowed a certain amount of leeway. I am curious to see what Dela's witness has to say."

"You are allowing your affection for this old pirate to influence your decisions."

"And you are sorely mistaken if you think speaking to me like that will change my mind."

At this Cellin's mouth slammed shut, and his face grew red. For a moment, just a tiny moment, his mask slipped. I saw his true self, the ugly soul behind his handsome face. He caught himself quickly, gave an obsequious smile, and sat back in his chair, momentarily defeated.

"As you wish, Councillor Wain. I have voiced my dispute and it has been recorded."

Councillor Wain turned to Dela.

"You may present your witness. Please note, Dela, if you have lost the support of your Region, we will need to start the election process. I am sorry, but this is fundamental to our system, and is not something I am willing to oppose."

Dela gave a short bow of respect to Councillor Wain.

"I agree entirely, Councillor. I would not wish to challenge it. I would only have you hear this man speak, and then debate a response. That is all I ask."

"Very well. Bring your guest into the chamber."

"He is already here, serving as my bodyguard." He gestured to me then, beckoning me into the circle. I made my way towards him, striding from my station nook, and moved around behind the Councillors and through the gap in the table until I stood next to him.

"I would like to introduce to you all... Baron Asheth Acellion."

There was a sharp intake of breath from Cellin, and I turned to glance at him. His face was red again, filled with fury, which surprised me. I had been sure that he already knew I was there. There was something else. A recognition of my name, which had not been generally known in Salis.

He looked at me with pure hatred in his eyes.

Others seemed to recognise my name as well but did not have as severe a reaction. There were looks of puzzlement, and disbelief. It was unlikely Dela was the only scholar in the group, so my name would not be entirely unfamiliar.

Dela left me on the stand and withdrew to his chair. We had agreed beforehand that I would not remove my hood and helmet until so directed.

"Greetings... Baron? Said Wain. She obviously knew my name and my history.

"Greetings, Councillor Wain, Council members. I apologize for my voice. I know it can be a little painful to listen to at first, but that will fade after a while."

Some of the chamber's occupants were pained immediately by the hollow boom issuing from my hood. The First Daughter jerked to wakefulness, nearly knocking over the cup of water in front of her.

"I have come here today, at the behest of my... friend, Councillor Dela Hevigne, to address you all on a matter of grave importance... if you will forgive the pun. Everything the Councillor has told you is true. Estwake has fallen to a cult that worships a dark god. They are sponsored and directed by the Emperor of Sechia, who is using dark magics to bolster his failing Empire. They experimented at first with crews for pirate vessels. Your sailors have encountered these for many years. Now they have their tendrils running through the lands of Estwake. I was part of an army of the undead. We invaded Tresh, and soon my former comrades will invade Salis, if they have not done so already. Every village, every town, every city they take increases their numbers. They will roll like a great dark wave over all of the Northern Shore if they are not stopped now."

Wain stayed silent. So did Cellin, although his mask had slipped entirely, and his rage was plainly visible. Councillor Yast was still arrogant, however, and questioned me with a mocking tone.

"You claim to be Baron Asheth Acellion?"

"Yes. That is my name, and the title I earned in war."

He laughed his false and forced laugh again. "Ridiculous. Utterly ludicrous. Dela, what mummery, what farce do you think to inflict on this Council? Are you deluded? Insane? Has the wine finally rotted what mind the brine hadn't destroyed already? Do you expect us to believe this man, this *fool*, is from the time of the Baronies? I have had enough. Councillor Wain, I demand that Dela and his costumed idiot be removed from this Chamber *immediately!* This cannot continue!"

I turned to Dela and he nodded his head. The moment had come. I raised my hands, pulled back my hood, and removed my helmet, exposing my bare skull to the coloured light streaming through the great glass dome.

It was as if a hungry feline had been thrown to land amongst feeding birds.

The secretaries and scribes scattered to the walls, screaming. Every bodyguard in the room drew their weapon. Captain Francyn grabbed his sword from the table and vaulted over it in one smooth movement, racing towards the stand to confront me. I heard a strangled-sounding "*Fuck me!*" and the Head of the Merchant's Union scrabbled backwards off his chair and fell to the floor behind it. The First Daughter bolted to wakefulness, leapt to her feet, and holding her chain of seashells before her she began to bellow prayers in a surprisingly loud and strong voice. I hadn't realised there was that much vitality left in her.

Francyn reached me and held his sword in front of him, ready to strike, both hands wrapped around the hilt. I made no move to defend myself. I had told Dela that I considered my ongoing animation to be forfeit to our plans. If I was to be destroyed there and then so be it.

The Captain of the Guard paused. He had seen me make no threat, nor even shy away from his charge, and he was a professional. He did not lower his weapon, but neither did he attempt to strike me down. I left my hammer strapped to my back, and stood with my hands outstretched, palms up, so he could see I meant no harm. It was a credit to him that he did not strike me. A lesser man may have simply attacked and allowed no conversation.

I allowed the panic in the room to subside. The First Daughter still chanted prayers but had lowered her voice, and Boris, the Merchant, had crept up from behind his chair and retaken his seat, trying to appear nonchalant. The various Councillors and functionaries and officials started at me in silent shock, but no one moved. The room felt quiet and still and heavy with tension. Councillor Wain's face was pale, her mouth open with no sound coming out. Yast was pale too, his head in his hands, his palms over his eyes. The only person not in shock was Cellin. His face was twisted with rage.

Dela spoke first. He raised his voice to be heard over the First Daughter's prayers. The Merchant leader patted her arm, and the old priestess fell silent, but did not take her seat, or lower her golden chain of shells.

"My fellow Councillors. The Baron means no one here any harm. He has come today to ask for help, on my behalf. He is proof of what we are facing. I ask only that you listen to what he has to say."

Dela rubbed his shaved head with trembling fingers and sighed.

"This is the gamble I have taken, and for which I give up my ambitions. Please do us both the honour of hearing our plea. You owe me that much at least."

"You *DARE*!" Cellin was on his feet. "You *dare* bring this *abomination,* this *disgrace* into our chamber? This is no place for such horrors! This thing, this, this…"

"*BE QUIET, CELLIN*!" Yelled Councillor Wain.

Cellin's mouth slammed shut, the sound of his teeth clacking together audible in the silent chamber and echoing around the walls. He opened his mouth to speak again and was immediately silenced by Wain.

"No." She raised her palm to quiet him. "You've said enough. Explain this, Cellin. You accuse Dela of telling ghost stories, and yet proof of his fear is stood before us. I can see it with my own eyes, hard to believe as it is. So what explanation have you?"

"All we can see before us is proof of *one* undead." Cellin pointed at Dela, his finger shaking with rage, "HE was removed from Salis because he was dabbling in dark magic! See what he has done!"

Councillor Wain lowered her eyes and shook her head, and then turned to look at Dela. "Councillor? How do you respond to this accusation?"

Dela stood again and brushed the front of his jacket with both hands, straightening his buttons. He seemed a lot calmer then than he had before.

"It's half-true. I did adopt some of Kroll's techniques, in extremis. My people and I may pay a price for that, someday. But our purpose was to give this man a voice. Perhaps we should let him use it? He will be happy to answer any question put to him."

Wain turned back to me.

"You are Baron Asheth Acellion?"

"Yes, Councillor."

"The Lord of Estwake, from the time of the Domint's reign?"

"Yes. I was Baron of Estwake for several years, after the Sechian Campaign. I was cut down by Frachia's men during his coup."

"I see. So how do you come to be stood before us?"

I gave my account.

It was late afternoon by the time I finished my tale. I was only interrupted by Wain in all the time I spoke. She asked for clarification and further detail when she deemed it necessary. The watching Councillors remained silent, as did the rest of the chamber. Even Cellin stayed quiet, although he was clearly boiling with anger. The First Daughter had retaken her seat, and watched and listened with more attention than I had thought her capable of. She still fussed with her chains of office.

After my account reached the recent past, and our arrival at the Western Gate, I bowed my head to show I had finished. The Council members looked at each other, some deep in thought, some reeling, some even showing compassion. Dela and I awaited their verdict.

To my surprise, Yast spoke first.

"Baron… Councillor Dela. Dela, I have never been your most ardent supporter. I hardly think this is a secret. I believe you gained your position through subterfuge and bribery. You're still the pirate you were before you took office."

He smiled a little then, the first real humour I had seen from him.

"Still a pirate. Yes. But not wrong. If even half of

this... of what Baron Acellion tells us is true, we have wandered blindly into great danger. At the very least this warrants further investigation, and some defensive preparation. That is my recommendation."

Dela looked genuinely shocked. He nodded thanks to Yast. Some of the other Council members voiced assent. Cellin bolted to his feet.

"How can you possibly believe this? I am Councillor for Estwake, and I tell you this is all *lies!* This thing, this ghoul... even if he is Baron Acellion, the Baron was Domint's man! He served a tyrant! He did the will of a brutal, conquering butcher, who ravaged an empire, who denied his kin, who..."

He quieted then, suddenly, as if he had said more than he meant to. His carefully crafted mask had slipped entirely. I was not sure then why he had exposed himself so.

"Cellin," Wain said, "this is a simple matter to prove. We will send a delegation to Tresh and to Estwake, to investigate and report back. Surely, if you have nothing to hide, you will agree to this?" The rest of the Council again voiced agreement.

"*HOW DARE YOU?!*" Cellin screamed and slammed his fists into the table in front of him, scattering papers. A glass of water bounced into the air, flew to the ground and shattered, splashing me. "*NO! I refuse! You have no right!*"

Captain Francyn had remained at my side, guarding against any aggression on my part. At Cellin's outburst he turned towards the angry Councillor. He didn't raise his sword, but the threat was clear.

"Councillor Cellin. Please compose yourself or I will remove you from this chamber."

"*I'll remove myself.* I won't have my reputation dragged through the mire by a pack of *fools!*" He turned, throwing his chair to the ground, which clattered on the marble floor. His bodyguard stepped from his post and both men strode from the Council chambers, Cellin screaming curses all the way.

Francyn resumed his post next to me and met my empty gaze. I nodded to show gratitude for his intervention. I spoke to him, as quietly as I was able.

"Watch Cellin."

Francyn frowned in thought for a moment, and then gave a quick shallow nod. I turned back to the Council members in front of me and saw Yast was watching us. He dipped his head too, having heard my attempt at a whisper.

Subterfuge is difficult when you have a voice like an echoing bell.

Wain addressed the chamber. "Councillors, I believe we have a matter of some import to debate. Captain Francyn, I would ask that you escort the Baron back to Councillor Hevigne's chambers. Place a guard on him. Baron Acellion, if you will forgive me, my practice is to trust, but verify. I hope you will not consider this an insult."

"Not at all Councillor. A most sensible policy. I will acquiesce to any demands of me made by this Council."

"Very well. Thank you for your testimony, Baron. I wish you well. We will speak again tomorrow."

Captain Francyn escorted me from the chamber, picking up a couple of Council guards from the corridors as we made our way back to Dela's quarters. He did not speak to me. I had replaced my hood and helmet before leaving the room. I did not want news of me to spread too quickly, although I doubted my condition would remain hidden for long. Francyn entered the suite of rooms with me, investigating them for weaponry and means of escape, but there was only one way in and out of Dela's quarters. He asked me for my hammer, and I unhooked it from my back and gave it to him head down. He nodded at me again.

"There will be guards posted outside the door. There are more in the corridors. Do not attempt to leave. My men have orders to kill you on sight if you step out of this room."

"I understand. Thank you."

"Don't thank me. I've never seen anything like you. My policy is not to trust. At all. If you do anything I don't like, I'll have you buried in the gardens."

"Fair."

I sat down on one of the chairs in Dela's study. The soldier turned to leave.

"Let me ask you, Captain. Do you trust Cellin?"

He stopped, and looked at me. There was perhaps the tiniest hint of a smile on Francyn's stony face.

"Not as far as I can throw him."

CHAPTER TWELVE

I waited in Dela's quarters, sat in his study chair. The sun was sinking now, early due to the winter season, and the garden overlooked by his window was shadowed and quiet, glinting with frost in the dusk light. The birds busied themselves to-and-fro, but their movements were slowing and their songs becoming intermittent.

There was a knock at the door. I had removed my hood and helmet, and my gloves, and had remained still in the chair, content to be patient and watch the light fade outside. I had not lit any of the lamps.

The knock came again.

"Enter, please." I said, expecting Captain Francyn.

Instead, the door was opened by a guard, and the First Daughter entered the room, her sea-blue robes swishing around her legs as she stepped inside. I noticed she was barefoot. She had removed some of the trappings of her office, and wore a plain white skull-cap in place of her head-dress, but she still had the golden chain of shells around her neck.

"Good Evening, Baron. I wish to speak to you." She said, looking around the darkened room.

"You are welcome to, First Daughter. I apologize for the darkness. I do not need light to see, my night vision is quite excellent. Please feel free to light a lamp."

She asked the guard to fetch her a light, and then lit only the lamp on the desk between us. She took up the seat opposite me and dismissed the guard, who began to protest but was immediately silenced by a stern look. Once he had left the room and closed the door behind him, the First Daughter turned back around in her seat to face me. I had thought her old and senile when I first saw her in the Council chambers, but the lamplight revealed her eyes, and they were intelligent, sharp, perhaps even kind.

"I would like you to perform a small act for me, before we engage in conversation. Would you consent to that for me?" she said, rummaging inside a pouch-bag at her waist.

This was not the way I had expected this conversation to go. My near execution in Salisson was still fresh in my memory.

"Of course. I am your servant."

"Hmph," she said, "Hardly. Here, I would like you to grasp this in your fist... gently, please."

She placed a small, ornamented shell on the desk between us. It was real, a spiralled, fluted and whorled mollusc shell, bound in silver wire and inlaid with pearls. It was beautiful, and even seeing it brought sudden visions of the ocean... the rolling sea, the waves tumbling upon each other, the tang of brine and seaweed, the cry of the soaring birds, the darkness of the churning depths. I could smell it, as if I was stood on the shore, and it was the first scent I had experienced since my awful awakening. The shock of memory and association nearly sent me to the floor.

I reached out, and my hand was shaking, another new-yet-old sensation, fear, nervousness, awe even. I picked up the shell gently with the tips of my finger bones and turned my hand, so it fell into my palm. Then I closed my fingers over it.

The vison struck me with overwhelming force. I was on the shore, buffeted by wind. I looked down at my bare feet. The flesh of my bare feet. They were covered by the waves of water rushing in, rushing out, rushing in again. I was naked on the shore but clothed again in muscle and skin. I looked out in wonder across the Scar Sea and saw a great, white-crested tidal wave rising in the distance. The water was sucked away from the sand and pebbles underneath my feet. I felt the grains moving between my toes. The gulls in the bright sky above me circled and cawed and screamed as a wall of water raced towards me. There was a shape inside the wave now, a huge dark mass with long and writhing limbs extending for leagues inside the rolling water. The shadow in the wave was lit by flashes and sparks of blue and green, but the lights did not serve to illuminate any more than tiny patches of silvery scaled skin.

I heard a distant voice call my name, over and over again.

I came to. I was still sat in the low-lit room, staring with empty sockets at the First Daughter. My hand was on the desk, palm up and fingers open, and the shell sat there, twinkling gently in the flickering lamplight.

"What did you see?" asked the First Daughter.

"The ocean. A wave... huge. It filled the horizon. There was... there was a voice."

"She spoke to you?"

"Yes. She called my name."

"Then... then she has a purpose for you, Baron. Tell me, on your journey here, did the sea treat you well?"

I bowed my head a little. "Not at first. We suffered storms early in our voyage, the weather was angered by our enemy's sorcery. After we repelled our boarders, after I struck down Hallek, the sea calmed and gave us fair travel."

"Then *you* did not offend Omma T'Lassa. The Mother was angered by the manipulations of Kroll's lackeys. I know of Kroll's god, R'Chun. He is a lord of darkness, and of the storm, and he oversteps his remit. He is not meant to rule the dead. He is angering the other gods, of the sea, the forest, the mountain, the north wind. He claims souls and prayers that are not his to take."

She picked the shell out of my palm and quickly hid it away in her pouch. Then she drew a small flask from within her robes, topped with a little cup that screwed on to it to act as a stopper.

"If you don't mind, Baron, I believe I'll have a drink. The winter chill gets to my bones you see... oh, sorry, no offense meant."

"None taken. My bones do not really feel the cold."

She smiled, poured herself a nip of liquor, downed it, and then poured another, letting this one rest on the desk between us.

"If the Mother accepts you then so shall I. I apologize for my reaction in the Council chambers, and for what happened in Salisson. The High Daughter there... well, every organization has its outliers. She is a devout woman, a great leader for her School, but she can be a little... lacking in perspective. Humour as well, for that matter. I try to encourage an open and accepting Temple, but you would be a step too far for anyone, I suppose. I know the young priestess you referred to as well. She is, unfortunately, an idiot."

She took a sip of her drink, sighed, and looked out of the window behind me, into the now dark garden. She was looking at her own face, reflected in the glass.

"Your story... I believe you. I am an old woman, and like Dela, and Wain perhaps, I have seen things... I have faith in the Mother, in Omma T'lassa. I have held that faith all my life and I have never heard her voice like you have. In many ways, Baron, I am older than you. You were a young man when you fell at Estwake. You still had a life to live, and I am sorry it was denied you. I will help you, if I can."

"Thank you. I am trying to have faith myself. That I have a purpose here. I hope that is enough."

"It will be, Baron."

I was tired of my title. Such things should not continue after death. "Please. Call me Asheth. My former position has no relevancy in this time or place. In fact, it serves only as a weight around my neck."

"Then so be it. Asheth. My name is Judith, and you may address me as such in private."

"Thank you, Judith."

We spoke for a long while. Judith was more interested in me, and my family, my history, than she was in the current crisis. She was most interested in the possible escape of my wife and children from Estwake, and how that may have been accomplished. I kept some details about that to myself, not trusting her entirely yet, and shared only what I thought to be pertinent. I was not sure if they had managed to flee.

I was able to speak of my family with warmth, and memories of love, rather than needing to prove myself to survive. She was a good listener.

We continued until Dela returned from Council, late in the evening, and Dela greeted the First Daughter warmly before the old priestess left us for the night.

Dela was exhausted by the day, and after a glass or two of wine he retired to his room and left me to my own devices. I entered my room and removed what armour I could, still finding my new garments a little impractical. I lay on the bed, a far grander resting place than the ones I had lain in recently, and I attempted to enter the fugue state common to my kind. I dearly wished I could sleep. Dreams can be fanciful and escapist. Memories can be a burden to carry.

At some time in the early morning, before dawn, I was disturbed by a commotion in the adjoining room and a pounding at my chamber door. I rose from the bed, less muddled than I would have been had I been sleeping, and opened the door to find Captain Francyn standing there, with Dela behind him rubbing his eyes. There were a handful of guards in the room as well, and they were accompanied by some member of the Temple I hadn't yet met. He was identifiable as such by his simple outfit of sea-blue trousers and white smock, and the small shell around his neck on a golden chain. In other regards he did not look like a holy man. His tanned head was shaved, and covered in white scars, some of which reached to his gnarled face. He was muscular, obvious even under his loose clothing, and his knuckles were calloused and scarred. He did not have weapons in his hands, but at each of his hips, attached to a wide belt, were two triangular scabbards that ran down his thighs and were tied by straps just above his knees. From the top of each leather sheath two parallel metal guards protruded, decorated with silver, which would lie along his forearms when the weapons were drawn. He watched me with intelligent and narrowed eyes.

"My apologies, Baron Acellion, for disturbing you. The First Daughter has suggested you join us, to see if you can shed some light on a difficult matter." Francyn looked weary, as if he had been woken with some haste, and his eyes were red with sleep. He was however fully armed and armoured.

"Of course, Captain. I was not sleeping. That is a pleasure I no longer partake in."

Francyn grunted, nodded, and turned to go. The guards, the newcomer, Dela and I left the room and traipsed after him down the corridors of the Council halls. Dela and I exchanged a look, and Dela, appearing even more weary than Francyn, shrugged his shoulders in confusion and shook his head. I was wearing only my padded clothes and my hooded cloak, feeling that if I was unarmoured, I would appear less of a threat.

It took us a little while to make our way across the Council grounds. We finally reached another set of chambers, a mirror of Dela's assigned accommodation. The doors were wide open, and two guards stood either side of the entrance. The men Francyn had brought with him regarded my warily and gave me a wide berth.

We all filed into the rooms. Inside was again a match to Dela's quarters.

Francyn addressed the group.

"I'd asked my guard to keep an eye on Cellin. He fled the Council halls around midnight with all of his entourage. Neither I nor my guard had the authority to stop him, for he has no crime proved against him, but you see how this looks."

Dela rubbed his face and took a deep breath, sighing to let it out.

"Captain… this is a serious matter, I understand, but surely news of this could have held until morning. Why are we here now?"

Francyn moved towards one of the adjoining chambers of the suite and beckoned us to follow him. We entered a room that was the twin of Dela's sleeping quarters on the opposite side of the grounds. The décor, however, could not have been more different.

The ornate bed was the same, but on the wall above a small dressing table was a dark mirror, half the height of a man, and framed with an assemblage of bones from many corpses. Fingers splayed out in many directions, protruding from a setting made of thighbones, too small to have belonged to an adult. A cage of ribs reached out from the edges of the frame, perpendicular to the surface of the mirror. At the top of the glass were set three small, infant skulls. All these grisly parts had been stained and rubbed with ash until they were a dark, grey-black colour.

On the dressing table, its greenish flame reflected

in the silver of the mirror, was a fat black candle. Judging by the coughing and spluttering of the living men in the room it gave off a noxious and choking smell. Dela covered his mouth with a corner of his jacket. The candle occasionally emitted a small green spark, and when it did so strange shadows raced across the walls, as if the candle produced darkness as well as light. The grizzled priest that had accompanied us clutched the shell hanging at his chest and began to mutter prayers in a deep, growling voice. He did so with an air of calm and control, unlike the panicked ranting I had seen from the priestess in Salisson. The atmosphere in the room was oppressive, and every man there who carried a weapon laid his hand on its hilt.

"This is beyond my experience, Dela," said Francyn, "there is clearly foul sorcery at play here and I don't know how to proceed. I was reluctant to leave this until the morning."

The candle and the mirror dragged at my gaze. I felt almost compelled to move towards it. Francyn watched me with suspicion, and Dela reached out to grasp my shoulder. I spoke to him.

"This is Kroll's work. I can feel him. It reminds me of the catacombs at Estwake. The darkness. The filth of his pit. This is not a place for the living."

I walked towards the mirror and saw myself. I

had already had a vision of my un-clothed face when Dela had given me my voice. This was much worse. To see myself, as other men saw me.

I had avoided this since I had awoken, and I had been right to.

My clothing was of the living, the padded leather and linen serving to disguise my form well. But beneath my hood I had the leering face of a dead man, and I drew back the cowl with the hands of a corpse. I could see the dim green light in the depths of my eye sockets, and some glimmer of it in the gaping hole of my nasal cavity. My cheekbones caught the light of the wicked candle and the edges of my jawbone gleamed in its glow.

I took it in, as best I could. I took in the reality of my condition, grabbed and held it with my mind, with every shred of will and wit I had left. I gazed into my own empty eyes and hated what I saw.

As I stared into the mirror, dark shapes moved under its surface, gathering around my reflection. Quickly the shadows obscured my ghastly skull and began to form a different image, that of a grey and straggly-haired, tanned and lined face. Colours bled into the image until Kroll spoke, his deep bass voice echoing as if he were speaking at the end of a long tunnel.

"So." he said. "The prodigal son. Why are you wasting your time with the living, Baron? I did not know who you were when I lifted you from the dirt, Asheth. If you had come to me, I could have re-instated you. Given you back your Barony to rule on my behalf. I have no interest in the daily matters of Estwake, nor do I have any interest in ruling the living. I would have left that to you." He smiled at me, sly and ingratiating.

"I would not serve such as you, Kroll. I sent your thrall Hallek to the bottom of the Scar Sea. I will send you back to the pit you spawned from." I felt the anger grow in my head, a sensation of heat and fury I could not feel in my bones. The men behind me remained silent, shocked and frightened by the apparition.

"Why such ill feeling, Baron? Hallek followed me willingly. He was no slave to me, but a faithful companion. He was a devout of R'Chun, as am I. You could have joined us and exalted in the glory and love of our God."

"Join you? In this, this madness, this horror... I am a man of honour... You are a murderer, an enslaver, and I will *crush your skull for WHAT YOU DID TO ME!*"

My rage grew from a spark to a conflagration, suddenly and with great force, as it had during the battle on the *Silverfin*. I lashed out at the mirror with one skinless fist, smashing my knuckles straight into the image of Kroll's face. Instead of cracking the glass, my hand passed through the mirror as if it were empty air. I felt Kroll's flesh under my fingers, a dull sensation passing through my hand as I struck him. He recoiled from the blow, and I withdrew my hand in shock from the mirror. As I did so it shattered, and shards and splinters of glass flew from its grim setting. A howling, wailing gale sprung up, and the room was suddenly filled with whirling shadows, trailing behind screaming dead faces made of vapour and smoke.

Every man drew his weapon. I turned away from the smashed mirror and saw that the warrior-priest had pulled a pair of wide-bladed, ornate silver punching daggers from their scabbards. The parallel guards I had seen at his hips now protected his arms, the plates that held the blades covering the knuckles of each hand. They were vicious, beautiful looking weapons.

The shadows lunged at us. A guard behind me tried to fend away one of the twisting spirits with his sword, but it ignored the blade and rushed at him, passing through the front of his head as if it were empty air. The man screamed and fell to his knees, dropping his sword and clutching at his face. His hands sank into his own flesh, which began to bubble and run like candlewax. Blood spurted between his fingers. He toppled over, and his hands fell to his sides as his legs jerked and his heels pounded the polished wooden floor. I looked down and saw that his skull was exposed, ribbons of bloody matter still clinging to the bones of his face, and his mouth opened and closed as he tried to scream. He could only make gurgling noises as the melting muscle of his tongue ran down his throat and stifled his agonised screeching.

The rest of the guards crouched and ducked, trying to avoid the destroying touch of the wraiths. Francyn was bellowing orders to withdraw, and the men started to exit the room as quickly as they were able. Dela was in one corner, hunkered down and unable to defend himself. The only man who seemed to be able to strike back was the warrior priest. He slashed at the spirits with his triangular silver blades, and where he struck the smoke of their forms parted and they shrieked in rage and pain. His teeth were gritted but his face remained passive, as if he were simply performing a chore. He made no sound.

There was a light behind me. I turned and saw that the green-flamed candle was now burning far brighter than it had before. The sparks it gave off were now striking the ceiling and the floor and were increasing in frequency. In an act of pure instinct I reached out with one fleshless palm and snuffed it out.

There was a booming sound, like a crack of thunder from a storm directly above, and the wraiths rushed upwards to the ceiling and span in a cyclone of screaming fury. Then they fled. Some seeped into the walls, becoming part of the shadows in the high corners of the room. Others rushed to the window overlooking the suite's garden and passed through the glass to escape. I swear I saw one fly into the sky and be caught by the wind outside as if it were a child's toy kite.

The room grew still. The guard on the floor, his face now an empty hollow, was dead. The other guards stood in the doorway, their weapons still drawn. The warrior priest looked around the room, grunted, and then sheathed his blades.

Dela broke the silence first.

"I don't know about the rest of you, but I could do with a drink."

It was midday again by the time we were summoned back to the Council chamber. True to his word Dela had downed another glass of wine when we had returned to his quarters and had then sank into a stupor. By some grace he had been left to sleep in to recover from the night's horror. He was called to speak to the First Daughter a little while before I headed to the conference.

I was escorted to the chamber by a handful of Francyn's men, but this time Fenna and Bor were summoned as well and assigned a seat with me at a hastily arranged table. Wain and Yast were present, Dela had his seat, and the First Daughter sat with Francyn at their post. However, the Merchant Quist was absent, and his chair was taken by the strange priest who had accompanied us to Cellin's quarters. The rest of the Council were not present. I noted that Cellin's chair had been removed.

Fenna leaned over to me as the places were set and the room prepared.

"What's going on? How did yesterday go?"

"As well as it could. I believe the Council is listening, and there were events in the night that may have strengthened our argument."

Bor grunted and said, "It's about time they woke the fuck up!"

He was a little loud, and Councillor Wain turned and gave him a stern look. Bor turned red with embarrassment, not an emotion I thought him capable of, and averted his eyes. Fenna mouthed *sorry* at Wain and the stateswoman nodded her head, a little smile at the corner of her mouth, and rolled her eyes.

The room settled down, and Councillor Wain stood to address us all.

"The Councillors for the other Regions have travelled home this morning, after some discussions with me. They go to make preparations for defence and will recruit what men and women they can to our cause. We do not have an army. We do have fighters, but they are fragmented and factional, spread far and wide, and joining our forces together to face the threat before us will be a difficult task. Councillor Yast has remained for this discussion but will be leaving this evening to gather his own troops. He wished to be part of this meeting today."

Wain sat, and gave way to Yast, who stood up.

"I must first apologize to you, Dela. I don't like you. I will never pretend otherwise. But you have done us a great service, and I owe you much. I want to assist you as much as I can before I return to Avania and begin recruitment. I will do whatever you ask of me in defence of our people."

Dela spoke softly. "I am grateful for your candour, Councillor Yast."

The Councillor sat down, his face still and pale, and Councillor Wain addressed the room. She remained seated as she did so.

"Cellin left us last night. As some of you are aware there was a… disturbance in his chambers. It is now clear he has been working against the interests of the Regions for some time. We are not sure of his motivations for this betrayal."

"I am." The First Daughter stood and moved towards the stand at the centre of the circle table. The warrior priest accompanied her and helped her as unobtrusively as he could by allowing her to lean on him as she walked. She looked older that day. When she reached the centre, she nodded her thanks to her companion, and the priest retired to his seat as the First Daughter cleared her throat and began to speak.

"I discussed the Bar... Asheth's history with him in some depth yesterday evening. I am assured... that is to say, I have faith, that he is the late Baron Asheth Acellion. He fell at Estwake, centuries ago. He had a family, a wife and two children."

I felt again the warmth of my love for them, as I had when I had spoken of them the previous night. I was glad of their memory. It gave me strength.

The First Daughter continued. "Asheth had a son, Ascas. I discussed this matter with Councillor Dela as well, who told me of a particular claim that Asheth has made. That Ascas was not his but was the illegitimate child of Emperor Domint... my apologies, Asheth, for having to speak to these facts with so little emotion, but we need clarity in this room." She turned her head to look at me, compassion in her eyes.

"No apology is necessary, First Daughter. I understand the need." I was confused however, as I did not understand then what bearing this had on our crisis. Fate can turn on you like a serpent.

"It appears to me," she continued, "That this claim is the truth. Ascas was Domint's son, and thus the last surviving heir of the Imperial line. It was this fact that started the civil war. I have attempted to trace the events after the fall of Estwake, and I believe that Ascas survived the siege."

This made me start from my seat in shock, and Fenna gave me a look of sympathy and reached out her hand to touch my shoulder.

"Ascas and Asheth's wife and daughter were captured by Frachia's men in the harbour at Estwake, although it is not clear how they arrived there. They were then taken to Frachia and held captive by him. I believe the Usurper intended to use them as leverage over any nobles who disputed his rule. After the revolt they were freed, and Ascas ended up residing in Nedra. When he was old enough, he had a family. Over the years the family name became corrupted, as such things can, through poor scholarship and sloppy penmanship, or perhaps… through subterfuge."

She straightened herself a little, as much as she could given her age, and glanced at me.

"Councillor Sern Cellin, or more correctly, Sern Acellion, has betrayed us for dreams of empire. Asheth is his adoptive grandfather, many times removed."

I felt then as if a yawning chasm had opened beneath me.

"I believe," she continued, "that Cellin knew of his provenance. He had access to all the writings I did. My Apostle, Quell," and at this she nodded towards the strange priest, "tells me that during the events in Cellin's quarters in the early hours of this morning, Kroll offered Asheth his Barony back, and professed to have no interest in ruling the Northern Shore. This was to be Cellin's role. Not just Baron of Estwake. Emperor. He is the last descendant of Domint and may believe it is his birth-right. A vassal ruler, serving the Sechian Empire, presiding over a land enslaved by the dead. A mirror of what Sechia has become."

Councillor Wain had her mouth open, all colour drained from her face. Dela was less shocked, having assisted the First Daughter in coming to her conclusions, but he did watch me. My face betrayed nothing.

Inside I was falling.

"Kroll seeks to undo centuries of progress." The First Daughter continued. "My view is that he intends to subjugate each of the Regions in turn, using the same methods he employed in Estwake and Tresh. The longer his unholy crusade continues, the greater his legions will be, a most terrible efficiency. If we do not design some strategy, here and now, to reverse his progress, he will become too powerful to stand against."

The First Daughter turned and nodded to Quell, who walked back into the circle and helped the old woman back to her seat.

"Baron Acellion," said Wain, "Would you please enter the circle? I believe we need your insight." She addressed me as if I were a visiting dignitary.

I stood up, glancing back at Fenna and Bor, who both gave me looks of support. I moved into the circle. I had already removed my hood and helmet. My hammer had been left in Dela's chambers. I missed the comfort of its mass.

"Councillor Wain. I will endeavour to assist you in any way I can. Please, address me as Asheth. Considering my current circumstances, and the heavy weight of my history, I no longer wish to claim my title."

She did not wince at the sound of my voice as she had the previous day, which gladdened me.

"Very well. Asheth. We have built a far more peaceful society than the one you served. That is not to say there is no conflict… there have been border disputes and aggression between regions, but it has never escalated to full-blown war. We are plagued by banditry and piracy, and most of the regions have their own forces to deal with that. But we are not used to mass warfare. You are. I know your campaign record is long and distinguished. If you were to wage war on Kroll and his followers, how would you proceed?"

I had thought on this already. Vengeance against Kroll and his cult has been on my mind for some time.

"I would not meet the dead on the field. Not without having weakened them beforehand."

"Weakened them? How?" she leaned forwards, listening intently, and the whole room hung on my words. I felt like a fly in a web.

I had been a professional soldier. A commander of many forces. In life it had been second nature for me to seek tactical advantage. I had already considered how to wage war against the undead.

"The Lesser Raised, the fleshed dead, and the Raised, the un-fleshed dead, are not great warriors. The Lessers fight like beasts and are driven at the enemy to break lines and splinter defences. But they have no thoughts and are easily slowed and distracted, if the defenders can hold their nerve and keep them at bay."

I warmed to my subject, and found myself gesturing with my skinless hands, as if I were briefing my old subordinates on campaign.

"The Raised, that is the skeletal warriors like me, are better fighters, but not by any significant margin. They fight by rote, with simple manoeuvres and tactics. A single trained fighter can kill a Raised easily if they hold their nerve and are not overwhelmed by numbers. In Tresh we... they took villages and towns by breaking the defenders first with a wave of Lessers, to terrify and disrupt, and then a wave of Raised, to stamp out any that had the nerve to stand. Raised cavalry was used for final sweeping strikes if needed and to run down survivors. This cavalry is not of a high quality either. To put it bluntly, the vast majority of Kroll's army is dim-witted, they are mere shadows of soldiers."

"But we are outnumbered." Dela said, "so their lack of skill is irrelevant." He sighed, leaning on the table in front of him.

"In the open field, or in a defensive action where the defenders are not ready for what they face, then yes. It is irrelevant. Quantity has a quality all its own. During Kroll's initial forays into Tresh we never raided a settlement where we had any danger of being outnumbered, and none of them were prepared for the kind of enemy they were facing. Few would be."

Councillor Wain looked pale. Yast had lost his arrogant air and had his elbows on the table, his head in his hands.

"What do you suggest, Asheth?" Dela's face was furrowed, his dark features ashen.

"Any army that fights the dead needs to know what it faces, and soldier's morale is ever a slippery fish to grasp. They need to have faith that they can carry the day and be armed to deal with their enemy. I have some idea of tactics that may be employed, but time is short to arm your forces correctly. The biggest concern is that fighting the dead will lead to casualties among your armies, and if Kroll's forces carry the day their numbers will be replenished in little time from those fallen in battle. Thus, every loss feeds the dead."

"Then how can we win?" Wain's features had drained of all blood, and she seemed old and tired.

"That is simple." I paused for effect. It is strange, how easy it is to fall into old habits. I remembered lectures I had given to my officers on campaign. Leadership is as much a set of affectations as it is a real skill.

"The dead rely on the living. There are only a handful like me, who have full retention of their abilities and memories. Kroll has living followers, but their numbers have not grown substantially since he came to Estwake. He must leave at least a few in every settlement he takes, else the dead there will revert back to wild savagery or witless animated bodies with no purpose or ambition, Any battle with the dead needs to have but one goal. To kill the living and the Greater Raised Commanders."

I paused again, and caught Dela's eye, who nodded at me.

"We must assassinate them all. A dishonourable strategy, to be sure, but the only one truly open to us. Every single member of Kroll's cult must die. The rot must be cut out."

I addressed the nascent War-Council for some time. They interrogated me about tactics, weaponry, disposition of forces, logistical challenges, and the myriad ways in which war can be waged. The assembled scribes in the room took copious notes, and Dela began to organise the structure of our defence with assistance from Councillor Yast, the two men often huddling together in frantic debate, all differences temporarily put aside. After several hours in conference my seminar reached a natural breakpoint, and Councillor Wain addressed me once more as a witness rather than an instructor.

"Asheth, I thank you for your advice and direction today. We will begin to assemble our people across the Regions as you have suggested, and in the meantime, you will remain a guest of the Council. Quarters will be assigned to you so we can seek counsel from you when necessary."

"No." I replied. "I will not remain here."

"You will not... Asheth, you are a prisoner of

this Council." Wain frowned. "As much as I have sympathy for your... condition, I cannot see what else we can do with you. We have offered you much trust already."

I lowered myself to one knee and bowed my head.

"I came here a penitent prisoner. I have partaken in the foulest actions since my awakening and find that even during life my dreams of honour and glory were simply the delusions of a young man. My past, my family line, my very *body* is forfeit to the ambition of the wicked, the vain, and the unholy. Now I have no Emperor to swear fealty to, no King to knight me, no noble brothers to join me in battle. I have been made an instrument of darkness. I cannot let this stand. I pledge myself to this Council instead, to the Northern Shore. I will be its servant and its defender. I will serve, and all I ask in return is that I am allowed vengeance."

I raised my head, gazing from my empty sockets into Councillor Wain's eyes. I raised my voice.

"Kroll has taken *everything* from me. My name. My family. My honour... and my rightful rest. *His head belongs to me.*"

The assembly remained silent. Then the First Daughter rose from her seat, and gestured to her Apostle, Quell, to stand. She turned to face the Council.

"I believe that Asheth's anger is justified. I also

believe he has been chosen, by Omma T'Lassa, to help us in our time of need. I have a suggestion." She gestured to the warrior-priest at her side.

"Asheth, Quell is a member of the Apostles of the Wave, the Temple's own warriors. He is a penitent as well, and was rescued from a life ill-spent, to use his skills for more righteous purposes. With the Council's permission I will assign Quell as your keeper. The Temple will house you for now, and when you go to war, Quell will accompany you, alongside his fellow Apostles. I believe they will be able to contribute greatly. Asheth, do you agree to these terms?"

"I do."

"Quell, will you perform this duty for me?" The First Daughter did not command him. The Apostle's features were unreadable. He was like a pool of still water.

"Of course, First Daughter." His voice was a whisper.

"Asheth, come here." I walked towards the old woman, out of the circle table, and knelt before her. She turned to Quell and held out her hand. The Apostle pulled the gold chain from around his neck, the blue and green light from the Council chamber's windows glittering from the links, and he carefully placed the seashell that hung from it into the First Daughter's palm.

The First Daughter placed the chain around my

neck, and in doing so she brushed my exposed skull, yet did not flinch from the bone. The shell was placed with care and reverence against my chest.

"Asheth Acellion, from this moment on you are in service to the Temple of the Mother of the Sea. You will be under my guidance and direction, and you will do as I command. Do you accept these terms?"

"I do." At least I did then.

"Stand, then. Omma T'Lassa welcomes you and will be glad of your service."

Bor made a whooping noise and clapped, and then was quickly silenced by Fenna, who rolled her eyes and sighed.

I left the Chamber with the First Daughter and her Apostle, having been congratulated by Dela, Fenna and Bor. As we left the Council grounds, we were joined by a number of others like Quell, Apostles all dressed in similar garments of loose blue clothing but wrapped in dark cloaks to keep out the winter chill. I replaced my hood and helmet so that I could walk through the city freely. We made our way down the other side of the island from where the *Silverfin* had docked. It was nearly dusk, as we had been in conference for some time, and the sun was just dipping below the horizon. There was still a glow to the west, and the sunset lit the underneath of the clouds with red, orange and purple, as the sun's last rays fought back against the encroaching darkness. As we made our way through the city the First Daughter leant on Quell for support.

Down at the sealine, alongside the westward-facing harbour, was a great spired building, the High Temple of the Sea. It was clad in white marble, with a mosaic of sparkling blue stone waves inlaid around its circumference. Its shape was that of a ship on the ocean, and the tallest spire sat where the bridge would be. We entered the Temple through a set of tall wooden doors set into the prow of the stone ship. Inside were lines of pews, each made of carved grey driftwood and made to look like the seats for oarsmen in an ancient vessel. The interior of the temple was lit by the setting sun streaming through the same blue and green glass windows that had adorned the dome of the Council. Opposite the entrance doors, at the far end of this place of worship, there was the figure of a woman, built from cut and sculpted planks of driftwood tied together with fine rope. The statue stood twice the height of a man. Carved fish and shells lay at her feet and her hands were outstretched to either side as if displaying the bounty she had brought from the sea. There was a small rock pool built into the floor around her, filled with brine, seaweed and shells that had been collected from the shore. A blessed offering from the ocean. The face of the statue was the image of a woman, but as we moved towards her the light on her face shifted and seemed to change her features. At first, she was a young girl, and filled with joy and life. Then she was older, motherly and nurturing but stern. Nearer still and she became a crone, grave and cruel looking but with wise, deep-set eyes.

When we reached the feet of the statue I could see its face up close, and could see that her features were just an illusion, a trick of the light in the temple. The carving was too worn for the face to be clear. Yet I could not take my gaze from her. I knelt before her for a moment and touched the shell that hung at my neck.

I had not been especially devout to any god in life. Having come from inland stock, our people gave some respect to S'Gara, the Serpent under the Mountain, and G'Rath, the Lady of the Forest, but I had only given cursory attention to the chantings of priests or any ideas of faith and piety. War had been my calling, until my family became my faith. But kneeling there in the Temple, at the feet of the icon of Omma T'Lassa, I felt a swell of reverence that had never risen in me before.

We left the main hall of the Temple. Making our way through a smaller side door we followed stone steps that wound down to where the building met the waterline. We entered a room that only had three stone walls, the fourth and far wall being open to the elements. The room served as an internal dock of some kind. The sea came in and lapped at grey stone walkways around a wide pool. At intervals around the rectangular bay were twenty or so iron loops embedded in the stone floor, holding chains that lead over the edge of the dock and into the water.

Our group stopped here for a moment, and the First Daughter turned to me.

"This is our graveyard, Asheth. Here, where we are alongside the sea, we offer back what we can. Any who serve the mother devoutly are here, rather than being buried in the dry ground. Sailors are buried at sea, sometimes with little care, but here we treat our offerings with more reverence. Look for yourself."

I walked to the edge of the water. There were torches on the walls around the room, providing light for the living, as the sun had finally dipped below the horizon. The flames reflected from the gently lapping waves and sent shimmers of golden light across the low ceiling of the room. Looking down into the water I could see that each chain that entered the brine had a body attached to it, posed under the surface in silent contemplation. Some of the bodies were relatively unmarked, if bloated, and seemed to have been recent additions. Others were almost entirely absent of flesh. Over and around the dock's occupants the crabs and fish of the small bay climbed and crawled and darted in and out, feeding on what they could.

To a man less inured to death it might have been a ghastly and awful sight. To me it looked like a peaceful reward. What better way to serve the sea than to offer your flesh as sustenance to its myriad creatures?

"You see, Asheth," said Quell, his whispering voice barely loud enough to be heard above the low sound of the moving water, "here we are used to the sight of bones and skinless skulls. Your appearance is not such a great shock to us."

"Though your animation does require some adjustment." Said the First Daughter. "Follow me."

She walked toward another door set into the grey stone, to the right-hand side of the room. We passed through a short corridor, that opened into a larger chamber than the dock we had left. The only light in the room was candlelight, although there were a great many candles spread around the floor and the walls, so it was not too dark for my companions.

This was a room of death, and its momentary resemblance to the catacombs at Estwake shook me. The walls and ceiling were decorated with many sculptures and ornaments, and all these things were made from the fleshless remains of the dead.

Here was a shelf of skulls, with feathered wings splayed on the wall behind it made from thousands of skinless fingers, the spine of each wing made from lengths of leg and arm bone.

There was a clam shell, constructed from layers of rib, each bone layered one on top of the other until the rippling texture of the shell's surface was formed in light and shadow.

Above us a candelabra hung from the high ceiling, below a rose of fleshless feet. It was a circle of skulls chained together, and the light from affixed candles shone from empty eye sockets.

There was a man stood in the middle of the room, and he stepped forwards and greeted the First Daughter warmly, bowing his head in respect. He was of middle age, with long dark hair streaked with white and a long greying beard, and he wore a blue skull cap on his scalp. His skin was pale, and his eyes were sunken, but they also seemed kind, amused even, and he looked at me with interest and curiosity and no fear at all. He smiled at me.

"I guess this is the one then, First Daughter?" he said, and he grinned at his obvious and rhetorical question.

"Yes, Terun." She said, with a little sigh, and then turned to me. "Asheth, this is Brother Terun. He is the Keeper of the Ossuary. His role is to take the remains of those offered to Omma T'Lassa after they have been sanctified by the sea, and to preserve them here, to make a permanent reminder of their sacrifice. He is well-versed in the art of working with... such materials. I believe he can help you to prepare for the coming conflict. Will you accept his help?"

"I will." I was not sure what was going to happen, but I was willing to do what the First Daughter thought was correct.

"Very well," she said, "Quell, please help Asheth to remove his garments."

It took Quell and several others in the First Daughter's entourage a little time to strip me of my clothing. It was well made, Shand's craftsmen were no fools, but it had not been designed for easy removal. Quell promised to bring it back, and even suggested he could investigate potential improvements, which I readily agreed to. The seashell on its chain was put to one side.

The rest of the group left, until just the First Daughter and Quell remained. She bid me goodbye, entrusting me to Terun's care, and she leant on her Apostle as they left the room. I stood there before Terun, naked of clothing, but feeling no shame.

I did not have anything he had not seen before.

Brother Terun turned out to be a strangely cheerful fellow, in a morbid sort of way. He whistled as he worked, and sang tuneless ditties, some that seemed quite bawdy for an ostensibly pious man. He engaged me in conversation on a number of different topics, never once treating me as if I were anything other than a living man. It seemed he drew little distinction between the living and the dead, being quite used to both.

I had followed him into an antechamber that served as his workshop and he had me lay on a bench, beneath a silver plate that he used to reflect the light of several oil lamps onto his work surface. The similarities between his work and that of Nisht in Estwake were startling, but there was a contrast between his neat and methodical surroundings and the grime-laden pit that Nisht occupied. There was a firepit in the middle of the room, and around the walls were many labelled shelves of jars, tools, screws, wires, nails, all well-organised and kept neat and tidy.

He examined Clasp's work on my ribcage, and was quite complimentary about it, saying that regardless of the reason or circumstances I had been repaired well. He reviewed the rest of me, finding many cuts, scrapes, cracks and assorted other signs of wear on my bones. He noted his findings down in a book, to help him plan his work. It made for a long list.

Before beginning his work proper, he had me get back up from the bench and take a seat in a long and deep stone trough that lay against one wall of the room. On the wall above it a small pipe, with some mechanical fitting above it, jutted from the stone. He turned the fitting, and a stream of water began to fill the trough, partially filling it until the liquid was roughly a hand-span deep. Then he boiled some more water in a cauldron hung over his fire-pit, and poured that into the trough as well, alongside some powder he retrieved from a large glass jar stoppered with wood. Once the warm, lightly caustic solution had been mixed, and the water was up to my chest, he proceeded to clean me, using dried sea sponge and stiff brushes of various sizes.

I found this a little embarrassing at the time, and I forbade him from cleaning my pelvic region. He laughed and said, "I've never had anyone complain before!".

I did that part myself.

I liked Terun a great deal. A morbid sense of humour suited my circumstances well.

After my ablutions were complete, I rose from the water, and Terun helped me back onto his workbench, where he dried me with a cloth. Again, I refused his attention in some areas, which raised more laughter from him. I laughed with him, but still did not give him any access to those regions. Then he began to make repairs. He mixed a small pot of a resin-like substance and brushed it into all the cracks and gaps in my bone. I had to allow then the indignity of him addressing some damage in my groin, and he did his best to appease me by singing his songs, to distract us both from the activity. He also examined my teeth, and he found several replacements for my missing ones in a drawer, which he then glued in place with more of the sticky resin.

Once he had applied several layers of his filling compound, he sanded the surface of my bones until they were smooth. Retrieving a different pot, he removed a copper lid from it and then varnished me with its contents, until my skeleton gleamed in the light from the lamps and the fire-pit. He took strong metal wire and using a small set of gripped pincers he wound it around and in and out of my ribcage, forming a protective lattice that gave the structure more strength, as if I had chainmail affixed directly to me. He wound the same wire around my upper arms and around my thighbones in coils, to add more protection there, and in and around the knuckles and joints of my hands.

Finally, he took a silver loop of wire, with the small golden seashell from Quell's chain in the middle. This was placed around my skull so that the shell sat on my forehead. Terun apologised and said that this had been at the First Daughter's instruction. He used small silver pins to tack the circlet to the front and back of my head. I told him I would accept whatever the First Daughter wished.

I stood then, and he retrieved a soft blue tabard for me from a cabinet in the corner of the workshop. He helped me lower it over myself, and I found it had a hood I could raise over my exposed skull. He tied the tabard in place with a length of fine, clean rope.

The silver mirror that hung above Terun's workstation was on a tilting mechanism, some sort of mechanical arm, so he moved it down, so it was perpendicular to the floor. I examined his work.

I was never going to be handsome again, but I was clean, and as well-presented as possible. The silver and gold I wore on my head, and the wire at my extremities and ribcage, caught the light and made me look like an idol that had stepped from some ancient frieze. I was a vision of death, but a reverent one.

I turned to Terun and saw the pride on his face at the fine work he had done. I moved to embrace him in thanks, momentarily forgetting myself. To my everlasting surprise and gratitude, he did not shy away, but returned the embrace with affection and respect.

I will never forget that.

I was assigned a chamber in the Temple's grounds, and I was treated as if I were any other pious member of the Order. It was a respite and a sanctuary for me, for a little while. I remained there for the rest of that moon and most of the next. Dela would visit me from time to time and update me on how preparations were proceeding. Some attempt at an army was being fashioned, with recruits being gathered from the guard forces of several nearby regions, and a ragged makeshift fleet was being assembled from privateer and trading ships.

I requested the return of my hammer, and it was given back to me after being cleaned and further ornamented at the order of the First Daughter. The head had been edged in silver and a shell decoration had been etched into the polished metal of its sides, alongside Dela's fin crest. I would go to the internal dock, where the dead gave their flesh to the sea, and practice with it, learning its weight and movement. It was different from the sword I had used in life, but I soon gained some skill with the awkward weapon. I found I did not tire of its weight. My strength was always at its maximum, as I did not have muscles to strain. Whatever animating force drove my movement never reduced in power with the action of combat. My hundredth swing was as strong as my first. I realised that I could easily break my own bones if I were not careful, and I gave silent thanks to Terun for his reinforcements.

In the evenings I lay in my cot, and read books brought to me by Quell, who often sat with me so we could discuss the teachings of the Temple. He was a quiet man, but clear and confident in his faith and knowledge. He was guarded when I asked him how he came to be an Apostle, and I felt it would take a little while to gain his trust, regardless of the First Daughter's faith in me.

I plunged myself beneath the waves of my new calling and absorbed all I could.

Quell also brought back my padded clothing, having had one of the local merchants make adjustments for me. Instead of dressing as a living man would, the garments could be strapped to me with buckles, and armour plates were fixed directly to the leather and cloth. A polished silver cuirass had been added to the assemblage. My helmet had been cleaned and polished also and etched with the same shell shape that decorated my hammer and my skull. It was a wonderful panoply and I thanked him deeply.

Near the end of my second moon at the temple, Dcla came to me, looking tired and distraught.

Salisson had fallen to the dead.

CHAPTER THIRTEEN

We travelled with Captain Shand again, although this time his ship led a flotilla of others. There were privateers like him, as well as merchant ships that had been pressed into service to hold what troops we could gather. Yast accompanied us in his own ship, the *Gemstone*, and we were to stop at the main harbour and capital of Avania, a city called Oese. This would allow Yast to retrieve his own men. Dela held out some hope that we would be able to gather together any Wardens who had escaped Salis before Kroll's invasion. It had come as an unpleasant surprise to Yast that Dela already had agents and safe houses in Oese where his Wardens could find refuge, and Salisson's Councillor looked more than a little embarrassed at having to give up this information. It had soured relations between the two men again, and they had not spoken further before boarding their own ships.

The crew of the *Silverfin* treated me with a great

deal more respect than they had upon our first voyage together. They were still wary of me but there was no cursing or spitting in my direction. I was able to be on deck and visit the Captain's quarters with no challenge to my presence, although I kept my hooded cloak on over my blue tabard out of courtesy. When a member of the crew saw the flash of my silver-circlet and golden shell under the hood they made the Sign of the Wave.

The passage to Oese went without incident, and even though we were at the tail-end of winter no storms troubled us and we had fair seas and wind in our sails all the way to the harbour.

Oese was a very different city to Salisson. Where Dela's home had a grey and dour temperament, Yast's was a bright and lively place. We made our way into the bay and docked alongside several other ships of the new fleet, and Yast sent runners to his hall to give and retrieve messages as we assisted with disembarkation. Dela, Fenna, Bor and I gathered our belongings and carried whatever we could to assist with unloading. I dressed myself completely before we left the ship, again assuming my disguise as Dela's bodyguard. A ramshackle army gathered underneath the long eaves of arched wood and stone that formed the edges of the dock, and they were hastily lined up in regiment order by their commanding officers.

We followed Yast and his personal guard through the city. I was struck again by the differences between Yast's domain and Dela's. Salisson had been a haven for privateers, only a hair's breadth from being a pirate enclave, and its geography and attitude reflected its untrustworthy and ruthless populace. In contrast Oese was a light and airy place, with architecture not dissimilar to the Western Gate, its buildings clad in marble and festooned with luxurious carved decorations of sea beasts and forest creatures. Dela had attempted to drag Salisson away from its violent heritage, but it would always be a grim place. Oese was golden.

We reached Yast's hall. Unlike Dela's adopted castle home, Yast's dwelling had been built for its purpose, and was a grand town building, much ornamented but lacking the fortified nature of the tower at Salisson. As we entered through its carved wooden doors Yast immediately began to issue instructions to various scribes and subordinates. He tasked his staff with turning several warehouses into barracks for the waiting army in the harbour, and they rushed off to have the buildings cleared and to acquire or requisition cots, bedding, kitchen supplies, chamber pots, wood for stoves, and all the other logistical supplies an army needs to station itself and begin a campaign. He wrote orders for tents and camping gear, rope, shovels, additional armour and weaponry, bows, arrows, horses and barding, wagons and barrows. He requested audiences with local carpenters and engineers to begin planning for the construction of siege weaponry, weapons that hadn't been built in three hundred years. All of this was based on advice I had given, but the cost was mostly coming out of Yast's treasury, other than some gold that had been assigned by the Council, and I saw him wince with pain at the bills that came back to him. He haggled over some, negotiating where he could and arguing for civic duty from his claimants, but other bills he had to accept with sighs of resignation and resentment. He knew the importance of his actions, and did not refuse to pay anything, but it clearly pained him to see so much of his wealth flow out of his coffers and into the hands of the gleeful merchants.

His last action of the day, which Dela and I were both present for, was to assemble his guard officers and entreat them to turn their men into part of the new army as well. They were not as unprofessional as the guard in Salisson, and did not quibble or refuse Yast's request, but neither did they overflow with enthusiasm. Dela and I remained in Yast's office as he dismissed the grey-faced officers. Yast's rooms were neat and sparse, with well-made, ostentatious furniture of carved inlaid wood and intricately patterned cushions, but an absence of the books and scrolls that Dela treasured. There was also, as Dela noted ruefully, no wine.

"Yast," Dela said, "Asheth and I are grateful to you for your hospitality, and I know you have arranged for us to stay here in your hall. However, I must leave you for the evening. I must make contact with my people."

"Your spies, you mean. Dela, I will put aside my enmity with you for the duration of this conflict, but afterwards you and I are going to have a long talk about your deviousness."

Dela looked a little embarrassed, but he forged on as calmly as he could. "I understand, but we have neither the time not resources to debate this now. I will take Asheth, Fenna and Bor out with me, and we will return in the morning."

"Very well. Do try not to cause any trouble in my city. The people of Oese are not used to your underhand ways."

Dela's lips were pressed together tightly, pale against his dark skin, but he said nothing more and just gave a shallow nod of the barest respect. We collected Bor and Fenna from one of the downstairs antechambers and headed out into the city.

Dela was ranting before we even turned the first corner.

"Stuck up, supercilious, arrogant *bastard!* Bah! He should try running Salis. We don't have half the resources Avania has. Look at this place!" he said, gesturing wildly with his hands, "He isn't responsible for any of this wealth, he just lucked into it! He started the card game three hands ahead and he thinks he's the best player on the Northern Shore!"

Fenna and Bor looked at each other and rolled their eyes, as we walked along the finely paved street. It was clear they had heard Dela sing this song before. Fenna tried to calm him and leaned in to speak into his ear.

"It's not important now, Dela. What's important is we're being followed." She whispered.

"*Of course* we are!" Dela hissed back, nearly growling with rage. "I saw that shifty little fellow when we left the hall. He's one of Yast's, the old crow wants to know where my spies are. *Hypocrite!*"

Bor was a step or two behind us, but he had caught the gist of the conversation and leaned in between the two of them. "I'll deal with him," he said, "I'll catch you up at the Wailing Sailor."

Dela paused for a moment, took a deep breath to try to catch his temper, and nodded agreement. We carried on walking as Bor turned back, whistling in a clumsy attempt to appear nonchalant. Just before we turned the next corner I looked back and saw him bump into the grey-clad man trying to follow us. Bor was far larger than the spy and the impact threw the other man to the ground. Bor leaned forwards to offer a hand, to help his victim off the floor, and when the man extended his hand for assistance Bor punched him hard in the jaw. He then dragged the unconscious spy into an adjacent alleyway.

It took us a little while to get to the Wailing Sailor on foot. I noted, as I had in Salisson, the brightness and strange structure of the oil lamps lighting the streets and walls. I asked Dela about them.

"Ah, those are an advancement since your day, Asheth. It's fish oil, mixed with some mineral solutions made from salts from the northern mines. It burns very brightly and with a great deal of heat, far more than just oil alone. Many of the cities now run it through pipes along the walls and below the streets, from reservoirs held at height to produce pressure. We've found lighting and civilization go hand in hand. Technological advancement has been one of the great benefits of not kneeling to Barons and Emperors... sorry Asheth, that was a little insensitive."

"Not at all, Dela. I was not always a Baron. I was a soldier first. I can appreciate engineering, although my experience has mostly been with weaponry."

"Well. There have been advances in personal weaponry. The Warden's crossbows are of a more mechanical nature than they were in your time. Easier and faster to reload. However, in a lot of ways, in terms of warfare, we have not advanced at all. We are in fact having to re-learn how to wage war. You have been a great assistance in this regard, Asheth."

"Thank you, Dela. I am glad to help." I nodded a short bow to my benefactor, and we carried on through the city, as I took in the marvels around me.

The Wailing Sailor was an inn of some size and luxury. We had been there a little while before Bor caught up and joined us, his knuckles red-raw. We sat at a table near the back of the Inn, which thankfully was dimly lit. Drinkers seldom want bright lights. Dela and the others ordered beers from a beautiful young barmaid, who reacted with a little confusion when I raised my palm to refuse a drink. She walked away with a puzzled expression.

Bor laughed and said "Looks like you've pulled!"

Fenna shook her head and sighed, but I remained silent. I was to be mute again unless in trusted company.

When the barmaid returned Dela's drink came

with a note, which he read and then stuffed into his pocket. He gave a nod of confirmation to Fenna and then we sat and waited. My companions drank slowly as the night went on, and the numbers in the inn thinned as people either left, drunk and sated, or fell asleep in their cups.

When the inn was nearly empty, barring some snoring drunks, the barmaid collected us and took us to a back room via a door behind the bar. There was a false wall at the rear of a shelf filled with tankards and glasses, and the space behind held a set of bare stone steps, that led down to a large cellar room that had been partitioned off from the main basement by a wooden wall.

In the cellar were several round tables, each with a few chairs, and a line of cots. Two of the chairs were occupied. A man with short brown hair and a beard sat at one. He was short and stocky, red faced and cheerful looking. The other chair was occupied by a woman who looked a little older than him. She had tanned, lined skin, with long braided white hair, and wore an apron over a patched and faded dress. She greeted Dela fairly warmly, nodded regards to Bor and Fenna, and then turned to stare at me with outright suspicion. Dela raised his hand and she glanced at him with not a little hostility.

"Please, Gerta, it's alright. This is Asheth. He is a friend and an ally, and I trust him. I ask you do the same."

She made a humphing noise, looking unconvinced. Dela introduced us.

"Asheth, this is Gerta, and her husband Eryk. They own this inn, and they also act as my eyes and ears in Avania and host my Wardens when their activities bring them into this Region. I apologise for Gerta's suspicion, but hers is a most difficult trade. Spy craft is delicate work, even amongst those who are ostensibly our allies."

"It's more dangerous the more who know of us. This is sloppy, Dela, very sloppy. You should not be here in person." Her voice was harsh and raspy, and she made no effort to conceal her anger.

"Needs must, Gerta. We are at war, and we have catching up to do. Asheth is here to help."

"His face is to be unknown to me?"

"For now. His role in this war is no secret to the enemy, that ship has sailed, but I would rather keep his presence here quiet for now. The less you know of him the better."

I guessed that gaining this woman's trust would be even more difficult if she knew of my true nature.

"Dela, you cannot keep me in darkness. A lack of knowledge can be dangerous."

"Too much knowledge can also be a threat. Put it

to one side for me, Gerta, for now. I need you to run some errands for me."

He sat at one of the tables, and after a moment, she sat opposite him, with a face like a gathering storm.

He outlined his requirements. He had a network of spies across Avania that Gerta managed for him, and they were tasked with gathering all of the Wardens that had been scattered into the Region by Kroll's advance. Dela was organising his own army, a parallel entity to the one that the Regions were assembling. His was to be the assassin's blade, at my advice. The Wardens were far more suited to the subterfuge and stealth we needed for my strategy to work. Dela spoke with Gerta into the early hours of the morning, and it was agreed that we would reconvene in two days, at the Wailing Sailor, to see who we had gathered and plan our next steps. We walked back to Yast's hall, where we were permitted entrance by the suspicious guards, and we were then taken to our assigned chambers. Bor and Fenna shared one, and Dela and I shared another.

He snored and muttered in his sleep, and his cot was too small for him. I sat cross-legged on the floor. I wiled away the hours by retreating into memories of better days. My family at the dinner table, a feast laid before us. Waking in the morning next to my wife, and watching her sleeping face, illuminated by golden sunlight pouring through the tower window. My children, playing and running freely around the castle, racing up and down the stairs and bumping into the servants.

I thought of how far I was from who I had been. At least now I had purpose, and that gave me some heart, so to speak.

Quell joined us the following afternoon. He had travelled on one of the other ships, with a group of his Apostle companions, and he had spent some time helping to organise the barracks with Yast's subordinates. He had led prayers and faithful songs for the gathering soldiers. He was dressed in partial plate and mail, trimmed in bright and polished silver, and covered it in a blue tabard, a match to the one I had worn at the Temple. He still had his strange, triangular daggers strapped at his thighs. He offered his services to Dela in his low, grit-filled voice.

"Councillor," he said, "I believe you intend to enter Salis soon."

"Yes, that is true. What do you wish to do, Apostle Quell?" Dela regarded him with narrowed eyes.

"I want to accompany you. If Asheth is correct in his assessment of how we should proceed, I believe the Apostles and I can help. The First Daughter believes you will need aid from Omma

T'Lassa. I offer myself as a test for that belief."

Dela frowned, which confused me at the time. He seemed reticent to accept Quell's help.

"You can accompany Asheth and Fenna, with the other Wardens." Dela said. "You won't be able to wear plate armour, we will find you Warden's garments. They won't offer as much protection, but stealth and swift movement will be vital and you will have to compromise."

"So be it, Councillor. Whatever the Mother of the Sea wills."

The Wardens gathered at the Wailing Sailor. They had crept into the city over a couple of days, in ones and twos, until there were twenty or so gathered and cramped in the dank cellar. They were a motley bunch. Most were brawlers like Bor, with wild eyes and uncouth language. I could see why Yast had such a low opinion of Dela's actions. His makeshift army was a rabble of thieves and cutthroats, and he had obviously ignored the boundaries of the Regions in his activities. However, for all their cursing and drinking, the men and women of the Wardens waited patiently to be addressed. They were polite to Gerta as she brought them beer and bread, and every one of them looked to be a capable and assured fighter. Dela's idea of an army may have not matched mine, but I could not deny that they would be a useful asset.

Word of my nature had already made its way around the ranks of the Wardens. Some of them had been present in Salisson during my short incarceration there. Gerta had finally found out and had been volcanic in her response, her red face in danger of setting light to Dela's garments while she ranted at him.

"What the *living fuck* do you think you're doing? The work I've put in to keep this place safe and secret and you bring this fucking *creature* in here!"

I kept my face hidden and stayed in the corner of the room. Gerta's husband Eryk put one hand on her shoulder, felt the heat coming from her, and decided to withdraw and shuffled quickly upstairs instead. I could not say I blamed him.

"Gerta, please calm yourself..." said Dela, holding up his palms to attempt to placate her, or perhaps preparing to defend himself. "Asheth has proven himself several times over. He is extremely valuable to our efforts. I ask that you try to accept him... if not for me then for the good of all."

I remained silent. I had not spoken at all while in the cellar, feeling it was best not to add any more fuel to the fire. The various Wardens regarded me with a strange mix of contempt and curiosity.

Dela let Gerta rant on for a little while, until her fire died down to grumbling embers. She left the room still growling, heading upstairs to tend bar after giving me a disgusted and withering look. She had no fear of me, that is sure. I pitied any man that caused trouble in her inn that evening. Dela turned to address the assembled Wardens, raising his hands for quiet. Bor had sat with them and Quell sat alongside him, but Fenna remained at Dela's side, as their commanding officer.

"Thank you all for coming so quickly. We have a lot to discuss, and only a short time to make our plans." He seemed a lot more comfortable speaking to these people than he had been in front of the Council.

"We are going to retake Salisson. Before we do so, we need to perform a scouting expedition to one of the undead nests. Wyrin informs me... " and at this point he nodded to a feline looking, shaven headed woman sat near the front of the room, who fiddled with a small sharp dagger as she listened to the briefing, "... that one of the villages just over the border of Avania has been corrupted by Kroll's forces, but is only lightly guarded as yet, as they are still in the process of... ah... recruitment. We are going to use this target as an opportunity to prove a theory of the First Daughter's. Quell is one of her Apostles and is here to assist."

Quell stood at this point to face the assembly and gave a short bow of his head. He got little response. The Wardens were not friendly to newcomers.

"This will be dangerous work," Dela continued, "and I don't want to commit all of you at once to it. Captain Fenna, accompanied by Bor, Asheth and Quell, will lead the mission. I need five more of you, but this will voluntary."

The gathered men and women looked around at each other, and with a susurration of muttered, resigned cursing, every last one of them stood up.

Wyrin spoke. "We've all lost someone. We'll all fight. But Dela..." and at this she tapped her dagger against the side of her face, under her right eye, and looked past Dela towards where I stood "...keep your dead pet in line. We've seen what his kind have done in Salis, and in Tresh. If he makes one wrong move I'll fuck him up."

Dela stared at her, stony faced. "I understand your reticence... however Asheth has earned my trust."

"Well... he hasn't earned mine. Tell him to sleep softly."

I admit, I lost my temper a little at that point. I had started to recover my pride and was not going to be spoken about in this way. From the corner of the room, still wearing my hood and helmet, I answered Wyrin. Perhaps a little too loudly.

"I do not sleep. I do not like threats either."

Wyrin jerked with shock at the echoing bell of my voice, but she recovered well. She slowly put her dagger back in its sheath and sat down, not taking her eyes off me once. Her stare could have melted glass.

The meeting came to a natural conclusion then, and Dela and Fenna sat at a table together to plan the raid.

CHAPTER FOURTEEN

Wyrin insisted on being part of the mission, if only so that she could watch me. Fenna relented, and the handful of others who were chosen sat around Wyrin, whispering, until Dela addressed the room again and they fell silent. He thanked the rest of the Wardens and dismissed them, asking only that they stay ready and local so that he could call on them quickly if needed. The small party remained seated as the rest of the Wardens left in ones and twos. They were still attempting to be unobtrusive and did not want to leave the Wailing Sailor as a single group. Dela went through his plan with the remaining volunteers, who listened intently and without interruption, even Wyrin. We were to collect a horse-drawn covered wagon and head to the village in the morning. It would be about a day's ride, but we would cross the border into Salis earlier than that.

The following morning, we took our places in

the wagon. Bor and Fenna sat up front, covered in cloaks to hide their skirmisher's wear, just a farmer and his wife travelling for their own reasons. In the wagon Quell and I sat with our backs to them, and the rest of the motley Warden crew were sat spaced as far away from me as they could get in the cramped conditions. The clouds above us were low and even, no shape or form to them, just a blanket of dour vapour pouring their contents over us. The roads were churned and muddy, ill-kept this close to the border, nothing like the well-built and paved Coast Road. The weather would help with stealth and subterfuge but would do nothing to aid our travel. The closer we got to Salis the worse the conditions and the road surface grew, until the wagon's progress became stilted and painful, and the covered back rolled and bumped on the uneven ground while the horses grew tired and whinnied wearily in protest at their load. We were lucky in some ways. The route we took wound through dark forests and the branches hanging over the trail gave us some cover from the rain and hail that bounced from the roof of the wagon. The gnarled and twisted branches also hid our passage from too many prying eyes.

There was conversation while we travelled, but neither Quell nor myself were invited to join in with any of the boasting, tall-tales or jokes that passed between the Wardens. If Quell even shifted position to make himself comfortable the movement was met with swiftly turned heads and suspicious stares. I was watched almost constantly, the Wardens taking it in turns to monitor my movements. Wyrin took the bulk of this responsibility.

We did pass some travellers moving in the other direction, and our travel towards the border was met with puzzled faces. All appeared to be refugees, of a similar nature to those who had camped in and around Salisson. I could see out of the back of the wagon from my seat, and most that passed us were in even worse condition that the ones I had encountered moons ago. Their clothes were torn and dirty, hanging loosely over underfed flesh and bone. They were soaked to the skin, and they were dragging or carrying barrows and sacks behind them which contained what few belongings they had been able to save. It was a desperate flight, and their wretched retreat only helped to stiffen my resolve. I hoped what I was doing would help them.

We dismounted from the wagon a little way from the village, as we needed to approach without raising any alarm. There were likely to be patrols, like the one I had been part of in Tresh. The Wardens lifted kit bags and backpacks onto their shoulders, strapped up armour and secured weapons, and prepared for travel. I carried very little, and my offer of assistance was met with scowls and curses. Quell was treated in a similar fashion. The Wardens led one horse with them and tied the other to a nearby tree, leaving one man behind to guard the wagon and its remaining supplies. The extra kit that I had offered to carry was lashed across the horse's back.

The Wardens were used to moving through dense forest and hard terrain, and I admit I struggled to keep up with them, as did Quell. I felt certain that, if she could, Wyren would have gladly abandoned us in the forest. It took some while to get to the edge of the wild wood. From the tree line we could see down into a small valley. The village below was called Rafe and was not dissimilar to any of the other dwelling places I had raided when I was still in Kroll's service. It was just a handful of buildings, surrounded by farmlands, and enclosed by a wooden wall of cut logs bound together to form a moderate defensive position. Obviously, this bulwark had not served the villagers all that well. The sun had just gone down, and we watched from the cover of the forest and waited to see what was in store for us.

Patrols came and went. They were difficult to see in the darkness, but occasionally we saw the marching silhouettes of skeletal soldiers cross the light of the torches at Rafe's gate. The Raised, like me needed no illumination to see where they were going, so carried none with them as they passed in and out of the village. The light was for the living only. It was very quiet, and the handful of Kroll's cultists we saw seemed to communicate only in whispers and gestures, unwilling to break the silence of the valley. The rain had relented at last, so the Warden's view of the gate was only encumbered by darkness. The gate was minimally guarded. We went ahead with our plan.

Quell and I got ready. Fenna and Bor helped us with our cloaks. Quell had swapped his fine garment for a dirty, mud-encrusted cloth, to help him look the part of one of Kroll's followers. I had my long black cloak but left it open at the top, so my armour was partly visible. I took off my helmet, so my skull was visible as well, but brought the hood of the cloak down over the circlet at my forehead to hide the gleaming shell. That would have been too much of a gap in my disguise. Before we left to enter the village, Wyrin crept over to us through the foliage.

"I'm watching you," she said, addressing both Quell and myself. "First sign you're up to something and I'll kill you. I don't give a *shit* if that gets me done by these dead fuckers, I'll be taking you with me."

"Have some faith, Mistress Wyrin," said Quell, "Omma T'Lassa will watch over us and guide us."

"I don't do faith, priest. I only trust the blade in my hand."

"Then let us be a blade for you." Quell brought up his dark hood and turned away from the woman, stalking towards the waiting horse. I clambered up into the saddle, with some assistance from Bor. It had been a long time since I rode. The horse shied from me a little and Bor had to calm it. It stomped and whinnied a few times here and there, distressed by my presence and nature, but I rubbed my gloved hand along the side of its neck, and Bor whispered gentle words into its ear until it decided it would submit. We set off. Quell and I moved through the woods, back to the main trail, and then made our way along until we reached the valley again and trotted down the hill to the village. We came across a patrol almost immediately, and the first test of our disguise was on us before I really felt ready. The four Raised who approached us lifted their weapons, guarded and ready for combat. Quell hung back as we had agreed. I bore some resemblance to one of Kroll fanatical commanders. In the darkness especially I would be convincing, or so Dela had hoped. We also had to rely on the mirror that Cellin had used being a rarity, and that knowledge of my allegiance was not widely spread.

As the Raised made their way towards us, unhurried but purposeful, I attempted to command them.

"*HALT!*" I made no attempt to lower my voice, and it seemed to echo through the valley around the trail, the loudest sound for leagues. Even I winced inside at the cracked bell noise of it. The dead stopped in their tracks, turning their heads to look directly at my face. I had never done this before and if this failed the rest of our plan would crumble.

There was a moment, fleeting but terrifying, where I thought we had failed. I experienced a feeling as close to panic as I am capable of. I had forgotten how deeply stupid the dead can be.

It took them a moment to process the instruction, and then they lowered their weapons, and stood dumbly in the middle of the road. I had been concerned that there would be some missing element in the command of the dead that I was not capable of. Clearly my fears were unfounded.

"Leave us. Continue your patrol."

They again paused, as if attempting to translate what I had said, though I knew they must understand me. Then they turned away from us and continued their march into the dark night. We knew our disguise would work against the dead. All that was left was to test it against the living. We carried on down the trail, the burning torches of the village gate growing larger and brighter in the distance. There were two Raised guards either side of the entrance, stood still and at attention, and there were still-living cultists hanging around outside the gate, fussing over some barrels and supplies on the back of a large barrow. As we approached the barrier the guards did not move, but the two living turned to regard us. There was a man and a woman, both in the usual bedraggled dress of Kroll's cult. We made to pass them without engaging in conversation, but the woman stepped away from the cart and addressed us directly.

"Sirc? Sirc? Apologies, but may I ask your name and business?" I had hoped that the usual deference for the commanders I had seen at Estwake would discourage any questioning, but clearly I had not accounted for the paranoia generated by war. I had two choices. I could remain quiet, and run the risk of further questioning and suspicion, or I could assume the role of a superior and dismiss her questions with the arrogant air I had witnessed Kantus use during his tenure as my commander.

"I am Sire Seth, and this is Drenk, out of Estwake. Lord Kroll has asked that I inspect the border conquests before we push into Avania. Although I do not see how that is any of your concern."

I put as much authority into my voice as I could muster, assuming the persona of a commanding officer. I had performed such a role in life, so it was not a great stretch for me. The woman looked puzzled, her malnourished and diseased face wrinkling into a frown, and she pushed one lank and greasy length of blond hair out of her face before responding.

"My apologies, Sire. We were not expecting anyone tonight. I thought I knew all the Greater Raised, Sire... I don't think I've encountered you before."

"A lapse of memory on your part does not give you the right to question *me.* Let us pass else your disrespect will be reported to our Master." Now I tried to let anger sound in my voice. I found it difficult. My emotions are not easy for me to display and faking them is doubly trying. I would not make a great touring player.

"Of course Sire," she said, averting her eyes from me completely and adopting a grovelling tone, "please accept my most humble apologies..." she backed away, turning to her companion and giving him a nudge with her elbow so that he hurriedly lowered his head alongside hers.

I neither accepted not rejected her apology. I needed to let her see that such niceties were beneath me. Quell and I moved towards the gate. The Raised at either side of the entrance stepped forwards and brandished their weapons, but I simply said, 'Let us pass". They resumed their positions with no resistance. Quell and I entered

Rafe.

The village was not lit well inside the wooden wall. There were a few torches dotted here and there for the convenience of the living, but this was now a place of the dead, and they took priority. Rafe did not look as if it had been a prosperous place. Its buildings were mostly of wood, with some having stone foundations and chimneys, and others being little more than shabby huts. It seemed to have been bedraggled and run-down before the dead had even arrived to claim it. We made our way to the centre of the village unchallenged. There were dead soldiers standing at attention at almost every corner but they did not move or question our presence. In the middle of Rafe there was a circular well, surrounded by a low stone wall and covered with an angled wooden roof. The rope and pulley that should have let the villagers draw water was broken, and the bar across the top of the well dangled into its open mouth, swaying gently in the light breeze that blew out of the dark sky. The well was surrounded by a roughly paved area, which had likely served as the main square of the village. On this uneven stone ground the remains of a funeral pyre hissed and popped, some small streams of smoke still rising from it. A few cult members were scurrying to-and-fro on their final errands of the day. It was nearly midnight now and the time of the living was reaching its end.

I dismounted from my horse, with some assistance from Quell, and I tied its bridle to a hitching post at one side of the smouldering pyre. Quell stood and looked down at the remains, his face hard and unreadable. We made our way around the defiled square to a large building, that looked like it could be a modest village hall. Where the stone of the square ended and the bare ground began, I could see trails that led to the door of the hall, as if feet had been dragged through the churned mud. I guessed this was our goal. Two Raised soldiers stood guard at the entrance, both armed with long polearms topped with rusted hooked blades. They crossed their weapons over the weather-beaten wooden doors of the hall as we approached, but at a command from me they withdrew their threat and stood silent and still. We entered.

We came into a long room with a tall, steepled ceiling, supported by a worm-eaten and ancient looking wooden frame. This had clearly been a meeting hall of some kind, but the long tables and benches that had served as furniture for feast days had been pushed to the sides. The rotted floorboards had been ripped up and the foundations dug out. Just like in the villages I had raided in Tresh, the hall had been repurposed as a birthing pool for Kroll's undead servants. The pit in the centre of the room had been filled with the foul and sorcerous Blood of R'Chun. Next to the pool was the customary cauldron, a smaller cousin of the one in Estwake, and this sat on a fire that made the caustic, flesh-stripping contents bubble and boil. There were two cult members in the room. One of them attended the pot, stirring it with a long-forked pole, occasionally lifting remains from the surface of the liquid to inspect the progress of the rendering process. The other was nearer to the door, against the right-hand wall, and he was moving bodies onto a pile, stacking the corpses in an orderly fashion and inspecting their condition. These were to be Lesser Raised, and he was assessing the work needed to repair them and make them ready for battle. This man looked up from his work as we entered the room and he frowned, his face alternating between subservience and confusion. He made to bow his head but did not take his eyes off us. We were unexpected, and we needed to act quickly lest we lose the advantage we had.

Quell paced quickly towards the pot-stirrer, while I moved to the man shifting corpses. A great-hammer is not a stealthy weapon, so I had left it slung at my back. Instead, I drew a dagger from beneath my cloak, one I had procured from the Warden's equipment, and I held it down at my side out of sight as I approached the industrious cultist. He stood up, and something about the way I was moving must have given him a slight warning, as he started to back away. He stumbled a little on the outstretched arm of a dead man at his feet. As he glanced down to check his footing, I lunged forwards and thrust my dagger up under his ribcage, clamping my other gloved hand over his mouth as I did so and stifling his cry of pain and alarm. Quell had reached the cauldron by then, and the pot-stirrer started to look up as the Apostle reached around his head to grip the man's face from behind and slice a blade across his throat. Blood sprayed across the cauldron, and when it touched the surface of the boiling white froth it hissed and sizzled. Quell's victim fell to the ground, dropping his forked stirrer as he did so, and Quell caught it before it tipped out of the cauldron and clattered on the remains of the wooden floor. He gave me a wry look as he lowered the implement to the ground, and then made the Sign of the Wave over the body at his feet, muttering a small quiet prayer as he did so. I had a momentary urge to do the same, although I did not particularly wish to ask for forgiveness.

We were alone in the hall then. Quell moved away from the Cauldron and knelt at the edge of the black pool. He reached inside his cloak and withdrew a small glass bottle from a pouch at his belt. He began to chant under his breath, low prayers and pleadings to Omma T'Lassa, and as he muttered, he removed the stopper from the bottle and began pouring its contents into the foul pit. The reaction was almost instantaneous. The dark liquid of the pool began to churn and roil, sending off green flashes and sparks of light where the contents touched its surface. A stream of milky, pearlescent fluid ran from the bottle, and I resolved to ask Quell about its provenance. The Blood of R'Chun moved as if it was trying to get away from the interloping liquid, becoming concave where the substance poured into its mass. A gale sprang up inside the hall, invisible whispers and cries rushing around the room and whipping our cloaks against us. A wave rushed out from the point where the stream entered the pool, forming a wide circle, until repeated waves lapped at the edges of the pit and met with the dirt of the dug-out ground.

The bottle emptied. Quell just stood there, watching the growing results of his efforts. The pool became still, the waves subsiding until the surface was like glass, and then it became dull and dry, and cracked in many places. Quell drew his dagger again and knelt by the results of his work, tapping the dark material with the tip of the blade. It was now like black mud in a drought-riven and crusted riverbed. Seemingly satisfied, Quell stood and nodded to me. We left the hall, the first part of our mission completed. This was to be the least violent part of the night.

The skeletons guarding the doors to the hall had not moved from their post and ignored us as we made our exit. I had been concerned that the noises of violence and the eerie wind that had blown through the building would have aroused their suspicions, but thankfully they lacked initiative like all their kind and were too dull-minded to investigate.

We made our way through the small village. The dead still stood guard or remained in their small formations, but the living had gone to their stolen beds, and the settlement was silent. We stole past the dumb Raised guards and crept through the few bare patches of ground between dwelling places, too small and ragged to be called streets. We entered houses and huts and killed those we found sleeping inside as quickly and efficiently as we could. My leather gloves were left soaked with the blood of Kroll's cultists. Some were still awake when I gained entrance but did not overcome the initial shock of my presence quickly enough to defend themselves, my appearance confusing the living as much as the dead. Others remained asleep, only a couple of them waking momentarily as I cut their throats, the last thing they saw in the dim moonlight being my leering visage looming over them. Even to those inured to the sight of the dead I must have seemed like something from a night-terror. I recalled the shame and horror I had felt at being part of Kroll's raids, the atrocities I had seen and partaken in. I felt none of that shame as Quell and I carried out our grisly task. There was a cold void then where my heart would have been, and it held no pity for these ravagers.

Quell's skill with blade and stealth shocked me. He was all but invisible as he made his way into each stolen home. Even with my superior night-sight I found it difficult to keep track of his movements. I wondered at this, resolving to question him on his history when the opportunity presented itself. For a supposedly holy man he seemed very well versed in the dark art of assassination.

The last building we came to was a large barn near the rear of the village. This was where the bulk of the Raised soldiers were being stored. Next to the barn, butted up against one of its wooden walls, was a cage of moaning, shambling Lessers, who shuffled towards us as we approached and reached out from between the twine bars of their enclosure. We ignored them and walked towards the barn doors, which were open. As we entered the building the first rank of the Raised stored there turned their heads to regard me but did not move to attack or even raise their weapons. I left them to their fugue and stepped back outside. We noted the barn's position and then made our way back to the well in the village square. I retrieved and mounted my horse, and then we left the village, passing the guards at the front gate without any hint of suspicion or response. We made our way back up the trail, out of the valley, back to the treeline and the waiting Wardens.

We hid either side of the path through the forest, taking cover behind trees and crouching in the undergrowth. The first patrol returned after a little while and as they passed, we leapt from our hiding places, Bor, Fenna Quell and myself on one side, Wyrin and her cut-throat posse on the other. We outnumbered the patrol more than two-to-one. I had my hammer in my hands then, and swung overhead at the rearmost Raised, crushing his skull to dust and shards with my first blow. Bor cut the legs out from under another and stamped its forehead as it lay on the ground, grunting with the effort. Soon all four Raised were in pieces strewn across the narrow path, and the Wardens quickly gathered up the remains and threw them into the surrounding woods. We resumed our positions. As each patrol came back to Rafe we repeated our actions, receiving only minor injuries and bruises in return. Wyrin's reavers were accomplished killers, and their history of banditry showed clearly. They were used to this type of work and ambushed their enemies in concert, with no need for thought, and no hesitation. By the small hours of the morning the Wardens were becoming tired, and we headed back through the forest to their camp and wagon. The living took some well-deserved rest. Wyrin remained on guard for the first watch, and would not let me be alone while the rest slept. She sat on a log, staring at me and playing with her dagger. It would be an uphill struggle to earn her trust.

We remained camped for the rest of the following day. I had talked at council about the process of refreshment, and I estimated that the dead had a few days of function before beginning to fail in their tasks. It was near midnight on the third day when Quell and I returned to the village, followed a little way behind by Fenna and the rest of the Wardens. They skulked down alongside the path, through the tall grasses and weeds that filled the valley. As we approached I saw that the skeletal guards that had held the gate to Rafe were missing. We entered the village unmolested, and found the two Raised inside the gate, standing and staring in opposite directions. Their swords were still in their hands, held limply at their sides. I walked up to the nearest and leaned in to look directly into his eye sockets. The green glow common to our kind was still visible, but he did not respond to my presence. I reached out, grabbing his jaw, and he still did not respond. He had been active with no respite for too long and had descended into complete idiocy. I pushed hard against his face, and he tumbled to the ground. Quell did the same with his counterpart. Then I used my hammer to crush both their heads, the sharp report of their cracking skulls echoing in the silence of the village. Still there was no other sound. Quell stepped back outside the gate and beckoned the others through.

We found Raised in various states throughout the small enclave. Some were frozen in place. The guards outside the main hall were clutched in an embrace, lying on the ground in front of its doors. They had their hands at each other's throats, and were attempting to silently strangle one another, a futile activity against an opponent with no windpipe. Bor and one of the other Wardens had to pry them apart, and their fingers flexed and grasped in the air as if they still had murderous intent. They were laid down and their heads were destroyed.

We reached the barn acting as an undead barracks, and several of the Wardens entered. The dead did not respond to their presence, and the men and women began to cut down the skeletal soldiers one by one, destroying them as quickly as they could. As the Wardens performed their grim task the Lessers in the cage outside the barn began to wail and moan. Bor and another Warden fetched barrels of pitch to the cage and poured it over the twine bars, emptying as much as they could over the shuffling animated bodies inside. One of the Wardens lit a torch and then touched it against the now extremely flammable prison. Most of the Lessers were immolated without any hope of escape, screaming and clawing at each other as they burned. As the structure of the cage began to give way some of the dead managed to stagger from the blaze, their hair and skin flaming and blackening, and the Wardens had to stand back from the conflagration and cut them down as the survivors approached. The Lessers couldn't move quickly enough to avoid the Warden's blows, or even show the sense to try, and their ligaments and muscles contracted with the heat of the flames, limiting their movements even further than usual.

We searched the rest of Rafe before we left and did not leave a single Raised capable of combat. The village was now a charnel house, and I could not imagine the living wishing to inhabit it again.

The journey back to Oese was nearly silent, the harsh jokes and tall tales of the Wardens hardly seeming appropriate after the sights they had seen. The Wardens were a hardy bunch, and used to violence, but theirs had been a morbid and macabre task and it had soured their mood.

The remains of Rafe were a stark reminder for them of what had befallen their homes and driven them west. The weather at least had relented a little, and we made fairly good time, partly because we could discard some aspects of stealth and just make haste for the border. No one wanted to remain in the wilderness for longer than they had to. When we finally made it back to Oese the Wardens dispersed after being allowed entrance to the city, not wanting to make straight for the Wailing Sailor lest they expose their sanctuary. Instead, they disappeared into the crowds, while Bor, Fenna, Quell and I made our way to Yast's hall to meet with Dela and report our success. He greeted us with relief, hugging Fenna and shaking Bor's hand, congratulating them on returning safely. Quell retired to his requisitioned chambers after giving a nod of respect to both the Councillor and me. Bor and Fenna left to get baths and clean clothes, Yast's servants running ahead of them to prepare their ablutions. Dela and I were left in his quarters, and I sat down on my cot after removing my cloak and armour. Dela fetched me a damp cloth so that I could clean my exposed bone, and he asked a servant to take my clothing and have it laundered. The servant made no attempt to enter our room. Word of my presence had already spread via the web of gossip and whispers that any workplace harboured.

Dela and I went over the events in Rafe.

"My disguise worked well, but we were lucky that no Greater Raised were present. I do not believe that my subterfuge would stand up to scrutiny from one of their number… however now we know that their pools can be destroyed, and their nests eradicated."

Dela had managed to procure a bottle of wine and a glass from one of the passing servants, and sipped at his drink slowly, swirling the liquid in its container and staring into its scarlet depths. "Yes. Yes, that is correct. It has given me another concern though."

He frowned, and shook his head a little, as if he were struggling to voice his fears. I waited patiently, and finally he sighed and looked at me.

"Asheth, I know you are finding the Temple a great comfort. They have given you sanctuary and reinforced your purpose. I do not wish to undermine this. But let me ask you this… how did they know how to fight the dead?"

I sat back a little. I must admit, this had not occurred to me. Dela swam in dark and treacherous waters as a matter of course, it was his natural habitat, and he questioned everything from a paranoid viewpoint. I was then, perhaps, naïve of such matters, and had not considered if I was being told the whole story.

"I am not sure what you mean, Councillor. Quell carried the Mother's blessing with him, but he felt he had to test it."

"Yes, of course. Except... his weapons, the silvered blades he carries... they were the only ones that affected the, ah, spirits, demons, that attacked us in Cellin's quarters. Of all of us he seems the most comfortable with your presence, apart from perhaps the First Daughter, after she overcame her initial shock. I question whether the Temple knows more than it has shared with us."

I thought on it for a moment.

"If that is true, Dela, why would they lie, or at least omit the truth?"

"I don't know, Asheth. I have spent some time trying to convince the Council of the threat, and only your presence finally forced them to accept the truth. Yet if the Temple knew that the undead existed, why would they not investigate my warnings immediately? I don't have an answer right now. But it needs addressing."

We returned to the Wailing Sailor the next evening, again taking a winding route so as not to give up the Warden's hiding place. Gerta and her husband scurried around fetching beer and food for the gathered Wardens and pointedly ignoring me, guessing correctly that I no longer required it. That is if she would have served me at all. I had taken up my position in the corner of the room, the least lit spot I could find. Quell sat alongside me, and although I was glad of his support, Dela's suspicions of the Temple lurked at the back of my mind. I tried not to let my concerns affect my interactions with the warrior priest. My dead face helped me to hide my worries, another unsought advantage of my strange nature.

When food had been eaten and beer drunk, Dela led a discussion of the outcome at Rafe.

"It appears we have at least the beginnings of a strategy to fight the undead. Asheth's assessment at Council was correct. If we can remove the head, the body will die of its own accord." He took a sip from the glass of wine Gerta had placed in front of him. Beer was not to Dela's taste.

"This will take time, and we cannot always rely on the subterfuge Asheth and Quell employed to enter Rafe. They cannot be everywhere. We will need to assemble small mixed forces, so each part of the army being raised will include a contingent of Wardens for reconnaissance and assassination purposes, as well as having a member of Quell's Order present to destroy any more birthing pools."

Wyrin stood up, having obviously assumed the

role of spokeswoman. I caught sight of Fenna turning to Bor and rolling her eyes.

"If you don't have any more corpse-pets knocking around, Dela, any attempt to get into another town will be a bloodbath. Rafe was small. The larger towns won't be so easy."

"I am aware of that, Wyrin. I am meeting with Councillor Yast so we can discuss tactics for dealing with the larger infestations. We won't be able to do it on our own."

The rest of the meeting concerned the breaking up of the Wardens into detachments, so that they could be added to the gathering army of the Regions. I stayed silent, not wishing to cause any more trouble than my presence already had. When it was over, we headed back to Yast's hall, and awaited an audience with him.

Yast was pleased with the results of the mission, although he was still not overjoyed at the presence of Dela's Wardens in his city. I was left in my room while the two Councillors discussed how to move forwards. The spread of Kroll's forces was too broad for me to be present at every engagement. We needed to strike many places at once, although Salisson remained the priority in the short term. Quell had gone to the local Temple of the Mother and was awaiting the arrival of more members of his strange militant order. He had also instructed the local priests to gather men and women from as many of the temples in Avania as they could. All would be required to accompany the missions into Salis and perform the same cleansing ritual that Quell had used in Rafe.

When Quell returned I asked to speak with him in private. Initially I asked him about matters of faith but then led the conversation towards how he came to be an Apostle. I wanted to know more about him, and in the process perhaps find out what the Temple was hiding. He was reticent to share any detail.

"I was a man of low morals. I worked for evil men and performed acts of violence on their behalf." His voice was still a whisper, almost a growl. He never seemed to speak louder than that, unless he was roaring prayers in combat.

"And the Temple... you joined it to get away from them?"

"I am a penitent. I joined the Temple to pay for the acts I had committed, and to wash myself clean in the waters of Omma T'Lassa. You are a penitent as well. The Temple accepts men and women like us, so that we can be cleansed. That doesn't mean we cannot fight for the Mother, if we have the skill."

"Even if we have committed acts of great evil?" I thought of the raids in Tresh. I thought of the children I had given to slavery, and the men and women I had killed.

"The sea is not good, or evil. It simply is. Evil is something *people* intend or do. The sea does not judge. It feeds life or it provides death. Both are part of its nature. The tide rises and falls, and washes over all."

"And what of the bottle you used to destroy the pool? What did it contain, where did it come from?"

"That is the Milk of T'Lassa. We do not share its origin outside the Order."

He fell silent then and would not be drawn further.

CHAPTER FIFTEEN

The campaign to retake Salis began.

I was given the horse that I had ridden at Rafe, which had grown a little more accustomed to me. Quell was provided with his own mount. A great caravan had been gathered. There were soldiers, raw recruits and guardsmen assembled from several different regions, a riot of different uniforms, armament and dispositions. It had been agreed that Captain Francyn was to be General, and I would act as one of his advisors alongside Dela. Yast was to remain in Oese and continue to raise recruits and gather resources. Francyn had made the journey to Avania not long after us, and he had brought a significant portion of the Western Gate Guard with him. They wore plate armour and mail, with tabard coverings of pale sand and gold trim. Yast's guard also assembled, their armour of a similar standard but with deep red cloth for their colours and their helmets crested with ostentatious sprays of black feathers. Alongside them the Wardens tried to appear as much like part of an army as they could, mostly failing in their attempt. Their numbers had grown again, with more and more of them making their way into Avania over the last moon, and they were split into small detachments to accompany the varied divisions.

Quell had gathered a handful of the Apostles, all dressed in similar silver plate, but armed with a variety of wicked and idiosyncratic weaponry; a mix of strange, curved swords, polearms, daggers, clawed gauntlets, and other vicious armaments that I did not recognise. The warrior priest only introduced one other of his order to me, a short, square-jawed woman called Chasten, who had a pair of small silver hand-axes dangling at her hips. She wore her red hair in one long braid, tied up into a spiral hill on her head and held in place with two long silver pins. She regarded me with cool and cruel green eyes, and only nodded acknowledgement of me when we were introduced, choosing not to speak. There was a scar running down across her lips, a slash that looked like a duelling injury. I nodded to her in return, exaggerating the motion as I had my hood up and mask on. As she walked back to join the rest of the waiting Apostles I asked Quell about her name, which seemed odd to me.

"We take new names when we join the Order. We choose them, to represent the change in our intent and purpose. Quell is not the name I was born with. I am not the man who had that name anymore. Chasten is not the person she was either."

Quell left me then, to begin assigning the other Apostles to their detachments.

Outside the city walls, the timber and mechanisms for siege weaponry had been cut and constructed and was being loaded onto long wheeled trestles drawn by teams of horses. The engineering skills of the Regions had advanced a great deal since the time of my death, but weapons of this type had not been constructed or used for hundreds of years, apart from on the privateer ships - and their armament was of a smaller and more specialised type. Many scrolls holding designs for these weapons had to be retrieved from dusty shelves in ancient libraries and handed to the craftsmen of Oese and the surrounding towns. Arms and supports for catapults were stacked together with siege crossbows and baskets filled with bolts and fittings that would need assembly at our target destinations. Counterweights would need to be added when they were constructed, gathered from what stone could be found near their final emplacements. The head for a ram had also been made, cast in dark metal, a cone-shaped cap for a log that would need to be found when we neared a suitable target.

Alongside the armoured guards of the regions were detachments of pikemen, men-at-arms, and a regiment of crossbowmen who had been supplied with quickly built replicas of the Wardens' armament. Training had been hasty and not comprehensive, and many of the men and women in these ranks wore faces that were grey and drawn and filled with unease. There were bowmen as well, but the military practice of training ranged fighters had been lost a little over the years, and most of these were conscripted hunters from villages across Avania.

A covered wagon near the back of the caravan carried a pigeon roost, so that communication with Councillor Yast could be maintained and supplies and reinforcements requested if necessary.

Our tactics were to be simple. The army was to be split into three detachments. The first would travel to the northernmost area of Salis and begin to cleanse the villages and towns there. The second would travel the same path the scouting Wardens and I had taken to Rafe and then push further inland, attempting to cross Salis entirely and get to the border of Tresh opposite, destroying all undead they found on the way and cutting the Region into northern and southern halves.

The final detachment, of which Quell and I were a part, would be led by General Francyn, and would push along the Coast Road to Salisson. There the Privateer Fleet, led by Captain Shand and his colleagues, would help us to take back the port. The Wardens, led by a number of Captains from different parts of Salis, would lead assassination missions while the main bulk of the army would draw out the undead forces, feinting where they could, to refuse engagements and avoid any protracted battles. I had helped devise some ways to remove the dead's advantages, but these had yet to be tested. The first such test would be at Hust, a small fishing town a few leagues or so along the Coast Road from Avania's border. Our third of the campaign caravan lined up outside the walls of Oese, and I rode in the vanguard ahead of more than two thousand men and women, soldiers, engineers and labourers, alongside General Francyn and his officers, Quell, Fenna and Bor. I was still in my disguise as a bodyguard, but now assigned to the General. He did not converse with me, still uncomfortable in my presence, and Quell was as silent as ever, but Fenna and Bor more than made up for his reticence to speak. They were openly affectionate in front of me now, often speaking to each other as if they were a married couple, and I even felt relaxed enough to tease them a little.

"When are you going to let Bor make an honest woman of you?" I was also taking the opportunity to practice my speech, so that I could converse without sounding like a cracked bell.

"Heh, he'll never manage that. He's hardly an honest man is he... he was a thief and a brute when I first met him, and he hasn't changed a bit..."

General Francyn resolutely pretended not to hear and simply stared down the road ahead of him. Bor bristled with mock outrage.

"Now listen Fenna, I've come a long fuckin' way. Look at us, marchin' with an army! I could be a respectable man now, I'm a soldier!"

"You've all the discipline of a wild pig. And the smell to match sometimes."

Bor sniffed under his arm and shook his head. "Aww, get away, it's fine. I had a bath the other day. I've just been workin' hard. Bit o'fuckin sweat never hurt anyone."

"I am glad I do not have a sense of smell." I said, and Bor gave me a dirty look while Fenna lifted the reins of her horse so she could stifle her giggles. "That being said, you are correct Bor. On campaign everyone smells. Getting clean is next to impossible. Although I do remember, there was one lad under my command who smelled of fish, all the time. The other soldiers called him Netty. Some of the officers did as well, behind tent flaps. No one would bunk with him in the end."

"What did you do about it?" asked Fenna.

"Do? Nothing. What can you do? Ordering him to wash did not help. We found out after the campaign that he had been carrying rotten fish guts in his shirt all the time. Turned out, he liked having a tent to himself, and he did not have a sense of smell either."

I heard a muffled snort from ahead of us, and could see that General Francyn's shoulders were shaking, although he did not turn around.

We set up camp just a short march from Hust. Sentries were posted, a mass of tents were raised, and the caravan of supplies and workers that marched with the army dished out rations of food and watered-down beer. The memories, the feelings of nostalgia I had, were almost overwhelming. I could have been on campaign in Sechia, nearly 400 years before. My reveries left me in a pensive mood. I was not at liberty to walk around the camp, still being, if just technically, a prisoner of Francyn's. I stayed in my tent, and read some books that Dela had gifted me, which

I had brought in lieu of the rations and supplies another soldier might have carried. They were recent histories of the Regions, and treatises on mechanics, alchemy, engineering, and art, part of an education I was determined to give myself so I would not be wrong-footed by any advances I encountered. Devouring this knowledge helped to steady my mind and gain at least the illusion of control over my situation. We had camped right on top of the cliffs, to the right of the Coast Road, and the sound of the sea and the surf crashing against the rocks below was soothing to me. I could also hear the revelry and loud voices of the camp soldiers, and this reminder of life helped me greatly. I had requested my tent be turned so that the opening faced the sea, and this allowed me to watch the ocean tide advance and recede in the moonlight until the sun came up.

Hust was a centre for the fishing trade in Salis, and its loss represented a significant part of the food supply for the Region, as well as a strategic opportunity for Francyn's army to establish their own supply lines. If we did not take it back from the dead, we would be leaving an enemy force at our rear when we moved on Salisson. The town had a harbour, smaller than Salisson's, and on the side nearest to us there was a long, rocky promontory extending out into the Scar Sea, that served as a barrier to both the sea's fury and our advance. Over the years the defences the town had employed in more war-like times had fallen into disrepair. It no longer boasted a moat of any kind, and even the ditch surrounding its walls had been filled in and built on, so just like Salisson its dwelling places and merchant buildings extended outside its original perimeter. However, the rocks that extended out to the sea also formed part of its walls, and surrounded the main gate, which was a stout construction of iron and thick wood. The rock had been mined through so the Coast Road funnelled straight towards this armoured entrance. This made the approach to the gate narrow and would make it harder for Francyn to bring his forces to bear. A scouting foray by some of the Wardens reported back that the dead had procured their own ranged weaponry, as bow-armed skeletons were visible along the crenelated walls of the town, and there had been a sighting of at least one of the ornately armoured Greater Raised. This meant any subterfuge, like the kind Quell and I had employed at Rafe, would fail, as my disguise would not stand up to the scrutiny of one of Kroll's fanatical commanders. A direct assault would be time consuming and costly.

I was asked to join Francyn and his officers in his command tent. I stayed in the shadows. They had been advised of my nature but I wanted to minimise their disturbance at my presence.

Fenna remained with me, as an escort of sorts, and in her capacity as Captain of the Wardens.

"We cannot be drawn into a protracted siege. The dead soldiers inside Hust vastly outnumber their living handlers, so they do not need the resources we do. Any extended delay will act in their favour, as they can out-wait us, out-supply us. We would lose momentum too quickly while Kroll builds his armies." I addressed General Francyn, again trying to quiet my voice as much as I could. Alongside Francyn stood Ulrich, Commander of the Avanian Guard, a tall, thin man with lank blonde hair. He hadn't taken his eyes off me for a while, and his mouth gaped like a fish when I spoke. I had not really taken to the man, but he seemed competent enough, if a little too easily startled.

"What do you propose?" Francyn leant onto the table in front of him. Laid across it was a roughly sketched map of the town that Fenna had provided. His hands splayed over the paper, his head tilted up towards me.

"There's a farmer's gate here," Fenna said, pointing to an area at the northern tip of the town, "it's surrounded by stables, a few huts. It's not big enough to get an army through, but it's hard to defend, there's a lot of cover outside the walls. My scouts say there are guards but they're thin on the ground. If the Wardens can get in here, we might be able to get to the main gate and open it from the inside. We'll have to be fast. Once we've opened it we'll have every Raised in the place after us."

"You will need a distraction." I said, and pointed to the main gate. "General, we need to bombard the gate. Set up your siege weapons here- " and I gestured to a clearing a little way in front of the gate, an open patch of ground that crossed the Coast Road, " -and your regiments alongside. We need to keep the enemy focused on the gate and draw as many away from the other walls as we can to give Fenna and her people the best chance of quiet access. If she can get the gate open, we can draw them out of the town. They will be funnelled by the walls and fighting on a narrow front. We cannot let them encircle us... we will need to withdraw when the time is right."

"It's going to be bloody work." Francyn looked weary already.

"It is. I am going in with Fenna and the Wardens. I confuse the dead. It may give Fenna the edge she needs."

Francyn stared at me, and then shook his head. He dismissed the rest of the tent, leaving just Fenna and myself.

"Asheth. I need you here. I've never done this before... no one in the Regions has done this in hundreds of years. We are not warmongers. I apologise for being so impersonal, but if you fall, we lose a valuable asset, and I would miss your counsel."

I stepped forwards out of the shadows, and into the circle of lamplight that lit Francyn and the table in front of him.

"General… I have only known you a short while, but in that time, I have already been impressed with your competence and fortitude. I have every faith that you can lead this army to victory, and simply put, I cannot stand by while others fight. Anyway, I have found so far that I am… remarkably hard to kill."

He gave a small, rueful smile.

Francyn acquiesced in the end, seeing that I was stubborn in my intentions and would not be content to wait in my tent as others risked themselves. I joined Fenna and the rest of the Wardens who had been assigned to Francyn's force, and Quell joined as well, to lend his skills in banishment to our mission. There were around twenty of us. We were to gain entrance to Hust just before sunset, when Francyn would commence his bombardment. It was a risk beginning the battle at night, but Fenna would need the assistance of the darkness. The dead have better vision after dark than the living, but often do not have the initiative to act on it. They make for poor sentries. We bound ourselves in dark cloaks and moved on foot, so we could pass through the night with as much stealth as possible.

We took a long and winding path through the surrounding countryside and made our way to the infested town. The terrain around Hust was far more heavily patrolled than it had been at Rafe. The smaller village had just been an outpost, a staging point for further progress in Kroll's expansion. Hust was a major hub for his invasion and would likely be filled with the dead, and the Greater Raised commanders were far more competent than Kroll's insane living followers. We had to go to ground often as the marching dead stomped past us on trails and paths through the forests and hills. We finally reached a thicket of trees on a hill, overlooking the northern end of Hust. We were high enough that we could see the whole town laid out, our vantage point giving us a slowly darkening view of thatched and slate roofs, smokeless chimneys, streets and squares, inns and market stalls, rolling all the way down to the harbour and the distant whisper of the ocean beyond. There were lights dotted here and there through the town, lamps and torches left burning for its few living inhabitants, but most of the buildings were dark inside and were lit only by the low-risen moon and the slowly dying glow of the setting sun.

Clustered around the northern entrance of Hust

were a collection of stables and modest wooden huts, and a small, paved area that lay just before the barred gate. We could see the dead at guard on either side of the gate, just a handful of them. More stood at the ramparts above, their quivers full of arrows visible in silhouette against the darkening sky. The defence here was stronger than I had hoped. A wide path led from the forest we occupied and down to the farmer's entrance, and it meandered through the hills behind us to fields of crops and grazing pastures used to feed Hust's inhabitants.

We had to wait for the sun to set completely before we heard the first sounds of Francyn's attack. The distant booms of stone missiles striking the main gate and the surrounding walls echoed around the hills behind us, making it difficult to tell where the sound was coming from. The skeletons guarding the outside of the gate remained at their posts, but there was movement on the ramparts, and we saw shadows run to the waiting bow-armed dead and then move away, ordering them to follow. This was our signal to begin moving towards the rear door. We scrambled down the hillside next to the farmer's trail as quickly as we could, still cloaked and difficult to see in the undergrowth. The guards did not notice us until we were already amongst the out-buildings, and we charged from the sides of the stables and huts and engaged the enemy. There were a dozen armed Raised to rebuff our incursion, but some of the Wardens carried crossbows, Fenna amongst them, and the shooters fell to one knee and put a dent in the dead's numbers before we even reached their line. The sound of their bolts cracking skulls open echoed from the walls. The stricken Raised fell to the ground, all animation drained from them instantly, but their fellows ignored the casualties and brandished their swords in response to our advance.

We fought in the shadow of Hust's walls. The bloodlust took me as it had on Shand's ship, and I let out a roar in my hollow voice, all thoughts of stealth momentarily absent. I had unhooked my hammer from my back, and I swung it in a wide arc. I broke the sword of one Raised as it tried to block my blow, and the deflection was not enough to stop me from shattering its skull. I followed the momentum of my weapon and spun with it, crouching low to bring it around again at knee level, and one of the dead was lifted from his feet and slapped onto his back. I brought the hammer up over my head and brought it down on his ribcage as he tried to get back up. His ribs exploded, shards of bone flying across the stone paving and spattering against my chest plate.

Alongside me Bor was grinning, never happier than when in the fight. He moved like an animal, muscled and lithe, pouncing when he needed to strike, darting back away from blows, then moving back in to slash with his sword and kick with his heavy boots. He wrestled one of the dead so that the skeleton's arms were pinned against his sides, and then head-butted it, breaking its jaw and sending teeth flying. As his victim reeled from the vicious attack Bor removed its head with a casual backswing and then turned to seek another unlucky opponent. His face was bleeding, he had a tooth embedded in the skin of his forehead, and he was smiling from ear to ear, overjoyed to be in battle.

The fight didn't last much longer. Quell crushed the skull of the last Raised under his boot and then we stopped so the Wardens could take a breath. We had no losses but one of the men in the group was bleeding heavily from a wound on his arm and Fenna went to check on him.

"Brack, you still with us?" She dragged a length of cloth out of her pack to use as a dressing and began to bind the wound, wrapping it tightly across the pale man's upper arm to try to staunch the flow of blood.

"I am Captain, but I'm not sure I can raise a sword. Load a crossbow for me and I can fire. Not sure I'll be any use inside."

"That's alright Brack, we need to set a watch on this door anyway, we'll need it to get back out again. Doubt we'll be able to leave by the front gate. Menz, Liston, you two stay with Brack and hold this door. Load your crossbows and give them to him, he can shoot if you need to defend it. We'll collect you all on the way out."

Fenna turned to investigate the Farmer's door. It was smaller than the main gate but just as stout-looking, and appeared to be barred on the inside. She spoke to another of the Wardens, a cheerful woman called Rake, who had apparently also been a thief in a former life. They dragged lengths of rope from their packs, which ended in what looked like a short metal pipe. They both made small twisting motions with their hands, and from each pipe sprang three hooks, to serve as a grapnel.

"All right Rake, you ready?"

"Yes, Captain, as I'll ever be."

Both women slung their crossbows across their backs, and then swung their hooked ropes in circles, faster and faster, until finally releasing them in an upwards arc. Their aim was excellent and both caught the crenelations above on their first attempt. They had clearly done this before, and I resolved to ask Fenna to tell me more stories of her exploits. The Wardens had a very interesting set of skills. The pair of them tested their ropes and then clambered up the walls of Hust with no difficulty at all, their shadowed forms disappearing over the ramparts above without any sound or disturbance. We waited. After a little while we heard a creaking noise, followed by the gentle sound of someone carefully placing a wooden beam on the ground inside the gate. The gate opened, just enough for a single person to squeeze through, and the Wardens, Quell and I all made our way into the town. We took positions in the shadows either side of the entrance. Brack and his comrades closed the door behind us, wishing us luck as they hunkered down to cover our exit.

I had been concerned that we had made too much noise and would be discovered. Certainly, I had not been particularly quiet during the melee outside. I need not have worried. The distant sound of Francyn's strikes against the main gate had covered the clamour we had made, the heavy impacts louder now we were inside the walls. It seemed as if most of the dead inside Hust had been drawn to the defence as I had hoped. Our primary mission now was to open the gate.

We had entered into an area of the town mostly dedicated to the storage of animals and grain, a mish-mash of stables, feeding troughs, corrals and store-houses. There was a wide clear area in front of the farmer's door where cattle would usually have been gathered. This ground was covered in straw soaked with blood and the offal and entrails from slaughter, and the Wardens with me covered their noses and mouths, discomfited by the stench. Even Quell, usually stony-faced, wrinkled his nose in disgust. We moved away from this area quickly, heading further into the town, unchallenged for now but racing quickly from cover to cover to minimise our chances of discovery. We hugged the walls and lurked in the long shadows. The streets of Hust were not paved as they had been in Oese but had cobbled centres that curved down into gulleys on either side of the road. These drainage ditches ran with filthy water and rats raced along them, sniffing the air at our presence but seemingly unafraid of us. The buildings around us seemed uninhabited, and there was only the occasional flicker of a torch to show that anyone still occupied the town at all. We began to come across small gatherings of the dead, skeletons marching in formation towards the main gate to join the defence. There were also several groups on horseback, their shoes clattering on the cobblestones, the bones of their steeds gleaming in the darkness. Kroll and his followers had worked hard to increase the number of cavalrymen they could field.

We were hidden opposite one long, low building, some kind of merchant's warehouse, when we heard a noise inside, a cry loud enough to be heard over the distant bombardment. Fenna and I exchanged a glance and then we broke off from the rest of the Wardens and crept up to the corner of a building opposite, so that we could get a good view of the entrance. We saw it was guarded either side by a pair of the undead, both armed with long, vicious forked implements, seemingly adapted farmer's tools. The doors to the warehouse opened as we watched and one of Kroll's cultists scurried out from inside holding a torch in his hand. In the glow from its flame, we could see the interior of the building, and it was filled with children.

They cowered on the floor, naked and covered in filth, huddling together for warmth as they had not even been given blankets. Not all of them were moving. Some seemed to be lying prone on the dirty, straw-covered floor, while others held each other, the only clean spot on their faces the lines where their tears had run. I only caught a glimpse of their forlorn forms, but I knew their purpose. Kroll would need slaves and converts for his occupation.

I remembered gathering slaves myself. Back during the invasion of Tresh. I was filled with shame and fury and loathing. I could not countenance leaving these children imprisoned. I crouched next to Fenna and spoke as quietly as I could.

"We cannot leave them here. The dead will murder them before Francyn can get this far. Kroll's followers are a spiteful breed."

Fenna shook her head. "We'll try to free them on our way back. The priority has to be the gate. No-one's getting out if we can't get Francyn in." Her face was stern, visible to me even in the low light of the town, and I could see she was struggling with her own conscience. I could see the logic of her decision, but still my hand clenched tightly inside my leather gloves, and my mouth clamped together so hard that the sound of my grinding teeth must have been audible even over the noise of battle.

We left the makeshift prison behind and made our way further towards the western side of town, and the gate that met the Coast Road. We found a hiding place opposite the barbican and watched as the dead moved to man the walls and gathered in ranks before the tunnel that led to the heavy, metal-bound wooden door. There were hundreds of them, and along the walls on either side of the fortified entrance there were cages, wheeled on the bottom so they could be drawn, and filled with a writhing mass of moaning and screaming Lesser Raised. Fenna coughed and covered her mouth and nose, and I heard several of the other Wardens trying to stifle retching in the shadows. The stench of death and decay must have been overwhelming.

The dead stood in quiet ranks with swords at their sides, or long pikes held upright with rusted vicious points catching the moonlight.

Dust rained down from the town walls as they were pounded by Francyn's bombardment, and fragments of stone fell into the courtyard and shattered at the feet of the waiting Raised. The skeletal soldiers were spattered with the spall of broken masonry, flying shards and splinters of rock clattering off their bones and ringing against what little armour they wore. If Francyn's army tried to gain entrance here without assistance the attack would falter. The force of undead arrayed at the tunnel mouth would stymie any incursion. Several of Kroll's cultists fussed around the undead, running here and there to tighten armour straps and straighten ranks, behaving as if they were overbearing mothers presenting their children for apprenticeships. At the rear of all of them a dark, armoured figure, cloaked and riding a skeletal steed, trotted to-and-fro along the regiment, inspecting his army and calling out organisational orders. This was the Greater Raised who had taken Hust. I recognised him by his overly ornate apparel, and the ridiculous winged and beaked helm he wore.

It was Kantus. I felt my rage boil up inside me. I owed him a debt I intended to pay.

Fenna crept up beside me and whispered, pointing towards a low structure to one side of the barbican.

"You see that building there? That's the gate

house. There's a winch inside that controls the gate, we need to get inside and get it open."

I couldn't see how the Wardens could make it across the Courtyard. If they stepped out of their hiding place they were bound to be noticed, and the gatehouse itself was guarded, two pike-armed skeletons standing either side of its small wooden door.

"I have an idea, but I will need a distraction." I said.

We remained in conference for a moment, and then Fenna turned to Bor, and started to give instructions. Bor pointed to a few of the Wardens and they made their way back through the streets behind us, collecting torches and whatever flammable material they could. He and his fellows started to light fires, placing them carefully so they did not spread too far. The town was still damp and cold with the late winter conditions, and I hoped that this would reduce the chances of a conflagration. We intended to do as little damage to Hust as possible. I suspected some would be unavoidable.

Soon the flame and ember-flecked smoke was visible from where we were hidden, and the living cultists began to react, pulling some of the undead soldiers from their ranks to assist in fighting the blaze. The Greater Raised on horseback moved towards the rear of the courtyard as his attention was drawn by the disturbance. A path opened for us, enough of a gap in the dead's lines for us to reach the gatehouse. Getting in would be another matter entirely. Fenna and the rest of her Wardens stayed in the shadows, while Quell and I re-arranged our apparel, so that we could mimic our enemy as we had done at Rafe. Quell covered his armour and weaponry in a dark cloak, while I removed my helmet, carrying it under my arm as we approached the low stone building. As we neared the guards, I did not look around or shorten my stride, instead pacing towards them as if I belonged there, my head held up in what I hoped was an arrogant manner and my hammer still in my hand. The courtyard was a mass of confused dead and panicked living, and we made it all the way to the waiting sentinels without our presence being noted. As we finally made it to the door both skeleton guards raised their weapons, and I said "Stand down! Let us pass!" in a loud and clear voice. Again, as at Rafe, the undead's dull wits worked in our favour. The two Raised lowered their weapons and resumed their posts.

The door to the gatehouse was not locked, and we walked past the guards, who paid us no further attention, and opened the door. Inside were two of Kroll's living followers, the dead not being trusted to look after the crucial mechanism inside. They turned towards us as we entered the room and the nearest one moved towards Quell and I, obviously wrong-footed by our arrival. I cut his voiced challenge short by crushing his face with my hammer, while Quell raced towards my victim's colleague and tackled him to the ground, plunging one of his punching daggers up under the man's ribs while clamping one gloved hand over his mouth to stifle any screams. I turned and saw that the door had a bar that could be placed on the inside to lock it, and I dropped this into its slot so that we could finish our work undisturbed. Once I had secured the entrance I turned back and walked towards the gate mechanism to examine it, replacing my helmet as I did so. It was designed so it could close quickly, using a counterweight to slam the gate shut, released by a levered wooden block. Opening the gate was a slower process, requiring the winding of a ratcheted gearwheel wound with thick chain. Quell and I looked at each other, shrugged, still a difficult motion for me, and then stood either side of the large wheel and grabbed a handle each. I was able apply more strength than Quell, but he was hardly a weedy fellow, and between us we managed to get the gate mechanism moving. Almost immediately we heard a cry of alarm from outside, even over the booming sound of Francyn's attack, and we sped up, turning the wheel as quickly as we could. There was a scrabbling sound at the door to the gatehouse, followed by a panicked pounding as Kroll's cultists frantically tried to gain entrance. This was interrupted by a handful of dull cracks and thumps, as Fenna and the other Wardens started firing their crossbows from the shadows to buy us time.

Now the gate was opening Francyn's missiles were re-targeted to strike through the portal, and I heard the heavy stones bounce through the tunnel of the barbican and pound into the front ranks of the dead. Determining that the gate was open enough I looked around for something to jam the mechanism. I found a metal bar with a tapered end, evidently some kind of maintenance tool, in the detritus on the floor of the gatehouse. I forced it into the gate chain just where it fed through a hole in the low ceiling. Once inserted I used all my strength and bent the bar until it looped on itself, trying to lock the mechanism into its open position. This released the counterweight, and instead of falling and reeling out its chain, the bent bar jammed itself into the wall, making the whole assembly creak and judder to a stop.

Quell and I turned back to the barred door, where we could still hear someone trying to gain entrance. I raised my hammer as Quell stood to one side of the door, his daggers ready in his fists. I brought the hammer down against the bar, splintering it in one strike, and the door burst open. A Raised soldier crossed the threshold, and Quell struck him under the chin, hard enough to remove his skeletal face and separate it from the back of his head. The dead man fell into a bundle of bones across the doorway and blocked the entrance for his comrades behind him. I charged across his prone form, hammer first, and barrelled into a group of the dead, scattering them with the impact. Quell followed close behind. I swept my hammer in wide arcs, trying to clear a path for us. The dead fought back but we had regained the initiative, and both Quell and I were able to take advantage of their startled state. We focused on movement rather than combat, and I tried to keep my bloodlust in check as we forced our way through the mass of bones. As we advanced I saw several of the Raised fall with crossbow bolts protruding from their cracked skulls, Fenna and the others helping to provide us with an exit route. We made it back to where the Wardens lurked in the shadows, and I turned around to see the results of our efforts.

The courtyard was in chaos and disarray. The neat ranks of skeletons had been broken, Francyn's strikes having driven a wedge into their lines, and their living commanders were struggling to restore order. Several of the cultists seemed to be arguing about what to do and were issuing conflicting instructions. Their attempts at re-establishing discipline were floundering.

I heard hooves on cobblestones and Kantus entered the courtyard and began to bellow orders. Even with his booming voice he was struggling to make himself heard above the din.

In the distance, outside the town walls, there was the faint sound of horns, cutting through the cacophony. This was Francyn's command to advance. Now our role within the town changed. With the gate open, our mission became one of assassination, while Francyn tried to apply the tactics I had suggested.

The cultists began to wheel the cages containing the Lessers to the barbican tunnel, intending to unleash their rotten contents into Francyn's advancing army. They opened the cage doors and began to herd their charges towards the gates with long-pronged forks. The Lessers loped towards our lines, ignoring the last few stones lobbed towards them by Francyn's catapults, and filled the Coast Road from side to side between the rocky walls that funnelled out from Hust's main gate. They moved as if they were one writhing, many limbed beast. As the rotten horde shambled down the narrow road, clawing the air and howling in animal rage, Francyn's men lay in wait for them.

Oese, like many of the settlements along the Northern Shore, had long experience in fishing, and the tools they used for this work were well-made and sturdy, having been perfected over many generations. I had suggested bringing some of this equipment along. As the decaying corpses shambled towards Francyn's lines a watching scout blew a high whistle, and two teams of men hiding at either side of the pass heaved on ropes that had been obscured by the mud and undergrowth. As the ropes grew taut, they raised a long, wide net across the road, and the idiotic dead ran into it, filling it as if they were a good day's catch. As the first of the Lessers got caught in its tangled weave the rest piled up behind them, and soon there was a crushing, writhing mass of decaying animated corpses struggling to reach the warm meat of the advancing soldiers. The first rank of Francyn's army had tall pavise shields held in front of them, and over their shoulders men with long pikes began to stab and pierce the wretched haul, quickly removing its offensive capability and reducing the net's contents to a twitching, stinking pile on the ground. I was told later that the stench was sickening, and the men at the forefront of this disgusting task were covered in filth, left retching and heaving behind their shields. As the movement in the netting began to die down the whole bundle was drawn as far from the road as the sweating and straining soldiers could drag it, trying to move their grisly catch out of the way of the besieging army's path. Once this foul obstacle had been removed Francyn's lines formed up again and advanced towards the open gate, banners showing the colours of multiple Regions unfurled to curl and snap in the chill sea wind, and horns blowing to signal forward march. Every tenth man in the line held a tall pole topped with a burning brazier, to help guide the army to its destination through the dark night.

Inside the gate, in the flame lit courtyard, the dead were struggling to reform their regiments. They were caught between the fires burning behind them and the resolute army approaching the breached entrance. Kantus cantered back and forth behind his forces, trying to get the apathetic and idiotic dead back into something resembling formation. He succeeded in getting the first wave of his troops through the barbican to meet Francyn's army, and I could hear the clash and clang of rusted weapons striking the advancing shield wall as pitched battle was finally met. This was our signal to switch focus, and Fenna and the rest of the Wardens, still lurking in the shadows of the courtyard's surrounding buildings, began loosing bolts towards living targets. They picked off and slew as many of Kroll's cultists as they could reach. Men and women in dark and filthy robes began to fall to the ground, but their deaths drew no attention from the dead around them, who continued to move towards the gate. A few of Kroll's fanatics tried to raise the alarm, suddenly noticing that they were under attack from their rear, but they were quickly cut down before their warnings reached their fellows. The cultists were caught in a trap, unable to move back out of the courtyard due to the fires behind them, and unable to move forwards due to the dense wall of bone funnelling through the gate. Silent and invisible bolts flew from the shadows and decapitated the command of the undead.

It was almost easy, and it could not last long. Finally Kantus noticed that we were killing his living subjects and ordered a unit of Raised towards our position. I turned to Fenna, now having to raise my voice over the sounds of battle and chaos.

"I have to kill him! We can't leave him alive, else this would have been for nothing!"

She nodded, and I moved out of the shadows and raced into the courtyard as fast I could. The Warden's bolts flew all around me, removing as many obstacles as they could and clearing the path for my charge. I heard footsteps behind mine and I knew Quell had followed. Raised soldiers fell to the ground, some with crossbow bolts in their smashed skulls, some from the wide swings of my hammer. I had to keep moving and not get trapped in the enemy lines. I pushed through, Quell close behind me, no longer quiet but screaming prayers in a rage filled voice. As we reached Kantus his skeletal horse reared on its hind legs, and the armour-clad and black-cloaked figure on its back turned to face us. The hooves of his mount came back down and tried to smash me into the ground, crashing against the paving instead and then rearing again at the command of its rider. I side-stepped, swooping low across the legs of his steed with the heavy head of my hammer, and my strike shattered the beast's foreleg, snapping it in two and sending shards of bone flying through the smoke and floating embers. The undead horse stumbled to the ground and pitched the rider from its back, but Kantus recovered before I could press my attack and got to his feet with his sword held in front of him. He adopted a wide stance, guarded and ready. I circled the still struggling body of his lame mount and he paced opposite me, neither of us willing to make the first move. I could hear Quell behind me, fending off any of the dead who tried to come to their master's rescue.

The Greater Raised lowered his sword, and then pounced, using all his strength to leap over his prone steed and strike from above. His speed and power shocked me. I had enjoyed the benefit of surprise against Hallek, when I fought him on the *Silverfin.* Here I was facing someone prepared and equal to me in their physical capabilities, and I had to react quickly to raise my hammer and block the blow. The impact of his strike nearly sent me to my knees, but I kept my feet and whirled away from his next attack. He was fast, and strong, but he was no great swordsman. His swings were wild and undisciplined, but no less dangerous for all that, and I could not avoid every one. He caught me with a smart blow to my head, which struck off my helmet and sent it tumbling to the dirt and ash-strewn courtyard, leaving me with the same vulnerability I had inflicted on Hallek. As I raised my head and displayed my skull face the Greater Raised stepped back, and although his face betrayed no shock his surprise was evident, and quickly became anger.

"Traitor! *Blasphemer!* You should be serving R'Chun, and here you are with these weak-fleshed fools. I will take your skull back to Kroll, and you can sit on his mantle until the *END OF TIME!*"

I do not believe he even knew he had been my commander.

"I have rejected your false god," I replied, still circling and preparing for his next attack, "My flesh was taken from me. You gave yours up for the insane dreams of a *madman!*"

"*You dare insult Kroll? I'll have your bones for my armour!*"

He swung at me then, but his rage and shock had made him clumsy, and I ducked the blow and struck up under his guard, shortening my hold on the hammer and driving its weight into his jaw. My strike split it in two. He staggered and did not raise his sword in time for my follow-up. Instead of aiming for his head I swept my hammer across at chest height. His breastplate crumpled under the impact, and I heard his ribcage shatter inside the metal shell, the bones within clattering against the armour. He fell to one knee, his sword still in his hand but laid on the ground as he tried to keep his balance. I looped the hammer up behind me with all the strength I could muster, swung it over the top of my head, and brought it down between the wings of his helmet, driving the top of it into his waiting skull. His face crumpled, his eye sockets split, and he slumped and fell to the ground. Immediately green flashes and sparks flew from the cracks in his face, and black smoke belched forth from his mouth and nasal cavity. His attempt to raise his sword failed and he dropped it, so it rattled against the cobbles.

I turned back to my comrades. Quell was still fighting at my rear, howling and bellowing prayers to Omma T'Lassa as he punched his blades into his undead opponents. He had racked up a fair tally, but we were in danger of being overwhelmed. The Wardens were retreating from the courtyard as several skeletal bowmen had joined the fray and had begun to target their position. The rear guard of the undead army had reached the Wardens' hiding place. Two of the Wardens had fallen. One lay prone on the ground, half in and half out of shadowed cover, and the slash across his belly was leaking glossy blood that glittered in the firelight. Another slumped against a wall, head down, the black feathered flight of a badly made arrow protruding from his chest. I barged through to Quell's position, fighting my way through the mob of Raised surrounding him, and he moved back-to-back with me as we hammered and sliced our way back to cover

Over the din of the battle and the advancing dead behind us I screamed at Fenna.

"NOW! Send the signal! We need to leave *NOW!*"

Fenna turned and yelled an instruction to one of her fellow Wardens, and he quickly lit the tip of a crossbow bolt, its head wrapped in alchemically-treated cloth. He tilted the weapon until it was pointed vertically and shot it into the sky above the gate, where it burned a bright, piercing blue. This was Francyn's signal to withdraw. The dead had no leaders left. We had killed every living cultist that commanded them.

We regrouped and then raced away from the carnage of the courtyard through the dark and filthy cobbled streets, the sound of bone-filled marching boots receding behind us. Our mission was complete, but we had further business to attend to. We could not leave the children here. Fenna led the way, finding the storehouse again with little difficulty, her sense of direction perfect even through the darkness and smoke of the dead town. The two Raised left to guard the entrance stood little chance against her wrath, and she did not slow her charge towards them as the rest of us raced behind her. She batted aside their first attempt to stop her with their forked, herding weapons and drove into them with a scream of absolute fury leaving her lips. Fenna was an orphan. The dead had forced the same fate upon these children. This was an injustice she would not let go unanswered.

She had destroyed them before we caught up with her. Bor put a hand on her shoulder to calm her, as she was still stamping the remains of their skulls into the stone below, the sound of her boots beating a rhythm on the ground as fragments of bone flew at her feet. She turned to Bor with wild, rage-filled eyes, nearly striking him as she did so, and then she caught herself. She took a long, shuddering breath, and then nodded to him, before entering the warehouse.

There must have been nearly a hundred children in the cold building, bound at their hands and feet. They were shivering and quiet. They had no blankets, and some of them were wearing very little clothing, having been taken with no care as to their comfort or safety. Some were crying but most watched the Wardens with suspicious and shock-filled eyes. I hung back in the shadows. I had realised my face was unlikely to be welcoming to them, and I had left my helmet in the courtyard. I raised my hood and pulled it forwards as much as I could to hide my features.

Fenna and the Wardens moved quickly through the children, cutting their binds and trying to organise them to move. Some of the younger ones were too small to run with us, and they were carried by some of the older children where they were able to manage. The Wardens picked up others, discarding what kit they could and tossing the limp, chilled bodies over their shoulders like sacks, trying to keep their hands free to fight. There were no children less than five years old. I knew what that meant, and it filled me with shame. I knew what I had done in Tresh. I knew what the dead had done in Hust. Freeing these captives was a small payment against what I owed.

We left the warehouse, a rag-tag assortment of frightened children and furious, hate-driven warriors. We raced through the darkness of Hust. We could hear the chasing dead behind us, close at our heels. They made no effort to be stealthy, and the clatter of their boots rang loud from the cobbled streets, echoing amongst the walls of the desecrated town.

We made it to the gate and found our rear guard intact. Brack was paler than before, his wound clearly telling on him. Despite his injury he still held the crossbow in his hands, and he and his companions helped usher the children and Wardens through the gate and past the outbuildings. We climbed the hill trail opposite the gate and made it to the treeline, the Wardens pushing the children through the undergrowth with care but as much haste as possible.

We left Hust behind us and ran through the night, taking a more direct route on our return journey so that we would not tire the children any more than we had to. We came across no patrols. We made it to camp just before dawn.

Francyn's army had returned. They had stymied the charge of the Lesser dead completely, and this caused enough of an obstruction on the Coast Road that the advance of the Raised had been blunted. It left Kroll's forces gathered into a target for missile fire from bows and catapult. The undead cavalry present had not been able to circumvent the blockage either, and when the dead finally made it to Francyn's lines they could only mount an ineffectual assault. We suffered some losses, but they were sustainable. When Francyn gave the order to withdraw the army did so in good order, and the dead did not have the initiative to follow far without guidance from their commanders and living custodians.

The men who had performed the horrific task of destroying the caught Lessers were the most shaken, and all of them were pale and covered in filth. They had set light to the corpse-filled nets as they retreated and some of them were still suffering sickness from the stench of burning flesh. Many of them took the opportunity upon reaching camp to strip themselves of their armour and undergarments and submerge themselves in the ice-cold water of the ocean, trying to remove the foulness from their skin. Their armour was taken to be sluiced and dried by disgusted looking camp workers, who held it at arms-length to avoid the smell of rotting matter.

The children were taken to a hospital tent, and the camp followers attempted to care for them. They were fed from supply rations and cleaned up where possible, and the men and women of the army brought what blankets and warm clothing they could spare. The frightened youngsters huddled together at one end of the enclosure, holding each other for warmth and comfort. I stayed away, heading back to my isolated tent. Fenna and Bor visited the young they had rescued, seeing mirrors of their own childhoods in the faces of the refugee orphans.

Brack died from his wound during the night,

having lost too much blood. Quell held a blessing ceremony over his body, and he was given an honoured burial at sea.

We waited.

As we had at Rafe, we kept watch. The patrols from Hust did not come out as far as our camp so Francyn sent scouts to observe the town and report back at intervals. It took a little longer than it had at Rafe for the dead to show signs of disarray.

A few days after the battle, Francyn, Quell and I, alongside a handful of volunteers, entered Hust through the still-open gate. I hid my face under my hood and wrapped it as much as I could with cloth, so the men with us did not find out what I was, and I tried to keep my distance from them. To gain access to the gate we had to clamber around the pile of ash, bone and rope still blocking the Coast Road. As we passed through the barbican we saw Raised who were still standing before the gate in ranks, awaiting commands that would never come. Others were fighting each other in a sleeping state, slowly exchanging blows and parrying strikes as if they were moving through syrup. Many of the dead rolled on the ground, clutching above them with bony fingers at enemies only they could see. It was raining that morning, the clouds low and dark overhead, and the deluge filled the eye sockets of prone Raised and ran in rivulets across their exposed bone.

Francyn looked around the courtyard in shock at what he had wrought. No bodies had been cleared, and the cold corpses of Kroll's cultists still lay where they had been cut down by crossbow bolt and blade. The devastation of Francyn's attacks and the hungry fires the Wardens had set had reduced this side of the town to ruin. I strode up to the broken form of the Greater Raised I had duelled. The dust and ash from the fires had coated his body in a thick layer of grey, and his sword still lay on the stone next to him, its blade dulled by the fire's residue but slowly being made clean again by the falling rain. My helmet was nearby, dented and lying in the dirt, and I picked it up, cleaning the thick coating of ash off it as best I could with the edge of my cloak. I turned to speak to Francyn.

"We need to find the birthing pool. General Francyn, could you please ask your scouts to spread out over the town. More than likely the pool will be in some shared building. They like to desecrate places where the living gather."

Francyn nodded, his face still pale, and began to issue orders to his men.

In the daylight the town was an atrocity. There was still much evidence of the violence it had suffered from the dead, and it seemed as if viscera and blood stained every street, every building, every home. Near the middle of Hust was a paved square, with a statue of some ancient noble still on a plinth in its centre. The armoured knight was riding a stone horse, its forelegs rearing into the air, and he had his sword raised as if he were celebrating victory. Surrounding the brass and marble edifice were the remains of a bonfire. It was a horror of charcoal and corpses. The men with me held their damp cloaks over their mouths and noses in an attempt to suppress the still lingering smell of scorched meat and death.

There was a temple to Omma T'Lassa by the square. Kroll's legion had befouled it. It was not as grand a building as the temple at the Western Gate, but what little grandeur it had once possessed had been polluted by the violations committed in and around it. At the fore of the ship-shaped building the paving stones had been ripped up, and a line of stakes pushed into the ground below. Atop each spike sat the rotting head of a Daughter of the temple, their faces frozen in an eternal scream of horror and pain. Their tongues lolled from their mouths like black and purple slugs, and their eyes had been taken by carrion birds scavenging for sustenance. Inside the temple the floor had been removed, the pews and boards ripped away, and the foundations dug out to form the cult's charnel pit. The pool in Hust was much larger than the one we had destroyed at Rafe. At one end of the temple, as at the Western Gate, there had been a statue of the Mother, that had stood in a small pond of gathered sea water. This had been toppled and smashed into many pieces of misshapen stone. In its place a crude support had been raised, made of floorboards hammered together with little care and propped up with chunks of the fallen statue. The body of the High Daughter that served this temple had been bound to it, almost as if she were a work of art on display. An offering from the cult to their abhorrent deity. She had been pierced in many places, with rusted nails and shards of broken stained-glass protruding from her pale and wrinkled skin. She had been partially flayed. They had begun with her feet and had made it to her vein-threaded thighs before they either became bored with the activity or her heart had given out. The sacred water below her was dark and soiled, the surface coated in a film of congealed blood and scraps of floating skin.

The men who had found her stood outside the temple and would not enter again. Quell and I were summoned, and as we passed the volunteers one spat at me. It seemed my nature was no longer a secret. The Apostle and I entered the temple. Quell performed the same ritual here that he had in the hall at Rafe. He knelt at the edge of the birthing pool, praying softly, and poured the Milk of T'Lassa from his flask into the foul ichor. Again, the black ooze reacted swiftly, and soon there was a layer of cracked and dried black mud where once there had been a liquid surface. Once this task was completed, I helped Quell to cut the High Daughter down from her wretched bindings, and we laid her on the floor in front of the broken statue as gently as we were able. Quell gave her back her dignity with a wrap of blue-dyed cloth he took from the altar at the rear of the temple. We carried her out with as much respect as we could, and then took her down to the harbour, where Quell said a short prayer. We lowered her gently into the waiting arms of the ocean.

The rest of the volunteers went through the town searching houses, merchant buildings and stores, searching for any living survivors and finishing any lurking dead they found. They noted any supplies they found in the abandoned and defiled warehouses so that they could be retrieved for use later. They found no-one alive. The town's inhabitants had been collected by the dead and either used as recruitment material or burned in the town square. A few people had fought back, and they were found either left in the rooms where they had been murdered, or hacked and mutilated and lying in the street, their wounds washed clean by the falling rain. Francyn and Dela's original intent had been to occupy Hust once it had been re-taken, and to use the town as a launch point for the next step in their campaign of resistance. This plan was quickly abandoned. The town was defiled. No man or woman would sleep there. The army set up camp as near to the walls as they could stand, and a team of camp workers and soldiers spent a few days removing the corpses from the Coast Road and clearing the entrance to Hust so that access was easier. This was filthy and demoralising work and the labourers often came back from their task and immediately dove into the sea to cleanse themselves, not caring that the chill waters left them with shivering flesh and chattering teeth.

There were a handful of ships in the small harbour, and these were investigated by some of the more sea-worthy men and found to be in good condition. These were then requisitioned and added to our forces. Francyn sent word of our victory back to Oese by messenger pigeon, and a few days later a response came in the form of the *Silverfin* appearing in the distance. The black ship sailed into the harbour, and Dela and his personal bodyguard of Wardens, including Wyren, disembarked. Francyn greeted them warmly, and then walked Dela through the town to give him a better idea of its condition. They reconvened for a meeting later that evening in Francyn's command tent, and I was invited to join them.

"Hust is dead. It's going to take a lot of work to make it habitable again, and I'm not sure anyone would even want to live here. I don't think we have the time to waste, we have to push on to Salisson." Francyn looked tired. He was used to being a leader of men, but the scale of this endeavour was clearly a strain on him. A constant stream of messengers passed in and out of the tent, carrying a barrage of requests, questions, complaints and requirements that pulled at Francyn's attention and ground on his nerves. When I had been in command of an army, I found that the greater part of my time was spent dealing with daily trivia. The fighting was the least of it.

Dela looked weary as well, and not a little concerned. He had been given a short tour of Hust and had seen the leavings of the undead and the horrors they had perpetrated on the town's inhabitants. The poor state of the settlement had not been improved by our attack either.

"Well," said Dela, reaching for his glass. "We must move forwards. I have had reports from our forces in the north and the mid-regions, their progress has been good, and our losses not serious... as yet. Most of the dead seem to be concentrated near the coast, and the inland villages were not as well defended... or defensible... as Hust. I do fear for my own city. Salisson will be difficult to take. I'm not sure how the dead gained entrance in the first place, Garet's guards may be incompetent, but I cannot believe even they would open the gates to such an invader. I insisted on making the city siege-worthy during my time there. The river Salis is split at the north end and encompasses it on both sides as a fast-moving moat, and the bridges into Salisson are narrow and easily defended. Only the harbour is a possible entrance point, and that would be the first place I'd garrison if I wanted to hold the city. I am afraid I have given a stronghold to the enemy that we will not be able to breach." He took a sip and placed his glass of wine carefully on the table, next to a map of the city he had brought with him.

"We have a small advantage. In my, shall we say, preparedness, I did have a tunnel made for the Wardens to make their way to-and-fro from the harbour in secret." I of course knew of this exit, as it was the one Bor and I had used to escape my execution. Dela looked a little discomforted at having to reveal its existence to Francyn, and the General gave Dela a wry and weary look. "Does your paranoia know no end, Councillor?"

Dela smiled sheepishly. "I believe my paranoia

has been well-justified, don't you think? Regardless, as you did here in Hust, we may be able to send in a small assassination force, although again they would need some distraction as cover. Success would depend on whether the tunnel has been discovered during the dead's occupation. It's possible, but unlikely. I think."

"Sounds great." Said Fenna, rolling her eyes.

CHAPTER SIXTEEN

It was decided that we would need more than one ship to take the harbour at Salisson. Dela departed on the *Silverfin* with as much haste as he could muster, taking the refugee children back to Oese with him to find them shelter. It took him a few couple of days to return, leading a small flotilla of privateer vessels, their crews made up of hardened-looking men and women who regarded the rawer recruits of Francyn's army with disdain. We broke camp, an activity that always looked chaotic to my eyes, and some of Francyn's detachments were loaded onto the newly arrived ships, marching up the boarding planks and then being directed into the holds of the creaking vessels with much griping and grumbling at the pressed conditions.

Fenna, Bor and I boarded the *Silverfin* again, and joined Wyrin and the rest of Dela's guard there. Dela remained with Francyn, and the land-based portion of our campaign force began the march to Salisson, heading along the Coast Road and passing the dilapidated and devastated ruins of villages and hovels that hugged the cliff edges and forests on either side. We sailed ahead, and anchored just outside Salisson Bay, giving the marching men time to catch us and set up their siege camp. The tired men and women had to rest, eat, and allow their officers time to plan the assault.

The harbour at Hust had been too small to carry out a raid from the sea. We would not have been able to land enough soldiers to push into the town, and our forces would have been caught between the ocean at their backs and the massed undead before them. Salisson was different. Its port was its largest asset, and there was room for us to dock several ships. The troops carried by Dela's ad-hoc fleet would first take the port by advancing on smaller boats, which many of the privateer ships carried. A huge chain was usually stretched across the harbour entrance to bar it, but this appeared to have been left sunken, so our men could advance without any barrier to their assault. As they landed the rest of the fleet would move in and begin bombarding the surrounding fortifications. Salisson's walls were lightest around the port, as usually it would have been protected by an armada of its own, and most of the ships that habitually berthed there were now part of our forces. It was determined that the attack would take place in darkness, well after sunset. Our scouts had reported the beacons at each side of the harbour were still lit, so passage inside its waters would not be too treacherous.

Quell and I would land at the harbour with a small contingent of Wardens and enter the disguised tunnel via its hinged crate door. The tunnel would take me back to the Sea Snake, where I had made my harried exit from Salisson many moons earlier. Our mission this time was simple. Kill as many cultists as we could.

Quell knelt on the deck of the ship while we awaited the order to depart, and he prayed and chanted softly, watching the sea swell and fall as the setting sun sent red and gold shafts of light through the clouds in the western sky. I knelt alongside him as he asked for help from his deity. The wind that whipped up off the ocean seemed sharp and cold with the chill of early spring, and I was glad I could not feel it. Quell was shivering even wrapped in his leather armour and grey cloak, and he brought the hood down close around his face to block out the biting breeze. I wanted to ask him more questions, about his nature, and his skills in fighting the dead, but I felt I would be interrupting his worship and instead kept my inquiries to myself. He finally bowed his head, and we got up from our knees, Quell moving far more stiffly than I did. The time had come to make our move on the beleaguered city.

The crew of the *Silverfin* hauled anchor, and as the army on the shore began its final march to Salisson, drawing behind them their huge siege weapons, we sailed for the port. As we approached the gaping maw of the fortified harbour we could see there were some ships present, although they sat in darkness, with no sign of life on board. One of the ships seemed more ornate than the others, though it was difficult to tell in just the glow from the beacons. As we drew nearer my view of it was clearer than my companions', my vision being superior to theirs in such dim conditions. It flew the flag of Estwake and was of a similar build to the *Silverfin.* I described it to Fenna, who waited on deck with the rest of her comrades.

"It's the *Fallen Son*. That's Cellin's ship."

"Why is he here?"

Fenna bit her lip, thinking. "Dela wasn't sure how the dead got into Salisson. There must have been someone on the inside...Cellin would have been able to dock here without being challenged."

I turned back to the ship in the distance. "If he brought the dead with him he could take the guard by surprise. Garet's men were a poor defence."

She rubbed her hand across her tightly woven hair and shook her head. "This is bad. We don't know what Cellin knows. If he's leading the dead in Salisson we could be in trouble."

"There is nothing we can do about that right now. We must keep pushing forwards."

By the look on her face, I do not think I gave her much comfort.

The wardens, accompanied by Quell and I, were lowered into the water just outside the harbour in two long boats, the winching mechanism used for our descent sounding loud to me even over the crashing surf. Once we were free of the hooked pulley-ropes we pushed away from the *Silverfin* and began to make our way between the long stone piers of the port. More troop boats were lowered from our other ships, and while we hugged the shadows at the edges of the harbour, they took a more direct route and headed straight for the centre dock.

The *Silverfin* and its accompanying ships began to loose their catapults, sending lit balls of tar and stone towards the quay to soften up any defences and help illuminate landing areas. I could see from our position in the shadows that there was movement on the dock, and the dead soldiers there were being drawn towards the edge of the water, awaiting the approaching assault. The Wardens did their best to stay out of sight, though I knew the darkness of the walls would not hide our presence from the night-sight of the dead. All we could hope is that their attention was drawn completely by the attack from our ships. At the same time I began to hear distant booms coming from my left, far from the walls of the harbour. Francyn was beginning his assault to take the river-bridge and the main gate to the city.

We reached a jetty at one end of the harbour, a mooring point for fishing boats, well away from the long pontoons that served the larger ships. This end of the wharf was quiet, any defenders stationed there having been drawn to the battle at the main dock. We hurried from our boats, dragging them up the slipway through the cold, lapping waves, and then scurried through crates, barrels, piles of rope and empty catch-baskets, making our way as stealthily as we could to the concealed entrance of Dela's tunnel. We reached it with no incident and crouched by the warehouse. The false crate sat at its rear, unobtrusive and unremarkable.

Fenna withdrew a brass key from one of her many pockets and pushed it into a small knothole at the bottom of the crate. I heard the mechanism *click*, and then Bor and Wyren got ready to lift the secret door on its hinges. Fenna and Rake pointed loaded crossbows at the opening, and then Fenna nodded, and the crate tipped back to reveal only a dark square hole, with no movement inside. While Fenna and Rake covered him Bor jumped down, and he came back up a few moments later, this time using the ladder bolted to the wall inside.

"There's no fucker here. The first chamber's empty and I can't see any recent footprints."

"Right." Fenna said, "Everyone in. Rake, you cover the rear."

We all descended into the chamber, using the ladder one at a time. Bor had lit a torch on the opposite wall, so the inside was illuminated, and the Wardens could see where they were going. He pulled the light from its mounting and brandished it ahead of him. I had not paid much attention to the chamber when I had first been there. It was larger than I had realised, and it had stone walls and a paved flagstone floor, a small shelf for storage, and even a couple of wooden chairs. It was still cramped by the time we had all made it inside and Rake had closed the crate behind her. She turned a handle at the top of the ladder to lock the exit. There were fifteen of us, and we were all pressed together in the small space. We started to make our way along the adjoining tunnel. We could only move along it two abreast. Fenna and I were somewhere in the middle of the pack.

"You know what Dela said about making this tunnel?" She whispered, as we paced as quietly as we could towards the hidden exit at the Sea Snake. Fenna could walk easily in the low tunnel, but I had to stoop, and I could hear Bor grumbling ahead of me, occasionally cursing under his breath as he banged his head on the ceiling.

"He said he made them for you and your Wardens."

"Yes… well that's not true. I think he wanted to save face a bit in front of Francyn. This has been here a long time, and Dela knew about it before he was Councillor. It's a thief's tunnel. He ran with some rough people when he was younger. They used to use this for smuggling, stolen goods, that sort of thing. We took it over when he set up the Wardens."

"And he told you this?" I said, slightly incredulous that he would admit this even to Fenna. Dela made a good show of being a proper gentleman.

"Well, he was pretty drunk when he did. I've not asked him about it since. It's none of my business what he got up to in his younger days. Anyway, he'd probably deny it if you asked him now."

The tunnel was not a straight line towards

the Sea Snake. There were numerous twists and turns, and there appeared to be other entrances to tunnels that led off from the main thoroughfare, which Fenna told me led to a few other exits hidden around the city. Bor led the way, torch in one hand, drawn dagger in the other. If the Wardens had not been there to guide me I would have become hopelessly lost, even with my superior night sight. The tunnel had a dirt floor and walls but had been lined with wooden supports that braced the passage at regular intervals. The wood looked old but sturdy, and there were signs here and there of repair and reinforcement that seemed recent. Now and then we came into open spaces with more storage and seating, and stone steps leading up. Bor knew where we were going and passed several of these exits before declaring we had reached our goal. He made his way up the steps and unlocked the door to the basement of the Sea Snake.

We all remained below, making as little noise as we could, in case our route into the city had been compromised. Bor had set his torch in a bracket on the wall, and using one hand to pull open the door he entered the adjoining room with the point of his dagger first. The exit was clear, and he beckoned the rest of us up the stairs. We followed him into the hidden basement room of the Sea Snake. We all piled into the

Warden's sanctuary. After some whispered and angry discussion between Fenna and Wyren it was decided to leave the door unlocked and open. Wyren was in favour of locking it as she did not want the passages to be discovered. Fenna regarded that as the least of our worries and wanted an escape route.

We remained as stealthy and quiet as we could. The basement room was adjacent to the storage cellar, accessed through another locked door that Fenna had the key for. We entered the storage room, its floor taken up by barrels and a coating of straw to soak up spilled beer and damp, and again we left the door behind us unlocked, against Wyren's protestations. I understood her argument. Exposure of these secret entrances undermined the Wardens. In war some needs can outweigh others.

We made our way up the cellar steps to the Sea Snake. The inn was empty and in some disarray. Tables and stools had been smashed into splinters, and there was broken glass and blood on the floor, only some of it soaked into the straw-dust. There was little light coming in through the windows, just the glow of a few still-lit bright oil lamps. Bor doused his torch so that our presence in the inn would not be detected. The inn had a front entrance and a smaller backdoor that led into an alleyway, and this was the exit we took. I returned to the cobbled, dirty streets of Salisson, and I could not help but wonder at the events that had brought me back. My escape from this place seemed more like a nightmare than a memory. Not that I have nightmares anymore.

Unlike the more open layout of Oese, Salisson was a rat-warren. We could make our way through the city without approaching any of the main streets, instead darting from alleyway to corner to alleyway. Even in darkness it was clear that Salisson had been occupied longer than Hust had, and the devastation wrought by the enemy was obvious at every turn. There was evidence of minor skirmishes and small-scale battles scattered throughout the city and judging by the reaction of my companions the stench was awful. Rotting viscera and black pools of blood and flesh lay decaying in the streets, and rats scurried down the gulleys either side of the cobblestones, feasting on the meals the invaders had left for them. Flies buzzed and swarmed in the cold night air and landed on any exposed skin, and the Wardens had to wave them away and pull their hoods around their mouths and noses. It was one of the few times I felt lucky to be without flesh.

We made it to the square where moons ago I had been prepared for execution. We passed the stone plinth, and the anvil was still there, a new body tied to it. As we drew closer, I recognised the High Daughter. She had been laid over the anvil, face up, and had been ravaged by blade, her chest flayed open, her ribs exposed and split so her heart could be removed. A dying scream was still fixed on her face, frozen there by the stiffness of death. Lying behind her on the plinth was the young priestess who had run from my cell. She had been beheaded as she knelt on the ground, her head rolling a few paces from her body, and she had toppled over onto her side so that the pumping blood from her open neck now dried around her remains. We moved on, silently, the grim faces of my companions betraying their rage and horror.

We reached Dela's keep. I had expected this to be the place chosen for the Birthing Pool, as it was an easily defensible position. Instead, I found it had been desecrated. The gate into the courtyard was open, and charred timber was piled up against the doorway to the keep, the remains of the bonfire's victims still visible as blackened husks amidst the burnt wood. Judging by the ash and scorched stone the flames had made their way inside, and the glass in the tower windows had shattered in the heat, their metal trace lines melting and pouring in rivulets down the stonework. The building was an empty shell now, its collected contents of art and learning destroyed.

I heard Fenna whisper to Bor. "This will break

his heart." Bor reached out and laid his hand on Fenna's shoulder, and I saw the quick gleam of tears in his eyes.

We walked away, still hugging the shadows of the alleyways, and headed down towards the harbour. We began to encounter both the living and the dead. Members of Kroll's cult still hurried about their business, comfortable in these ghastly surroundings, and the Raised marched towards the harbour and the main gate to defend their prize. We hid in the shadows, and watched, and began to strike where the opportunity presented itself. We needed to do as much damage as we could before we were driven out and give Francyn's forces the advantage. When we found a cultist without company Fenna or one of her comrades struck them down with a crossbow bolt, their accuracy unerring even in the patchy light of the remaining streetlamps. Where we found a small group together the Wardens padded quietly behind them, treading carefully to avoid alerting their victims before cutting throats and piercing hearts. I hung back a little during these attacks, as I did not have the Wardens' skills in assassination. My role in this group was defensive. If we were discovered, I would be the one to fight in the rear-guard as we retreated.

The Wardens eliminated a number of their enemies in this way but finding them all in the darkness of the town would be difficult. We needed to find the birthing pool, as destroying that would give Francyn the upper hand. We finally came to an inn, called the Wave Crest, that had a significant guard outside, more than a dozen Raised and several living cultists who were busy carrying bodies inside. Fenna asked Rake to investigate, and the nimble and stealthy woman darted across the darkness of a nearby alleyway to peer into one of the inn's grimy back windows. She came back and whispered urgently to her Captain.

"I think this is it… but there's a problem. They're carrying the bodies downstairs."

"So?" said Bor, leaning into the women's huddle. "We'll just have to get down there, makes no difference. Same deal fighting the fuckers upstairs as downstairs."

Fenna scrunched up her face, closing her eyes tightly and taking a breath.

"Bor… don't you get it? If they're in the cellar that means they could find a tunnel entrance. This is one of Dela's inns. If they know about the tunnels we could be in trouble. We won't be able to use them again once we're done tonight."

Realisation dawned slowly over Bor's face. I liked Bor a great deal, but he was hardly the sharpest blade.

"Right, yeah, you're right. But there's nothin' we

can fuckin' do. We just have to fuck 'em up as much as we can now."

As simplistic as this was, he was not wrong. We had to do what we could in the time we had.

We heard a commotion, and from our hidden vantage point we could see that more cultists had arrived at the inn. They yelled orders and drew away a part of the Raised guard, and then marched them down to the harbour to assist with the defence. Our army was still trying to get access to the city via the docks. We waited for the sound of their marching boots to recede a little, and then the Wardens raced across the street and struck at the remaining dead sentries. Stealth was momentarily discarded as a consideration and Quell and I led the charge for the door, with Bor close at our heels. We struck down the few Raised that held the entrance to the inn, smashing them into the damp cobblestones and destroying their skulls, and while Quell and I finished off our opponents Bor kicked his way into the building. We followed after him as the rest of the Wardens either barged through the door themselves or took up positions outside, their crossbows at their shoulders and loaded, ready to cover our exit.

Inside, Bor was treating our attack like a night on the town. He roared, his sword drawn, and picked up a bar stool. He threw it across the room to smash against the head of one cultist, and then launched himself over the bar to bring his sword down and cleave another fanatic in two. Quell and I swung and stabbed at the handful of living still on this floor of the inn, and Bor ran the length of the room behind the bar and shoulder-barged one screaming, bedraggled woman standing in front of the cellar door. His blow smashed her through the door behind her and sent her tumbling down stone steps into darkness. I heard her bones crack against the stairs as she rolled, and she became instantly silent when her head connected with the hard flagstones at the bottom.

Rake and two other Wardens raced upstairs to search the inn's bedrooms, returning quickly and declaring them empty of threat. We descended into the cellar. Downstairs the main storeroom had been cleared, the barrels, rotting sacks of vegetables and haunches of salted meat moved out of the way so that a space in the middle could be used. The old damp flagstones of the cellar floor had been wrenched from their places and propped up against one wall, and a pit had been dug to serve as a receptacle for the Blood of R'Chun. As Quell knelt at the side of the pool to begin his ritual Fenna moved to the back wall of the cellar and pulled aside a set of shelves that opened on a hinge. Behind it was the door to the tunnels, and it was open. I was standing next to Quell, and I could see from where I was that the lock was broken and surrounded by splintered wood.

"Cat's out of the bag then. The tunnels aren't secure." Fenna's eyes were narrowed, and her lips pressed tightly together. She ran her hand over her rows of braided hair, a gesture I had come to recognise.

"That's just one. They didn't find the one under the Sea Snake." Wyren looked worried as well and was fidgeting with her dagger again.

"Didn't they? They all join up. We don't know what's down there, and we can't use this one to get out if it's compromised. We're going to have to go back to the Sea Snake and block the exit at the harbour if we can. By the *Mother!*" she yelled, and slammed the shelves against the wall in frustration.

The noise made Quell jerk backwards and he looked up from his prayers. I was still watching the pit, and as he turned back to the pool, I saw a ripple moving towards him in the black ooze. As the first drops of white liquid fell from his bottle and touched the contents of the pit the surface of the pool convulsed. Instead of curving away from the strange pearlescent blessing and trying to escape its touch the black ichor rose to meet it instead, and an open-mouthed, silently screaming face erupted from the dark slime. It snapped its jaws shut around Quell's bottle and reached out to grab him. I grabbed the back of his hood and pulled him out of the apparition's reach, and we both tumbled backwards, me landing on the padded bones of my backside and Quell lying on top of me, both of us scrabbling away from the pool on our hands and our heels.

The slime-coated figure started to climb out of the pool, rivulets of black and flashing-green ooze falling from its joints as the Blood of R'Chun did its profane work. As it clambered up the side of the pit the contents of Quell's bottle emptied into its gaping mouth and rained down through the dead man's jaw, splashing over his exposed shoulder joints and ribcage. Where the Milk of T'Lassa touched the black slime it hardened into plates, like the scales of a snake, and these then cracked and burst into fragments and dust as the Raised lunged forwards and reached for a victim. It grabbed the ankle of one of the Wardens, a man named Grent, and pulled as hard as it could. He toppled backwards and fell to the floor, cracking his head on the flagstones. He was too dazed to resist as the dead man dragged him into the writhing black liquid. Bor and Wyren reached for his arms and caught hold of him, turning the struggle into a tug-of-war. I had regained my feet, and I struck out with my hammer, hitting the Raised in its face and splintering its skull. It tumbled backwards into the slowly congealing pool. Bor and Wyren pulled Grent free of the pool just as its surface solidified, and the destroyed Raised was caught in the cracked black mud, its broken skull just visible above the crust, one hand reaching into the air it as if it were asking a question.

Grent's face had been submerged, and he choked and spluttered, trying to get to his feet and spitting out black and green slime. Fenna ran over to him from the tunnel door and knelt at his side, reaching out to help him clean the filth from his face, but before she could touch him I snapped out my hand and grabbed her wrist.

"WAIT! Do not touch it!" I had seen what small drops of the Blood of R'Chun could do to living flesh, and I feared the effect on Grent would be profound. I was not wrong.

The man staggered to his feet but then bent double and made a strangled, high-pitched squealing sound. The visible skin on his face turned red, then purple, then nearly black. He stood up straight again, his limbs stretched out and shaking as if he were having some sort of spasm. He was mouthing words, "No, no, no..." and his eyes rolled into the back of his head, the whites starting to darken as threads of black and green crawled towards his irises and pupils. The flesh of his face started to move of its own accord. Black and yellow-green pustules started to erupt from his cheeks and his forehead, and as he brought his hands up to cover his face, we could see the same boils rising on the backs of his hands. The cysts burst and ran with red and yellow pus, the foul fluid swiftly turning black as rivulets of the Blood of R'Chun ran down his wrists and seeped into the sleeves of his undershirt. The skin on his hands began to split and tear away from the bone, enough that we could see the tendons that moved his fingers swelling and unravelling like frayed wet string. Grent gave a gargled scream and clenched his hands into claws, pulling at the flesh of his face, the skin parting from the front of his skull with a wet ripping sound. Underneath his swiftly dissolving features the muscles of his jaw and cheeks writhed with black worms, threads of darkness that burrowed deeper into the meat and into the soft jelly of his eyes. His decaying orbs shrivelled in their sockets, gruesome blue-black slime pouring down the remains of his face.

I must admit I did not react as quickly as I should have as the man suffered. Bor did. He drew his sword and beheaded his comrade in one swift and unhesitating movement. Grent's struggles ceased, and the head rolled into one corner of the cellar. The poor man's body stood still for a moment, trembling and shaking, and then fell to the ground. The dead flesh continued to boil and tear. His hands split apart completely, gobbets of black and red matter flying across the flagstones.

The man's severed head ruptured, bursting like fruit left to ripen too long.

The room fell silent. Bor spoke first.

"I'm done. Let's get the fuck out of here."

We came back up out of the cellar, and assembled in the inn upstairs, ready to make our run back to the Sea Snake. The Wardens were sombre and pale with shock at what they had witnessed. They were hardened and brave warriors, no doubt, but the mind can only stand so much horror before retreating from sense. We left the inn and began to make our way back through the dark, oppressive streets and alleyways of Salisson. Wyren darted across the road into the opposite alley, back the way we had come, and then beckoned the rest of us to cross. We could still hear the sounds of battle in the distance, as our ships launched flaming missiles at the harbour defences and Francyn's siege engines pounded at the city gates. I thought that the occupying forces would be distracted enough for us to escape Salisson unchallenged. I was wrong.

As Wyren left the next alley she ran in front of an entire regiment of Raised marching towards us, preceded by a drawn cage of Lessers and its entourage of handlers. The procession was led by a single armoured figure on skeletal horseback. She scrambled back into hiding but it was too late, and a shout went up from one of the cultists. We turned to take another route but heard the wet slapping of decayed feet and wailing moans behind us. The Lessers had been unleashed and were being driven towards us by their handlers. The Wardens tried to lose the hunting dead in the winding labyrinth of Salisson's streets. We doubled back on ourselves several times as we tried to reach our escape route, but now our presence was known and the attack on the harbour had not cleared our path. Too many of the dead were still in this part of the city, and the living cultists drove patrols towards us as we raced for sanctuary. Their net began to close on us. Where we could we struck down the living men and women who commanded the Raised, every one of them we could kill another small victory, but the undead would quickly overrun us if we tarried too long in one place, and our numbers dwindled as we tried to reach the tunnel exit. A man at our rear, Hans, was caught by a pack of Lessers and they dragged him to the floor screaming. They began to tear at his leather armour, trying to reach his warm flesh. Bor turned to go back for him as Hans struggled, but it was too late. One of the Lessers was on top of him, its thumbs buried in the howling man's eye sockets, and his screams rose in pitch and volume before being cut off by rotten jaws at his throat. Rake fell when several Raised lunged from the darkness of an alleyway and struck at her as she ran past. She did not even have an opportunity to raise her sword before she was run through, her stomach and chest pierced in several places by rough-edged, poorly made blades.

By the time we reached the Sea Snake less than half of our party were left, and the few remaining were cut and bruised and panting with exhaustion. The dead were still at our heels and there was no time for my companions to rest. We got inside the inn, and the last thing I saw before I closed the door behind was a dark shape on horseback cantering down the street towards us. He called out. I have no flesh, and yet a chill ran down my spine when I heard him speak.

"GRANDFATHER! GRAAAAANDFATHER! Is that you, oh Baron?"

His voice was hollow and echoing like mine, but I could still recognise his accent and tone.

It was Cellin. He had been made into a Greater Raised. He had fallen under Kroll's control completely and been reborn as one of his undead commanders.

I felt compelled to face him. I opened the door to the inn and stood there at the entrance, my hammer in my hands. He sat on his horse, perhaps twenty paces away, and a hundred Raised stood behind him in formation.

His armour was more refined than that of the other dead leaders. Instead of the spikes and affectations the others adorned themselves with, his armour was polished and well-made, its silver surfaces reflecting the lamps and torches dotted around. It was trimmed with gold, and he still wore his green cloak, the colours of Estwake when it had been a Barony. He had left his skull face visible and had ornamented his bones with circles of gemstones, set around his eye sockets, that glimmered in the flickering light. He wore a black crown, also bejewelled, with an emerald that sat at his forehead.

"You're not *reeeeeallly* my great grandfather though, are you? I'm sure that old fool the First Daughter told you who I am. I know my heritage, I know what my birth-right should be… and you, you and your ridiculous fellow Barons, threw it away. All your talk of honour. Such silly fantasies. I will take back what I am owed. Kroll will make me Emperor, and the Scar Sea and every shore that borders it will be mine *forever!*"

He had lost his wits. I replied to him, raising my voice as much as I was able so that it boomed across the street and echoed from the leaning walls of the surrounding buildings.

"The dead have no business ruling the living. The old Baronies are gone, and you and I are remnants of a time best left in the grave."

"NO! No. Kneel before me. Wield your weapon in my service or your allies will suffer the consequences." He dismounted from his dead steed and drew a long, double-handed sword from the scabbard at its saddle. He began to stalk towards me, seeking a response to his demand.

Fenna answered for me. She barged me out of the way, levelled her crossbow, and shot him in the head. Her shot was true, but the bolt deflected from the emerald at Cellin's brow, knocking his pretender's crown to the floor and staggering him. She grabbed me by the shoulder and pulled me inside the inn, yelling right into my face, "We have to go NOW Asheth!", before pushing me towards the back of the room and the cellar steps. We both clattered down them and found Bor at the bottom holding the door to the tunnels open. Fenna descended first, and then Bor nodded to me, gave a little grin, and gestured down the steps in an exaggerated manner as if he were letting me go first out of politeness. I rushed down the stairs without thinking, shaken by the encounter with my descendent, and as I reached the bottom I looked back up to see Bor run through, Cellin's long sword in Bor's belly, the end of the blade protruding from his back. The insane Councillor was gripping my friend around the back of the neck as he plunged his weapon deeper.

I howled and moved to go back up the stairs,

my hammer brandished in front of me. Bor screamed "You *FUCKER!*" and head-butted Cellin, making him stagger back and relinquish his hold on the Warden's neck. His sword was left lodged in Bor, and I could see the blow was not survivable. The dying man turned to me, as I stared up at him out of the darkness.

He yelled "Get the *FUCK* out of here!" and slammed the door shut.

I ran up the stairs and pushed at the door but Bor had put his weight against it, and before I could force my way back out I heard Fenna behind me, a slow keening wail resounding through the gloom of the tunnel. There was no light, but I could see the tears streaming down her face in the grey half-vison my dead state afforded me. There was no time to go back. My role then was to protect the living, not avenge them. I strode back down the stairs, grabbed Fenna, and dragged her towards escape.

Our flight through the tunnels was a desperate, miserable gauntlet. Now the alarm had been raised we heard the distant tread of the undead echoing through the adjoining tunnels, and they were heading to our position from every direction. I had to push Fenna ahead of me. She was insensible with grief, but it swiftly turned into a quiet but incandescent rage. She wanted to stand and fight, to lash out at those who had taken her lover, but if were caught in the darkness we would fall. I drove her on instead, as if I were one of Kroll's cultists herding Lessers, pushing and dragging her with all my strength as she beat at my arms and cursed me and my forebears. At the head of our much-reduced party Wyren held a torch, and without her guidance we would never have made it out. We got to the hidden entrance at the docks and the Wardens clambered up the ladder one by one. Wyren forced Fenna to climb the ladder as Quell and I covered the rear. I was last up, and I climbed from the hole with a wave of screaming filth clutching at my heels. Cellin had released the Lessers into the warren, and I had to beat back one who had instinctively climbed after me and was trying to claw his way out of the exit. I slammed the head of my hammer into the face of the howling corpse and it tumbled back down, landing on the writhing mass of wailing creatures below it. Wyren slammed the false-box door shut. I threw myself across it and held it shut with all my weight as Wyren fumbled at the lock, and then both she and I lay prone there for a moment. She was sweating and shaking, panting with fear and exhaustion. We had little time to rest. The false door was already creaking, and we could hear pounding and rotten scrabbling claws on the other side of it. We stood, and I took Fenna by her shoulders and pushed her on as we fled back to our boats.

CHAPTER SEVENTEEN

Francyn's attack had stalled.

Our troops on the dock were holding their position, and we saw them still entrenched as we left the harbour. The defences had been damaged but not enough for Francyn's men to gain entrance. Our forces could not advance, but neither could the dead rebuff them without giving up their advantage. Our ships remained in the harbour, and we boarded the *Silverfin*. Captain Shand took us back up the coast a little to a small cove where we could disembark and join Francyn's camp. We made our way up a stone walkway, and Wyren and the surviving Wardens took Fenna with them to their part of the encampment, Wyren holding Fenna with one arm around her shoulders. The loss of Bor hung heavy on the Captain of the Wardens, and I did not know if she would be able to continue the fight. Quell left to get unarmoured and cleaned, and I joined Francyn and Dela in the command tent. The mood was sour. The ground assault had also made little progress, and an attempt to gain entrance through the main gate via use of a ram had failed. Francyn had lost many soldiers, and morale was low. Both Dela and the General looked tired and drawn. Dela leaned on the table, his hands splayed across the map of his home, his head hung down.

I briefed them on our disastrous mission, and informed Cellin that Bor and many other Wardens had been killed, and that his tunnels had fallen into the hands of the enemy. Dela remained silent throughout, and when I was finished, he stood quietly for a moment and then made an angry growling sound. He slapped out with his hand, smashing a wine glass from the table and shattering it across the floor of the tent.

"We have no means of gaining entry now. My own secrets have been turned against me. I am an old fool and I have lost my way." he rubbed his face with his hands, pulling at the skin and dragging his cheeks down.

"What of our other armies? How goes the rest of the campaign?" I tried to steer the conversation back to practical matters. Francyn answered me.

"We're stymied on all fronts. We've been able to take some of the smaller villages in the north and in the midlands, but I have received messages from our commanders. Whenever we reach one of the larger towns we are rebuffed. We cannot besiege them, we have neither the time nor the resources, and they can out-wait us easily. Salisson is just one example of our failure. We have many more. Even if you destroyed their only birthing pool, which we can't be sure of, there are still many more of Kroll's fanatics in Salisson and thousands of the undead. We cannot root them out. We've lost many men already just trying to take the harbour and the main gate, and we still haven't gained entrance."

I sat on a stool at the table, looking over the map that Dela had brought. His city was a well-fortified position. Its original builders had been clever. The river surrounded it, and its tunnels were a significant advantage to defenders.

"Cellin circumvented your defences. You could not have known what he would do."

"He let them in, and *I should have foreseen it!*" Dela reached for the bottle of wine he had with him and took a drink straight from it. "I have not been near as cunning as I thought."

I looked at the map. Dela had labelled different areas, and I traced one gloved finger along the walls and up to where the river split at the north of the city. There was a clear area at the top of the map, just inside the black lines of the city border, that seemed to be empty of settlement. There was just the outline of one building there, and this had been labelled 'OR'. I tapped it with the tip of my finger.

"Dela... what is this?" He walked around the table to stand next to me, sloshing the wine in his bottle a little as he did so.

"That's the oil reservoir. The city lamps are fed from there. See, there's pipework along the walls that lead back into the main streets so that we can light the city."

"This is where the oil is made?"

"No, no. We have a refining centre to the East. It's brought in on ships as a regular delivery, and the barrels are brought to the reservoir. We keep it all in this area, away from homes, so that if there are any accidents the fire would be contained. The pipes are fashioned to close if they get too hot, the joins melt, and the reservoir is built into the wall behind it so the oil can be vented into the river if it needs to be emptied. It's a wonderful piece of engineering. Cost a fortune."

I traced the wall with my finger again, and then moved my pointing digit along the river. There was a crossing bridge just north of the city, a stone's throw from its battlements. I followed the winding river to the top of the map where it disappeared at the edge of the paper.

"Where does the river spring from?" I asked, and Dela frowned a little.

"Eh, up in the mountains somewhere. I don't know. The land is quite craggy to the north, most of our farmlands are to the east and west. We don't have much cause to go up there."

"So. It is a single river, where it splits to meet the city walls, and then forms a moat around the town."

"Yes. That's correct. What are you getting at?"

"The river is our largest barrier. We cannot get troops across, so we are forced to attack the main gate, which is too heavily defended to take. It is too fast moving to ford, especially at this time of year as the spring thaw has fed it. We can use it, though."

I stood up straight and turned to face both men. If it were possible to read my expression, I believe I would have looked hopeful.

"Tell me, gentlemen, have you ever been farmers?" Both men shook their heads, slowly and with some confusion.

"I knew some, and on occasion I would visit them working on my land, and even lend a hand if the mood took me. Sometimes, when a new field was being prepared for planting, there was a stone in the way. If it was small enough, then it could be removed by wrapping rope around it and having strong horses drag it out of the way. if not, it needed to be broken into pieces. The farmers had an extremely clever method of performing this task. They would dig a pit underneath the stone and light a fire. Once the stone had been heated, hot enough that the air around it shimmered, they would douse it with ice-cold water. The shock would split the stone, and the small parts could then be removed by hand."

I turned back to the map. My shadow was cast over the paper. It was as if I were a giant, standing outside the city walls, silhouetted by the sun.

"Fire and water, gentlemen. That is how we take Salisson"

I laid out my plan, and then left them to rest.

The next morning was bright and clear. Spring was now starting to take hold. I could tell the ocean breeze was chill, based on the shivering hands and steamy breath of the camp's occupants, but the deep blue sky was clear of clouds, and I could see all the way to the distant horizon as I looked out over the Scar Sea. As I looked out across the water I could see our ships returning. Francyn had pulled them out of the harbour. Trying to hold that ground was a waste of effort and the men who disembarked were disillusioned and worn down by the failed attack.

My nature was now an open secret. My tent was

still a little way from the main encampment but Francyn and Dela were concerned that someone would attempt to attack me, so had selected trusted guards to stand in front of my quarters. This did not stop curious soldiers from investigating, and many of them seemed to run errands that brought them near to my lodgings, the men and women going out of their way to try to get a peek at me. I remained in my tent, content to wait, read the books I had brought with me, and sit looking at the sea. Although I was somewhat ostracised, I could tell that the mood in the camp was sour. This grim malaise was not improved by the arrival of a message from Salisson.

The message arrived pinned to the back of a man riding an ill-nourished and sick looking horse. He had been bound to the horse's back, face down. The guards at the edge of our encampment had watched the poor old nag traipse towards them along the Coast Road, and once they had discerned the nature of its rider they had reacted with horror and raced through the gathered resting soldiers to Francyn's command tent. The General then summoned Quell and I, and we made our way towards the guard-post. My assigned guards followed me, and the soldiers of the camp gave me a wide berth, as a feeling of dread descended upon me. The runner who Francyn had sent to summon me had been pale of features and clearly disturbed by something. The General met us at the guard-post and handed me the letter, which had my name written on its folded page in neat and flowing handwriting. I did not read it immediately. Instead I stepped forward to investigate our visitor.

The man on the horse had been quartered, his limbs removed, and the wounds crudely stitched shut with rough black twine, the holes in his skin tearing in places from the tension on the criss-crossed cord. Some of the stitches split open completely as he writhed and twitched and moaned, and pus and rotting matter dripped from the rents at his shoulders and hips. One of the guards nearby bent double and heaved the contents of his stomach onto the ground, and the living around me covered their mouths and noses. Insects could be seen landing and crawling on the man's flesh, feeding and laying their eggs. He made bestial and unthinking sounds, his mouth opening and closing as if he were trying to be understood, but I knew this was just an illusion, and that he was without sense. His eyes rolled blankly in his sockets as Quell and I cut him down from his mount and he fell to the ground. He lay face up and stared blindly into the blue sky, as the flies that surrounded him scattered into the wind.

It was Bor.

The wound at his belly was still open, and his decaying guts were exposed, coils of black-grey entrails hanging from the opening. Francyn gagged at the sight of that. He started to order the surrounding soldiers away, attempting to minimise the impact on his men, but more were coming towards us, curious as to the source of the disturbance. I turned my back on my dead friend and read the letter he had carried from Salisson.

Dear Baron,

The pool you destroyed was not our only sacred hollow. Salisson is a large city and we had many offerings to make to R'Chun, and we have brought a great supply of the Blood of our God with us. I thought your friend would make a suitable servant, but unfortunately our lord has rejected him. If he cannot be with R'Chun then perhaps he can still be of some use to you. May he serve you in death as poorly as he did in life.

Yours Faithfully, your adoptive descendant

Lord Sern Cellin

I screwed up the letter, dropped it to the ground and stamped it into the dirt of the road until it was ragged torn scraps. In my anger I did not notice Fenna approach, and I only realised she was present when she gave out a high, mournful moan. I stepped forwards quickly and tried to grab her, to stop her from approaching, but she had already passed me. She knelt at the side of the mewling, squirming, rotting thing that had been her lover. It could barely move but still tried to lunge for her, its blackened teeth snapping together as it gnawed fruitlessly at the air. She stared at its face, into its eyes, searching for any sign of the man she had known, but it just gibbered and growled, pulling idiot faces and lashing its tongue across its lips. I knew that its stupidity was a mercy. It would have been far worse if Bor had found himself aware in this ruined body.

She knelt there, and thoughtlessly I put one hand on her shoulder. For just a moment I forgot what I was and tried to give her comfort. She accepted it for a few shuddering breaths and then she shrugged away my hand and stood up. She did not look at me, and she did not make a sound. She gazed down at the awful form lying on the ground, her cheeks still wet with tears but her eyes blank. She drew her sword and took a single step back. She raised the weapon over her head and then struck, beheading the corpse of the man she loved.

She walked away without saying a word.

We sent a messenger on a fast horse back to

Oese, with a request for Yast. We needed tools, barrels of pitch and oil, stonemasons, carpenters, and the best engineers he could find. While we awaited his response we sent scouts up the river, looking for a suitable site for the work I proposed. They found a point upstream where the river passed through a small ravine, and after investigation we determined this to be an ideal place for construction to begin. We were going to dam the river Salis.

It was half a moon before the ships from Oese landed at Hust and the men and equipment we had asked for were carried overland to our camp outside Salisson. Francyn briefed the arriving engineers and craftsmen, and they poured over the rough maps our scouts had made, arguing and planning, until a consensus was reached. A regiment accompanied them up the trail along the river to protect them while they worked. It was going to be a difficult and dangerous task anyway, without having to fend off the attentions of the roaming undead patrols.

While we waited the rest of our army encircled the city, attempting to stop any effort by the undead to leave or reinforce themselves further. Several regiments marched the long route around the walls, crossing at the bridge where the river moat split and making their way to the eastern side of the city, camping across the Coast Road as we did at the western wall. I remained with our army in the west. Dela instructed Shand and his fleet to blockade the harbour.

We may not have been able to get in, but we were not letting the dead out.

There were still patrols left in the hills and crags around Salisson but the Wardens hunted them through the wild terrain, Wyren leading them temporarily while Fenna remained at camp, unwilling for the time being to leave her tent. Francyn's army grew restless waiting. Their spirits were low, and word of Cellin's ghastly missive had spread around the camp. Francyn had tried to suppress rumours of it under pain of corporal punishment, but no secret could be kept by soldiers for long and the story was whispered around fires and in tents at night. Each morning several men were missing, having fled their duty under cover of darkness. Rumour had it some had been taken, but no evidence for this was ever presented, and my own feeling was that desertion was more likely than capture.

One evening, just as the sun was setting in the west, the guards at my enclosure were approached by a visitor who sought an audience with me. It was Quell. He entered my tent and addressed me.

"My apologies for disturbing you. May I take a seat?"

My tent was not too small, but it had little in the

way of furnishings, and I had to fold a blanket for him to have a place to sit. I had no need of such comforts but kept a blanket over me in the night anyway out of habit.

We sat there for a moment, watching each other. He had always been a quiet man unless in battle, and he seemed reluctant to speak. I waited for him. Patience is one of my strengths.

"I… I wanted to thank you. You saved my life in Salisson. If not for you it would have been me dragged into that pit, not Grent. I wish I could have helped him too. I've lost people in battle before… I have seen death many times."

"As have I. May I ask… how did you come to be in service to the Temple? I know I have asked you about this before. I wish to know more about you."

He lowered his head, staring at the grey woven blanket, and even picked at it a little with his fingers. He looked like a guilty boy, being interrogated by his father over some childish misdemeanour.

"I was a killer." He said, and then raised his head to look at my uncovered skull.

"So was I. I did it in the service of an Emperor, believe I was performing just and honourable deeds. I am no longer as certain as that as I was when I lived."

He shook his head. "I knew what I did wasn't honourable. I served the Men of the Web, a league of thieves, blackmailers, brothel-keepers. I was their blade." He picked at the blanket again, his fingers pulling threads from its edges. "There came a point where I had forgotten how to be a good man."

He leaned back. There was little light in the tent, but his eyes glittered in the darkness.

"You can't live that life for long. Most die by a blade in the back. Mine was in my front. I was asked to… remove… a merchant, a man who had crossed the Web. Taken what they regarded as theirs. They thought everything was theirs. The man was prepared for me. At the end of it I lay in an alleyway with a knife in my shoulder and my blood pouring out of me. I could… I should have died there and then."

"What happened?" These were the most words I had ever heard Quell speak. I had known he had a dark history from the way he had fought, but still I felt shocked at the matter-of-fact way he talked about these things.

"I was found. By a Daughter of the Temple. She took me in. Saved my life. I didn't deserve it."

Perhaps he thought in the darkness of the tent I could not see his tears, for he made no effort to wipe them away.

"I have sought absolution ever since. My past is

as bloody as yours, and I have no illusion of honour to cling to."

I felt for the man. But I needed an answer to a question, and this was my chance.

"You say you are penitent… that you try to live as a good man now. So why have you lied to me?"

He jerked with shock, as if I had slapped him. For a moment I worried I had pushed him too far. A wave of anger passed across his face, but then his head sagged, and he retreated into himself again.

"What… what do you mean?"

"You knew what I was. You knew the threat from Kroll was real. That the dead were walking the Northern Shore. So why did Dela have to force the issue?"

He did not reply, and all I could hear was his heavy, shuddering breaths in the darkness of the tent. I did not relent.

"*Answer me*! Men and women have died because you remained silent! Regions have fallen because you did not *act!* I need to know *why!*"

He refused to look at me. I waited in the darkness. My patience would outlast his resolve.

Finally, he spoke.

"There are things I am forbidden to speak of. The Temple's secrets are not for outsiders. I cannot answer you."

"You say I saved your life. Your answers are the payment I demand for this debt. You were prepared to fight the dead, before I ever came to the Western Gate."

Even as I said it, I felt shame at having to use that leverage. His knowledge was too important for me not to bend my own morals. He still would not meet my gaze.

"It is... not for me to say. I can say that what you state is true. Yes, the Temple knew. I am armed and armoured to fight the undead. All the Apostles are. But I am oathbound to deny you the answers you seek. Only the First Daughter can speak on this matter. It is her orders I follow, and she would have to tell you why."

"And the blessing you use to destroy the pools? The Milk of T'Lassa? What is its source?"

"I cannot say. Please, Asheth, do not ask me to break my oath. It is all I have."

"Your oath, and the Temple's secrecy, have cost us much. My promise to her is forfeit because of her deceit. When my work here is completed, Dela and I will speak with the First Daughter. We deserve an answer."

He did not dispute me, and instead gathered himself and left the tent. Afterwards I sat in silence, gazing at the stars until sunrise, and watching the waves roll in.

The spring tides were high, and although the chill coming off the sea was still enough to have the men and women of the camp wrapped up and shivering while performing their duties, the days were becoming a little warmer, and there were bright sunny mornings where I looked out to sea and could pretend I was not preparing for battle. At least for a little while.

We had received word from upstream that the dam across the ravine was complete. Yast's engineers were talented, and the evidence of their success could soon be seen. The rushing river-moat slowed, the level of the water lowered, and within a day the carcasses of animals, the remains of tipped wagons, and the flotsam and jetsam of a living city using the moat as a means of disposal could be seen. Shapes both identifiable and not appeared from the mud beneath the swiftly shallowing waters. Once the water had gone and the muddy riverbed was exposed, Yast's men investigated the northern end of the city, watched from the walls by bow armed Raised who loosed arrows upon them but struck nothing.

As predicted by Dela, the vents that served as safety valves for the oil reservoir were exposed, just below the original surface of the moat. Once the water had cleared enough teams of men were sent in under palisades, the ineffectual bowshots of the dead failing to pierce the wooden covers, and the men laid sandbags and planks across the mud so they could gain access to the vents. Each vent was broken open, the rusted metal grates torn from the walls and discarded, and they were packed with rags soaked in the flammable, bright-burning oil that the Regions used, a supply having been brought from Oese. More barrels of the stuff were sat at the base of the wall, stacked against it to form a pyramid under each vent. The dead were now dropping chunks of masonry on their attackers, and the work grew more dangerous as the stones crashed against the palisades, breaking through in places. The wounded and dead of Francyn's army were dragged out of the mud by their comrades and replaced with more workers. While the bonfire was being built Francyn set up catapults on the opposite shore and stood on the bridge crossing to survey the work, out of range of the unskilled dead bowmen. Once Yast's engineers were satisfied with their work they and their assisting soldiers withdrew, and moved to either side of the moat, making smaller dams there so that the water could be channelled towards the bonfire. Many men died there in the mud and filth of the river bottom, either caught unawares by shots from above, or crushed under the assault of falling stonework. One of the teams broke and ran, and had to be replaced, when the dead resorted to throwing the unused carcasses of dead city-folk into the moat. I heard the whispers in camp of the dead's foul actions. They did not waste any bodies they could use, so the corpses they threw at their attackers were those of the very young or the very old that had not yet been burned. Disease then became a threat to our forces, as many men and women in the camp were struck down with fevers and loose bowels, and again I felt a little comforted by my immunity to the stench. There were many physical effects that no longer troubled me, but I could hear the moans of those afflicted in the night, and I often heard racing footsteps as men and women stumbled down the winding path to the seashore to seek relief in the ocean.

One day, as the sun was high overhead, the construction at the walls reached completion and the men and women withdrew. Francyn gave the signal, and a single flaming missile was sent by catapult towards the barrels. I stood with the General and Dela on the crossing bridge to witness the result of our efforts.

The barrels broke and caught fire, and even I had to shield my eye sockets with the bones of my hands as a bright star of intense heat and light shone at the bottom of the wall and then grew until it reached the open rag-filled vents. The rags lit and the fire crept up inside, heating the tanks kept on the other side of the wall. We did not have to wait long for the oil inside to react. There was a thunderous noise, as if a god clapped its hands, and a tall pillar of fire erupted from inside the city. A wave of heated air rolled towards us from the walls, and all of us on the bridge staggered and then ducked behind the low stonework as a hot wind threatened to drive us into the muddy riverbank below. I was unaffected by the heat and was able to stand up sooner than my companions. Through the glare of the raging inferno, I could see some fractures had appeared in the opposite wall already, and where the burning oil seeped through the cracks it lit them from within, as if they were threads of lightning crawling on the surface of the stone.

We let it burn for a while. The air above and around the walls shimmered and shook. The defending Raised who had stood at the battlements above the tanks had gone, destroyed by the blast, but we could see more had arrived, their shapes twisting and warping in the heat haze as they moved through the smoke and flame. As they moved to take their shooting positions their bowstrings snapped in the heat, their bows charred, and their kilt-wrappings caught fire and fell from their bones. The stone gave off so much heat that Francyn and Dela were sweating, despite the chill sea wind. As we stood watching I heard the distant sound of chanting, and clouds began to gather. The cult was trying to raise a storm, as they had when

I helped assault Gallin the previous year. If we waited for the storm to come the fire would be put out and the wall cooled slowly before we could strike. It was time.

Francyn sent a rider up to the dammed ravine. It was a most clever construction. Wooden logs had been placed at intervals with hooks embedded in their ends, tied to strong horses by thick ship's rope. Yast's engineers had performed their task admirably. The dam held back a river that was becoming a cauldron of force and rage, the spring thaws having fed it and fed it until it was like a wild beast waiting to charge. A signal was given, and the horses were driven, straining and heaving, pulling on the long ropes at either side of the ravine, the men with them whipping their hinds and screaming encouragement. The dam creaked, stone and sand and wood shifting and groaning, until finally its supports and keystones gave way, and the water was unleashed.

My companions and I moved away from our position at the crossing bridge, and stood well back from the riverbank, awaiting the arrival of our weapon. I heard a distant roar, swelling quickly to a thunderous, almost overwhelming howl as the rushing water pushed a wave of air, earth and stone ahead of it in an unstoppable torrent. The uncaged, swollen river came towards the city at incredible speed. I saw it strike the crossing bridge and the stone structure ceased to exist, obliterated in an instant. The tidal wave reached the city walls. Corralled by the smaller dams either side of our target it did not lose any of its strength to the moat around the city. It struck the searingly hot stone of Salisson's battlements, and a huge cloud of steam erupted from its touch and rose swiftly into the air, obscuring our view of the city momentarily. There was a series of sharp, cracking reports, and then a booming sound, and pieces of shattered rock and masonry flew from the mist and began to land in the swiftly filling moat and on the opposite banks. The wall collapsed, and the water pushed through the gap and forced its way into the streets of Salisson. It drove all before it, the living, the dead, the homes and hovels, buildings of both stone and wood annihilated by its passing.

We waited as long as we dared for the water to cool the stone and settle to a fast-moving river rather than a raging torrent. It was still flooding over the remains of the wall but we could now see the exposed masonry of the foundations, and Francyn began to yell orders and prepare his assault. The long wooden palisades were brought to the riverbank, this time to cover ramps that were moved into position either side of the still racing water. They were pushed towards the breach and their heavy hooked ends were lodged over the remains of the wall, to serve as new, temporary bridges. The General's army began to advance across, raising their shields as they left the cover of their wooden tunnels, defending against the pitiful bowshot from the remaining dead archers. Most of the Raised near the breach had been washed away by the water. Quell and I followed the army into the city, accompanied by the trusted guards Francyn had assigned me. They lifted their shields to cover us, as Quell and I had none, both of us armed in such a way that we could not carry our own. Quell wore his full, silver armour instead, and I wore my Warden's garb, but did not cover my face. I wanted Kroll's cultists to see who opposed them. I wanted to find Cellin.

Francyn had left forces at both the west and east gates to stop any attempt the dead made to escape, and we drove back any Raised left standing by the flood as we assaulted the breach. We waded through rushing water that came to our knees as we attacked the waiting dead. My kind were not suited to this kind of combat. They were not used to moving in the water, finding it hard to keep their footing, and Francyn's guards were brutal and efficient, unleashing all their pent-up misery and rage at the Raised soldiers. They advanced in an orderly shield wall, cutting down any that tried to stand against them, and if any of the skeletal defenders tried to flank us

Quell and I lashed out, slashing and smashing away those that made it to the rear of the guard. It was a gruelling slog, but we made good progress, grinding our way into the city.

We pushed the dead back, Francyn's army taking the city street by street. Hordes of Lessers floundered in the flood waters and were stabbed and cut by pikemen, held underwater so that men could cut off their thrashing limbs and separate their gnashing heads from their shoulders. The water around the army was quickly filled with the filth seeping from the animated corpses. The Raised staggered under assaults from our furious soldiers, cries of rage and disgust loosed from the men's lips as they broke bone and splintered skulls. The dead were in disarray and were being driven down towards the harbour. As our forces passed the east and west gates they took the gatehouses, opening the way for the rest of our regiments to enter the city. At either side of the gates were cages filled with more Lessers, befouling the waters around them, but in the rush of the flood there had been no time for their handlers to release them, and they pawed and clawed at the wooden bars, trying in vain to reach our men as they passed through the gates. A unit of pikemen attacked each one, destroying the bestial creatures before they could escape their prison.

If our enemy had been a living army they would

have routed or sought terms by now, but the dead do not break, and we had to fight our way all the way to the harbour walls. On the docks we found the undead cavalry, their skeletal steeds slowed by the still flowing water and hemmed in by the dense storehouses and work buildings of the dock, unable to fight effectively or mount a competent charge. They and several of the living cultists still with them were driven into the waters of the harbour, the un-fleshed sinking like a stone, the living splashing and panicking in the churned and filthy waters. They drowned as their dead servants were driven onto them. Cellin was on the dock, his fine cloak soaked and ragged, his armour stained with mud and streaks of blood, and he rode his skeletal mount back-and-to, slashing with his greatsword and screaming garbled and panicked commands at the few warriors he had left. In a last desperate attempt to escape his fate he charged our lines, and his horse tried to clear the shield wall in one great bound. Its leap fell short, and it crushed several men underneath its armoured bulk as it clattered and fell to the ground, its hooves slashing through the water as it lay on its side. Cellin was pinned underneath, and his sword fell from his hands and was lost in the deluge. His head was under the water. I saw him fall, and I pushed through the swirling tide, reaching down to grip his skull by his eye-sockets and drag it up out of the water. He could not drown, I knew that, but I wanted him to know who had him.

"Haaaa, Grandfather. How good to see you…." He said, and his voice filled me with fury. I dragged him out from under his mount, fully intending to crush his skull there and then. I raised my hammer high over my head but Quell caught my wrist. He had to raise his voice to make himself heard over the water and the dying sounds of battle.

"He might be useful! Stay your anger for now. We can take him back to the General."

I held my hammer above me for a moment, fighting the overwhelming urge to kill the treacherous bastard anyway. I got control of myself and gently lowered my weapon, placing the head of it right next to Cellin's gem-encrusted face. Quell looked down at the traitor, his nose wrinkling with disgust.

"I believe Dela would have words with you." He said.

Cellin was stripped of his armour and bound by his hands and feet to a long pole, so he was hanging from it like a hog for the roast. As the rest of the army worked their way through the water-logged streets of the city and tried to clear it of the remaining dead, Quell and I accompanied Francyn's guard back to camp. They carried Cellin between them and paraded him through the gates and back out to the siege line. This raised cheers and hurrahs from the gathered men and women, and several of them spat at the traitor as he passed the bridge over the muddy moat and up the Coast Road. When we reached camp a small storage tent was cleared, and Cellin was bound to its central support. Quell and I left our prisoner there, guarded by several of Francyn's capable men, and we made our way to join the General and Dela in the command tent. I had re-covered my face by this time and found that although the soldiers were still giving me a wide berth, I was not attracting the insults and abuse I had previously. Word of my actions in the siege was spreading, and there was a grudging respect there now. When we entered the command tent the two men were sat at the map table, Francyn exhausted and still wearing half of his armour, Dela with his customary glass of wine. I took a seat at the table and advised them of our captured prize while Quell fetched himself a drink of water and sat in the corner on a stool, hanging his head in weariness.

"We need to question him. If he has insight into Kroll's greater plans then he may prove a useful asset." Dela rubbed his face and then slid his palm up over the dark skin of his hairless scalp.

"That being said... I don't know how we can verify anything he tells us. I had similar difficulty when I came to question you for the first time, Asheth. How do you trust the word of a dead man? I can't offer him freedom for his co-operation. He has betrayed the Regions completely... he needs to be imprisoned or destroyed. I don't know what pressure I can apply to get answers. Would threat of violence work?"

Dela turned to me, and his lips were pressed tightly together. He looked at the floor.

"Asheth, I'm sorry to ask, but... if it were you in that tent, what would work to persuade you?"

It was not the first time I had thought on this subject. Back in the first days of my new existence, when I had still been Kroll's slave, I had considered how I could be tortured by him if my true nature were discovered. I knew the answer to Dela's question, but felt some apprehension sharing that knowledge, no matter how much I trusted him. No matter what friendship had grown between us over time, Dela and I were still a living man talking to a dead one. The two will never be on even ground, and I did not relish the idea of sharing my fears. Nevertheless, our needs outweighed my trepidation. I shook my head, as if to clear away my doubts, and answered the man.

"I do not feel pain. Neither will he. So, torture of the kind I would have employed against prisoners in the past will be useless. We could have threatened him with violence against a loved one, but I doubt Cellin loves anything apart from his own ambitions. We have no-one to use as leverage against him. Finally, he worships a god of death, so the possibility of destruction may not sway him. However, if Cellin is as I am, he would fear one thing… time."

Dela frowned. "I don't understand. Time?"

"Yes. I am, apparently, immortal, unending. I can only be… killed, by destroying my skull or removing it from my neck, and even then, I cannot be sure that I would cease to think or feel. My limbs are dead bones, with but little sensation. When I hid my nature from Kroll… at first it was because I denied what had happened to me, I thought I was moving through a nightmare. Later I feared the torture he could inflict, simply by trapping my soul in a place I could not escape. He could put me in a grave for all eternity and leave me to lose my wits in the dark earth. Or… there were severed heads, mounted on spikes, adorning the walls of Estwake. I do not know if they are aware, or if they can see or hear. It is possible that they gaze out across the land, bound to the castle walls in solitary, unceasing torment."

Dela and Francyn looked at each other, their expressions filled with absolute horror, and in the corner of the tent Quell began muttering a prayer under his breath. Dela drained his glass of wine and immediately refilled it.

After some muted discussion, Quell, Dela and I went to the tent where Cellin was being kept prisoner. I asked Francyn to remain behind. I felt he should not sully his character by partaking in the interrogation. He was a noble man and did not deserve such a black mark on his soul. As we approached the tent where Cellin was being held we could hear him. He was singing, some bawdy song about a sailor's wife who sought solace from loneliness while her husband was away. The traitor's spirits seemed high, considering his circumstances. He appeared to think he could not be harmed. I was about to correct him.

We entered the tent to find him sat with his legs and arms still bound around the central pole, and he was being as loud and obnoxious as he could possibly be. Dela asked the guards to wait outside, and they were obviously relieved to get some distance from the sound of Cellin's voice, if only to gain a brief respite from its cracked bell tone. I do not know what his singing was like when he was alive, but in death it was a grating dirge.

Dela took up a small stool just in front of the captive, and Quell and I flanked him, our weapons in our hands. The traitor ignored us and carried on bellowing his ribald ballad.

"Cellin, please stop that. We'd like to talk to you." Dela was polite, his manners not dissimilar to those he had displayed during my interrogation.

"What about? What do you think I have to say to *you*, you wine-soaked pirate *shit?*"

He snapped his jaws shut a couple of times, the crack of his teeth almost as infuriating as his singing.

"We need to know Kroll's plans, the extent of his forces. If you have any loyalty to the Regions left in you at all you will help us." Dela remained calm and spoke quietly. He did not respond to Cellin's insult.

"Loyalty? To this, this *hive* of *hypocrisy*? Why would I have *loyalty?* You of all people, Dela, should know what a festering hole the Regions have become. We were an *EMPIRE!* We ruled the Scar Sea and beyond, and now we are just… we are just squabbling fishermen and farmers, led by bureaucrats and scribes. Where is the *glory* in that? Where is the *magnificence?*" Cellin was becoming more animated, straining against his bonds, and Quell and I took a step forwards. He ignored us.

"I have no loyalty to your politics, to your ridiculous Council, to this weak and feeble host of coin counters. *I should have been an Emperor!* Kroll and R'Chun have offered me an eternal throne, and you offer me *nothing.*"

I took another step towards him then, and crouched down in front of him, balanced on the toes of my boots. I set my hammer on the ground, head down, so its handle stood between us.

"I have served an Emperor, Cellin. I have been made aware of his faults. His goals may not have been as just or honourable as I believed when I lived. But you are no Domint. You are no leader of men. You are a mewling, wretched turncoat, a traitor to your people… and believe me when I say this to you, you *will* help us."

He quieted a little then, but he was still showing bravado. He did not know the nature of the pain I could inflict on him.

"You can't hurt me, *grandfather.* Kroll has given me the gift of undeath, the same blessing you have spurned. You cannot turn me against him." He shook his head. "We are both eternal, grandfather, and even if you destroy me, I do not fear the true death. I will gladly fall into R'Chun's embrace and be at his side."

"You will never meet your god." I said, and stood, picking my hammer back up off the floor.

Dela called in the guards from outside the tent, and each one grasped a limb of the dead man while his bonds were cut. They held him on the ground while he struggled, his arms and legs extended. I swung my hammer and cracked it against his thighbones, shattering them and leaving splinters of bone like broken twigs protruding from his hips. As he tried to wrench himself free from the men holding his arms the remnants of his legs writhed and twisted in their sockets, and he howled and screamed and cursed. I repeated my blows at his arms, breaking them in two above the elbow, leaving their stumps to thrash uselessly from his shoulders. All that he had left to move with any purpose was his head, and he started to slam his skull against the floor, desperately trying to crack it open and release his soul. The floor of the tent was not hard enough for this, and as the guards stepped back all Cellin could do was wriggle, his spine curling and his head turning from side to side as he attempted to bite the retreating men. Threads of the animating Blood of R'chun dangled and floated from the open, fractured ends of his broken limbs.

He wailed and screamed but I ignored his protestations and reached down to turn him onto his front. I hooked my hammer to my back and then picked him up by the base of his spine. He tried to writhe free from my grasp, but I held him firm, and he could not turn his head enough to look at me. I walked out of the tent carrying him.

We had an audience as I carried him towards his destination. More of the soldiers had come back from the city by now to rest and eat, and they watched with silent and hard faces as I carried the screaming corpse through the camp. His identity was not a secret, and some of the observers spat and made the Sign of the Wave or called out insults.

Outside the camp, about twenty paces beyond our perimeter, a small team of men had dug a hole. I took him to it, and when he saw what had been prepared, he gave out a wail of anguish. He began to beg and plead, finally realising what fate I had planned for him. I lowered him into the grave and dropped him face down onto the dark earth at the bottom. He tried to turn over, his broken and useless limbs cutting rents in the soil but failing to right his body. Worms and beetles and all manner of crawling, skittering things were visible in the churned earth. The hole was a little shallower than a grave would usually be, but deep enough that it took a while for the men to bury him completely.

While we waited, Dela and I headed back into Salisson.

Most of the flood waters had receded. The temporary dams at the river fork had worn away from the force of the torrent and the moat was starting to refill. Inside the city the water was draining into cellars, and into the network of tunnels that Dela had so carefully maintained.

Slime and mud and filth coated the cobbled streets. The blast from the oil reservoir had blackened the buildings around its clearing, and the rushing water had knocked down what the fire had not. The remains of both the old and the newly dead were everywhere, the drowned and smashed bodies of Kroll's cultists lying in the road or pinned against stonework by debris, and soldiers from Francyn's army gutted and torn and left to rot in the morning sun. Streams of befouled liquid glittered and sparkled and caught the sunlight.

We reached Dela's keep, and he paused for a moment in front of his ruined home. He did not shed a tear or speak a word, but his face was a mask of pain, and I felt for him.

It was as we neared the execution square that he finally spoke. The High Daughter's body had been removed along with that of her acolyte, but the anvil was still stained with blood. The congealed marks had not been cleaned away by the deluge.

"This isn't going to work." He said.

"What do you mean?" I waited for him to elaborate. He took several deep breaths, and then turned to look at me.

"We didn't save this place. No-one will live here again in my lifetime. It is corrupted, cursed."

He kicked a chunk of muddy rock at his feet, sending it skidding along the slick and slime coated cobbles.

"My home is a place of death now. We didn't win this battle. Fighting the dead has cost us too much. This isn't even our last fight, but the first of many to come. Salis may be re-taken... Kroll had only just established his hold here. But Tresh is lost, and Estwake is no longer part of the Regions. We can drive the dead back, but all we will get in return are the corpses of towns and villages. We've already lost."

"We can stop his advance. Hold them here." I tried to comfort him, but my mood was also low, and I was fighting my despair as much as he was fighting his. I could not help the doubt in my voice.

"Perhaps. But Estwake is now a Sechian stronghold. Tresh too, most likely. Even if we can hold them here, Kroll can bring in reinforcements with impunity. It will be difficult to blockade his harbours completely, especially this far from the Western Gate. We need an advantage, some insight. We need something that will halt his advance."

"We will get it. Cellin will have broken."

"You're sure?"

I hung my head, and lifted my hood back over my skull, even though I knew the shame I felt at my actions would not show on my face.

"Trust me, Dela, I am sure." I said. "His fear of life now outweighs his fear of death."

I waited two days. I returned to Cellin's shallow grave, accompanied by a handful of Francyn's men. They began to dig. Even under the tight-packed soil Cellin must have heard the disturbance above him. As the dirt was shifted away a low, mournful sound issued from the ground, not a scream but a constant moan, echoing up from the pit. When Cellin's spine and ribcage became exposed I stepped down into the grave and grasped him, pulling him free from the last layer of earth. He babbled and shook in my grip, his head lashing from side to side, and he began to shriek.

"Be quiet." I said. "Do you want to remain here with the worms, or do you want to help me?"

"PLEASE! *Pleasedon'tputmebackpleasenonoNONONOOOO!*" He coiled and twisted in my hands like a serpent, then his mouth snapped shut and he became still. He made a low whimpering sound.

"Do as I say, and I will give you to your god. Lie to me and you will remain in your grave for eternity, with only the crawling things for company. Do you agree to my terms?"

"YES! Yes. Please. I can help you. Please."

"Very well."

I stalked back to the tent where we had held him before, carrying him in front of me. Dela and Francyn were there waiting for us, both sat on camp stools for comfort. I set Cellin down against the central post, and then bound his torso to it with a length of rope so that he was sat up facing me. His bones were stained from his burial and wet clods of earth and mud dripped from his ravaged skeleton. As I watched a small beetle skittered out of one of his eye sockets, falling to the ground on its back. It managed to roll and right itself and raced through the open tent flaps.

"Councillor Dela and General Francyn are going to question you. You will answer truthfully. If you do not, this grave will be your home. Do you understand?"

I stood opposite him, to the side of my comrades. My helmet and hood were removed so he could see my exposed skull. I felt little mercy towards him, but I was ashamed of my methods. I had inflicted my own worst fear upon him.

"I do understand, I do, I'm sorry, please don't put me back there pleasePLEASE*PLEASE*-"

"Be *QUIET*!" I raised my voice as loudly as I could, and from the edge of my vision I saw Francyn and Dela both wince.

They proceeded to question the traitor.

The interrogation took most of the day. Cellin was out of his wits, half-mad after the torture I had inflicted, and I often had to interject with further threats to focus his mind and bring him back to sensible conversation. If I had flesh, I would have shuddered at the thought of what I had subjected him to. I had no intention of repeating my actions. Burying him the first time had meant putting aside my honour, and I could not countenance doing it again. Permanently entombing him was beyond even my rage. What I had done was cruel, no matter how much circumstance demanded it.

Cellin revealed much to us.

Kroll was over-extended. He had brought many of his living followers with him when Cellin had let him settle in Estwake, but some had to remain in every village and town he took, lest he lose control of the dead stationed there. The numbers he had meant he could only push so far without drawing strength from behind his lines. He had many soldiers but few leaders. Tresh was fully occupied, but Estwake was now only sparsely held. There was an opportunity there, but time was not our friend.

"Kroll has sent word back to the Sechian Emperor of his success. Their ships have begun to dock at Estwake Harbour." Cellin has calmed, no longer babbling and moaning. It had taken some encouragement from me for him to cease his whining.

"How did he send word back? Are the ships he has taken from Gariss making the Great Crossing?" Dela leaned from his stool, his elbows on his knees. He looked tired.

"No, we have other means of communicating with the Emperor."

Dela frowned, and then his realisation dawned on his face.

"The mirrors. The same method he used to direct you in the Council chambers."

"Yes. There aren't many of them. They are a gift from R'Chun, that have been brought here from Sechia. They are meant to allow us to speak with him, but they can be used to pass messages between mortals as well."

"You can speak directly with R'Chun?"

"Kroll speaks to the Emperor, and he communes with our god and passes on his edicts."

"And what has Kroll told the Emperor?" Francyn asked, leaning forwards, the stool he sat on tilting on its legs, his heavy boots planted in front of him.

"That he is winning. He had hoped to make it all the way to the Western Gate, but if he doesn't it does not matter. All Emperor Velst required was a weakened Northern Shore. We've taken three

Regions already, and they have been desecrated. They will be of no use to you now, and the Northern Shore will starve like the Sechians have. Soon the Emperor will send more ships, filled with the dead. Kroll is not the only Priest of R'Chun. More wait in Sechia. More will come."

Francyn sat back, the legs on his tool touching the floor of the tent again. He turned to Dela.

"If the Sechian Emperor sends his forces before we defeat Kroll, we will be fighting on two fronts. We've left the Western Gate and the surrounding Regions unguarded. The war for Salis has cost too much already and we haven't even begun our advance on Tresh." Francyn wiped his brow. The spring was near its end and summer was on its way. The tent must have been warmed by the sun, and Francyn was sweating in his armour. I felt no warmth.

"We must withdraw." Said Dela.

"And give up all our gains? All of the progress we have made against the dead?"

"What progress? Fighting them will always be a losing battle. Defeat costs them little. We can contain them in Tresh, use Salis as a buffer to stop any further advance. But re-taking Tresh will over-stretch us. Salis is a wasteland, and Tresh and Estwake are *lost.* We cannot afford to lose yet more soldiers, and risk simply feeding the beast we fight." Dela lowered his head, looking at the dirty floor of the tent.

"Believe me, I don't want to give up all I've built. This is my home, my legacy. It is no more. I have walked the streets of Salisson and I no longer recognise it. We cannot sacrifice more men for worthless territory. This place is dead... and the further east we go, the worse it will be."

"And what of the Emperor?" I spoke as softly as I could, as my voice had jarred them enough that day.

"We need to at least delay his invasion. We don't have the strength yet to launch an attack, so all we can do is withdraw to the west and protect what we have." Dela looked old to me, then. The events of the last few moons had been a great burden on him.

"Perhaps we can stall him. Send a message... a warning." I walked back to where Cellin's remains were bound to the tentpole.

"Cellin. Where is the mirror that Kroll uses to speak to the Emperor?"

The treacherous corpse lifted his head to look at me. I could sense the fear in him, like a low tinkling bell ringing just below my hearing. If he had eyes he would have been crying.

"It's... it's in his chambers. In the catacombs under Estwake. But the castle is still held. You can't get in." Cellin tossed his head from side to side, and something like a laugh, tinged with madness, escaped his gaping jaw. "You can't *win*, grandfather… hehe… R'Chun will rule all of this land."

"R'Chun is nothing, as are you. Estwake Castle once belonged to me. It has secrets only I know."

The corpse hung its head, its useless and shattered appendages hanging limp.

"Please. End this. You promised me death… I have told you all I know. I have been truthful. Please let me die." His voice was quieter now, and he began to make sounds almost like sobs, little whining grunts that filled me with disgust.

"I did. I believe you have told the truth. So… I will release you to your god. When you see him, tell him I reject him."

I unstrapped my hammer from my back, fully intending to destroy his head. As I raised the weapon there was a commotion at the entrance to the tent. There had been two guards posted there, and one of them stumbled through the tent-flaps, holding his face. Blood was running through his cupped hands and was soaking into his shirtsleeve and chainmail. He tried to speak, babbling out a warning through his broken nose and teeth, but he was too late. Fenna came in behind him and kicked the heel of her boot into the crease behind the guard's knee. He dropped to the floor, groaning in pain.

Dela stood up from his seat and made as if to grab her, but she rounded on him and screamed "Don't you *dare! Don't touch me!*"

She stood alongside me, gazing down at the moaning carcass I was interrogating. She looked up at me, her face stern, tears of rage rolling down her face. Her lip was cut and bleeding from fighting with the guards.

"Is this him? The one you buried? Is this the one who killed Bor?" Her voice came out in short, angry bursts, and her teeth were bared and clamped together, the muscles in her jaw standing out and tense under her black skin.

"Yes, Fenna. This is Cellin. He has answered my questions, and I am going to end his life now, as I promised him."

"After what he *DID? That wasn't your promise to make.*" She hissed the last through her teeth.

"Fenna…"

"He doesn't deserve mercy Asheth. He'll get none from me."

She pulled a dagger from a scabbard at her belt, knelt down, and cut the bindings that held Cellin to the tent-post. Then she reached under his ribs and lifted him.

"Fenna, stop." Dela went to bar the exit from the tent. Francyn had not moved, his feelings obviously divided on the matter.

"Get out of my way Dela. He has to pay for what he's done."

"He has paid. He's a pitiful, forlorn creature, Fenna. We must put him out of his misery."

The traitor's corpse was trying to twist out of her grip, and flailed his ruined arms towards her, unable to strike a blow with what was left of them. He let out a wail and rolled his head back and to, his jaws clacking open and shut as he began to beg.

"Please, please, *letmedieletmedie…*"

She ignored him and moved towards the tent exit, barging the protesting Dela out of her way. He reached for her shoulder to stop her, and I grabbed his hand. Fenna left the tent, and I followed her. I walked behind her as she carried the writhing and sobbing corpse through the camp. The men and women of the camp watched her at first, but each one of them bowed their heads as she passed and made the Sign of the Wave, muttering prayers to Omma T'Lassa.

At the rear of the campsite, near where my quarters lay, the cliffs fell steeply down into the waiting ocean, high white walls of stone and lichen where seabirds made their roosts. There were sharp rocks at the base of them, but also deep whirling pools where the water rolled and tumbled but then sank into dark abyssal depths. Fenna walked to the cliff's edge, leaning out over the drop with her squirming, screaming cargo. She found the place she wanted, and stood there, holding Cellin out into the sea air with the churning ocean far below him. I spoke to her.

"Fenna... do not do this. It will stain your soul. Trust me, you will not be able wash away this mark."

She looked over her shoulder at me, her voice struggling against the wind and her arms still straining against the flailing dead man trying to twist from her grip. I could hear the seabirds cawing and crying in the sky above us, and the deep rumbling bass of the waiting sea below. She was silhouetted against the horizon, and behind her I could see a rising anvil cloud, black against the swiftly greying sky. The wind gusted and whipped the tears away from her face.

"I'll wear the stain, Asheth. Bor was my love. My lover, my friends, my *home* is dead because of this foul *thing.* I will wear the mark this gives me and treasure it."

She turned back to gaze into the Cellin's eye-sockets, and he wailed in madness and terror.

"PLEASE DON'T! PLEASE! I'M SORRY! I'M SO SORRY!"

"Tell it to the sea."

She threw him, just far enough that his remains did not touch the cliff walls as he fell past them.

I got to the cliff edge quickly enough to see his bones disappear into one of the deep, roiling pools. I do not know whether he had luck on his side. If he did, then the water will have smashed him against the rocks and ended his existence.

If not, then he might wait there still, in the darkness.

CHAPTER EIGHTEEN

Councillor Yast joined us at Salisson, arriving in the *Gemstone* and disembarking onto the ruined docks. He toured the city with Dela and an armed guard. We had moved the camp closer to the city now the dead had been evicted and the flood waters had fallen, but we had no intention of occupying Salisson apart from using its harbour. When Yast finally returned to the command tent from his tour he was pale and looked shaken by what he had witnessed. This was his first encounter with the undead beyond speaking to me. The desecration of Salisson had obviously disturbed him. He was trembling with anger and horror when he took his seat at the table, his attitude far removed from the arrogant air he had displayed at Council.

"You see my point." Said Dela.

"Yes" Replied Yast. "If this is what they leave behind… they have ravaged this place. Salis and

Tresh won't be a home for the living for a long time. It weakens the Regions as a whole. We'll have to rebuild, make new steadings for the farmers, the harbour needs re-opening for fishing and trade… this is disastrous." Yast ran his hand down his short beard, bringing it to a point with his fingertips, and his forehead creased in a tight frown.

"If Emperor Velst sends more abominations to our shores… we cannot afford to reclaim the fallen Regions right now. We must fortify what we have, protect the harbours, and reinforce the Western Gate, as soon as possible. Any time we can buy will be precious. We don't know how long we have."

"Cellin didn't have much information about timing. He seemed to think the invasion was imminent." Dela took a sip from his glass, although out of deference and respect for his company he had filled it with water not wine, and grimaced as he swallowed.

"What of Cellin? Is he still here?" Yast asked, and at this Dela glanced at Fenna, who sat silently at the back of the tent, her head down.

"No. Cellin answered all he could and was then… removed. That is no longer a line of inquiry we can pursue."

Yast sat up a little and looked at Dela with a quizzical expression. Dela shook his head a little and mouthed *don't ask* to dissuade any further questions on the subject.

"We need to delay Velst. Asheth has made a suggestion, and I think we should consider it." Dela turned to me then, and I stood to speak to the assembled leaders, tempering my voice as much as I could. Yast was someone we needed in our side, and I had no wish to disturb him further.

"Kroll is in communication with Sechia, using the same sorcerous means he employed to direct Cellin. I propose we assassinate Kroll. If the Emperor sees that we can strike at the heart of his forces here it may convince him that the price of invading us is too high right now. That we have not yet been sufficiently weakened for him to conquer us easily."

"Assassination? A bold idea, Asheth, but how do you propose to carry it out? Kroll is safely ensconced in the catacombs under Estwake Castle, behind legions of madmen and undead. I don't see how he can be reached." Yast had recovered well from the sight of Salisson and the arrogant tone was creeping back into his voice.

"I can get to him. I need a small group with me, just a handful of warriors. I do not wish to say any more than that. This would need to be done in utmost secrecy. We cannot risk Kroll finding out and leaving his burrow. I know I can get into

Estwake Castle, but I will need help, for it will be dangerous. We will likely not return."

"A suicide mission." Yast shook his head.

"A sacrifice. I have lived my life, Councillor. My time now is a gift for me to give. Assassination is best accomplished if one is willing to exchange their life for another."

"And we are meant to trust you? Who was Kroll's servant?"

"I trust him." Dela spoke softly, but with conviction. I nodded my respect and thanks to him.

"As do I. We would not have made this much progress were it not for him." Francyn said, and I nodded to him as well, heartened by his support.

Yast sat back in his chair, steepling his fingers under his nose, deep in thought.

"Do you have anyone in mind to accompany you?"

"I volunteer." Fenna spoke up from her dark corner. I turned to look at her, ready to argue against it, but she met my gaze with hard eyes that smothered my words. She had made her decision, and I doubted any man could have turned her from it.

"Very well," I said, turning away from the rage-filled woman. "Quell will most likely join me as well. I will ask him. Possibly Wyren will come, although I will not demand it of her. She is well versed in the skills we require. We will need a ship as well."

"The *Silverfin* is in the harbour. Shand will take you." Dela was not looking at me, but watching Fenna instead. He seemed on the verge of tears. I believe he thought of her as a daughter. He had no children of his own.

Wyren agreed to come. Fenna spoke to her. I knew the Warden did not like me very much, but she had lost many friends and colleagues in the recent battles, and her yearning for revenge outweighed any caution she had concerning me. I spoke to Quell instead.

"I will join you, Asheth. Was there ever any question? It is my calling."

"I did not want to speak for you, Quell. You understand we are likely to end our days in the bowels of Estwake? Assassins often must trade their lives for victory. That is what makes them difficult to stop, in my experience." I was adjusting my armour as we spoke. It tended to work loose after a while. Seeing me struggling the Apostle knelt behind me and helped tighten the buckles at my calves.

"I told you, Asheth. I have sworn my life and my blades to seek forgiveness. What better way to find absolution than on such a quest? To strike at the very centre of this darkness. You have given me a gift."

He stood up, his work on my armour finished, and I turned to face him. There was no sign of fear in his eyes. He looked at peace with the choice he had made. I held out my gauntleted hand, and he clasped it, then moved to clasp my wrist as I did his, as the warriors of old greeted each other. We embraced then, pounding each other's backs, and when we parted he gifted me with a rare smile.

"We are brothers now, Asheth. I go where you go."

I am not capable of much emotion. My feelings can be distant and numb, as if layered in sheep's wool. But at that moment, if I were capable of such a physical act, I would have wept. I felt more at peace in that instant than at any moment since my awakening.

"Then we go to Estwake, and fight the dead, for the sake of the living."

The next morning was grey, overcast, and the rain splattered from my hood and mask and ran in rivulets down my breastplate. The four of us boarded the *Silverfin,* while only Dela waited on the dock, watching us walk up the gangplank in silence. He looked old, and his face was drawn. Shand's crew paid us no attention, having only been told the bare minimum about our endeavour. I noted that I was no longer a source of any interest. They had become used to me, which I found strangely comforting. My companions were given their own quarters, whereas I chose to spend my time in the hold, not needing a bed to rest or blankets to warm me. In the evening I was invited to Shand's cabin, and we talked into the early hours, him drinking roughly-made spirit while we swapped stories of our lives and battles. He told me of the wild times Dela and he had lived, when Dela was Captain and Shand his First Mate, and they plied their privateer trade across the Scar Sea, up and down the Jagged Coast, and on the sea beyond the Western Gate. Dela and Shand were more than just friends. The Captain spoke with a sense of loss and regret, for Dela had chosen the land in the end. I believe the old sailor missed his companion greatly. He had to concede that Dela had seen further than him, and the fears the Councillor had carried for years had come to pass.

At twilight, nearing our destination, I stood at the prow of the ship, watching the frothing, glowing surf break around it as we ploughed through the waves. I prayed quietly to Omma T'Lassa. I spoke into the wind.

"I do not know why I am the one to carry this

burden, Mother. Is it chance that I was awakened and not another? Or do you have some design, a fate in mind for me? I have lost so much, and now I risk the lives of yet more people I care for. I need your help. Please let us succeed. Please help me!"

No answer came from the sea, nor the howling wind that filled the sails, nor the black skidding clouds that passed over the rising moon and darkened the surface of the water. I turned to stalk back to the hold, content to lie still and wait for us to reach our goal. But as I moved away I heard a sound behind me. The prow of the ship was ornamented with the head of a sea-creature, some great-jawed fish that served as a figurehead, and a large white seabird was stood upon it. I did not recognise its kind, though not having spent a great deal of time at sea that was not surprising. It was a raptor, certainly, a fish-eater, with a long, sharp, spearing beak, and dark eyes that glinted in the light from the ship's lamps. I walked back towards it and it shuffled a little on its perch but did not fly away, simply tilting its head to one side and regarding me with what appeared to be some intelligence. I reached out, seeing if the bird would allow me to touch it. I thought it would depart but instead it spread its wings wide, swept them back and then lifted itself into the air with a hopping motion, alighting on my outstretched arm. It looked directly into my mask, gazing through the visor and into the empty sockets that served me as eyes. We remained like that for a little while, neither of us moving. It felt as if it were trying to commune with me in some way, and I could almost hear its spirit talking to me, though I could not relate what words were spoken. I do not know how long we were there. Finally, it gave a loud, screeching cry, and with one sweep of its wide wings it launched itself into the dark night sky, the light from the moon illuminating white flashes from its feathers as it disappeared over the waves.

It took us a little while to reach our destination. We could not take a direct route and simply follow the coastline, for our passage would have been marked and could have been reported back to Kroll. Instead Shand took us out into the Scar Sea, and then looped back so that we could travel up the eastward coast instead, its rocky mountainous shores devoid of harbour or landing spot and hopefully clear of spying eyes. The closer we got to Estwake the darker the skies became, even during the day. The gloomy, despondent darkness that I had noted when I resided in my former Barony now extended further along the Northern Shore and out to sea, the weather affected by the presence of Kroll's sorcery. The clouds above us loomed low and black, and squalls of wind and driving rain became more and more frequent as we neared our goal, the sea rising and falling with much severity and the waves battering over the bow of the *Silverfin*. Storms rolled over and through us. Green forks of lighting danced in the sky and glowing flames of emerald light ran up and down our masts, curling around rope and sliding in waves across the deck. The thunder that accompanied the bright flashes above cracked overhead in constant retorts, the maelstrom shouting its warnings at us again and again.

As we neared Estwake Harbour, approaching from the southeast, the lights of the port showed the shadows of tall black ships silhouetted against them, and Shand and his crew knew them to be of Sechian manufacture. Some of the invasion forces were already beginning to arrive, a vanguard at least, and the dock was laden with a number of these warships, their contents having been spilled into the infested harbour town. Alongside the port, by its walls on the eastern side, was the entrance we sought. The Scar. The great ravine that split Estwake in two and ran along and below the high Sagaran Mountains. Its mouth opened here into Estwake Bay, and the water of the Scar River ran down from its source leagues away and emptied into the Scar Sea, the tributary that had fed this body of water for aeons long past. Its cliff sides rose high on either side, and the entrance to the Scar River was hidden by the rocky faces, so that we could gain access if we could sneak past the harbour.

Stealth was going to be difficult, but it had already been determined that the *Silverfin* would serve as a decoy for any local ships to chase, hopefully being fast enough to get away, or if caught by sorcerous means then tough enough to fight. If we succeeded in our mission, we would have to make any escape by land, as Shand's ship would not be able to wait for us but instead needed to draw ships from the harbour mouth and allow us access to the ravine.

The light was fading, and the sun must have been setting, though it was not visible behind the dark gathered storm clouds. Quell, Wyren, Fenna and I said our farewells to Shand and his crew. The Captain clasped my gauntlet in his, and gave me a respectful nod. We clambered into a small boat that had been lashed to the side of the ship, and we were then lowered into the rolling water by the crew, who strained and heaved at the long, wet ropes as we moved a finger-length at a time down to the surface of the waves. Quell and I took position at the oars to either side of the skiff, and Fenna and Wyren held loaded crossbows, guarding our backs as we pushed off from the hull of the *Silverfin* and began to make our way along the eastern coastline. We had a single lantern at the prow of our little vessel, and as we got closer to the mouth of Estwake Bay Fenna reached forwards and doused it, leaving us to approach in near total darkness. I was able to guide us across the water, having no need of light to see. Our oars had been muffled with lengths of cloth to reduce their impact in the waves, so we made little noise over the sound of the surf as we approached the entrance to the Scar.

As we began our journey, the *Silverfin* turned away, and began its charge towards the port, intent on raising the alarm and pulling the hounds away from their kennel. From our position to the left of the harbour we watched as the privateer vessel lit the missiles loaded on its catapults and began to fire on the stationary ships in the dock. Some of the enemy boats caught fire, the flames illuminating the sudden chaos on the wharf. We could see racing shadows carrying buckets, attempting to put out the fires, and several of the ships began to cast off, their crews suddenly called to action and determined to drive off their attacker. A number of the Sechian vessels put to sea with some speed, and immediately began to press the attack on Shand's ship. He turned tail, intent on simply leading them on a merry chase rather than engaging in an extended melee. The hounds took the bait, and what ships were not burning followed the *Silverfin* out into the wider ocean, determined to punish their attacker.

We could see the mouth of the Scar River at the end of the harbour nearest to us. The shore on our side of the river outlet was unused, being of a rocky and treacherous temperament, and it had claimed many unwary boats over the years. We looped away from this ship graveyard and turned ourselves so that we could pass between the cliffs of the Scar. This was the first true trial of our quest. If we were seen from the dock we would be attacked. We had to hope that Shand's diversionary tactics had drawn all attention. Quell and I rowed as quietly as we could whilst still making forward progress against the current, and all four of us kept as low in the boat as possible, so our shapes would not be exposed as shadows against the soft glow of the churning surf.

We were close enough to the harbour that we could hear the shouts of its occupants, Sechian voices raised in alarm and command, the march of undead boots and the clatter of armour and industry. My companions held their breaths, though I doubted it would make a difference. Quell and I had to fight the flow of water from the ravine's mouth, the current there being very strong, and he was sweating with exertion. Thankfully the spring thaws had passed now and the river, though powerful, was not swelled with meltwater from the mountains. We were able to pass between the canyon walls without notice from the shore, and we left the commotion and threat of Estwake Harbour behind us.

The ravine was deep and steep-sided, and even were the moon not covered by the dead black clouds no light would have reached down there. Wyren and I swapped places so that I could lean from the prow of the boat and guide us through the treacherous passage. Our goal was a way upstream, but we made good progress, and I was able to keep us away from the walls of the crevasse and the many sharp rocks that broke the surface of the river. Far up in the mountains the Scar River was a raging, rushing, white-water torrent, which had claimed many lives in the past. Nearer the sea it was still fairly wide, and its power was diminished. Though the current was against us we were able to make good headway.

It was past midnight when we reached our second goal. We pulled into the cliff-face to our right. There was a deep and shadowed overhang, arching over us, and beneath it was a set of stone steps that led up out of the water and onto a dock carved directly into the cliff. At one edge of this worn stone structure was a hole, bored straight through the rock, that served as a place for us to secure our boat, and I fed rope through it so our little ship was tied fast. We disembarked and took our packs from the boat. Then we made our way into the shadows underneath the cliff, where there was a chamber with one wall open to the river. At the rear of the chamber a set of steep and narrow steps disappeared into the shadows, carved into the rock. They led up to a cave opening that led deep into the roots of the mountains above.

"What is this?" Fenna whispered, though it was unlikely anyone would hear us there.

"This... this is an ancient place." I said. "It dates from well before my time at Estwake, from before the Castle was even built. The keep above was built into the mountains directly behind it, and there are catacombs below that my family and earlier generations used for many things... but the mountains are riddled with cracks and caves, streams that run underground, caverns of crystal and stone that have barely been explored. The stairs run up through narrow passages and winding galleries all the way up to the rear of the keep."

Memories assailed me. This place had been dear to me once.

"This has been used as a means of exit for the Lords of Estwake for centuries. When the Castle was besieged, this is how my wife and children escaped. We had a boat tied here for them, and they left the keep and tried to sail past the harbour. They failed, and they were captured."

Fenna must have sensed my sadness and put one hand on my shoulder.

"I'm sorry, Asheth."

"Thank you, Fenna. My children used to play here. They used it as a secret room for their games, under warning of staying away from the river. Being here... I have played at this riverbank with my children. We used to make model boats, of wood and parchment, and my children would set them in the water to watch them sail away down to the sea. We would make up stories of the sights their crews would see, and the strange people they would meet."

I had spent a long time trying not to think of my family too much. I had kept my mind focused on the role fate or the gods had assigned to me and had tried to trade action for memory. In that place my bargain failed, and the weight of my history seemed too heavy to carry. I sat quietly away from my companions as they recuperated and prepared themselves for the battle ahead.

Once they had rested themselves, Quell, Fenna and Wyren stood up, shook off their stiffness, and collected their packs and weapons. I took the torch from Quell and led us up the narrow stairs, into the dark.

CHAPTER NINETEEN

Neither the living nor the dead had discovered the passage through the mountains. The dust of time unremembered coated the floor, and no footprints were visible barring the tiny trails of pattering rats and skittering insects. The rodents were cowards and only occasionally showed a pair of glowing eyes in the shadows as they watched us pass. Overhead bat colonies roosted in the natural eaves of the cavern rooves, and they shook their wings and squeaked and flew back and forth, leaving the tunnels to hunt for food, incensed at our trespass. The journey up through the mountain roots was a long and winding one. We passed through corridors of crystal, flashing blue and violet reflections drawn from the walls by the torchlight I carried. We walked over rushing streams, with wide stone bridges that had crumbled in places, unmaintained for centuries, the brickwork that had supported them now dust and fragments.

We reached a large cavern, its roof marked by long spikes of deposited mineral. The fat drips of water that fell from these formations echoed through the hollow, so that it was almost like being caught in the beginnings of a storm, the sound of the droplets' impact bouncing from one wall to another over and over.

Against one wall of the cavern was a statue, carved into the rockface. A pillar reached from the floor of the cave and up into its ceiling, twice the height of a man. Around the pillar curled a serpent, covered in many tiny scales, and it twisted around and around until its face loomed out from near the top of its perch. It did not have the face of a snake. Instead, there was a mass of smaller serpents, with small, fanged mouths on eyeless faces.

I spoke to my companions.

"This is S'Gara, the Serpent under the Mountain. In ages past he was worshipped up and down the eastern Sagaran Mountains, and this shrine to him is one of many that were made, in caves and catacombs all along the eastern side of the Baronies and up into the mountains of the north. His power has waned while the Mother of the Sea grew strong."

"Was this your god?" Quell asked, his face stern. He looked at the statue with a hateful expression, his lip curling in disgust.

"No. I did not worship any god. I was a noble, a Baron. Religion was for the peasants and the poor, a means to keep them satisfied with their lot. I was meant to be above such things."

Quell glared at me then, finding offense in my blunt reply.

"And now? Do you have faith? You gave yourself to the Temple, Asheth. Did you do so under false pretenses?"

"No. I believe the Mother of the Sea has set me on this path in some way, and I will serve her needs as I promised. But it is still in my nature to question the gods, Quell. I had blind faith in a leader once. I will never be so blind again… and I was not the one who was false."

He grunted then, and withdrew from me, unsatisfied with my answer but unwilling to press his argument in such surroundings.

The rest of our journey passed uneventfully, and I remembered the way easily. From my perspective, I had only been in the tunnels a year or so ago, and they had not changed all that much, even in nearly 400 years. There was a last set of steps, and then the passage doubled back on itself to form a long corridor. At one end were the decayed remains of a wooden door, its fittings long since rusted to almost nothing, its petrified wood grey and covered in dust and cobwebs. More insects and long-legged spiders raced and crawled out of our path as we approached the secret entrance.

I gestured to my companions to be quiet, and then I doused the torch and padded as softly as I was able up to the rotten portal. There was a small hole at head height, and I leaned forwards to peer through it. The room beyond seemed unoccupied. There was a chain that served to open the door, fed through the stone wall at the side, and I pulled it gently, hoping that it was not rusted shut or decayed so much that it would snap. It creaked and squealed a little, but luck was on our side and the mechanism still functioned. The door moved, and I waited to hear if the noise of its opening would raise a response. Hearing nothing, I moved it forwards again, a small measure, and repeated this until I was confident the room was unused, and the door was fully open. No one raised the alarm. Behind the door was a rotted tapestry, its colours faded, and its surface coated in cobwebs and accumulated dust. As I pushed it gently aside it fell to the floor and collapsed into many pieces, its threads finally crumbling. The room beyond was dark and devoid of all life. There was a large bed, a post at each corner holding up the decaying remains of panel and curtain. There was a wardrobe and cabinets, the doors and drawers of them ransacked, damp eating what remained of the wood, and mushrooms and other carrion growths protruded from their surfaces like a forest of decay. The floor of the room had partially collapsed, and a rug on the floor, threadbare and decomposed, dangled through the ceiling of the room below. The exposed stone walls of the room were slimed with damp and crawling fungus. The shutters over the windows were missing, only the rust-stain marks where their hinges had been still visible, and the cold mountain wind blew through the wide openings, making my companions shiver and forcing them to wrap their cloaks around them and cover their faces. We were near the very top of Estwake Castle, and this high in the mountains the wind was chill all year round. The gusts howled into the room and snapped our cloaks around our heels.

When I had lived at Estwake this had been the room I shared with Helena. The torrent of memories nearly broke me. I could remember the smell of her perfume. I could recall her warm breath on my face. I had a vision of her, stood before the windows in the morning sun, the light shining through her night-gown, the shape of her body beneath. I remembered her soft voice calling my name, and the love sparkling in her eyes.

I knelt on the floor and removed my hood and helmet. I could not find release from the pain.

I held my fleshless face in my hands, unable to weep, unable to cry out, trapped in my dead body. I could not even shed a tear for the wife and children I had loved and lost.

Fenna, my friend Fenna, knelt beside me. She had guessed where we were, and of all people she understood my anguish. She put her arm around me, and I leant against her, and she against me. We embraced and she silently sobbed on my shoulder, her tears for me and for herself. We were brother and sister in grief.

After a short while we stood together, our arms still around each other, and she wiped the tears from her cheeks. Then she took the crossbow from her back and loaded it, and Wyren did the same. Quell drew his pair of daggers and I unstrapped my hammer from my back. We edged around the hole in the floor, single file, with me leading the way. We made our way down through the castle.

I had guessed that most of Kroll's followers that had remained would be in the lower floors, as I had known the heights were in a state of disrepair, like many towers across the Regions. I was correct in my assumption. The dishevelled state of the keep had made it unsafe for the living, and Kroll and his cultists would not be expecting a strike from above. This part of the castle seemed unexplored, and so the passage through the mountains had remained undetected. As far as I can tell most of the castle was unused. The majority of its defensive forces were underground, in the catacombs, and in its surrounding grounds.

We made our way down the winding, spiral staircase from my old chambers. Two floors down we started to find evidence of occupation, but no resistance. It was still the early hours of the morning and the living needed sleep. We passed rooms filled with snoring piles of rags and filth bundled on cots, the floors covered with scraps of food and carelessly discarded clothing. My colleagues wrinkled their noses and covered their faces against the stench, and again I found small comfort in not having a sense of smell. We let the cultists sleep. We did not want to risk raising the alarm, and we were focused on our goal.

We did not encounter any guards until we reached the ground floor. Wyren scouted ahead, padding silently along the paving stones with boots wrapped in cloth to muffle her tread. She came back to report that four of my brethren stood at the entrance to the catacombs.

"If we try to fight our way past we'll raise too much noise. We need to deal with 'em quick and quiet." She hunkered down on her heels, her crossbow across her knees, and we were all hidden in the shadows at the foot of the main staircase.

"It is a risk, but I believe I can move them. If they act like the ones in Rafe they should obey my commands... unless Kroll has accounted for that. I would think he is not prepared for it, but we shall have to be lucky." I was doing my best to whisper but my voice seemed very loud to me in the silence of the sleeping castle.

"Don't like relying on luck much." Said Wyren. She had never really warmed to me, but she had a sardonic grin on her face, which I was able to see even in the darkness.

"Me neither. Regardless, we must try."

I stood up, and left our cover, walking as carefully and as quietly as I could to the guard's position. My companions crouched and crept slowly behind me, ready to react if my scheme failed. I turned the corner into the main thoroughfare of the castle, onto the path that led down into the catacombs, and I stood up straight and walked purposefully towards the guards as if I had every right to be there. Which, in a sense, I did. The skeletal soldiers reacted immediately and raised their pikes to stop my advance, each of them taking a step forward and assuming a fighting stance. I held up my left hand, leaving my hammer dangling at my side in my right, and said in a clear voice, "At ease. You are dismissed.

Take yourselves to your regiments to refresh."

They ignored my orders and began to advance purposefully towards me.

I spoke again. "You are *dismissed.*" By now they were surely able to see my skull face and recognise me as one of their own.

Instead of obeying my command, they charged, and I realised quickly that luck had deserted me. The first one to reach me lunged forwards with his pike, and I had to turn to avoid the blow, the weapon coming within a fingersbreadth of taking my head from my shoulders. Before he could reset and strike again a crossbow bolt appeared in one of his eye-sockets. The momentum of his thrust took him straight past me, and I side-stepped out of the way. The rest of his body realised his head was shattered and he fell to the floor behind me. I had no time to appreciate the skill of Wyren's shot as I had to defend myself from the next guard's attack. As I parried his strike with the head of my hammer, shattering his pole-arm blade, Quell rushed past me and charged the remaining pair of dead. We were going to win this melee, easily, but we were making too much noise, and as the last guard fell to the floor in a pile of bones we could hear the distant sounds of footsteps and yells of alarm coming from the upper floors of the keep.

Fenna yelled "*Move!*" and we rushed down the

central hall, racing for the back wall and the entrance to the depths below.

The long, steep tunnel was much as it was when I had been here last. We passed the alcoves where the regiments of undead Kroll had created stood in silent ranks. Their numbers were much diminished, as many had been sent west on campaign, but there were enough left to decrease our chances of escape from the pit. We ran, down into the deep dark earth, down to the profane birthing lake that lurked in the bowels of Estwake, a foul mother much larger than the children it had spawned across the regions. The cavern was lit by torches along its walls. The great cauldron was still there, bubbling on its fire, and its dull metal sides caught some of the golden light from the flames. The living were present in the pit as well as the dead, and they were already aware of our presence. The cultists had been roused from sleeping litters around the edges of the cavern and were moving towards us. The woman that served Kroll as his flesh seamstress, Nisht, ran down the passage from her workroom with a wicked cleaver in her hand. She yelled in rage, and then darted towards a cage of Lessers that sat next to her workshop's entrance and slashed at the rope that bound its door shut. She screamed orders at the contents of the cage as they lurched out onto the cavern floor.

"Kill them! Kill them all! *Rip them apart!*" She howled, her pale face twisted in a mask of utter hatred, and she pointed towards us as the Lessers tumbled out of their prison and began to shamble and claw their way towards us. If we were caught by them, it would take too long to extricate ourselves. If we tarried our mission would fail.

"Go! You need to find Kroll! *GO!*" Fenna drew her sword and pointed it at me, desperation in her eyes. "There's no time, you have to go now!" She turned her back on me, and she and Wyren charged the filthy horde shambling towards us. Both women had discarded their crossbows and drawn their swords, and were hacking and slicing at the advancing tide of rot.

Quell and I turned away from the melee and circled the other side of the black lake, kicking, hammering, cutting and barging the cultists there out of our way. I swung and knocked one woman into the Blood of R'Chun, and there was a gargling agonised scream as she sank into the foul morass, her flesh already melting from her bones. The passage on that side of the lake was narrow, but this worked to our advantage as the cultists were not accomplished warriors and were not able to stand against us without bringing their numbers to bear. I killed the last of our living opponents and approached the entrance to the western antechamber. This was a room I had never seen. This was Kroll's lair.

The sound of battle behind us became muffled, the grunts and cries and moans of the combatants echoing in the cavern and along the short dark tunnel to Kroll's chambers. There was a dim and flickering light at the far end of the roughly made corridor, by turns yellow like natural flame, then green like the sparking glow of his sorcery. We entered the chamber and found it to be a small, simple room. There was no bed, just a bedroll on the floor to serve as a resting place, no different than the ones Kroll's followers used. There was an old wooden chest, open, that contained some clothing and bric-a-brac, and was surmounted by a row of glass bottles, each filled with more of the black-green sorcerous slime. There was a wash basin in one corner, filled with grey water. On one wall, opposite the bedroll, was a large, bone-framed mirror, the twin of the one that been in Cellin's quarters at the Western Gate. As before there was a large black candle set before the mirror, and it was this candleflame that was illuminating the room. It burned yellow but occasionally flashed with green sparks.

Kroll stood before us, barefoot and dressed in a simple black smock that served as his nightgown. He made no move to attack us or defend himself, but instead remained calm and composed, as if we were simply guests come to engage him in conversation. He had tied his long, dirty-grey hair behind his head, and it was tight against his skull. His face was lined with age, and his eyes were red, their sockets stained with blood. He had spent too long over the rising fumes of his rending cauldron. He seemed more a dead creature than some of the Lessers in the cavern. I stepped towards him, my hammer raised, Quell close behind me. The sorcerer spoke.

"So, the prodigal son returns. Such a pity. You could have been the greatest in our army. You aren't a simpering, arrogant fool like Cellin... our other Greater Generals are nothing compared to you. Your skills would have served R'Chun well. It's not too late, Baron. You could still serve willingly as his warlord."

"I have no intention of serving you. I am here to kill you." I lifted my hammer high over my head, ready to end the man's existence. Instead, my arms locked in the air, my weapon shaking and trembling as I strained to strike him down. I willed myself to move but my limbs would no longer heed my commands.

"I created you, Baron. You cannot hurt me. You were made to do my bidding." He made a small gesture, flicking his hand at the wrist and pointing to Quell behind me.

"Now, kill your friend."

I heard the order in my head, and it pushed out all other thought. The hammer moved of its own accord, swinging down and around in a sweeping curve, and I watched it as if it were held by someone else. The heavy head of the weapon struck Quell in the face, the surprise of my attack giving him no opportunity to parry the blow. The Apostle crumpled to the ground, his nose and cheekbones smashed, his forehead crushed in, and blood poured from the broken crater where his features had been. I tried to cry out, but my voice was no longer mine. Quell lay on the floor of the cave, unmoving, and I was compelled to turn away from his body and face my master.

"You belong to me, Baron. You will remain by my side, and you will watch as I crush the Northern Shore and the living are made to serve the dead. All will serve R'Chun. You cannot stop this. You will be witness to the death of all you hold dear."

My body shook as I fought and howled and screamed inside my skull, my will battering against the walls of my bone prison. No matter how much I raged I could not move. The sorcerer walked towards me, until his face was pressed up close to mine and he was gazing into the caverns of my eyes. His will bored into mine, my mind assaulted by the waterfall force of his command. I was helpless and would have been lost there and then.

Kroll's expression suddenly changed. He threw his head back, let out a cry of pain, and then staggered and fell backwards. I was able to see his ankle was pouring with blood. Below me I could see the point of one of Quell's daggers. The Apostle had crawled to the sorcerer's feet leaving a trail of blood behind him, and had forced his dagger into the man's foot, slicing between his bare toes nearly to his ankle. The agony had broken Kroll's control over me, and I moved as swiftly as I could, afraid that if I hesitated, I would succumb to his will once more. I raised up the hammer. Kroll extended one hand, his palm out, trying to defend himself against my wrath. He failed. I struck down with all my strength, battering through the man's hand and snapping it at the wrist, the head of the hammer embedding itself in his forehead and obliterating his skull. His blood ran into the dirt at the floor of the cave. He did not move again.

I spun and knelt at the side of Quell. His face was a ruin. One eye peered out from beneath a mask of blood, the other obscured by torn and mangled flesh and bone.

"My friend, I am so sorry. He had me in his grip. I could not stop. Please forgive me."

The Apostle tried to speak through a jumble of broken teeth and shattered jawbone. I do not know how he still clung to life.

"All's well. I know. I am glad to have helped. Perhaps I have finally… paid my debt. You still have to pay yours."

I held him for a moment. He gestured to me with one of the daggers in his hands, urging me to take it. I did so, along with its twin, and he reached down with one trembling, blood-stained hand to unhook his belt, handing me the scabbards for his weapons.

"Take these… back to the Temple. I only borrowed them for a short while."

I nodded and stood to put the belt around my padded waist, hooking my hammer to my back. I sheaved the left dagger but kept the right one in my hand. I knelt again, hoping to hold him while he passed, but he was already gone. He had completed his penance.

I turned away from his body and stood over Kroll's corpse. His head was broken but his features were still his. I sawed Quell's silver-lined dagger into the dead man's neck, severing it, and then picked it up by a handful of blood-soaked grey hair and let it dangle from my hand like some ghastly censer. Then I strode towards the mirror on the wall. I did not know how to make it work. I need not have worried. A swirling grey and green cloud formed in the glass, as if the mirror was aware of me, reacting to my gaze. The mist coalesced into the face of a gaunt, pale, thin man, with cruel, emerald-green eyes and long black hair hanging down to his shoulders. He wore an emerald gemstone at his neck on a gold circlet, which flashed with pulses of putrescent verdant light. He regarded me with an arrogant air, as if I were some slave come to petition for my freedom. I had no intention of begging.

"Who are *you?* Where is Kroll? Let me speak to your master, corpse, or else I will have him break you into pieces!" His voice was deep and accented like Kroll's, and dripping with scorn, clearly used to being feared and obeyed. I would do neither.

"I am Baron Asheth Acellion. Here is your whelp." I held up the head of Kroll, blood still dripping from his roughly cut neck. The man recoiled, but recovered his composure quickly, and gave a small smile.

"So, you are the millstone around Kroll's neck. He has spoken of you, Baron. A dead man amongst the living. Why do you fight? You will never be one of them. You should be serving me."

"My motives are my own... and I will never serve you, or the god you obey."

At this he laughed, a cold, mirthless sound, tinged with madness.

"*Obey?* I do not obey R'Chun. I am his Emperor, and I rule him, just as I rule Sechia, and just as I will rule all the Scar Sea. That pitiful, whining old hag, the First Daughter, knows the truth.

R'Chun is the blade in my hand. What power he holds serves *ME!*"

I did not know then if he lied. My face betrayed nothing of my reaction. Another small benefit of my lifeless skull.

"It does not matter. I will defend the Regions. I am here to tell you… *do not come here*. You may believe you bring death to us. Believe me, death is already here, and it waits for you. Every man and woman, every walking, wretched corpse you send to the Regions… we will give them to the sea. But this man… this man you can have back."

I threw Kroll's head into the mirror then, and it passed through the sorcerous glass as my fist had done in Cellin's chambers. I had aimed my throw well, and the wet and ruined chunk of flesh and bone struck the arrogant emperor full in the face. He recoiled as the dripping stump of Kroll's neck covered him in blood, and his mouth flapped open, gaping like a landed fish.

"Halt your invasion, Emperor. *Or I will come for you.*"

He did not voice a reply. Instead, his face still smeared with Kroll's remains, he lifted his hands. Black smoke began to rise from his palms, flickering with green light. The smoke joined together into one thick stream and began to reach his side of the mirror, passing through the glass and creeping towards me through the air. I reacted quickly. I still had Quell's punching dagger sat across the knuckles of my right hand. Avoiding the questing tendrils of smoke, I struck it into the mirror as hard as I could, hoping to reach the sorcerer and end the invasion there and then.

Instead, the silver point of the dagger struck the glass barrier, and from its centre a circle of green-white lines spread across the portal. The image of the Emperor disappeared, and the smoke slithering towards me was cut in half, dissipating now his will no longer drove it on. There was a sound like a distant wail, and then a crash of thunder as the mirror shattered into thousands of shards. A sudden wind blew up, and the black candle snuffed out in the tempest. The shadows of spirits clawed their way from the broken pieces of glass scattered across the floor of the cave, screaming skull-faced clouds of rage and spite. They swirled into the air around me, hundreds of them, thousands, overlapping, flying inside and through each other. They tried to latch on to my face, my armour. The silver shell pinned to my brow became suddenly heavy and pulsed with a heartbeat rhythm I could feel through my skull. The metal became freezing cold, the chill of deep water where sunlight does not reach, a sensation I never thought I would feel again. The spirits clawed and howled, and their keening screech rose in intensity until it was all I could hear. I began to strike and slash at them with Quell's daggers, drawing the left one as well and sweeping them both around me in wild blows, and the billowing clouds of dead parted and flew away from the reach of my weapons. I started to push my way through the storm, back along the tunnel to the main cavern, suddenly conscious that I had left Fenna and Wyren to defend themselves against the dead. I feared I had tarried too long to help them.

I made it out of Kroll's chambers, the wailing shades still churning the air around me, their shadowed talons dragging at me every step of the way. I could feel something wrong with my body. My joints seemed loose and weak, and even my gloved hands struggled to grip my weapons, as if my fingers were becoming limp and unconnected to my will. I stepped into the main cavern and saw that all of the dead there were screaming. The last few surviving Lessers were on the ground, writhing and twisting in what seemed almost like agony. Their rotten flesh was being pulled from their bones by the rough stone floor and the force of the foul wind that roared through the enclosed space. The flames of the torches on the wall whipped back-and-to and struggled to stay lit. On the opposite side of the black lake Nisht was on her knees, trying to stop her guts from falling from a slash across her belly. Blood was pouring from her eyes and mouth, and the spirits that had failed to hurt me took their frustration out on her. The shadows swooped towards her and circled her screaming body. She coughed and choked on her own blood as rents from astral talons appeared across her face and arms. She tried to bat them away but soon lost her strength and fell to the ground.

I shambled to the edge of the lake, my limbs now becoming unruly and impossible to control fully. I felt as if I were coming apart. I made it to Wyren and Fenna, surrounded by a pile of slashed corpses. This was where they had made their stand. Wyren was dead. Her eyes were still open but there was no life in them as they stared sightlessly at the roof of the cavern. Fenna was still alive, but cut and bruised in many places, and she was down on one knee, using her sword for balance so she did not topple over. She had destroyed many of the Lessers but it had taken a toll. I knelt beside her, unsure if I could get up again. Whatever sorcery that held the dead together was being removed from this place by the anger of the seething wraiths. I called her name over the storm, and she looked up. One side of her face was sliced open, and blood was running freely from the wound. Her armour was hanging from her, her pack only barely clinging to her shoulders, its straps torn in many places.

"Did you kill him?" She asked, through panting breaths.

"Yes, Fenna. Kroll is dead. I believe I have also angered his master."

"Good. We need to go." She got to her feet with some effort.

"I am not sure I can, Fenna. I believe this is where we part ways. I am falling apart. The sorcery here is rebelling, and so too is my body."

Tears appeared in her eyes.

"No... no, you can't, you have to come back!"

I was about to reply, in an attempt to comfort her, but my voice was drowned out by a thunderous, wet bellowing behind me. I turned to look, even that motion now difficult, and I saw that the black liquid of the lake was moving.

At first there were gentle waves. Then they became furious ones, like a storm out at sea, a whirlpool that breaks ships and swallows up their crews. Green flashes and sparks and bolts of lightning flew from the wave crests as they formed and broke and formed again. The liquid was receding from the edges of the lake and turning more viscous as it did so. It had turned to thick, rancid oil, and the waves became rounded and lapped together with a sloppy wet sound, now joining and reinforcing each other rather than crashing apart. The surface of the lake rose in the middle, like a waterspout, twisting and turning faster and faster, but its consistency was clotting by the moment. It formed into a central tower, the lakebed now just mud, as all remnants of the Blood of R'Chun threaded towards the growing monolith and joined with its mass. The tower threw off long branches at its base and head, inconstant questing limbs that split and re-joined and split and re-joined again and again, as if seeking purchase in the mud of the ground and the stony surface of the cavern ceiling. Bubbles began to form on the trunk of the tower, and each one flashed with green light. I knew, in my soul, that this thing was a creature of some kind, not simply a sorcerous creation but a living animal, and that the glowing emerald orbs forming in its skin were eyes. I felt as if it were looking through me, and my wits nearly fled. The threads that held my skeletal form together were being called back to re-join their source. My limbs twitched, and my hands and feet felt loose in their bindings, as if the bones could rattle free at any moment and fall from my clothing. Cavernous holes opened around the glowing orbs in the black tower, mouths that yawned wide and smacked grotesque lipless edges together, and the creature roared and screamed, a sound like a hundred horns and whistles being blown together in a discordant, cursed cacophony. The spirits that had attacked Nisht were now circling the tower, adding their wails to the din.

The writhing black column pushed upwards, and the cavern began to shake with its straining movement, as it unleashed all its fury at its surroundings, finally free of the sorcery that had held it captive and unformed. Dust and splinters of rock began to fall from the roof. Fenna cried out in fear, terrified by the creature, and even though my body was betraying me I knew I had to act. I looked away from the looming tower of slime and saw that the bubbling, caustic cauldron still sat at the side of the pit, the mist of fumes above it swirling in the gale that still rolled around the cavern. I had to marshal every fragment of my willpower to make my way towards it, tottering on barely functioning legs, stumbling and lurching from side to side as I dragged my body towards my goal. I was on my knees and crawling by the time I made my way behind the cauldron and had to fight to stand. I pressed my hands against its back, heedless of the heat of the flames that burned beneath it. I grasped the edges of the bowl and pushed forwards with all my strength. It rocked forwards and a little of the milky corrosive liquid sloshed over the side opposite of me and then settled back again. I heaved once more and this time the cauldron reached its tipping point, and slowly rolled forwards. The contents flowed out, the grisly remains of Kroll's last victims still visible in the rending fluid. The white and smoking substance emptied from its container and flooded one end of the pit, rushing toward the screaming column of black and green sludge.

The caustic solution reached the nearest of the black tendrils, and the creature let out a howl of agony and indignation. Where the white froth touched its black-green ooze the surface bubbled and smoked, and began to visibly decay, first becoming dry and then crumbling into glittering green dust that mixed with the white liquid and disappeared. The creature redoubled its effort to destroy the cavern, its cries and screams and whistling howls becoming louder as its base was eaten away. The black tower started to change, becoming indistinct, and parts of it were nearly transparent, the flames from the few still-burning torches visible through its form. Some of its mass began to vanish, as if it were feeding portions of itself into holes in thin air, pulsing black and green muck disappearing into passages that did not exist.

I fell to my knees. I could feel my strength had gone, and the black threads that tied me together began to creep out of my clothes, appearing at my sleeve ends and the collar of my leather armour. My sight began to dim, the edges of my vision black. I was prepared to be destroyed. I had already had my life, and I had made good use of the extra time afforded me. the last thing I could see was Fenna, crawling towards me through the dirt and debris of the shaking cavern floor. I wished I could help her escape. She was bound to be buried down here with the dead, and there was nothing I could do to prevent her fate. She made it to where I knelt.

"We need to go, Asheth."

"You need to go, if you can. I am done, Fenna. I cannot move. Whatever vigour was present in me has gone. It is time for me to die."

"Please... please. I can't lose any more. Please stand up! *Stand up!*"

She was sobbing, her heart broken by what she had endured. Bor was dead. Her friends were dead. Now I was to leave her alone in this dark place. She grasped my gloved hand in her left, lifting the blood covered fingers of her other hand to touch my skull, stroking the side of my head with affection and sorrow.

Her touch changed everything.

Immediately the black threads ceased their attempts at escape. My body became locked together again, my vision clearing, my limbs regaining their strength in a moment. I raised my head and looked at her in shock. She stared back at me, and some vital force, some feeling of power, passed between us. My mind was thrown back to the ritual she had performed in my cell, back in Salisson. The same feeling came to me, as if I were being born again, made complete and whole by her will.

I stood up and held my hand out to where she knelt.

"Come with me."

She got to her feet, and we started to make our way to the cavern entrance, avoiding the falling chunks of stone from the ceiling as the last remnant of the Blood of R'Chun raged against its prison. The last few dead still in the cave were rolling on the ground and were convulsing and shaking as streams of black and green slime and filth streamed from their mouths and ears. Fenna leant on me as we staggered out of the dead pit, and we began to claw our way back up the tunnel to the castle. We passed the alcoves where Kroll's regiments waited, and the skeletons were all on their knees, black threads flowering from their joints and eye sockets. Some of them tumbled to pieces as we passed, all motion leaving them, and they fell into piles of bones and dust. The refuse of dead men, rolling skulls and crumbling ribcages. We drove on, staggering our way up the shaking passage, and it felt like we had been trudging for days before we finally reached the ground floor of the castle. This too was shaking, masonry cracking around us and dust falling from the shifting upper floors. The whole castle was about to fall. There was a huge, thunderous boom outside as we reached the main door and I saw that one of the corner towers had fallen into the courtyard.

There were living cultists outside, panicking in the grey attenuated light of the rising sun, but in their distress they ignored our dust-covered forms as we made our way through the falling rubble. I saw Rack, on his knees, tears rolling down his cheeks and cutting swathes through the filth on his unwashed face. He looked at us and seemed about to cry out to stop our progress, but then the courtyard wall behind him collapsed, and he scrabbled and failed to get out of the way as the falling masonry crushed him.

I managed to get us out of the courtyard and onto the bridge into the town. Cultists passed us, racing towards the castle to try to rescue what they could and paying us no heed. I heard my old home die behind me but did not turn back to watch.

In the town there were dead still moving and obeying the orders of their masters. The effect of the creature's anger did not seem to extend past the immediate grounds of the castle. They marched past us, driven by the cultists, running to try to pull their colleagues from the wreckage, and we were able to make it through the crowd in the confusion. One man near the rear of the throng was driving his horse and cart to the disaster, and letting go of Fenna for a moment I reached up and dragged him from his seat, slamming him into the cobblestones and knocking him senseless. He wore the same filthy black cloak as the rest of the cultists and I wrapped Fenna in the dirty garment and lifted her onto the cart. I patted the horse's side to try to calm it, and then clutched at its saddle and mounted the skittish beast, taking the reins in my hands. I turned the cart around and drove my stolen transportation away from Estwake Castle as fast as I was able.

The sun was nearing its apex by the time we reached the border of Estwake. We had passed several patrols, but they had paid us no attention, as I appeared to be just another follower of R'Chun, rather than an interloper. At these moments I bade Fenna to hide as low as she could in the back of the cart. We finally reached the ruins of the watchtower overlooking Estwake Harbour. The skies above had cleared a little, the grey and dour clouds having parted as we headed west along the Coast Road. The harbour below us was still occupied by Sechian ships, but none of their occupants had ventured up onto the clifftops, so our route into Tresh was clear. The sea was blue and green, the waves tipped with white and sparkling in the bright sun. Summer was coming. The seabirds floated and flew over the cliffs and down towards the harbour, riding the warm sea breeze, cawing and calling to each other over the distant sound of breaking surf. It was beautiful.

I dismounted from my steed and went to check on Fenna. She seemed stronger, and the cuts on her face and arms had ceased to bleed. She had taken ointment from her pack and had applied it to her wounds, some old recipe the Wardens used to ward away infection. I handed her a skin of water I had found tied to the horse's saddle, and waited as she drank a mouthful, grimacing at its warmth.

"How do you feel? Probably not a sensible question I know." I took the skin of water back from her trembling hands.

"Like I got the shit kicked out of me. That's what Bor would have said". She lowered her head and gave out a long, shuddering sigh. "I miss him."

"I know. I miss him too. He was my friend. I do not know how that came to be. How anyone could befriend such as me."

She looked up at me, her eyes filled with tears again, but her expression stern.

"You're a good man, Asheth. Alive or dead. It doesn't matter how you look. You do what you can to help. That's all anyone can do."

I nodded and offered her the water again. She took a little more and then I hooked it back on to the horse's saddle. There was a feedbag in the cart, and I hung it around the horse's mouth and let it eat.

"Asheth, can I ask you something?"

"Anything."

"Do you still want to die?"

I thought on it for a moment. The Regions were still threatened. The First Daughter had lied to me. I had questions that required answers. I looked out over the Scar Sea, over the Great Crossing. It was a clear day, and I could see on the horizon tall white clouds that seemed to rise from behind the ocean and reach up into the deep blue sky.

"No," I said. "I have things to do first."

End of Part One

EPILOGUE

Councillor,

When you instructed me to find Baron Acellion,

I must confess I thought you were jesting with me for a moment. I had read the history of the Scar Sea wars as a young boy in school, but as I grew to adulthood, I had dismissed the accounts of an undead warrior fighting for the Regions as just stories, tales for children. It was only when I began to trace the history of those times through surviving documents that I found there may be a seed of truth in the legends.

The Baron was a difficult man to find. It was through sheer luck that in my travels I heard of an old man, living in a remote village I have been asked not to name or place on a map. There were rumours of some strangeness about him, and travellers I met said that he was an unnerving character who never showed his face. When I reached the village, the locals were tight-lipped, seemingly protective of him. It took some time for me to gain their trust, and one evening, as I sat in an inn with a warm flagon of beer, I was approached by a young woman, dark of skin and beautiful. She told me the man had heard of my interest, and was willing to speak with me, with the understanding that his location was not to be revealed. I was told he would make me swear an oath to keep his secret.

I agreed to those terms, and I was blindfolded, and led on a winding and circuitous route to his dwelling place.

I do not know if it was a house, or some large,

underground construction. There was little light and no windows. A lamp was lit for me out of hospitality, for the Baron himself did not need it, being able to see as easily in darkness as he could in daylight. The walls of the room were covered in shelves filled with books and scrolls, parchments and maps. There were assorted weapons and armour hanging in cabinets, and drawers filled with tools and instruments of all kinds. There was a jeweller's bench, surmounted with a wide magnifying glass on a mechanical assembly so that its position could be changed, and the bench itself was strewn with beautifully made silver and gold rings, brooches, necklaces and bangles. In the far corner of the large room was an anvil, and there was a blacksmiths forge, unlit.

The Baron was a gracious and kind host, though it took a little while for me to overcome my fear of him. He agreed after some debate to give me an account of his 'life', for the want of a better word.

He told me he had found this refuge some years ago, with assistance from some long-standing allies, and that the townsfolk knew who he was and why he hid himself away. He had lived, as it were, for a long, long time, but said he was not tired of his existence yet. At village festivals he would dress as legends from folklore, like many of the men and women of the village did, and he would wander the streets with other revellers, more comfortable when he could go about amongst others masked as he was. He would play games with the children, who loved him, though he did not show his face lest they be frightened of him. He would even, on occasion, go to the inn, and sit in a corner nursing ale he could not drink. He would listen to the conversations, and the music of the local men and women there as they played instruments and sang songs into the small hours of the morning.

I asked him, perhaps impertinently, why he did this. He was not alive and could not partake in any of the pleasures that a living man would take for granted.

He told me that to take pleasure in the life of others was enough.

I enclose the first volume of his memoir. I am going to stay here a while with him. He is a wise and kind man, and I feel I have a lot to learn from him.

Regards

Your Servant

Meil Facilus.

Printed in Great Britain
by Amazon